THE HAUNTING OF BECHDEL MANSION

ROGER HAYDEN

❀ Created with Vellum

RETROSPECT

The Redwood Murders: Twenty Years Later

By Anthony Moore, Staff Writer, *The Dover Sentinel*

By 1975, the Bechdel mansion, located in the town of Redwood, Indiana, was considered the height of opulence. Lush acres surrounded the mansion, which dated back generations. Reportedly of Dutch descent, the Bechdel's ancestors immigrated to America with virtually nothing, only to build a family dynasty that tragically came to an end on one quiet summer evening.

During the 20th century, the Bechdel's wealth, power, and influence knew no bounds, but within their rise, there was also a disturbing pattern of loss. By the 1950s, however, The Bechdel bloodline dwindled after illness, disease, and death left a young George Allen Bechdel as the sole remaining heir of his family's enterprise.

Throughout his early years, George's twelve other siblings all perished in separate tragedies. His parents, Eugene and Reba Bechdel, were later killed when their driver lost control and jettisoned a vintage Rolls Royce into a lake with them inside. To most, it was unthinkable that a family could suffer so much loss, and a theory developed of a curse that had doomed the family line to extinction.

The "Bechdel Curse" has fascinated folklore and urban-legend enthusiasts for years. Perhaps this is why the Redwood mansion continues to bring tourists to the area to this day. There has to be something out there. There have to be answers to explain the mystery behind the curse. Whatever the reasons, the 1970s saw the last living heirs of the family name.

While running his family's land-developing enterprise, George Bechdel found love with socialite, Anabelle Brackman. The two married and had four children. Together, they prided themselves as being among the town's most influential families. They had three sons and one daughter. Their eldest son, Travis, was engaged to be married to a young real-estate heiress. The recent engagement was the toast of the town, and though the merging of two wealthy families wasn't front-page news, everyone in town had heard about it.

On June 25, 1975, the Bechdels hosted a dinner party to celebrate the engagement. The parents of the bride, Victor and Holly Drake, were in attendance with their daughter, Katelyn. It was meant to be a night of new beginnings and good cheer. Instead, it ended in tragedy and disaster. Even the skeptics had to admit that the existence of a family curse made some kind of sense. Some just didn't want to admit it.

The brutal murder of the Bechdels and their dinner guests by unidentified gunmen in the late hours of the evening shocked the small lakeside town to the core. Bodies were found the next morning by authorities in one large, bloody pile in the ballroom. Fifteen people were murdered that evening, and after lengthy investigation, the killers were never found. The case had gone cold, which to many, was something as unthinkable as the crime itself.

Much has been written about the "Redwood Massacre," and countless theories as to who had committed the slaughter have yielded few results. The killer, or killers, are still out there, and this possibility has since casted a permanent cloud over the seemingly peaceful town of Redwood. From the onset, investigators had a variety of suspects, but nothing ever materialized, and over time, all the hype and fascination surrounding the case naturally faded, leaving behind an unending mystery.

There is no doubt that the unsolved murder of fifteen people has since torn the façade of innocence and harmony from Redwood. And many residents say that things have never quite been the same. Perhaps there is still hope in bringing the killers to justice. Only time will tell.

THE NIGHT OF

Redwood, Indiana
June 25, 1975

Julie Bechdel sat on her bed, bored, as sounds of laughter and music echoed throughout her room, rising from below. Her parents were entertaining again, marking the engagement of her older brother, Travis, to a girl from a family even more wealthy than his own, the Drakes.

To Julie, the engagement seemed too soon. Her brother had just graduated high school, and his fiancé, Katelyn, was just entering her senior year of high school. But both Julie's parents and the Drakes not only supported the engagement, they had insisted on it. Everything seemed to be happening very fast, and Julie had her suspicions.

That evening, she had been sent to her room after dinner so that the adults could "have their time," as her mother put it. And even though her room was outfitted with plenty of games, books, and magazines, she was more curious about what was going on downstairs.

Her older brothers were all allowed to stay up, and she

resented having been banished to her room only because she was eleven. Whatever the reasons, she found the party distracting. She couldn't sleep if she had wanted to, and it was time to get a closer look.

Wearing her nightgown, Julie got out of bed and approached her door, where she could smell the cigar smoke from downstairs before even opening it. With the turn of a knob, she carefully ventured out of her room and down the hallway, which led to a winding staircase. She stopped at the railing and looked below into the smoke-filled lounge.

Guests sat among plush green sofas, conversing, or stood on the white tile floor admiring the artwork that adorned the walls. Men in suits and women in their glittering gowns all looked elegant. Julie's brother, Travis, stood near a window, talking with her other brothers, John and Alex, all in long-sleeved tuxedo shirts and bow ties. A record spun on the turntable, booming with jazz music.

Julie knew every nook and cranny of the two-story mansion and its fifteen rooms. She was born there. Her parents were protective of her and rarely let her have a social life beyond the few friends they approved of. She had spent a lot of time within the mansion and had discovered all sorts of ways to move around undetected, and with such experience under her belt, she decided to do some investigating.

From below, guests cupped wine glasses and sipped periodically as they talked and laughed. Julie could hear her mother, Anabelle, laughing out of view. Everyone seemed to be having a good time. She crept down the stairs without a single head turning in her direction. The entire affair seemed strange to Julie. She reached the bottom of the stairs, shielded from view by a nearby palm, and stayed low. No one had noticed her yet.

She rushed behind the nearest couch to her right, where a couple sat talking. She felt over the top of the couch with a certain thrill in her spying. She turned to the gaming room across the lounge and saw her parents standing next to a billiards table, mingling. Her father, George, puffed on a large cigar, talking with some men, drink in hand, as her mother chatted with the women.

Adjacent to the gaming room was the library—her favorite room in the house. She could see inside. Katelyn, her brother's fiancée, stood next to a bookcase in conversation with her parents. Julie wanted to get a listen. She moved along the side of the room, staying close to the thick red drapes that adorned the windows behind her.

She dropped to her knees next to a china cabinet as one of her brothers walked past her from the opposite direction. She was sure she had been spotted, but his black pant legs kept going as she sighed with relief. She crawled to the corner of the room and crouched behind a vacant sofa chair, ready to sprint toward the library.

The music stopped for a moment as the record ended and another dropped down, taking its place. Julie waited until the next song came on and then ran across the room with stealth, reaching the open double doors of the library. The Drake family was within an earshot. Julie stuck her head into the room, careful to not expose herself. The parents had their backs to Julie. She saw Katelyn's brown wavy hair over her parents' shoulders.

"Well, you love Travis, don't you?" Katelyn's mother asked, her permed red hair bouncing up with a nod, as if to provide an answer. Her blue silk evening gown shimmered in the low light.

"Of course I do, but—"

"Then what's the problem?" her mother asked.

"This is all happening too fast," Katelyn said.

Julie crept closer to the side of a tall bookshelf, taking cover.

Katelyn's father interjected with his own thought. "I understand that you're nervous. That's only natural. It will all pass soon enough."

Katelyn shuffled in place, shaking her head. "It's not just that. What about college? I'm graduating high school next year, and all this talk about children... I don't know if I'm ready."

Katelyn's father put his hand on her shoulder. His gray hair was thinning on top, but his stance and attitude were that of a strong and confident man. Julie couldn't see the parents' faces but could still detect their own worries in their daughter's concerns. "That's enough of that talk," he said, slicing the air with his hand. "You have your entire life to do whatever you wish, but you *will* be marrying this boy. Our family's fortunes rely on it."

"Listen to your father, dear," Kate's mother added. "This is about more than…" She paused in hesitation.

Katelyn was quick to respond. "More than what? My future? My own happiness?"

Her father tilted his head back, laughing. "Of course not. Your happiness is very important to us."

"Very much so," her mother said. "But we all have our little parts to play for the greater good. For the family."

"Well said, dear," her father added.

"Thank you," her mother said.

Katelyn threw her arms down in frustration. Julie couldn't believe what she was hearing. Her suspicions, it seemed, were true.

She recalled Travis expressing similar doubt at the breakfast table the morning prior. In response, her father had said he would not hear of it. *The marriage was going to happen*, as her father had put it. As she listened to Katelyn and her parents, Julie did her best to remember every word of what they were saying so that she could write about it in her diary.

In the midst of her eavesdropping, her mother's voice suddenly rang out from behind her.

"Julie Lynn Bechdel!"

Julie spun around in a panic when she saw her mother, Anabelle, standing in the doorway, pearls around her neck, glass in hand, and her face enraged. Julie struggled to speak but found herself frozen.

"What are you doing in here?" her mother asked.

Katelyn's parents turned around, surprised to see Julie hiding nearby.

Julie thought quickly. "I-I couldn't sleep. I was just going to grab a book."

Anabelle moved to Julie like a hawk and yanked her by the arm. "We told you to go to bed an hour ago!"

Julie struggled to get loose as her mother turned to Katelyn's parents, blushing. "I'm very sorry."

"Quite all right," Katelyn's dad said with a smile. His wife, however, stood stone-faced and unamused.

"Let's go," Anabelle said, pulling Julie out of the room.

"You're hurting me," Julie cried out as heads turned in their direction from the lounge.

Her mother's grip remained as she dragged Julie toward the staircase. She saw her father peer out from the gaming room, wearing a stoic frown. She was in trouble, that much was clear. Her mother stopped at the bottom of the stairs and released Julie's arm.

"Now go to bed and stop this bad behavior," she said.

Julie felt angry and defiant. Her brothers watched her from across the room, not getting involved. Guests attempted to turn their attention away, but it was clear that the scene had gotten their attention.

"How can I go to bed with all the noise you're making down here?"

More heads turned, and Julie could see the embarrassment and inner rage in her mother's glazed eyes. She could hear her father's dress shoes clicking against the floor as he approached from the gaming room.

Her mother extended her long, skinny arm toward the stairs. "Go!" she hissed.

Her father stopped beside Julie and stared down at her. "What are you doing here? We told you to go to your room after dinner." His bow tie was undone, and his short black hair was messy. Like her mother, there was a slight slur to his speech.

"I've got this under control, George," Anabelle said.

He raised his hands defensively and backed away. "If you say so." He turned and rejoined the party as a new jazz track came blaring from the turntable speakers.

Julie took one step up the first stair and could feel her mother's stare. She turned her head slightly to see her still there, arms crossed.

"I'm going!" Julie said.

"Good night," Anabelle said in a steely tone, walking away.

Her parents could be both loving and cold depending on the situation. That evening, they seemed to have little patience with her. Julie walked halfway up the staircase and peered over the side as the party resumed and guests returned to their conversations.

She then ran up the stairs and into her room, eager to write about the incident in her diary. She closed her door behind her, muffling the music and obnoxious laughter reverberating through the halls. Her blinds were open, and the night sky was a blanket of tiny stars. She approached her window and looked out into the courtyard below. Beyond the flowing fountain she saw a line of luxury vehicles, a few limos among them. Then, from the shadows of the road leading into the courtyard, she saw headlights.

PARTY CRASHERS

Julie watched as a large white van pulled into the courtyard and parked. Its rusty exterior and rattling engine made it out of place among the other guests' vehicles. Perhaps the driver was lost. That happened sometimes as far out as they were. She kept watch as the van's headlights shut off. The doors opened, and three figures emerged. Beyond the glow of the fountain, she couldn't tell who they were, but she could see that they were all dressed in black.

A troubling feeling stirred in her gut. Something wasn't right. Something hadn't seemed right about the entire dinner party. As they got closer, she could see that they were also wearing black ski masks and were carrying guns. Panic gripped her. She turned around and rushed outside her room in hopes of warning her parents.

From upstairs, she heard someone kick open the front door as the three men rushed inside, storming past the bottom of the stairs. She crept to the railing, frightened with uncertainty. Everything felt so surreal. She couldn't move, and as she opened her mouth, not a sound came out.

She crept back up the stairs, peering over the railing, as

the three large and menacing intruders came back into her view. For a moment, everyone below remained oblivious to their approach as the music continued. One of the masked men suddenly rushed to the turntable and kicked it over, instantly gaining the attention of everyone in the room. Julie's mother screamed, and everyone stood frozen as gasps followed. The intruders circled the room as the tallest among them waved his rifle around, corralling the guests toward the center.

"Don't make a move!" he shouted through his mask. "I want everyone to get in here, right now. *Every swinging dick!*"

Julie crouched down behind the railing in a panic. She hadn't been seen yet, but that could quickly change. She thought of the nearest phone—in her parents' room at the end of the hall next to her. She wanted to act, but her legs wouldn't move.

"All of you. That's right, come on out," the lead gunman continued as terrified guests packed into ballroom the below. Julie then peeked over the railing. . Her brothers were in view with their hands up, shaking. The lead gunman paced from side to side with the rifle against his shoulder with assured cockiness.

"Where's George Bechdel?" He paused, looking around, and then aimed his rifle at the group. "Let's go, Georgy boy. Front and center!"

From the stunned crowd, George stepped forward. He was sweating, and his hair was even more of a mess than it had been a few minutes ago. Another gunman pulled him closer, pushing him to the ground as the guests screamed in panic. Things then got even worse when her mother stepped forward.

"Leave him alone!" she shouted. "Who are you, and what do you want?"

From his knees, George raised his hand, urging her to be

calm. The lead gunman, however, had his own ideas. He stepped forward and smacked her across the face, sending her stumbling backward. Further startled, another woman shrieked in response.

George jumped up, infuriated. "You son of a bitch!" he shouted, lunging at the man, only to receive the paralyzing thrust of a buttstock against his back. He then collapsed to the floor, groaning in agony. Julie shook against the railing, trying to build up the nerve to run, but her legs were locked in place.

"Don't make me do that again," the lead gunman said.

Anabelle held her reddened face, glaring at the gunmen with contempt. She bravely approached George and placed a hand on his shoulder as he lay on his stomach, twisting and grunting.

"He'll be okay," the gunman continued. He then looked to the rest of the crowd with a sweeping gaze, preparing to address them. "Is everyone here?" He glanced at Anabelle as she stroked George's head, pearls dangling at her neck. "Is this all of your guests? Is there anyone in the can?"

Anabelle looked away without response. She then flinched as the gunman stepped closer. "Come on, Mrs. Bechdel. My men don't have the time to search every room." He took a knee, inches from her face. "Be honest with me, and no one gets hurt. Fair enough?"

Tears trickled down her cheeks as she nodded and looked around the room. "Everyone is here."

Pleased, the gunman stood up. "Where's the Drake family?"

After a brief hesitation the two parents raised their hands from within the huddled group. "Great," the gunman said. "Come out here and join your friends."

Fearing for her family and herself, Julie knew that she needed to run and call the police before it was too late. She turned from the staircase and could see that the door to her parents' room was closed.

The lead gunman continued with demands for wallets and purses. "Everything you have, just put it in the bag," he said as one of his men held out a burlap sack, approaching the crowd.

Katelyn's father, Victor, tossed his thick billfold into the bag, a creeping fury in his eyes. "Just take it and get the hell out of here. Damn punks."

"In time, Mr. Drake," the gunman said. He then shifted toward George and kicked him lightly in the side. "Get up, Georgy Boy."

George grunted in pain as Anabelle glared at the masked man. "You don't have to kick him, you monster!"

The gunman stared down with indifference. "You too. Both of you on your feet."

Anabelle helped George up, holding him as he looked at their remorseless assailant and spoke. "We're willing to cooperate with you. Please stop pointing your guns at us. You're scaring people with this nonsense."

The lead gunman nodded, seeming to consider it. He then raised a gloved finger, signaling further instructions. "Everyone get closer. Huddle together tight." As he spoke, the other two gunmen took places at both sides of the group. "My men are going on a little pillage mission, and we can't have any of you running off. Got it?"

The terrified guests looked at each other in confusion. They were hesitant, and no one seemed to fully understand the situation, or the intent of the gunmen as they boxed them in like cattle.

"Come on, people," the gunman continued. "Don't make me have to ask again."

The guests reluctantly inched closer to each other,

forming a tight huddle. "Great!" the lead gunman continued. "Now we can wrap this up."

Julie carefully ascended the stairs, but no matter how light her movements, the steps creaked. She ducked down immediately as silence followed. She could feel the intruders listening as her heart beat wildly.

"Go upstairs and check it out," she heard the lead gunman say to one of his men. "The rest of you, prepare to fire."

An ocean of screams followed. Julie jumped up and looked over the side to see two masked men aim their rifles into the huddle as another one moved toward the stairs, closing in on her. She turned and ran the moment she heard her father's voice scream out, begging the men not to shoot.

Gunfire erupted in a cacophony of deafening blasts. Julie stormed to her bedroom, not looking back. She closed the door, locking it. Her hands were shaking, and she could barely breathe. The shooting continued amidst the screams, initially rapid but then more widely spaced, and then one final shot. Julie couldn't believe any of it.

She heard footsteps outside the door, nearing her room, slow and methodical. She turned off her bedside lamp and looked to her window. It was her only chance to escape. She ran over and unlocked it, without concern for anything she was leaving behind. Though her diary had crossed her mind. It was sitting on a nightstand in view, but there was no time. Her doorknob rattled from the other side. Someone was trying to get in. Her heart raced as she pulled the window open, feeling the night breeze hit her face. She looked down over the ledge to the thick grass below.

She could climb down the trellis on the side but doubted she had time. A loud bang suddenly came at her door, startling her further. She had to run. She climbed out the window, legs dangling in the air, closed her eyes, and said a quick prayer.

She leapt out just as her door was kicked open. She hit the moist grass like a deadweight. A pain shivered up her leg as she looked around in panic. Her adrenaline was in overdrive, but she couldn't shake off the confusion and disorientation.

She turned to run and collided with the waist of a man, smacking her face into his thick belt buckle. She flew back, feeling dazed. She covered her face in pain, blocking the man from sight. She couldn't tell whether he was friend or foe. However, she learned quickly as soon as he spoke.

"Where you off to, little darlin'?"

It was the same man as before. The lead gunman downstairs whose voice had sent shivers down her spine. She looked up and could see him towering over her, no longer wearing a mask but with his face nearly concealed by darkness. She shuddered as he held his rifle up and pressed it against her forehead.

"I have to give it to you—you almost got away."

Her legs locked as she shook in fear, tears streaming from her eyes. She felt cold. Sheer terror tore her stomach into knots. "No..." she said with a trembling voice.

The man paused with the barrel still pressed against her head. She could see his long jaw and the thick stubble on his face where he had a noticeable scar on his left cheek. Shaggy hair hung to the side over his forehead. His eyes appeared as two black holes, as though there were nothing underneath.

"Don't worry. It'll be quick. You won't feel a thing."

"Why?" she cried out.

After a heavy sigh, the man spoke. "Nothing personal, sweetheart. Just business. Now close your eyes and go to sleep."

She clenched her watering eyes as a white burst of light pummeled her, followed by a silent darkness that consumed everything around her.

WELCOME TO REDWOOD

For the longest time, the Bechdel Mansion had remained an old, dusty, and vacant shadow of itself. There was always some morbid fascination with the place in the decades that followed. The town of Redwood had grown weary of the association and tried to distance itself from the mansion and the family's supposed curse. The Redwood city council tried several times to have the house demolished and leveled but was met with resistance every time.

George Bechdel's will awarded all of his financial assets and properties to his bank, in the unlikely event of just the sort of catastrophe that had, in fact, occurred. Assets were to be invested, and undistributed to distant relatives or charities making claims. The estate, he contended, must always remain intact. He explicitly forbade the destruction of the mansion and/or liquidation of the property. This, Bechdel's lawyers explained, was non-binding, but the will could be broken. What was the bank going to do with a hundred-year-old mansion with such a history? Apparently, and surprisingly, they had several offers.

Boris Sokolov, a wealthy Ukrainian businessman, leased

the mansion with his family one summer day in June 1992. He had high hopes of remodeling the property and suiting it to his family's elegant needs. Two weeks after moving in, the Sokolovs were out with no explanation for their hasty departure. All of their furniture hadn't even been moved in yet.

In 1996, Christopher Taylor, a famous Hollywood director, leased the mansion to shoot his latest horror movie. It only took a week for the troubled production to immediately shut down, and Taylor was on his way back to California with his demoralized cast and crew. Nobody ever explained the reason why, as though they had been sworn to secrecy. Taylor never made a movie again.

Five years later, the Bechdel estate found another purchaser—a wealthy Manhattan magnate who had big plans for the mansion. Eugene Garland moved his wife and four children, oblivious to its history and the lore surrounding the mansion. Garland, himself, didn't believe in that kind of stuff. He died in his sleep from a heart attack three weeks later.

Then, for a while, there were no buyers. No tenants. No renters. No one wanted to go near the house. Each owner had fled, for some reason or the other, and no one could ever understand why.

UNTITLED

* * *

October 9, 2016

Mary Malone woke up when her head bumped against the car's passenger window. It was afternoon, and her fair-skinned face felt the heat from the flashing rays of sunlight beaming through the oak trees along the leaf-strewn road. Her husband, Curtis, was at the wheel of their Ford Expedition SUV. A twenty-six-foot moving truck followed behind them. Soft rock played from the stereo as Mary tilted her head and squinted against the blinding sun. Her neck ached, and she didn't know how long she had been out. She reached for her sunglasses on the dashboard as Curtis glanced over from behind his own shades.

"Hey. You're awake."

Mary felt her neck and shook her head. "How long was I out?"

"'Bout three hours," he answered.

Her eyes widened. "Really? Oh my gosh. I'm sorry!"

"Don't worry about it," he said. "We crossed the state border about an hour ago."

Mary looked around. A forest of trees, barren of leaves, lined both sides of the rural, two-lane state road.

"We're in Indiana?" she asked.

"Sure are," Curtis said as they continued down the road, blowing leaves to the side.

A fresh, familiar vision entered Mary's head. She could see a large boarded-up door with vine-covered pillars on either side. Beyond the entrance sat an empty fountain in the center of a cracked courtyard, weeds sprouting all around it. "I saw it," she said. "In my dream, I saw our new house."

Curtis pulled at the collar of his white polo shirt. His black hair was slicked back, and his face was clean-shaven, with the lingering musk of aftershave still there. They had been married for two and a half years. They had a happy marriage and good jobs and lives back in Chicago. Recently, however, all of that had changed, and they were looking to start over.

They had fled the city for a reason: a new beginning under new and better circumstances. The town of Redwood afforded them that opportunity, as Curtis had explained to her. He was the primary force in their sudden relocation, and Mary had felt like a simple bystander as of late.

She continued describing her dream and its unsettling visions.

Curtis nodded along, interested. "Really sorry that you never got a chance to see the place first, but I wanted to lock the deal in as soon as possible."

"I understand," she said. "You've done a lot for us the past couple of weeks." She smiled and took his hand. "You've been very busy."

"I certainly wasn't going to sit around with you in the hospital. This is good for us, trust me."

Mary looked out the window with a slight uncertainty in her gut. "It's just… it looks so old from the pictures you showed me. And it's so big. What are we going to do with all that space?"

"Whatever we want," he said, flashing a smile as sunlight reflected against the dark lenses of his sunglasses. "They've been renovating all week. It's going to look a lot better now."

"I was reading about the people murdered in there," Mary said. "At first I thought you were crazy to even consider moving here, but I feel drawn to the place. It's hard to explain."

Curtis waved her off. "You know a good deal when you see one, that's all. Besides, those murders took place forty years ago." He looked up, thinking. "Ancient history."

"It's still creepy," Mary said. She released his hand, brushing her blonde hair to the side and looking back out the window.

Curtis slowed at an empty intersection. They hadn't seen another house for miles. It was all forest, and Mary loved the stark contrast from the busy streets of Chicago where they had resided for years.

"Don't tell me that you're softening up," he said. "I thought you loved crime stories and the supernatural."

Mary shook her head. "I don't know anymore. My mother thinks we're crazy for doing this."

Curtis turned to her as they continued through the rural terrain. "It's a ten-acre *mansion,* Mary, for nearly the same price we were paying for a two-bedroom apartment in Chicago. This is a miracle."

"I wonder why it's priced so low," Mary said with a tinge of sarcasm.

"I don't care," Curtis said. "I feel good about this. After all we've been through, we deserve it. A small town with a clean slate. It's perfect."

Mary turned to him, half-convinced. Before their marriage, she had never gone into great detail about the visions she would have. Half the time she didn't understand them herself. They came in spurts, starting as far back as her childhood. Then again, she was an artist working as a free-lance illustrator for children's books. Having "visions" was part of the job.

Curtis began to speak of their future with sheer optimism. "I'm looking into setting up my own practice out here. You'll have all the room you need to work. We'll have everything we need. He stroked the surface of her jeans above her knee. "We're going to be okay."

She looked up at him with a faint smile, struggling to find the right words. "I know. It's a great deal. It's just… something feels off now. Maybe I should have come out here first."

"You were in no condition for that," Curtis said, looking into her blue-green eyes. "I told you I would handle everything. We're out here now and that's all that matters."

Mary nodded, holding her emotions in. It was hard to believe how quickly things had fallen apart over the past year, but she did love him and felt committed to their future together.

Curtis slowed as they neared a faded traffic sign on the side of the road that said, Redwood 5 Miles. They were close. The moving truck behind them followed, headlights filling the rearview mirror. She wondered if there was still time to return to their former lives before it was too late. But there was no turning back now. This was their new home.

The moving truck was filled with everything they owned, packed and loaded in haste. One day they were in their apartment eating dinner, the next day movers were loading up their things.

They passed over bumpy railroad tracks, just as a long semitruck, the first vehicle they had seen in miles, roared past them from the opposite direction. As they neared Redwood, Mary still had questions. She should have asked from the get-go but didn't.

"How did you first find out about this place? It's so... out here," she said to him as they passed a small gas station and country store. There were a few people in the parking lot and a car at one of the two pumps.

"I told you this, remember?" Curtis said. She didn't, so he continued. "A buddy in real estate, put me in touch with a realtor in Redwood, Bob Deckers. Bob told me all about it. Mansion has been sitting dormant for over a decade." Curtis laughed to himself, then continued. "Lots of superstitious people out there, I imagine."

"Can you blame them?"

"We got lucky, Mary," he said. "And we should be grateful for that."

Rolling prairie fields and lush forest encompassed the surrounding area. The rural isolation was disquieting but comforting at the same time. They had truly escaped. Up ahead on their right was an old wooden billboard. It overlooked a deep, watery canal. Etched on the sign were giant letters: Welcome to Redwood Est. 1826. A small wooden sign hung below the big one on small links of chain: Population: 1,600. Mary wondered how accurate the numbers were. Perhaps she could adjust to life in the country after all. She would have to see the mansion first. Not in some kind of dream or vision but right in front of her. She would make up her mind from there.

* * *

Curtis turned onto Main Street, an old-style brick road along the so-called "historic" district. He slowed as Mary took in all the quaint shops and buildings around them.

There was an old theater with a marquee that read, Autumn Celebration VC Fairgrounds OCT 15 & 16.

Next to the theater was a green building, three stories high, with two American flags flapping from its midsection. A red canopy hung over the first floor of a furniture store that was open for business. As they continued, Mary took notice of a grand mural sprawled across the side of the building, detailing a herd of frontiersmen journeying up a hill of bare pine trees.

There were other historical markers along the way, including some statues set among benches and trimmed bushes. They passed a deli and a crafts store—both resembling mom-and-pop shops. They certainly weren't in Chicago anymore.

The police station was a small brick building with a sloping teal roof. To the left was the town square, where a large fountain sprayed water, mushrooming out on all sides. Across from the fountain was a domed stage with several rows of empty benches. Past the dome, Mary could see a park with fading grass and fall leaves strewn across the ground. Because the weather was still warm, people walked about wearing sun visors and shades, pushing baby strollers or walking their dogs. There was a serene quality to the town unlike anything Mary had felt in some time.

Heads glanced in their direction, young and old. Their mini-convoy did not go unnoticed. It was a Saturday afternoon, and there were plenty of people visiting shops, having lunch, or just out for a stroll. There was an old village vibe to the town, slightly modernized but still steeped in the history of old buildings and roads. The brightness of the town resembled nothing in Mary's own visions, and for the time being, she felt at peace.

"Nice little town," Curtis said.

Mary nodded along, observing shops on her side among

bike racks and newspaper stands. Aside from its humble and welcoming aura, the town so far looked like something out of an amusement park. Though Mary kept such thoughts to herself. The intersections ahead had old-fashioned traffic lights on each side of the street, attached to poles. Their light was green, but a young boy on a bike rode across right in front of them, not even looking.

"Look out!" Mary shouted.

Curtis slammed the brakes, and the car screeched to a halt. Mary flew forward, and then was thrust back as her seat belt locked. Bags catapulted from the backseat. Mary's purse hit the dashboard. The moving truck behind them slammed its brakes just as Mary glanced into the rearview mirror, startled.

Frightened, the boy lost balance and tipped over, falling onto the pavement as the grille of the SUV came within inches of him. Their moving truck screeched to a halt. Mary grabbed her armrest and closed her eyes, bracing herself for the impact, but nothing happened. She opened her eyes and turned to see the truck right at their rear bumper.

"Crap... that was a close one," Curtis said in a dazed state.

Mary then turned to see the boy struggling on the ground in front of them. She opened her door, stepped outside, and rushed to the front as heads turned from pedestrians around them.

"Mary, what are you doing?" Curtis called out as her door slammed shut.

The boy was in the process of pushing himself up when she came to his aid, arms out and instinctively protective of him.

"Are you all right?" she said, kneeling down.

The boy's shaggy red hair bobbed up and down with a nod as he tried to speak. With the bike pinning him down, he looked plenty distracted.

"Here, let me help," Mary said, pulling his bike up. The boy was able to move more freely and seemed less panicky than before. She heard Curtis's door open as he stepped out and approached them.

"Is he okay?" he asked.

Mary took the boy's hand and carefully helped him up, brushing his thick bangs out of his eyes. "There. Everything's okay. Your bike's fine, and it looks like you just have a tiny scratch on your elbow."

"Uh huh," the boy said as his big eyes looked downward with slight embarrassment.

"You need to be more careful, little buddy. That was a close one," Curtis said from behind them.

The boy nodded again as Mary rubbed his shoulders. He then turned from them and got back on his bike as though nothing had happened.

"It's all right," Mary said. "We're just glad you're okay."

"Thanks," the boy said, glancing up at her. She knew that they were complete strangers in his eyes, but she maintained her friendly smile as the boy quickly pedaled away without looking back.

"Can you believe that?" Curtis said with his hands on his hips. "My heart is still racing. Should have a talk with that kid's parents."

Mary rubbed his chest as she made her way back to the car. "Let's just keep going. We already have enough people looking at us."

Curtis turned and followed her back to the idling car and got in. Still shaken, he slowly accelerated and then drove off as people continued to stare. There was no doubt that they had already made an impression in town. That was, if anyone made the connection with the moving truck behind them. They passed a few more buildings and then turned left off

Main Street onto a road that ran along a glistening lake that stretched for a mile into the distance.

Some locals were fishing around the lake, in ankle-high grass as endless forest stretched behind them on the horizon. Curtis steered along the wide curve in the two-lane road, still frustrated.

"Can't believe he just came out in front of us like that. Where were his parents?"

"He's just a kid," Mary said. "Be grateful nothing bad happened."

"Nearly had a heart attack," Curtis said, shaking his head. "You just don't dart out into the road like that."

Mary said no more and looked out her window as they drove past homes concealed within the forest brush, spread out, with No Trespassing signs posted on guideposts and gates blocking the dirt-trail entrances. The rural home-owners seemed to revel in their privacy, and privacy was exactly what Curtis and Mary were looking for.

"How much farther?" Mary asked.

"About five miles down here," Curtis said. "Excited?"

"I am," she said.

Curtis looked away, convinced enough. Mary glanced at the dashboard clock. It was a little after three.

As they continued down the road, the homes became more sporadic. Soon Mary didn't see any. Were they really going to live out here? What were they going to do with a two-story, ten-thousand-square-foot mansion? Mary closed her eyes, trying to calm her nerves while telling herself that she had to give it a chance.

She then had a sudden vision of a large hall with open windows and thin white curtains blowing in the wind. A distant voice called to her from the darkness at the end of the hall, where she could see the faint glow of red eyes. Her heart seized, and she couldn't move. She snapped out of it, clutching her chest with a gasp.

"What is it?" Curtis asked, looking over with concern.

"Nothing..." she said, rubbing her head. "I was... just thinking about that boy. How terrible it would've been."

Curtis took her hand again and squeezed. "No need to worry." He tapped his steering wheel. "You're looking at the model of a safe driver here."

Mary smiled even though she still didn't feel right. The closer they got to the mansion, the worse she began to feel. She squeezed her forehead again while holding Curtis's hand. She felt dizzy, frightened even. Curtis must have noticed something wrong with her as she nodded forward.

"Mary? Mary!"

Before she knew it, her head dropped down and hit the dashboard and she was out cold.

HOMESTEAD

Mary woke up, reclining in a chair inside a large, empty room, with an icepack over her forehead and a paramedic at her side, checking her vitals. She had no idea how long she had been there. From the window, the sun was still out, and she could hear movement all around her. Curtis was nowhere to be seen.

"Take it easy, ma'am," the young male paramedic said to her as she began to rise. "You passed out a little while ago and your husband called us out here."

"Where am I?" she asked, looking around the room in wonder.

"You're at your new house. We brought you in about twenty minutes ago." He paused, shaking his head. "Weirdest thing. Our ambulance wouldn't start. I'm going to have one hell of a word with the maintenance department." He then looked at her with a matter-of-fact demeanor. "We wanted to get you somewhere comfortable, so your husband suggested the house."

Having heard enough, she rose from the chair, touched

her sore neck and scanned the empty room where boxes were strewn across the floor.

"You should give yourself sometime," the paramedic said, handing her a water bottle. "Your husband told us that you two have been through a lot. Could have been a panic attack or stress fatigue. Anything's possible."

She took the bottle and drank from it, thanking him.

"My name's Chet, by the way. Welcome to Redwood."

"Thank you," she said, walking past him and looking around the room. Its faded walls and vaulted ceiling seemed familiar to her. She had the strangest feeling that she was in the living room.

The paramedic followed her, concerned, as she left the room and walked through large double doors which were propped open, revealing the busy courtyard outside. So many people! She shielded her face as she walked down the steps and through the crowds of unfamiliar faces who were moving around the courtyard in a dizzying bustle, purposeful and busy.

She turned to face the mansion as it towered over her. Its faded gray walls were covered in winding vines, growing from the green brush which spread on all sides. Its windows were thick with grime and dust. Its arching roof was covered in leaves and debris, gutters full. A deck on the second floor overlooked the entire property.

An empty fountain sat in the middle of the courtyard, filled to the brim with branches and dead leaves. Mary turned back to the mansion, taking in its looming presence. This was it. This was where they were going to live. It didn't look nearly as dilapidated as it had appeared in her dreams.

They had hired a renovation team weeks ahead. There were several landscapers on site, eradicating decades of over-grown foliage. Men with pressure hoses sprayed the front of the house, gradually turning the hard exterior surface from gray to white. There were also painters on site, janitorial services, carpenters, and other renovation teams. Mary lost count of them all. She shuddered to think of the cost. Financially, she hoped that it would be worth it.

Their moving truck was parked next to the courtyard fountain, backed in near the front door. Curtis stood at the rear, directing the movers as they unloaded their living-room set, placing various pieces of furniture around the courtyard. Mary felt strangely detached, and she couldn't pinpoint why.

The sun was temporarily concealed by passing clouds, providing some much-needed shade. She looked to the driveway circling the courtyard, where a line of vans and trucks were parked. Even with all the work going on, there was still a lot more work to do. The thought of cobwebs and rodents alone made her queasy. Despite her lingering apprehension, she couldn't help but feel the excitement in the air. They actually owned a mansion. Everything that had brought them to this moment seemed unreal.

She walked along the pebbled ground toward the moving truck to talk to Curtis. She had seen pictures of the mansion before, but now within its presence she felt as though she had walked the same path many times before. She stopped beside the moving truck and looked up at the center balcony, where a white curtain flowed into the air from an open window, its fabric torn.

A pest-control van pulled up next to her, out of nowhere, and parked behind the long line of vehicles. She took in the disorienting sounds of the pressure washers, gas-powered hedge trimmers, and lawn mowers around her. There was so much activity going on, she didn't know what she could do, if anything, to lend a hand. Everything had already been set in motion. Curtis had seen to that. What could she do but accept their brash relocation?

She approached Curtis as he directed the movers from the rear of the truck. "What happened?" she asked, startling him.

The paramedic following her then cut in. "I explained to your wife the best I could. All her vitals are good. She just needs to take it easy."

He turned around with sweat stains showing through his white polo shirt. "You gave us quite a scare," he said. "That's what happened."

"When did I pass out?" she asked, struggling to form the question.

"About five minutes from here. Your head hit the dashboard, and you were out cold. I pulled over and tried to wake you."

"I don't understand," she said, confused.

She turned to see the ambulance in the courtyard with its hood open and another mechanic tinkering with the engine.

Curtis turned away from the movers and placed his hands on her shoulders. "I'm just glad you're okay. Maybe it's the heat. I can't believe the ambulance broke down. Strangest thing I've ever seen."

"I'm very sorry, sir," the paramedic said. "That's never happened before."

Curtis shrugged. "Not your fault. Maybe it's time to trade her in."

"Maybe..." the paramedic said.

Mary said nothing as Curtis looked into her eyes with genuine concern. "How do you feel now?"

"Better," she said with a faint smile.

He then turned to her, and with a flourish he extended his arm out toward the mansion. "Well, then. Would you like a personal tour of the premises now, Mrs. Malone?"

"A tour would be great."

She put her arm around his as they walked off together,

past the courtyard, toward the marble steps leading inside. As the hired workers moved around them, Mary felt invisible. Arm in arm, they ascended the front steps, leading to the large double-door entrance. The more she saw of the mansion, the more she felt at home.

Anticipation for what lay ahead increased with each step. Mist from the pressure washer fell onto her arm from afar. Much of the grime and buildup on the right side of the house had already been removed. They reached the top step, and Mary could see a darkened foyer ahead.

"Oh," Curtis said. "Still trying to get the power on out here." She followed him inside and could see rays of light hitting dusty hardwood floors from the open windows. "Got the water turned on, though," he added with pride.

"So… no power?" Mary asked.

Curtis let out a nervous laugh. "Trying to get 'em out here today, but it's not looking good."

Mary thought to herself for a moment. "Maybe we should just find a hotel for the time being."

"Nonsense," Curtis said with a squeeze around her waist. "It's our first night. We have to stay."

"But there's no power," Mary said. "And this place is a dust bowl."

She looked down the vast empty foyer and observed its cobweb-covered chandeliers hanging from the high ceiling above. Ahead of them was a long, winding staircase to the second floor. There were halls at both ends of the foyer, leading to a variety of different rooms. Though there was plenty to explore, she felt a strange knowledge of the layout without even looking.

"Shall we continue, my dear?" Curtis asked.

She turned her head, smiling and feeling slightly overwhelmed. "Sure. I just don't know where to start."

Curtis released her and backed away, pulling a folded

paper from his pocket. "I've got a layout here." He unfolded the paper as Mary looked down the dark hall to their left.

Curtis pulled a mini flashlight from his pocket and shined a light on the map. The endless symphony of pressure washers, hedge trimmers, and leaf blowers continued outside, unabated. Mary walked to the center of the foyer. Her soft shoes barely made a sound on the dusty hardwood floors. She looked to her right toward an adjacent room that could very well be considered an extension of the foyer, though she found something peculiar about it.

"The lounge…" she said softly. "Is this where it happened?"

"Sorry?" Curtis said, holding the layout under his mini flashlight.

"Nothing," Mary said. "How big is the kitchen?"

Curtis scanned the layout, trying to answer. "Kitchen?"

Mary turned to her right and began walking.

"Yeah, that way," he said, looking up. He hurried to catch up with her as she continued down the dark hall. Mary stopped in her tracks and looked up as Curtis stopped beside her.

"You okay?" he asked.

"Yeah…" she said in a distant tone. She closed her eyes and touched her forehead, sighing.

He caressed her shoulder with concern. "Maybe you should lie down. I don't want you to pass out on me again."

"I'm fine. Let's see the kitchen," she said, walking ahead. She then looked up to the ledge of the second floor and stopped as though she saw something.

Curtis halted as his shoes squeaked against the floor. "What is it?"

"Just thought I saw something," Mary said. "Never mind."

"Well, that's creepy," Curtis said. He then put his arm around her and pulled her closer. "Just remember, a long time has passed, and we should have nothing to worry about."

She looked at him with a smile. "I suppose you're right. I just want to find out more about it."

"How about we go to town tomorrow? They have this library. It's so quaint, you'd love it."

Mary nodded and continued down the hall and entered a long, empty room with two windows on each side—caked with enough dirt and grime to block the sunlight from entering.

"This is the dining room," Curtis said, shining his flashlight around.

Mary looked around in awe. "Enormous…"

The air was stuffy and smelled of old wood. Curtis went to the first window at his right and tried to open it, but it wouldn't budge. He handed the map and flashlight to Mary and turned back to the window, pushing up against it. "This is ridiculous," he said, grunting. "We need to get all these opened and air this place out."

Suddenly, the front doors swung wide open down the hall at the foyer and the movers entered, looking for Curtis. Curtis looked up and turned to Mary. "Oh, right. I almost forgot about them. Can we continue the tour later?"

"No problem," Mary said. "I'll keep looking around."

Curtis walked off and met with the movers, leaving Mary to explore on her own. She approached the window he couldn't open and ran her hands down the warm glass, trailing lines of dust. Now that they had started, she felt the urge to explore every room in the house, top to bottom. She approached a set of double doors at the end of the dining room, eager to see the kitchen beyond, with its simple amenities.

She turned both knobs and pulled the heavy oak doors open, and dank, musty air hit her. Like the rest of the house, all the windows were closed and caked with years of dirt and mildew buildup. She entered the kitchen, switching on the flashlight. Dust rained down as she moved the light through the darkened room. There were several countertops, and cabinets that reached the ceiling. The kitchen looked as though it could have been considered at one time the height of elegance.

There was a large industrial-sized antique stove in the corner. She wondered if it was still operational. To her immediate right was a sink the size of a bathtub and flat, dusty countertops that stretched the entire length of the room, with more cabinets overhead than she would ever know what to do with.

She walked along the tiled floor past the thick granite countertops and came upon a vast pantry with dozens of shelves bolted to plaster walls. There was energy in the room that she couldn't quite pinpoint.

She walked away from the pantry, exploring the rest of the layout, when suddenly, a jolting clang rang out as something hit the floor a few feet ahead of her. She jumped and raised her flashlight, only to see a metallic ladle on the ground, fallen from a nearby hook on the wall. The kitchen needed work. That much was clear. She had seen enough, though, and walked with haste back through the dining hall to the foyer, where the movers were carrying in boxes. Curtis stood to the side talking on his cell phone, pacing back and forth.

"Yes, but I was scheduled for activation yesterday." He paused, annoyed. "Your company was given plenty of notice to turn our power on."

It wasn't looking good. Mary said hi to the movers as they breezed past her. She wasn't sure what was in each box that they set down. She and Curtis had packed everything the prior weekend, and her head still wasn't clear. Once their possessions were inside, she figured they could decide where to move things later.

To almost anyone, she thought, the mansion would seem excessive in its size. Everything they owned could probably fit in the downstairs ball room alone. The thought of having so much space was overwhelming, and the thought of living behind these walls felt unreal.

Curtis had spent the last few weeks convincing her they were making the right decision. She knew him to be impulsive, but in the end, she agreed to it. As she stood in the foyer, surrounded by boxes, she wondered when the reality of their choice would settle in.

"Just send someone out today. Please," Curtis said on the phone. "We can't wait until Monday. That is final." He hung up the phone and shook his head in frustration.

Mary gazed up the staircase, eager to see the rooms above, but before she jaunted off into the unknown upstairs, she approached Curtis for an update.

"Everything okay?"

Curtis turned to her, flustered. "Yeah, the power company is playing games. Completely dropped the ball on us."

She touched his arm. "I'm going to look around some more. Want to join me?"

Curtis brought his hands up to his head, massaging his temples. "Nah. That's all right. Why don't you go check out the master bedroom while I have them move in the rest of our stuff?"

"Sure thing," she said with a smile.

She walked away toward the stairs and climbed the white marble steps, which curved to the second floor. The faded brass railing had circular see-through patterns that ended at two thick rail posts at the top of the stairs. A crystal chandelier hung within eye level over the floor below. She could see the foyer below as well as the lounge, where they had been standing. Everything had a strange and familiar feel to it that she could not look past.

She turned to the right and went down the hall toward the master bedroom. The doors on both sides of the hall were open halfway, exposing dark, empty rooms. She pushed the master-bedroom door open and walked in with a sense of awe and wonder.

There was a pair of long windows at the end of bedroom that overlooked the backyard. They were less dirty than most, and sunlight beamed in, illuminating the bare hardwood floors, which were so dusty, she left footprints as she walked across. The white ceiling was high, and the walls were gray-patterned, with tarnished sterling light fixtures at intervals along the way.

She approached the windows, curious to see the view from their bedroom. The backyard was enormous, with grass so high it covered a stone walkway that led to a sizable gazebo covered in vines. Beyond the gazebo was thick forest, seemingly untouched by man. With its abundance of trees and underbrush, there was no denying that the backyard needed considerable work. She couldn't imagine the amount of upkeep it was going to take to keep everything under control. She attempted to quell her doubts that they could afford it all. They belonged here. This was their home.

She turned toward the bathroom at the other end of the room, and decided to have a look. With a click of her flashlight, the room brightened, and she looked inside, taking in its vast size. There was a bathtub, a standing shower, a bidet, an old toilet, and a long counter with two sinks.

"Mary, where are you?" Curtis's voice shouted from the hall.

"Back here," she said, walking out of the room to meet him. He was leading the movers down the hall as they carried a mattress.

"We should really clean these floors before moving anything in here."

The movers stopped with a large sigh between them as they lowered the mattress. Curtis stood nearby, dazed but understanding. "Yeah, I guess you're right." He turned to the movers. "Hold up, guys. Sorry, we're going to have to get the cleaners in here first."

They leaned against the mattress and shrugged. Curtis went back down the staircase as Mary followed. They walked through the foyer and back outside, where the collective work of a dozen landscapers, painters, and movers continued.

As she walked into the courtyard, Mary glanced up into the window near the second-story balcony. She could see someone standing there watching them. At first, she assumed it to be one of the movers, but it wasn't. Her attention went to the front door, where both men walked outside. Her heart seized as she glanced up to the window again, but no one was there.

* * *

With most of the moving and work done, Mary and Curtis sat on the floor of their master bedroom, their first night in the house. Their mattress sat in the corner with blankets strewn over it. On the floor close by sat two burning candles, a pizza box, and an open bottle of wine on the floor.

"I heard some scratching in one of the rooms downstairs," Mary said, taking a sip of wine from her glass.

Curtis tipped his wine glass with a smile. "Not to worry, my dear, pest control is on it."

Mary looked around the room, still feeling overwhelmed. The floor had been cleaned, and there was a startling difference from what it had looked like a few hours ago. The same couldn't be said of every room. There was still a lot of work to be done.

"A lot of things still don't make sense to me," she said, looking up at the high ceiling.

Curtis scratched his head. "Like what?" he asked.

"Like why we moved here," she answered, touching her forehead. "Everything happened so fast, I really never got a chance to think about it."

Curtis smiled, took both empty wine glasses, and stood up. "I know you're concerned, but you need to stop worrying. I don't like to see you like this." He paused and looked into her eyes. "Everything is going to be okay."

"I hope you're right," Mary said. "I really do."

Curtis set the wine glasses on their dresser, walked over to Mary, and took her hands in his, pulling her up. "There's nothing to worry about," he said. "We are going to make this work."

"Part of me wishes that we just waited a little longer," Mary said. "Now it's too late." She then backed away as Curtis tried to hug her.

Slighted, Curtis threw his arms down. "Mary, you need to stop this!"

Suddenly, both candles erupted in a bright burst of flame and then immediately extinguished, leaving the room pitch black. Mary and Curtis stood silently for a moment in the darkness.

"Just great," Curtis said, leaning down. He pulled a lighter from his pocket and tried to relight the candles, but the wick wouldn't catch fire on either one.

"What the hell's wrong with these candles?" he asked with increasing frustration.

"I don't know," Mary said. "But that was really strange."

He slouched onto their bed, deflated. "How about we just call it a night?"

"Might as well," she said, feeling exhausted herself. She joined him on the bed as he kissed her forehead. Slivers of smoke flowed from each candle in the darkness. She still couldn't wrap her head around it.

"That was so weird..." she said softly.

"Did you feel a draft?" Curtis asked. "I felt a slight draft."

"Me too," she said.

"Must've been from outside," Curtis said, pointing to their open windows. That would have made sense, but the air that evening was still, and there hadn't been a breeze for hours. They sat together for a moment, lost in their own thoughts. Their first evening in the house was a quiet one, and Mary couldn't shake the feeling of an unexplained presence. For the moment, she kept such thoughts to herself. There was no sense in trying to convince Curtis of something she couldn't fully explain herself.

We can make this work, she thought, drifting asleep. *I know we can.*

A STROLL THROUGH TOWN

Mary awoke to sunlight beaming into their room, feeling disoriented. Curtis's side of the mattress was empty, and she could hear movement downstairs. For a moment, she lay in bed and stared up at the ceiling. It felt strange to wake up in a new place, especially when she remembered where she was. To her, the Bechdel mansion was a repository of undiscovered secrets, and she found what little she knew about its history to be fascinating.

As she lay in bed alone, she heard a large thud downstairs followed by several voices. She stretched and leaned over the side of the bed, retrieving her cell phone.

"Oh no..." she said upon seeing that it was five past ten. She had overslept, and there was still much work to be done. Settling in seemed a mammoth task that could take weeks. She remembered that Curtis also wanted to go into town that day.

It would take a good shower and a big cup of coffee to get her up and moving. She sat up as she heard footsteps clamoring up the stairs and the sound of Curtis's voice. "So far, only a few rooms have power. We might have to gut some of the wiring. It's an old place."

She heard them shuffle around in the room next door and stepped out of bed. Her bare feet touched the warm hardwood floor as she went to the door and closed it, muffling the commotion. She turned around and looked at the two open windows across the room overlooking the backyard and felt a slight comforting breeze.

She walked to her suitcase and placed it on the bed, unzipping it. Hastily packed clothes were crammed inside. The double closet in the room was large enough to hold her entire wardrobe and then some, but for the time being, she was living out of a suitcase.

She grabbed a T-shirt and white shorts and headed for the bathroom, where she would find out just how well the plumbing worked. A small window illuminated the vast bathroom, and as she walked toward the standing shower, loosening her nightgown, she heard the bedroom door open.

She froze and held her nightgown on. "Curtis?" she said, feeling nervous with the bathroom door open a crack. The footsteps continued as she walked to the door, calling for Curtis again. As she pushed the door open, she was taken aback to see a large bearded man, sweaty and panting, wandering through the room like a lost child.

"Excuse me," she said, backing into the bathroom.

She heard the man halt. "I-I'm sorry, ma'am. I was just looking for a restroom."

She clutched her chest and backed against the wall. "Well, this is *our* room. Please talk to my husband and find another."

The man apologized and stumbled out of the room, closing the door behind him. Mary remained half-clothed and pressed against the wall, her heart pounding. She lowered her arms, sighing in frustration, and closed the door fully. She then went to the shower, which the cleaners had scrubbed down the day before.

The orange-and-white checkered tile inside looked old-fashioned, to say the least. There were two knobs below the showerhead. She turned the left knob, assuming it was for hot water, and the pipes rumbled and shook, spraying out water intermittently.

She held her hand into the spray and felt a dash of warmth. After a moment, more water began to flow, but it had an almost sulfuric smell. The last thing she wanted to do was to have a strange odor on her. Beyond the unwelcome intruder from a moment ago, she had the feeling that she was being watched.

She then heard the bedroom door open again. Her head whipped around, but she heard nothing else. She turned the water off, frustrated. "Damn it, Curtis. That better be you."

"What are you so afraid of?" an unfamiliar man's voice asked.

Livid, she pulled her T-shirt over her head, put her shorts on, and rushed to the bathroom door, swinging it open, prepared to give whomever it was a piece of her mind. But their room was quiet and undisturbed. The bedroom door was closed and there was no one there.

She darted to the open windows and looked below into the lush, overgrown backyard. There was no sign of anyone. She didn't know what kind of game someone was playing, but she didn't like it. Her hands leaped at the windows and pulled them shut. She scurried across the room and locked the bedroom door. Taking a shower had never proved so difficult. Feeling safer but annoyed, she walked back toward the bathroom, stopping at her suitcase as a thought crossed her mind.

She leaned down and tore through her clothes in a frenzy. Her hands stopped as she slowly pulled a .38 caliber pistol from the bottom. She was probably over-reacting, but she wasn't going to take any more chances. She took the gun with her to the bathroom, locked the door, and set it on the gray tile countertop.

The showerhead dripped as she tried her hand at the knobs again. Water spurted and gushed for a moment before flowing naturally in a warm, steady stream. The strange smell had subsided as well. She stepped inside, feeling an immediate and much-needed relief. It was only morning, and already she felt that she was being tested in some way.

Showered and dressed, Mary walked downstairs, apprehensive about running into any of the movers. There were several men around, but Curtis wasn't among them. She politely gave them a "good morning" and continued her search, walking outside into the bright light of morning shining down onto the concrete courtyard.

There were dozens of people outside, while a short time before, there had been none. Many of them were busy with lawn work, trimming the trees and hedges surrounding the mansion. There was a roofing team above, walking along the ridge and tossing rotted panels into a pile below. That day, Mary imagined, would be much like the day before. Ahead, next to an electrician's van, she saw Curtis. He stood in the shade with a tall, skinny man who wore a red netted hat.

She walked over to Curtis, incensed.

"Good morning," he said, smiling. His smile, however, dropped once he noticed the serious look on her face.

"What's wrong?" he asked her, eyes brimming with concern.

"Can I talk with you in private?" she asked, glancing at the electrician.

Curtis looked around, taken off guard. "Yeah... Yeah, sure." He excused himself and followed Mary around to the other side of the truck. Once they were alone, she leaned closer and spoke in a soft but forceful tone.

"Someone came into our room earlier when I was in the shower."

Curtis's eyes widened. "What?"

"Yeah," she said, shaking her head. "The first guy came in by accident. Then someone else just walked in, said something to me, and walked out."

Curtis covered his mouth. "*What?*"

Realizing she might be making too much of it, she raised her hand as if to stop herself. "If it was an honest mistake, I can understand, but the whole thing gave me the creeps."

Curtis nodded, biting his lip. "There's some electricians in the house now. I'll talk to them. I'm so sorry, honey. They should know better."

"He said, 'What are you afraid of?' Those were his exact words. I thought it was you at first, but when I opened the door, no one was there."

Curtis looked around with his hands at his sides, growing increasingly frustrated. "Well, that's it. Whoever that was, they're gone. I'll talk to Skip now." He took her hand and squeezed it. "I'm so sorry." His face then brightened with a smile. "How about we go into town for a little bit? I'm getting a headache with all this commotion around us."

"Sure," she said. "That sounds nice."

She wanted to get out, but above all there was a burning desire to find out more about the Bechdels. Perhaps there were people in town who could help her.

* * *

They drove into town on a blue-sky day, prepared to get the lay of the land and meet some people in the process. The mansion was roughly five miles from any home, store, or gas station, and it was nice to escape all the activity at home and rejoin civilization. Mary tried to put all the recent strangeness out of her mind and enjoy the scenic beauty of the town before them, a stunning contrast to the traffic and noises of the city. They had entered a different world.

It was a Sunday, and they passed a quaint white church that looked like something out of a storybook. Amidst its fresh green lawn and picket fence, a congregation flowed out of the double-door entrance toward a side parking lot. A wooden sign sat in front of the church with First Christ Church of Redwood neatly painted over it.

Mary turned and looked at the church as families in their dress clothes, men and women, old and young alike, slowly exited the building for Sunday services. She couldn't remember the last time she had been to church.

"It looks nice," she said. "Maybe we could go there some time and get to know some people."

"Sure," Curtis said. "You have fun with that."

Mary turned to him, mouth agape. "As if it would kill you to go to church." She then leaned back against the headrest and placed her sunglasses on. "I think it would be good for us with everything that's happened."

"Too boring," Curtis said matter-of-factly.

Mary laughed. "This coming from a lawyer," she chided.

Farther down the road, they passed a park where children climbed a jungle gym and a corner store to their right where an older man stood at the gas pump fueling up his boat, which was hitched to his truck. Downtown was in sight, with its brick-paved roads, vintage light posts, and quaint buildings. "Historic Downtown," they called it. There was a fire station to their left, small like everything else, that had its bay doors open revealing a shiny red fire truck. A sign at the end of the driveway said, "Redwood Fire Department."

A few blocks past the fire station, they saw the police

department, where two officers in beige uniforms were talking outside the door. Their heads turned toward the car as Curtis passed and the two officers waved. Curtis gave them a wave back and smiled.

"This town sure is something," he said.

"It does seem like a safe, nice town," she said. There were plenty of places to go for a run. She had even spotted some nature trails by the park, perfect for jogging. Back home, Mary was an avid runner, and she tried to make the time at least three times a week. It refreshed her and made her feel focused, an important part of her weekly routine. She scanned the buildings ahead, hoping to see the library. Then she wondered if it would even be open on a Sunday.

"You could use this place in one of your stories," Curtis said. "Take your sketch pad out here and capture it."

"I plan to," Mary said, "but it'll be for fun. I don't write the stories."

"Have you called anyone at work yet to let them know you're settling in?" he asked.

The thought so far hadn't crossed her mind. She was a professional illustrator for children's books, and mainly worked from home. It was a dream job that she couldn't be happier with, though she'd been on maternity leave for a few weeks and hadn't talked to her publisher in some time. "I'll call them tomorrow," she said.

"That's what I like to hear," Curtis said. "Relax and put it off." He scanned the shops as they drove down Main Street. Mary knew that he was looking for a potential spot to set up his own practice, but their dwindling finances concerned her. During the drive from Chicago, she had suggested that he find a partnership in Redwood. There had to be a law office out there somewhere. He had originally balked at the idea, but they would have to start somewhere.

They came to a parking lot near a pizza place aptly titled

Bricklayers Pizza, complete with an old-fashioned hanging sign above the door. American flags, pizza places, parks, and nature trails, Redwood seemed perfect.

"This looks like a good place to park," Curtis said, turning in. "Library's just up the street." He then parked between a truck and Jeep and turned off the ignition while glancing up at the rearview mirror. "Hey, it's Bob Deckers!" he said, excited.

Mary turned her head. There was a man in a suit smoking under the canopy of the building behind them. "Who?" she asked.

"Our realtor. That's his office," Curtis said. He opened his door and stepped out as Mary put on her sun hat and exited the car, her sandals touching the hot pavement.

They walked toward the rear of the car while Curtis kept his attention on Bob Deckers, who hadn't noticed them yet. He looked to be in his fifties, with gray slicked-back hair and a dark tan.

"Let's go talk to him," Curtis said, taking her hand. "I want to ask him about leasing some office space."

Mary shook her head. "I'll meet up with you guys later. I want to check and see if the library is open."

Curtis turned, frustrated but understanding. "At least come say hi. He really helped us out."

"I will later," Mary said. "I promise."

"All right. Don't go far."

"Okay," she said, pecking his cheek with a kiss.

"Have fun," Curtis said, walking away. She watched as he hurried to the building, calling out Bob's name and shaking his hand. Bob looked startled and surprised to see him. They exchanged words, and then Bob slapped Curtis on the back, opening the door to his office and leading him inside. Mary then felt free to walk through the town on her own to get a feel of the place. Someone had the answers she needed.

She was, in fact, a believer in the supernatural. She had seen many strange things in her life, dreamlike visions of the future as far back as when she was a teenager. There was a lot Curtis didn't know about from back then, and she was determined to keep it that way.

She approached the sidewalk and moved past the pizza place, passing a closed consignment shop and, next door, an art gallery. Redwood seemed to have a little of everything, and she was excited to see a crafts store with art supplies in the window. It was closed as well, but she made a note for later. A few people passed her by as she smiled and nodded, but there weren't nearly as many people out as on the previous day.

She heard the church bell toll as the library came into view in the distance—a long gray building with a flat roof and large tinted windows. It was surrounded by vertical metal railing and nicely trimmed bushes. She didn't see anyone around the building, but something told her to keep going. The open gate in the center was a good sign.

As she walked past a closed bar, an old woman stepped into her path from an alley, startling Mary. The woman looked frazzled with long, dirty hair, a green jacket and a plain dress about two sizes too large.

"Oh! Excuse me," Mary said, carefully moving around the woman.

The woman stared her down, shaking her head and not saying a word. Her gray hair sprouted in all directions. She wore bright-red lipstick and had heavy bags under her glazed eyes. As Mary passed, the woman turned and followed her, wagging her long finger in the air.

"You and your husband," she said in a low, scratchy voice.

Mary stopped and turned around, facing the woman, dumbfounded. "What did you say?"

"You've made a terrible mistake," the woman said.

Mary stepped forward, upset. "What are you talking about? How do you know my husband?"

"You don't belong here. Outsider..." she hissed with contempt.

Despite the woman's shoddy appearance and rudeness, Mary felt an urge to probe further. "What can you tell me?"

The woman shook her head, lost in her own thoughts. She then opened her mouth to speak, when a nicely-dressed man approached her from behind and placed a hand on her shoulders. "That's all right, Evelyn, let's take you home."

The woman jumped as the man looked at Mary with a smile on his face. He was clean-shaven with thick white hair, neatly brushed to the side. His dark-blue three-piece suit was a stark contrast to the woman's tattered clothes.

"Hi, I'm Phil," he said, extending his hand.

Mary nodded and shook his hand. "I'm Mary. Nice to meet you."

The woman looked down and mumbled to herself, her train of thought broken.

"I apologize if ol' Evelyn gave you a scare. She wandered from the retirement home again." He squeezed the woman's shoulder. "She's been missing for hours, and the staff has been worried sick."

Mary smiled. "Well, I'm glad she has somewhere to go."

The man narrowed his eyes in curiosity at her. "You and your husband just moved here, correct?"

"Wow. Word gets around," she said.

"It sure does," Phil responded.

"That's correct," she said. "We arrived yesterday."

"And you're staying in the old mansion, eh?"

"We are. It-It's been interesting so far," she said.

Phil smiled again, exposing bright white teeth. "I certainly hope you get settled in okay." He paused for a moment and stepped closer to Mary as Evelyn rocked in place, muttering.

"I'm the pastor at the First Christ Church of Redwood. Pastor Phil, they call me. I sure hope you and your husband can attend our services some time."

Mary nodded politely with a smile. "We'd love to."

Phil snapped his fingers as though recalling something. "We're having our annual summer barbecue next week. You should come on out and see everyone."

"That sounds... really nice," she said.

Seeming satisfied, Phil turned back to Evelyn and took her by the hand. "It was nice meeting you, Mrs. Malone, but I gotta take ol' Evelyn here back home."

"Pleasure meeting you as well," she said, though she didn't recall telling him her last name.

He waved and walked off with Evelyn in tow and then turned around, calling out to Mary. "I look forward to meeting your husband!"

Mary waved back and watched as they crossed to the other side of the road. A few cars passed as she stood there thinking about the woman's words. They could have been the ramblings of a mentally damaged woman, or they could have meant something more. Mary turned back to the library, ready to investigate and uncover whatever was behind the creeping strangeness that seemed to follow her wherever she went.

UNEARTHED

Mary was glad to see that the library was, in fact, open. There were a few rooms with rows of old bookshelves and several empty chairs and tables in the center where patrons could sit and read. There was an older bespectacled man at the check-out table sitting on a stool and reading a newspaper. He wore a striped button-down shirt with the sleeves rolled up and looked up at Mary as she walked in.

Inside, the library was eerily quiet. Sunlight shined through the slats in the blinds covering the surrounding windows. She found the vintage aesthetic of the white plaster walls and faded red carpet comforting but also felt nervous being the only person there—or so she thought.

"Good morning," she said to the man, approaching his counter.

He gave her a polite smile that lifted his wrinkled face and eyed her like the stranger she was. His thinning hair was slicked back, and his skinny neck hung down in folds. Like her, she assumed that everyone in town was from somewhere else. Or maybe some people had lived in Redwood their entire lives. It was exactly what she intended to find out.

"Morning," he said back. "Welcome to the Redwood Public Library."

"Thanks," she said, looking around. "I wasn't sure if you were open today or not."

"Seven days a week."

"That's great," she said. She didn't want to draw attention to the empty tables and aisles, but the man seemed to have read her mind.

"Sundays are our slowest in the morning. Big church community and all. By afternoon we usually get a good crowd," he said.

Mary approached the counter and placed her hands flat on its mahogany surface. "I'm Mary. My husband and I just moved here from Chicago. I'd like to get a library card if I could, please."

The man nodded and leaned down, retrieving a large, dusty binder and setting it on the counter. "All right, Mary. I'm Hal. I'm sure we can get you set up." There was an old computer next to him, but he didn't seem interested in using it. He asked for her full name as well as her driver's license.

She pulled her wallet out from her purse and opened it. "Oh. It still has my old address on it."

"That's fine," he said, taking her license. "Just let me know the new one."

He began scribbling onto a sheet in the open binder, taking down Mary's name. The subdued quiet of the library had her thinking that she'd be spending a lot of time within its walls. It was soothing and pleasant. "I live at 513 Weatherford Lane," she said.

Hal stopped writing and looked up at her. "Weatherford Lane? The old Bechdel mansion?"

She was surprised that he made the connection so

quickly. But then, the mansion and its story surely were known by most people. That much seemed evident in the few interactions she had experienced so far. "Yes, that would be the place," she said.

His eyes immediately fell back onto the binder as he continued writing. "Didn't think that place would ever sell," he said.

Curious, Mary leaned in closer. "And why is that?"

Hal looked up again, taken off guard. "Well, it's just... It's an old place. Too big for most people. Not really practical in today's modern world."

"But it's so inexpensive," Mary said. "Hard to believe they'd have a hard time selling it."

Hal tore a slip from the binder and handed it to Mary. "I wouldn't know. Just seems it was held up in probate forever." He then handed her a pen. "Sign the card here, and you're all good to go."

Mary took the card and signed it, not entirely satisfied with what he was willing or not willing to reveal. "Mister... ?" she paused waiting.

"Hal. Just call me Hal," he said, sitting back down on his stool.

"Hal. I actually came here today to get some information."

Hal went for his newspaper and then paused, looking up with an arched brow. "What kind of information?"

"About this town. About our new house. About the Bechdels, if possible."

Hal leaned back with his arms crossed, more reserved than before. "You some kind of reporter? Been a while since one of them have come here asking questions and all."

"No, I can assure you that—"

Hal cut her off with one arm in the air, pointing. "Because if you are trying to dig up some dirt under false pretenses, I'd like you to kindly leave."

Mary shuffled on the carpet, eager to set the record straight. "I am not a reporter. My husband and I just moved here, and I'd like to do some research."

"Oh…" he said, calming down. "Of course. Well you can't blame me for being suspicious. Folks in Redwood don't bother anyone. They just want to live in a nice, safe community. We're not spectacles for big-city types to come down here and judge us. I think you can respect that."

"I can," Mary said. "This is the exact kind of community my husband and I were looking for."

"It's a long shot from Chicago, ma'am. I can tell you that."

She felt restrained from revealing anything more, or taking a chance on making him even more suspicious. She wanted to tell someone about the visions she had, the unsettling feeling the mansion gave her, and her overall apprehensiveness, but Hal seemed all business, and that was exactly how she decided to proceed.

"Can you direct me to nonfiction, please? As I said before, I'd like to read some history about the town."

"Plenty of books over there," he said, pointing to a row of wooden shelves in the corner across the room. "Lots of local authors there." He then paused and looked up, pushing his glasses back. "Of course, if it's records you're looking for, you might want to visit the courthouse. They got an office of records there dating back a hundred-some odd years."

Great, Mary thought. She was beginning to have her work cut out for her.

"Do you have a newspaper archive here?" she asked.

"Sure do," Hal replied. He then paused and eyed her suspiciously again. "You sure you're not a reporter?"

Her face flushed as she placed her hands on the counter. Hal noticed and reversed course with a laugh.

"Sorry. Can never be too sure around here."

He then pointed to a darkened room off to the left side,

behind glass-paneled doors where stacks of newspaper where piled on shelves. "That's our news room there."

There were also several old monitors lined up next to a microfilm cabinet.

"Thank you," she said, walking away.

Even with her back turned, she could sense him watching her. Perhaps he was reaching for his phone to alert the others that a newcomer was snooping around—an outsider. She stopped at the newspaper room and glanced behind her, only to see Hal going back to his own paper.

She turned the light switch on as she walked inside the room where there were two old beige sofa chairs with a circular coffee table between them. She scanned the years labeled on each microfilm, unsure of where to start.

There was a history that the residents of Redwood seemed very protective of, though she was curious how long Hal and his wife had lived here. Maybe if she got to know him better over the coming weeks, she could find out. She turned to the newspaper shelves with wonder. There were papers dating back to the 1950s, but she was looking for one particular decade—one particular year.

She reached the end of the aisle and turned to walk between the shelves the next aisle over, eyes scanning up and down. In the middle she could see a label on one section for 1974-1975, encompassing over five shelves from top to bottom. "Well," she said to herself. "Here we go."

Suddenly, her cell phone rang inside her purse. She paused and pulled the phone out. Curtis was calling her. She answered, speaking softly even though there was no one in the library at the moment to disturb.

"Hey! Make it to the library okay?"

"I sure did," she said. "I'm there now."

"Great-" His voice cut out a little as a gust of wind blew

into the phone. *"Hey, listen. Bob wants to take us to lunch at this cozy little diner. We'll come over and get you."*

"That's fine, but not right now," she said without hesitation. "I've got to finish what I came here for."

"Come on, Mary. It's Sunday. You'll have plenty more times to go to the library this week."

"Sorry, I'm in the middle of something. I'll meet up with you when I'm finished."

"And how long will that be?"

Mary paused and looked around. "Thirty minutes or so? Not too long."

Curtis sighed but held his tongue. *"Okay. I'll text you what they have on the menu."*

"Sounds good. Thank. Love you. Bye."

She hung up and guided her hands along some newspapers on the second shelf dated between June and July of 1975.

"Perfect," she said, walking away toward one of the sofa chairs. She took a seat with a few papers in her lap as a young couple walked inside the library wearing their Sunday best. She could see them through the glass window. They walked in and said hi to Hal, continuing toward a line of bookshelves.

She carefully opened the first paper, *The Dover County Sentinel*, scanning some articles. Dover was the county in which Redwood was located, but the town seemed to exhibit a boundary all its own. The closest town over, Jasper, was at least twenty miles away. Its headline displayed national news on inflation and gas prices.

It was interesting seeing the advertisements for old television sets and refrigerators, right next to news articles with men dressed in vintage jean jackets and turtlenecks and women with their long, button-down granny dresses. As she flipped through more old news and captured moments of the past, her eyes stopped on one tiny article in the local section.

She recognized the man in the picture. He looked much younger of course, but there he was wearing a plaid jacket and tie and with dark-brown hair, brushed back the same way as now. It was Pastor Phil, and he was standing at a podium with several microphones attached to it. The headline verified her suspicion immediately:

Local Pastor Calls for Peace and Calm during Time of Tragedy

She brought the paper closer and read the article, completely engrossed.

"Following the tragic murders at the Bechdel estate, Pastor Phillip F. Evans led his congregation in vigil for the victims while urging the town not to fall prey to elements of darkness and fear."

She lowered the paper, thinking to herself. She pulled the next paper and found herself engrossed immediately by the bold headline on the front page: "Massacre at the Bechdel Estate."

She didn't know exactly what the articles would tell her, if anything, but she felt that she was closer to fully knowing what had happened, and why, than before. She stood up in haste with the newspapers in hand and walked out of the room, approaching Hal's desk.

"Do you have a copy machine here?"

His eyes rose up with their usual uncertainty. He examined her for a moment, hesitant, as she stood, arms clutching a stack of old newspapers.

"Back there." He pointed.

She turned and saw a large copy machine next to the restrooms, off in the far corner, past the newspaper room.

"Ten cents a copy," he added.

She set the stack down on the counter and fished through

her purse, handing him a few dollar bills for change. He stopped and sighed as his hands slowly went to the cash register and counted her change. She thanked him and went to the copy machine, feeling satisfied, even excited.

After about ten or so minutes of fishing through relevant articles detailing Redwood or the Bechdel mansion, she made her copies, one by one. Once finished, she returned the newspapers to the shelf and strolled through the rest of the library with her copies in hand.

She scanned the bookshelves, looking for anything crime-related in the nonfiction section. She came across a few Redwood travelogue books from independent publishing presses. She wondered if the authors were the locals Hal had mentioned.

Hal looked up from his newspaper as she approached with ten books in hand, plopping them down on the counter. "This'll be it for today," she said.

"Well, all right, then," Hal replied, marking the books with his scanner. She had more than enough to keep her busy. For the time being. She called Curtis to find out where they were when he informed her that Bob Deckers got a call and had to cancel their lunch plans.

"*We can still go to the diner if you want,*" he said.

"Sure," she said. "Let me just put these books in the car first."

"Meet you there," he said.

She walked out of the library with her curiosity about Redwood piqued. She wanted to go home and start reading more than anything else, but it was a nice day out and a perfect opportunity to see more of the town and look for secrets, perhaps, that existed beyond its cheery façade.

* * *

Later that evening, Curtis and Mary took a breather in the master bedroom, admiring the furniture arrangement of their dressers, nightstands, tables, and bed. Mary's bookshelf was intact along with their television stand and flat screen. Their next big step was to unpack the many boxes lying around the room.

"Well, this room's almost ready to go," Curtis said, falling back onto the bed. "That leaves us about... fourteen more rooms."

"There's no furniture left," Mary said, pacing barefoot through the room in her shorts and T-shirt. The power was working in their room. From above, their ceiling fan rotated. Two standing lamps in each corner lit the room.

Curtis sat up and grabbed the remote, turning on the TV, and receiving a screen of white static instead. "Oh, I forgot," he began. "We don't get cable or Internet until tomorrow." He turned the TV off and tossed the remote aside.

Mary continued to pace the room with a worried look on her face. "This house is going to need permanent upkeep. Are you really sure we can afford it all?"

Curtis grabbed a notebook lying on the bed and opened it. "I've charted out our finances right here for the next year. At minimum. I'll need clients here soon, but we can make it."

She felt less than reassured but didn't want an argument. "What's the plan for tomorrow then?"

"Well..." Curtis said, thinking to himself. "The painters will be here. The electricians still need to sort out some of this bad wiring. Lawn maintenance still ongoing." He paused, thinking to himself. "I think that's it."

"Who are we kidding?" she said, taking a seat next to him in bed. "We'll be broke by next week."

Curtis put his arm around her and laughed. "So how'd it go at the library?"

"I got most of what I needed." She gazed up, staring at the

ceiling. "I still can't believe it all happened here. All those poor people murdered. That little girl. She must have been terrified."

Curtis gently tugged at Mary's ponytail. "Terrible things happen, Mary. But this is our house now, and we have to move on."

"The man at the library suggested that I go to the office of records near the courthouse," she said.

"For what?" Curtis asked.

She turned to look at him. "To find out more about this town."

"I knew it," Curtis said with a laugh. "You're planning on writing a book."

Mary waved him off. "I wouldn't even know where to start. I told you, I'm not a writer."

He took her hand, kissed it, and pulled her closer to him, kissing her soft lips. With a heavier embrace to follow, Mary backed up, holding him at bay. "Honey, please. I need to jump into the shower"

"I do too," he said with a devilish smile.

She fell back into his arms as they kissed with deep-seated passion. His hands caressed her back, moving her shirt up. She broke away and raised her arms as he pulled the fabric off and tossed it on the floor.

Mary awoke in the dead of night, curled up on her side of the bed, lying next to Curtis. The sheets were pulled up halfway, and she felt a dryness in her throat that she could not ignore. The room was dark except for the blueness of the moon, shining through the open windows. The overhead ceiling fan was on, making a strange buzzing noise. The air conditioning unit needed to be replaced, and Curtis had told her to expect a new unit within the week.

Feeling spirited, not to mention thirsty, Mary rose in her

nightgown and stepped out of bed, leaving Curtis fast asleep. She wasn't sure which lights downstairs worked yet, so she picked up a flashlight next to the TV stand and left the room to venture toward the kitchen, where there was plenty of bottled water in their new refrigerator.

She crept down the hallway, flicking a light switch on the wall that did not work. She then turned on her flashlight and continued down the hall. The house was quiet, with nary a disturbance. The noise of their old city seemed like a distant memory. At the moment, she would have done anything to hear a car engine, a siren, or a train. She came to the stairs, hesitant to enter the black abyss below.

She knew when to stray away from danger, especially living in Chicago, but if she was afraid to venture through her own house alone, day or night, she feared that she could never make the transition work.

"Come on. What are you waiting for?" she asked herself in a soft voice.

She pointed the flashlight down the stairs and walked down, step by thick marble step. She reached the foyer and was met with a stack of unpacked boxes sitting all over the room. The boxes cast shadows against the light, which put her on edge. She couldn't deny a slight pinch of fear coupled with her increasing heart rate. Her mind was playing tricks on her. She was seeing things, shadows that her mind gave life to.

She rushed past the stacked boxes and headed toward the dining room, closing in toward the kitchen. She flicked on the kitchen light switch in haste. A series of long fluorescent bulbs overhead flickered on, much to her relief. Their new stainless-steel refrigerator hummed in the corner next to the dishwasher. She approached the fridge with the intent of grabbing a bottle or two and going back to bed, but the grumbling in her stomach told her otherwise.

She swung the fridge open and grabbed two water bottles from the middle shelf, setting them on the counter. Inside, the fridge was practically empty. There was half a tuna-salad sandwich Curtis had gotten her from the diner earlier, a loaf of bread, and some cold cuts. Not wanting to spend too much time in the kitchen alone, she grabbed the to-go box and closed the door. Sandwich and water in hand, she left the kitchen, leaving the light on behind her.

As she passed through the dining room, Mary felt more at ease and less afraid of the bare, looming walls where her shadow moved along with her, a companion of sort. She turned the flashlight back on, balancing her sandwich and drinks, and suddenly heard an unmistakable sound coming from the foyer. She slowed her pace and listened. It was the familiar scratching sound from before, coming from another room.

Rodents, she thought.

Pest control had done a sweep of the house earlier in the day, but their work was far from over. The scratching ceased, and she continued on, when another sound stopped her dead in her tracks: the faint cry of an infant. She couldn't believe it. She had to be dreaming. She slowed again and followed the sound, past the staircase and toward the rooms on the other side of the hall.

The crying grew louder with each step. Shining her flashlight ahead, she looked down and saw that her hands were trembling. As she stopped at the first door to her right, the crying became clearer. There was no door to muffle it. The sound was coming from the living room. She peeked inside, waving the flashlight around. The crying stopped. The hairs on the back of her neck stood up in unison.

What the hell was it?

She bravely moved forward and entered the living room, clutching the bottles of water and to-go box against her chest. Ahead in the corner, just beyond the beam of the flashlight, she saw something huddled in the corner. It looked small and furry. Too large to be a rat or a feline. Too small to be human. The cries resumed. Whatever the thing was, it was most definitely making the noise.

She stopped within five feet of the thing and tried to steady her flashlight. A loud screech from all around startled her, just as the figure came into view, turning its gleaming yellow eyes and fang-ridden face in her direction, hissing. She screamed just in time to see the figure scurry off to the other side of the room, burrowing into a small hole above the baseboard.

The figure had ears, whiskers, and a striped tail. She stumbled back, dropping her food and water, and bolted for the door. She ran without turning back, vaulting up the stairs and into the bedroom, adrenaline flowing through her veins.

She closed the door and threw her back against the wall, breathing heavily. "A raccoon…" she said, exasperated. "That's what it was. A freaking raccoon."

A NEW DISCOVERY

Mary woke the next morning still feeling rattled. Curtis had just walked out of the bathroom in his robe with steamy mist following him as Mary sat up, agitated. "I saw a raccoon last night when I went downstairs," she said.

Curtis stopped and dried his bushy hair with a towel, curious. "Are you serious?"

Mary flipped her legs over and onto the floor as she moved to the edge of the bed. "It hissed at me and ran into a hole it had burrowed in our wall."

Curtis's eyes widened. "You have got to be kidding me. A raccoon in our house?"

"We need to get pest control back out here."

"I'm on it," Curtis said, moving to his phone on his dresser.

"There was more, Curtis," she said, stopping him. "I heard an infant crying. Clear as day."

Curtis shook his head. "What are you talking about?"

"Downstairs, right before I saw the raccoon, I heard this crying noise. I'm pretty sure it was a baby."

"Well, there's not much pest control can do about that," Curtis said.

"I'm serious!"

Concerned, Curtis approached her and sat on the bed. "I'm sorry that happened to you. It was late, and you were probably hearing things."

She opened her mouth, prepared to object, when he cut her off.

"Listen. We'll set up some traps and get rid of any rodents still remaining in this house. I promise."

"It's not just the raccoon. I'm getting strange vibes from this place, and I want to find out what it all means."

Curtis took her hand and squeezed it. "I'm not saying that I don't believe you. I just think your nerves are a little shot with everything going on. That's why I want you to relax today."

"I'm not crazy. I know what I heard."

Curtis laughed and rose from the bed, standing in the sunlight. "I never said that. Just take it easy, please. For your sake and mine."

Mary nodded. "I'm going to get to the bottom of this. Mark my words."

"I think you should. You have an excellent intuition."

"This one woman in town yesterday knew about us moving into this house," she said. "She looked rough. She told me that we made a terrible mistake. How did she know anything about me?"

Curtis shrugged. "It's a small town." He turned to his dresser and then spun around. "Speaking of which, we've been invited to a barbecue next Sunday at the church."

"How'd you hear about that?" Mary asked.

Curtis put on shorts and a T-shirt, checking himself in the mirror angled on top of the nightstand. "I met someone at the diner before you arrived. He's the pastor at the church we passed." He thought for a moment and then snapped his fingers. "Pastor Phil was his name."

"I met him too," Mary said. "He approached me on the street. Seemed like he already knew who I was. Same with you."

"I admit, he did seem very friendly and outgoing.

Maybe too much?"

"He's been living here since the seventies. Can you believe that?" Mary said.

Curtis turned with a shrug. "From what I hear, once people move to Redwood, they don't want to go anywhere else."

"I'm sure they don't," Mary said softly.

Curtis moved toward the door, ready to get started with his day. "Plenty of warm water left in the shower," he said. He paused, hand on the doorknob, and turned back to Mary. "So are you in for next Sunday?"

"The barbecue?"

"Yeah. You said so yourself that we should go to church more often."

Mary arched a brow. "And I'm sure this has nothing to do with you fishing for prospective clients."

"It has everything to do with that," Curtis said with a laugh. "I've got to try to make a living somehow."

Mary nodded. "Sure. Next Sunday. Let's do it."

Curtis seemed happy and said he had work to do, leaving Mary in the room as he left. She looked around their nearly setup master bedroom, wondering exactly how she was going to spend the day. It was Monday, and she expected more of the same—landscapers, roofers, movers, and all the like, working in unison. Granted, they were there to help Mary and Curtis fix their dream house, but at the moment, she had never felt so alone.

Mary showered and went downstairs dressed in her

sneakers, pink sleeveless button-down shirt, and jean shorts, just in time to see Curtis talking with the pest-control team in the foyer. There were two men, lanky and young-looking, with red polo shirts and hats. They nodded as Curtis pointed out the place and explained to them what happened to Mary. He then stopped and looked up as she came down the stairs.

"Ah, there she is," Curtis said. "Honey, could you kindly show these gentlemen where you saw the raccoon last night?"

"My pleasure," she said, signaling to the hall at their right. "This way."

The two men thanked Curtis and followed Mary as she led them to the living room. It was empty, just as before, and less ominous in the daytime. Two bottles of water lay on the floor along with a to-go box. Mary carefully picked up the box and saw that the sandwich was still inside. Regardless, it was going into the garbage.

She then went to the far corner of the room across the hardwood floor, to the place where she had seen the raccoon. As expected, there were tiny scratch marks on the wall, clear as day.

"Right there," she said, pointing. "That's where I saw it last night."

The pest-control team eyed the wall, hands on their chins, as Mary went across to the other side of the room. "It ran over here and crawled back into the wall." She stopped at a hole near the baseboard, about five inches wide. She couldn't say how the raccoon squeezed in there so quickly, but the hole was evidence enough.

The men approached as the taller one with a goatee shined his flashlight inside the hole. "Damn," he said. "We can get in there, but it's gonna be tricky."

"Whatever you have to do," she said. "This particular raccoon seemed very mean. I don't want to mess around."

The two men turned and looked at each other. The goateed man scratched his head and spoke with careful consideration. "We have a bunch of traps in our van. Of course, we can try to lure it out instead of banging up your wall, cutting a hole..."

"She could have babies, Earl," the other man said. "It's best to take a look."

"Fine," the goateed man said. He then looked at Mary. "That okay with you?"

Mary thought of Curtis and all the effort and money they were putting into fixing the place up. "Keep the destruction to a minimum please." Though she was eager for them to tear into the wall and get whatever was living inside of there out.

Earl looked up, scanning the room. "It's a big house, ma'am, but we'll try our best. No telling where it's at. Could be a maze of tunnels in these here walls."

They left the room as Mary paced around the center of the floor, stricken with worry. The infant cries were coming back to her. There was no way that any kind of animal could have made a noise so distinctive. It was yet another strange, unexplained occurrence. She walked to the living room window, looking outside at the front courtyard.

Curtis was by the empty fountain, talking with some contractors. The pest-control team was at their red van, pulling out equipment. Earl had a crowbar in hand and some kind of snare. She assumed that was how they were going to do it. She turned and walked back to the hole on the other side of the room. The faded and stained beige walls needed a good painting.

She pulled a mini flashlight from her pocket and shined it into the hole out of curiosity. She could barely see a thing beyond the light, but as she held her hand against the hole she felt faint, cool air against her palm. She took a knee and tried to get a better look, and then she heard something. She froze, just as a man with a noisy leaf blower passed by the window, distracting her. She pressed her ear against the hole, listening, as the sound of the leaf blower finally passed.

Silence returned to the room. Mary remained still, eyes looking upward and trying to make out the faint noise inside the wall. It sounded like a groan. She pressed her ear closer, practically inside the hole. It was the long-winded groan of a man, fading but clear enough.

The sound soon vanished just as quickly as it appeared. Mary backed away and clutched the side of the hole, trying to pry bits of the wall off to make the hole larger. Something came over her, a need or obsession, and she pulled and pulled until she tore a piece of hard plaster from the wall and fell back in surprise.

"Whoa. What's going on here?" Earl said, entering the room with his partner.

Mary looked up, startled and clutching a piece of the wall in her hand. "Nothing. I thought I heard something."

"You leave the busy work to us, Mrs. Malone," Earl said. "Pete and I have this."

His partner, Pete, set a small cage next to the wall as Earl set down his toolbox. He knelt by the hole and asked Mary politely if she could give him some room. She stood up and backed away, intending to watch them chip away at the hole, piece by piece.

Earl held the crowbar in hand and then turned to Mary with uncertainty. "You sure your husband is okay with this?"

She felt taken aback by the question and simply narrowed her eyes in response.

Earl stuttered nervously. "I-It's just. He's the one who called us out here and all."

"Yeah, no offense," Pete added.

Mary crossed her arms. "It's quite all right," she said. "My husband doesn't mind, nor do I."

Earl nodded with a gap-tooth grin and then turned back to the wall. He stuck the crowbar in the wall and pushed against it like taking off a hubcap. A big chunk flew out as Earl fell back, regaining his balance. The hole was nearly large enough for him to put his head through, but he kept chipping away. Mary heard the front door open and shut, and looked to the side, half expecting Curtis to walk in the room and flip out at what they were doing.

Earl set the crowbar on the ground and held up his long steel flashlight. Mary walked closer as he turned the light on and scanned the inside of the wall.

"Yep..." he said, nodding. "Just like I thought. She's got babies."

"How do you know?" Mary said, hovering over his shoulder.

Earl scratched his face. "There're droppings everywhere." He leaned over, head halfway in the wall, shining his flashlight inside and blocking Mary's view. She imagined the raccoon spiraling out of the hole, attacking them, and kept a careful distance.

"Hello, what's this?" Earl said, reaching down. He backed out of the hole holding a dusty booklet of some kind. Mary moved closer. He shook the dust and bits of wall from the book and held it up for everyone to see. "Looks like someone lost their book in there."

Mary extended her arm to take the book as Earl reluctantly handed it to her. It was extremely dusty, despite his shaking it off. Mary carefully examined the leather-bound cover, which had a drawstring tying it shut. The pages looked warped and dry. It looked decades old.

"Let's see what else we got in here," Earl said, looking back in the hole. He shined his flashlight around as Mary felt along the book's rough edges.

She was hesitant to open it, as it seemed so fragile, and

didn't want it to disintegrate, though her curiosity quickly got the best of her. She turned from the men and gently untied the tattered string binding the book together. She slowly opened it, finding pages with faded cursive handwriting, barely legible. Mary held it closer, trying to read the words.

Tuesday, May 20, Today father said that we have to all put on a good face at lunch with the future in-laws. His words not mine. I'm so sick of putting on a good face around here when they keep me locked in my room half the time. I got a record player for my birthday, but they won't even let me play it half the time. Mother says that my music is too loud and distracting.

Mary lowered the book, a dozen questions leaping to mind. Earl had discovered a diary of some sort, and the raccoon had led them straight to it. What was it doing inside the wall, and how old was it? She ruminated over these questions, knowing that a delicate piece of history rested in her hands. She looked over to Earl as he continued scanning the inside of the wall with his flashlight.

"See anything else?" she asked.

Earl grunted and then spoke. "Nah. Just a bunch more raccoon droppings. Might even have some rats down here too."

"Wonderful," Mary said with a sigh.

Earl leaned back from the wall and turned toward her, face covered in dust. "I'll leave a trail of pellets leading to the trap. Lure the mother out come feeding time." He then paused, thinking to himself. "Course, we may have to put a fogger in there for the babies. Maybe as many as five kits."

"You mean kill them?" Mary asked.

"Yep," Earl said matter-of-factly. "But they might come out looking for mom."

She didn't like the idea of a fogger, but Earl and Pete were the professionals. Raccoons had no place in their walls, regardless of age. She flipped to another page in the book, almost on instinct, and began reading.

In trouble today. Mother found out I've been taking scraps of food and feeding raccoons in the backyard. She told Father, and he told Lawrence, our groundskeeper, to kill any 'rodents' he saw on sight. Those raccoons are the only friends I have left, and they won't even let me have that. I need to get out of this house. I need to get away. Need to get away before it's too late.

Mary raised her head and nearly dropped the book. Her mind went right back to the night before, when she had encountered the raccoon. She remembered its yellow eyes, long, sharp canines, and wondered what connection it might have had, if any, to the girl's writings.

"That was no normal raccoon," she said out loud.

"What was that, Mrs. Malone?" Pete asked.

She turned to see both Earl and Pete looking at her. "Nothing… You gentlemen do what you have to do. I have to make a phone call." She excused herself from the room and went right toward the stairs, clutching the book and rushing up the steps to evade being seen, though she couldn't understand why.

She fled into the master bedroom, and closed the door. The diary would make a good addition to the books and newspapers she had already acquired, and beyond those references, she felt that the most definitive view into the family's history could, in fact, be found in the words of a young girl.

She went to the bed and sat, prepared to read the diary in one sitting. She turned the pages carefully and saw that some of them were so deteriorated that she couldn't read the writing no matter how hard she tried.

She then turned back to the very first page. The ink had smeared almost entirely, but she was able to read mid-sentence as it carried on to the next page.

...said that we had to. They're so demanding. They gave me a diary for my birthday just like I asked, but they also wouldn't let me have any friends over. They're so protective that it's driving me crazy. Happy birthday to me, I guess.

A knock came at the door, and Mary's head jolted up.

"Mary, you in there?" Curtis called.

"It's open," she said, tucking the diary under the sheets.

Curtis walked in, red from the sun and sweaty. "You all right?"

"Yeah. Why do you ask?"

"The pest-control guys said you took off in a hurry. I told them to go easy on the wall. I don't think we have to tear this place apart to flush a couple rodents out."

"I agree," Mary said. She put on her best face with hope that Curtis would be satisfied and go back to whatever he was doing, but he persisted.

"They said they found an old book. What's with that?"

Mary waved him off. "Oh, it's nothing."

"Nothing?" he said, walking forward.

"Well, we found a diary, but it's nearly impossible to read," Mary said.

"Really? Wow," Curtis said, waking to his dresser. He grabbed a pair of sunglasses. "You'll never believe who stopped by."

"Who?" Mary asked.

"Pastor Phil. He brought a welcome basket for us. Can you believe it?"

"Wow, that's nice," she said.

"I told him that you'd come down and say hello," Curtis continued.

Great, she thought.

Curtis walked to the door, whistling, and told Mary to come down when she was ready. As he closed the door behind him, Mary pondered the arrival of their new guest.

He seemed awfully interested in making their acquaintance. Maybe he was just a really nice guy. However, her instincts told her differently.

She wondered if she should mention the diary to the pastor. He seemed familiar enough with the Bechdels, and she knew from the newspaper that he had been a pastor of their same church since before the family was slaughtered. There was something there, and the more time she spent in Redwood, the less she believed in coincidences.

She walked down the hall to the stairwell, and below, saw the top of Pastor Phil's white hair as he chatted with Curtis, his back turned toward her. He wasn't wearing a suit this time but was dressed in a checkered short-sleeved button-down shirt and tan Dockers. He pivoted on his heels while laughing along with Curtis, and whatever Curtis was telling him. In his hands he still held a basket of fruit with plastic wrapping over it. *The Redwood welcome wagon in the flesh.*

She slowly descended the stairs as Curtis looked up, causing Pastor Phil to turn and smile at her.

"There she is," Curtis said.

Phil nodded as she reached the bottom, holding the basket out to her. "Good morning, Mrs. Malone. A pleasure to see you again."

"Hello," she said, unsure how to address him. He hadn't told her his last name, but he sure seemed to know theirs.

"A welcoming gift from our church," he said, thrusting the basket toward her.

Mary smiled and took it with both hands. "You shouldn't have," she said, feeling the plastic crinkle in her hands. "That's very thoughtful of your church. Thank you."

"When was the last time someone ever gave us a welcome basket?" Curtis asked with a laugh.

Phil waved him off. "Ah. It's nothing. We just like to make our neighbors feel at home."

Mary turned and set the basket on a nearby table at the foot of the staircase. She thanked him again, noticing his eyes wander around the grand foyer surrounding them, taking in the boxes, furniture, and work in progress.

"Just a beautiful mansion," he said.

"Still have a ways to go," Curtis said. His demeanor suddenly changed as he looked at his wristwatch. "Oh, and I gotta get back to work. Said I'd lend a hand. Sorry. Thanks again, Pastor."

They shook hands, and Curtis waved to Mary and hurried out the door. Phil looked at Mary while wiping a bead of sweat from his forehead with his handkerchief. There were several windows open and portable fans blowing throughout the house, but the outside heat was inescapable. "Air conditioner on the fritz?" he said with a smile.

"It's the air conditioner that never was," Mary said with a sigh. "We should have a new unit here in a couple of days."

"One modern convenience at a time," Phil said.

"Indeed..."

From the living room, Pete and Earl entered the foyer chatting and carrying a tool bag and two more cages. Their voices lowered as they tipped their hats to Mary and Phil.

"The wall doesn't look too bad, ma'am," Pete said. "A little drywall, and you'll never know we were in there."

"That's fine," she said as they walked by.

"We'll give your kitchen a good look," Earl added.

"Don't forget about the attic," Mary called out as they continued on.

"Oh no," Pete assured her, turning his head. "We're saving the best for last."

Mary turned back to Pastor Phil, who stood patiently waiting with a polite smile. "Pest control," she said.

"Ah, I should have known," he said.

"Thank you again for the basket. It was very nice of you."

"My pleasure," he said. "Your husband sounds pretty excited about the barbecue next Sunday. Can we count on your attendance?"

Mary placed a finger against her lip and then pointed at him. "So *that's* why you came out here."

Phil's smile widened with a measured laugh. "You figured me out and uncovered my scheme." He bowed his head like a royal subject. "Forgive me, madam."

"We'll put it on our calendar," Mary said.

Phil looked up, pleased, as Mary leaned in closer, preparing to pursue her own agenda, which was filled with questions. "You've lived here for some time, haven't you?"

Phil's smile straightened out as his blue eyes looked up in thought. "Well… darn near half my life has been spent in Redwood, yes."

Mary paused, trying to choose her next words wisely. "And did you know any former owners of this mansion?"

"I did, actually," he said. "Place has been vacant a long time, but I've known families who lived here at one time."

"Families?" Mary said. She didn't know that anyone else had lived in the mansion, and this new information gave her another path to research. "So. You knew the Bechdels?"

For the first time since she had met him, Pastor Phil's face went completely blank. He seemed to have realized this, and quickly turned his expression into a smile. "Yes. The Bechdel family. A terrible tragedy back then. Worst thing to ever happen in our humble town."

Mary seized the moment and moved in closer, first glancing outside, where the hammering continued loudly. "Pastor Phil," she said. "Is there something about this house we should know? I've heard things in the night, seen things I can't ignore, and we've only been here a few days. Do we have anything to worry about?"

Phil stared back at her, long and hard, in contemplation. He then took a step back, motioning toward the door. "To be honest with you, Mrs. Malone, it's an old creaky mansion that needs a lot of work. I've seen families come and go, some of them even going broke, trying to make this place into something it was never meant to be." He paused and scratched his chin, looking around. "In the end, I think you and your husband will be fine. I can see it in you."

Before she could say another word, Phil shuffled to the door, excusing himself. "It's been a pleasure talking with you, Mrs. Malone. Have a wonderful day, and I hope to see you at the barbecue."

Mary stood still for a moment, surprised by his hasty exit. "Call me Mary," she said as he neared the door.

"Sure thing, Mary," he said with a wave and a bright smile. She didn't know what she had said that might have prompted him to leave so suddenly. Her question was one that any new homeowner might ask. One thing was clear; Pastor Phil was being evasive. After he closed the door, she walked toward the living room prepared to see what damage had been done to the wall at her behest.

Was Pastor Phil right? Would they face a fate any different from the others who had tried to make a home there? The questions were mounting as Mary stood dazed with thoughts of a little girl who once lived within the same walls.

SUNDAY BARBECUE

The new air conditioner was up and running, much to the collective relief of Mary, Curtis, and the various work crews tasked with renovations. Painters, cleaners, pest control, and electricians had been busy throughout the week modernizing the old mansion, transforming its faded grimy, walls and dusty, spider-webbed interiors into something entirely different. Mary could hardly believe it herself. Their home was beginning to look downright livable and even elegant.

The attic had been cleared out of resident rodents that for so long had made the space their own. The pipes running through the walls had been nearly repaired, the septic system replaced, and the electrical wiring brought up to standard.

The downstairs study had been turned into her own art studio, where she could work in the sunlight from a large bay window. The room looked out onto their shaded backyard and its long, stone walkway that wound its way through the freshly cut grass and was lined with bushes trimmed to perfection. Her agent had lined up a new children's book for her to illustrate. She had a three-week deadline and by mid-week she hadn't even started.

Mary was doing her best to adjust, even though normality had long since recused itself to a different time and place. Redwood seemed the perfect town to live in, their mansion, a dream come true, but it seemed there was something lurking beneath the surface, troubling and grim, that she couldn't shake off.

The week had rushed by, and by Sunday she couldn't believe all the work that had been done on their home. Things were quieter, with fewer people parading through the house, and Mary knew that she and Curtis would soon be the only two people inside their vast dream home, living like royalty without the bank account or prestige to show for it.

That morning, she had almost forgotten their Sunday engagement at the Redwood church. There had been no visitors to their house since Pastor Phil's unexpected visit, and when she opened the drawer to the nightstand to get her cell phone, she was greeted once again by the sight of the child's diary that had been captivating her attention the past week.

Curtis was just coming out of the bathroom after a shower, when Mary quickly closed the drawer. She stood in a T-shirt and underwear as he greeted her with an optimistic smile on his face.

"Morning," she said back in a tired voice. She hadn't been feeling that well for the past few days, chalking it up to exhaustion.

"I got my first client today!" he said with excitement.

"Really? Wow, that's wonderful. Congratulations, honey," she said.

"Just called me this morning. Wants me to represent him in his custody battle with his ex."

"That's so great," Mary said, stretching.

"And he'll be at the barbecue too, so I can talk to him then."

"I'm so proud of you," she said, walking away from the bed.

She felt ecstatic for him even as her mind drifted to other thoughts. She had her reservations about Pastor Phil. He knew things, he had to, and he had taken an interest in her and Curtis in ways that she couldn't exactly understand.

Curtis went into the walk-in closet and then emerged in a pair of cargo shorts and polo shirt.

"What do you think?" he asked. "Too casual?"

"It's fine," she said, sitting back on the bed. Her straight blonde hair rested just above her shoulders, strands matted to her neck from deep sleep. She was clearly not in the mood for social activity, but she put on her best face for Curtis's sake. Despite her efforts, however, he noticed something wrong.

"Are you okay?" he asked, noticing her lack of enthusiasm.

"Yes," she answered quickly. "Nothing a big cup of coffee couldn't cure."

"I'll make you a cup in a minute," he said, walking back into the closet.

As he continued talking, her eyes shifted back to the nightstand where the young girl's diary was hidden. Reading the diary, Mary began to feel closer to her each day. Her name was Julie. She was the youngest victim of the massacre. She seemed very bright and caring, an adorable child whose life was tragically cut short. Mary would have done anything just to talk to her.

The week had been an exhausting blur, and in that time there hadn't been any visions or anything out of the ordinary, and she hadn't had much time for any research. Her publisher had called in need of a series of new illustrations. A routine was gradually forming, one that was pulling her away from the answers about the house she so desperately desired.

"Service starts at ten thirty," Curtis said, brushing his hair in the mirror. "We have a good hour. I can make us some breakfast too if you want."

"Coffee's fine," she said with a faint smile.

Curtis looked at her with near suspicion as his own smile dropped. "You need to eat, Mary. Don't think I haven't noticed."

She looked down at the floor, embarrassed. "I'm fine," she said. "I'll save it for the barbecue."

"At least eat a bagel or something," Curtis said.

Mary rose from the bed, and headed toward the bathroom, her spirits lifting for a moment. "*All right*… You're so pushy," she said, closing the door.

She went to the mirror and wiped her hand across its foggy surface, staring at her reflection. There were noticeable bags under her eyes, and her lips fixed in a downward slope.

Strands of blonde hair curled up at her chin as she took note of her gaunt cheek bones. The more she looked at herself, the thinner her face grew, almost as though she were fading away.

Mary backed away from the mirror, terrified, and then glanced back at her reflection. She was normal again. Gone were the bulging eyes seated in a skeletal face of almost visible bone. She panicked, wondering if what she had seen was just another vision brought on by her current surroundings or by something else, more sinister. She went to the shower, pulling her T-shirt off, and turned the nozzles on, evening out the hot and cold water. Nothing felt right. *She* didn't feel right. Troubling anxiety flowed through her no matter what she did, and she always felt as though she was being watched.

* * *

They drove to the First Christ Church of Redwood on a bright, sunny morning, amid rolling green fields and lush forest. The town, was instantly comforting with its natural beauty and lack of anything resembling a major city. This was a place people moved in order to get away from it all, and it showed.

Its old-fashioned, Victorian nature was endearing. A brochure Curtis had given to Mary earlier heralded Redwood as a "family community." All of that was fine, but Mary wasn't interested in all the good things about the town. She wanted to find out its secrets.

Curtis was upbeat as always, handsome with his blue shirt, gray tie, and slicked-back dark hair. Gone was his five days' growth of beard, his cheeks bare now. Wearing a neon coral summer dress and sandals, Mary felt better after a shower and coffee. Her hair was tied back into a ponytail, and she wore a light foundation on her fair face.

They were a young couple, married only a few years, and she dreaded the questions she was sure to get while introducing themselves to the townspeople. They would probably ask why they moved into a mansion that could house a large family when they themselves had no children. She suppressed her anxiety as they drove to the church, hoping that she wasn't being too paranoid. Curtis, however, easily saw through her silence.

"Nervous?" he asked.

"A little," she replied, moving the passenger visor aside to block the glare of the sun.

"Well, you shouldn't be," he said. "There are good people in this town. I can feel it."

Mary stared ahead, convinced that, for the most part, Curtis was probably right. If Pastor Phil seemed reserved in discussing the Bechdels, she assumed it would be the same with anyone else. Maybe it was just something people didn't talk about. Lost in her thoughts, she felt Curtis's hand touch hers and squeeze.

She squeezed back and smiled, feeling more anxious as they neared the church ahead on the right. Its painted white exterior, modest size, and pointed steeple looked like something out of a storybook. The front parking lot was full, and a sign had been mounted in a square section of freshly cut grass. There was forest on both sides of the church, making it appear isolated.

Mary looked at the dashboard clock. It was 10:35, and services had already begun. The onus was on her, however. She had been in a morning funk and took too long to get ready. Taking notice of the time himself, Curtis assured her again that they would be fine.

"We'll find a spot in the back," he said. "No one will even see us come in."

Mary ran her hands down her face with a sigh. "I don't even remember the last time we went to church. Remind me why we're doing this again?"

Curtis jokingly scoffed. "We're trying to fit in. It's that simple." He slowed the car and turned into the parking lot as Mary's heart raced. The church seemed inviting enough, and maybe it would be good for them. She knew that she needed to shake off her suspicions and embrace the small-town life before them. Something, however, kept holding her back.

They parked in the far corner where Curtis had finally found a spot. They exited the SUV and walked hand in hand toward the church where they could hear the faint hum of an organ playing inside. A sloped concrete walkway with a railing running up the middle led to the double doors of the church, with two elegant door handles, one on each side.

Curtis pulled the door open for Mary, revealing a red-carpeted lobby where an older woman was seated in one of two chairs separated by a highly polished table with a vase of fresh dahlias. The woman looked up and smiled at them, her white hair trimmed and her large glasses magnifying her pupils.

Behind her was a window with vertical blinds open, revealing the backs of the congregation standing in the pews and holding hymnals and singing. Mary approached the woman first as she stood, holding out a leather-bound hymnal.

"Welcome to the First Christ Church of Redwood," she said with a smile and hushed tone. "My name is Barbara."

Mary took the hymnal and introduced herself as Curtis approached from behind. A font in the corner of the room gently bubbled. The surrounding white walls were adorned with paintings of saints, and a door to the side led to a darkened room identified as the Reading Room.

Curtis shook Barbara's hand and apologized for their tardiness. She waved him off and then told them that they could go inside once the hymn ended.

"You recently moved here, yes?" she asked.

"We sure did," Curtis answered.

Barbara looked them over and then asked if they were the couple who had purchased the old mansion on Weatherford Lane.

"That's us," Curtis said.

"Wow," Barbara commented. "I didn't think anyone was going to buy that old place."

Curtis was quick to respond. "Trust me. It's taken us a lot of work."

Barbara turned to Mary with a smile. "I hope you're planning to stick around for the barbecue. It's our first one this year."

"We're looking forward to it," Mary said.

The singing ended, and the congregants took their seats. Barbara turned to the door to their right, opening it for them. "Enjoy the service," she said.

Mary and Curtis thanked her as they walked inside, heads turning toward them as they searched for a place to sit. Mary went to the third pew from the rear, which had two empty spots right at the end. A stained-glass window filtered the bright rays of the sun, and Mary looked ahead as Pastor Phil approached a pulpit overlooking the crowd.

Curtis smiled at an older couple seated next to them as he sat with Mary at the end. She sat there as the room went quiet and Pastor Phil, wearing a beige suit and blue tie, adjusted his thin rectangular glasses while looking down at his open Bible below. He looked up and seemed to make direct eye contact with Mary, causing her to look down.

The seated patrons consisted of adults of all ages, with most, however, older and gray. Pastor Phil spoke with clarity and conviction, and Mary could tell he had been doing this for a while. He gave blessings for the peaceful Sunday morning and then read from the scriptures, discussing faith and sacrament.

"It is our duty to love one another while adhering to the message of our Lord and Savior." He paused, holding a finger in the air. "Let us never forget the sacrifice bestowed upon us in this world of sin. Let us come together under the banner of truth and love, which are natural elements of His plan."

As his sermon proceeded, Mary's mind couldn't help but wander. She thought of the diary back home and how she had neglected to do her research or study the materials she had checked out at the library. It had been an exhausting, busy week and she couldn't blame herself entirely.

She had time. The pieces were there. All she had to do was put them together. Pastor Phil continued, as his audience sat silent, seemingly captivated by his small-town charm and charisma. Mary could see that he was an experienced speaker, with a gravelly voice and careful, measured words, that streamed persuasively over the speakers in the ceiling.

Mary looked around the room and at its stained-glass windows, wondering how long the church had been there. Ultimately, she just wanted the entire affair, the service and the barbecue, to be over with. They were newcomers to the town, and the thought of putting on a friendly face and making a good impression among strangers was nerve-racking.

Perhaps she wasn't completely out of her funk just yet. She noticed an elderly couple turn their heads in unison from three pews ahead and make eye contact with her. What had prompted them to turn around? They nodded as she smiled back. She turned to Curtis, who was trying his best to pay attention to Pastor Phil's sermon.

On the wall next to the organ was a small board with three hymn numbers listed on it. Pastor Phil took a step away from the pulpit, holding his hymnal in hand, and instructed the congregation to prepare to read from page one fifteen. The organist began playing as the people rose from their pews. Mary and Curtis stood up as well, sharing the hymnal and singing in barely audible voices. As the congregation broke out in a joyful chorus, it was clear that the newcomers were unfamiliar with the music.

* * *

When the Sunday service had ended, most of the congregation convened in the field behind the church, where picnic tables had been set up, and hot dogs and hamburgers were already smoking on a nearby grill. There were several families already seated, wearing their Sunday best. Children played together, running around with colorful streamers, as Mary and Curtis made their way outside, where close to a hundred people mingled together, talking and laughing.

Mary walked toward the group, her hand on Curtis's arm, feeling almost invisible to everyone. Pastor Phil was talking to a young couple under a canopy that offered much-needed shade from the sun, and waved at them to come over.

As they approached, Curtis extended his arm to shake Pastor Phil's hand.

"So nice of you two to make it," Phil said with a tight, firm grip. He shook Mary's hand more lightly, while complimenting her dress.

"Thank you," she said. "We're glad to be here."

Phil gestured toward the smoking grill smiling widely. "I hope you brought your appetites. Looks like we have more than enough food."

"That's great," Curtis said. "Excellent sermon by the way."

Phil seemed to take the compliment in stride. "Thank you so much," he said. He then looked at Mary, half expecting additional praise, and then signaled to the couple standing next to him. "This is Lucille and Steven Hardwick. They moved here roughly six months ago."

The attractive couple turned to Mary and Curtis and shook their hands. The woman was short and petite with long red hair and freckles. Her husband was much taller and lanky, with curly blond locks. "Welcome to Redwood," he said.

"It's a pleasure," Curtis said. "I just love this town so far." He looked at Mary as her tight-lipped smile began to wane. "We really struck gold with this find. That's for sure."

"I heard you bought the old Bechdel mansion," Steven said.

"Yes," Curtis responded. "We sure did!"

Suddenly, the woman, Lucille, took Mary's hands in hers and spoke. "I simply have to introduce you around. These are some of the nicest people I've ever met."

Mary nodded and then looked to Curtis. "Go meet some of the folks," he said, clearly more interested in engaging the newly-introduced Steven Hardwick. "Enjoy yourselves."

Mary allowed Lucille to guide her toward a cluster of other women as the aroma from the grill made her stomach growl. She was getting hungry after all. They approached a group of five women in Sunday dresses, fanning themselves.

"Ladies, this is Mary Malone," Lucille said. "She just moved here from..." Lucille paused and turned to Mary. "Where is it that you're from?"

"Chicago," Mary said to the group.

The women nodded back with inviting smiles as Mary shook their hands. They were middle-aged, slightly older than she was, and distinctly reserved, like women out of the Victorian age. Their husbands, it seemed, were gathered around the grill behind them, in their own huddled conversations, full of cheer and laughter.

The women introduced themselves as Trish, Ellen, Madison, Beatrice, and Allison. They each wore a fair amount of makeup, and all had sparkling, drop earrings that looked expensive. Two of the women looked nearly identical in both physical appearance and clothing. They both wore sun hats and large, designer sunglasses. Mary glanced at them, taking in their shoulder-length auburn hair, slender necks, and matching pearl necklaces. Ellen, the woman on the right, smiled

"Yes, we're twins," she said. "But our matching wardrobes were *not* planned, I can assure you."

Her sister, Madison, tilted her head back, laughing and touching Mary's hand. "Do you have any siblings?"

"Yes," Mary answered. "One brother and one sister."

Madison leaned in closer with a crooked smile. "So you can understand what it's like. We've had this problem since we were children." She paused, shrugging. "After a while, we just embraced it."

Mary was curious. "You mean to tell me that you dress alike without even realizing it?"

Ellen stepped in. "It's like looking in a mirror sometimes, I tell you."

Madison waved her away as the other women laughed. "Of course, I'm the more attractive one."

Mary smiled as the group continued laughing. A pack of small children ran past them, with their good clothes already looking disheveled. They were the same bunch she saw running with streamers only minutes before. They were all boys, elementary school-age, and that was when it dawned on Mary that she hadn't seen a single young girl anywhere in the crowd.

"Tell me, Mary. How are you and your husband settling in?" the oldest of the women, Beatrice, asked. Her gray hair was permed, and she had pinned a rose brooch to the dark-blue blazer that she wore over her flowered dress. Her face was caked in bronze makeup, and dark mascara fringed her blue eyes. She had the brightest of bright-red lipsticks that Mary had ever seen any woman wear. Her eyes remained on Mary with intense, unblinking focus.

"Just fine," Mary replied. "It's been a very busy week, and we're just glad to get out and meet some of the townspeople."

"Tell me, my dear," Beatrice said suddenly, "what are you and your husband going to do with all that space?"

"It-It's daunting, that's for sure," Mary said.

"What made the two of you want to move into that old relic in the first place?" Beatrice asked, holding her hands out, chubby digits extended.

"Beatrice, please," Lucille said.

The soft curls of Beatrice's faux bob bounced as she waved Lucille off, leaning closer to Mary, as though she were addressing her in confidence. "You *do* know what happened there, don't you?"

"Beatrice! That's enough," Lucille warned.

Beatrice paused and looked around at the disapproving faces surrounding her. "Sheesh. It was just a question."

"What do you know about the Bechdels?" Mary asked abruptly, addressing the group, then looking directly at each one. Nobody said anything, and an uncomfortable silence filled the air.

"That's not really appropriate church talk, if you don't mind," Lucille said in a polite but stern tone. She then took Mary by the wrist and began to lead her away from the group as the women waved.

"Don't mind Beatrice," Lucille whispered. "What she lacks in simple tact she makes up for with some of the best peanut butter cookies this side of the state."

Mary turned back to glance at the women as she was guided through the crowd, faces growing blurry in their quick pace.

"Here," Lucille said. "I want to introduce you to some of the other ladies." They reached a group sitting at a bench under another canopy, all older than the ones Mary had just been introduced to. They sipped from bottled water and nibbled at fruit plates of watermelon and strawberries resting on their knees.

Their long, sleek dresses looked elegant but out of place to Mary. Their jewelry added to the impression of wealth and prestige: arms, necks, and fingers with heavy burdens of gold. Mary glanced down at her own arms realizing that she had forgotten to wear any jewelry at all. The small diamond on her wedding ring sparkled in the sunlight, the only thing she had to show for herself.

A gray-haired woman, the only one who had not fashioned an orange tint over her perm, looked up at Mary as she approached. She and the others smiled as Lucille introduced her.

"Mary, these lovely ladies run the local chapter of the Redwood Women's Association."

"It's a pleasure," Mary said, shaking their hands one after the other. The name sounded generic, but Mary could tell just by their posture and demeanor that they fancied themselves power players in Redwood.

Sylvia, the woman introduced as the president of the local chapter, looked up at Mary and spoke with a low, scratchy voice.

"You and your husband are quite the word around town" she said, pulling out a cigarette from a silver case.

"I suppose so," Mary said. "I ran into Pastor Phil just the other week, and he seemed to already know our names."

Sylvia shrugged and lit her cigarette. Lucille turned to the stage and signaled Mary to follow her as Pastor Phil took the stage.

Mary waved to the table of aging socialites as they waved back. A sizeable crowd had already gathered around the stage, plastic plates in hand, digging into their grilled lunch.

"Welcome all. Thank you for being here," he said. "Now, why you'd want to hear me speak again after an hour-long sermon is beyond me, but here we go."

The crowd laughed as Mary looked around, searching for Curtis. She caught a glimpse of him in the back near the grill, having joined a huddle of men deep in conversation. It looked as though he was making friends just fine. Lucille seemed nice enough, albeit a tad pushy.

"I'm glad to see so many smiling faces here for our Redwood Annual Fall Kickoff Barbecue!" Pastor Phil continued, swinging an arm through the air as the crowd clapped and hollered.

"I just love him," Lucille said loudly into Mary's ear. "Isn't he just the best?"

Mary nodded with a smile.

"Now, we've got plenty of food and drinks for everyone. Games for you and your kids, or tables where you can just sit and take in the beautiful scenery that surrounds us. And before we hear from a special guest speaker, I want to welcome the newest additions to our lovely town, Curtis and Mary Malone! Everyone welcome them with a hearty applause." He looked downward, arm outstretched to Mary, zeroing in on her from the crowd. "Stand tall, so we can all see you," he urged. Mary felt her face flush. She looked around nervously with a wave as the crowd politely applauded.

"Let's show them how we treat each other here in Redwood," Phil continued, "with love, kindness, and respect for one another. The way neighbors are supposed to."

The applause continued as Mary looked around for a way out. Phil leaned into the microphone with bravado. "Now, I'd like to introduce a very special guest. Ladies and gentlemen, the mayor of our fair town, Mayor Taylor!"

The crowd cheered as a tall silver-haired man in a suit climbed the steps and waved, smiling. The very sight of him was making Mary dizzier and the last thing she wanted was to have another episode in front of so many people.

"I'm sorry. I need to find Curtis," Mary said to Lucille as she worked her way out of the crowd. Lucille nodded, distracted by the mayor's introductory words.

"So nice to see all your lovely faces on this beautiful Sunday morning! It's a true pleasure to be here," he began.

Mary snuck away as Lucille continued clapping,

squeezing herself through the crowd and excusing herself along the way.

She broke free and quickly moved to the grill, where Curtis handed her a plate with a hot dog on a bun, beans, and coleslaw.

"Dig in," he said, bobbing his head along with the music.

She took the plate, thanking him. She felt flushed and a bit light-headed as the music continued on in the distance. Curtis must have noticed and asked if she was okay.

"I'm sorry, I need to go home," she said. She looked over his shoulder past him, and for a minute it seemed as though all heads were turned in their direction, staring at them. She squeezed her eyes shut and rubbed them. Upon opening them, she saw no such thing. No one was watching them. All attention was on the stage.

"You need to meet some of the guys first," he said. "Bob's around here somewhere. The realtor, remember?"

"I remember," she said. "Maybe some other time."

Curtis gently placed his hand on her shoulder as his smile faded. "What's wrong, Mary?"

"Nothing. I just... I'm not feeling well. I'm so sorry."

Concerned, Curtis crouched down and grabbed a cold water bottle from a cooler below, handing it to her. "Why don't you take a seat, have some food, and relax a little."

She took a step forward, inches from his face. "Please. It's the dizziness. It's back."

Curtis paused, stunned. He then looked around with his hands out, in a gesture of helplessness. "Okay, okay. We'll get you out of here."

"I'm sorry," she said again, walking beside him as he gripped her shoulder.

"Don't worry about it. You don't look well. Your face is losing color."

Curtis led the way at a quick pace, around the side of the

church and to the parking lot as the music faded and the general cheer grew more distant. She felt instant relief upon entering the parking lot and couldn't understand any of it, but something told her that the answers lay in the diary back home... somewhere.

WARNING

Curtis was quiet but tender as they drove home, clearly perplexed. He rubbed her leg as Mary's gaze remained fixed on the long stretch of encroaching forest on their way back to the mansion. Away from the heat and the crowd, she felt a little better as cool air blew on her face from the dashboard vent.

"Feeling better?" Curtis asked.

"Yes, thank you," she said softly. "I'm so sorry."

"Enough of that, Mary," he said. "We don't want to take any chances. Just make sure you drink plenty of water, and we'll get you home."

She felt too tired to talk, surprised and disappointed with herself in the process. Regardless of Curtis's assurances, she knew that their hasty departure could very well be considered a rude gesture. They turned onto the concrete path leading to the mansion and bypassed the rusty automatic gate that had yet to be repaired.

They pulled into the empty courtyard, free of work crews. It seemed as though they were going to have a quiet day after all, which was good enough for her. There was much research to be done, and she wanted to prove to Curtis that something was indeed wrong with the house and the town he had whisked them away to.

With one glance toward the front door, Mary's heart seized. Something bloody looking, a curious marking eight feet tall was painted down its surface.

"Stop the car!" she said.

Curtis hit the brakes fifty feet from the door as she flew forward, constrained by her seat belt.

"Are you all right?" he asked.

"Oh my God..." she said, cupping her mouth with both hands.

Curtis followed her gaze, unsure of what to say. Painted down the middle of their double doors were two thick, red intersecting lines in the shape of an upside-down cross.

A police cruiser with the Chief of Police and his deputy showed up about twenty minutes later. What looked like simple vandalism had a more ominous meaning to Mary. The driver, an older man, stepped out of the car and introduced himself as Chief Benjamin Riley. His partner, Deputy Alex Ramirez, extended his hand as well.

Chief Riley was older than his young deputy by at least twenty years. He was tall and lanky with a gruff demeanor, and his silver hair and wrinkled, leathery face fulfilled a stereotypical notion of a small-town sheriff. He wore aviator sunglasses, a gray, short-sleeved uniform shirt, and dark slacks. At his side were a pistol holster and radio.

Deputy Ramirez was shorter than the chief, with boyish good looks and a short crop of black hair. Mary remembered seeing both of them standing outside the police station the week before, and wondered if they alone made up the entire police force of Redwood.

All business, Chief Riley held his clipboard as they stood

at the end of the courtyard next to the steps leading to the vandalized door. Ramirez admitted that they both came not only to investigate but also to meet the new couple everyone was talking about.

"I didn't realize that we were such celebrities," Mary said.

"You certainly are in this town," Ramirez said, flashing a smile.

Angered, Curtis pointed to the red upside-down cross on their door. "I want to press charges against the punks. Not even here two weeks, and our home has already been vandalized."

"Anyone get inside?" the chief asked, scribbling onto his clipboard.

"Not that I know of," Curtis said. "I searched every room. No signs of any break-in."

"Whoever did this had to know that we would be gone," Mary said.

Deputy Ramirez glanced up at her with a raised brow. "What makes you say that?"

Curtis suddenly cut in. "The point is, I want whoever did this charged with trespassing and vandalism!"

Ramirez walked up the steps to take pictures of the door with his pocket-sized digital camera.

"You might want to get that gate fixed outside first and foremost," the chief said.

"These weren't kids," Mary said.

Their home had been marked with an inverted cross. There was nothing subtle about it. She wondered if it was yet another warning bestowed upon them by unseen forces.

Curtis turned to her with his hands on his hips, shaking his head. "I don't care. I want whoever did it to face charges."

"It's a message," she continued as Riley and Ramirez stood to the side, reluctant to offer their own take. She approached the door and ran her hand down the dry red paint on the hard wooden surface. "Either a warning, or something else."

Curtis walked up the steps and stopped near her, clearly not having it. "Mary, please. Someone is toying with us. Probably kids."

She glanced at him, unconvinced. "I wish that were the case. I really do."

Curtis went back to the two police officers with his hands out, and shrugged. "Shouldn't be too hard to find the perpetrators, right Officers?"

Deputy Ramirez nodded while scribbling into a pocket-sized notebook. "We can run a search on paint purchases at the hardware store."

"Good thinking, Deputy," the chief added. They both seemed satisfied enough and turned to leave with an assurance that they'd try their best to find the vandals.

Mary then spun around from the front door, calling after them urgently. "Chief Riley!"

They both stopped, and Riley turned around. She hurried down the stairs, passing Curtis and approached the officers, hands folded together and a worried look across her face.

"Yes, ma'am?" the chief asked, waiting.

"How long have you lived here, if you don't mind my asking?" she asked.

Chief Riley looked up, thinking to himself. "Hm." His head shifted back in her direction. "About fifteen years."

"How about you, Deputy?" she asked Ramirez.

"My wife and I moved here about five years ago," he answered.

Mary turned, signaling toward the mansion. "I'm sure you're both familiar with the history behind this place."

"Sure am," the chief said, putting a piece of gum in his mouth. "But that was a long time ago."

"The Bechdel murders?" Ramirez asked.

Chief Riley nodded.

"The case was never solved to my knowledge," Mary said. "This house is trying to tell us something. I can feel it." She looked squarely at the chief, imploringly. "Is there anything we should know about this place? About this town?"

Chief Riley cocked his head and scratched his face. "Well... All I can say, ma'am, is that there's one cold case that's just never seen the light of day. But from what I've seen we're certain that nothing like that is going to happen in Redwood again."

"Pretty cryptic there, Chief," Ramirez added.

"I'm asking for your help," Mary said, determined. "Is there something I should know?" She paused as his blank expression showed a clear unwillingness to elaborate. "This vandalism is just the latest in the strange occurrences we've experienced since moving in."

Deputy Riley flashed an understanding look. "I can tell you this, ma'am. You're not the first family to raise concerns about this old place."

"Interesting..." Mary said

"'Bout ten years ago a family moved in here," the chief said. "Weren't here very long, from what I hear."

"See," Mary said to Curtis. "I told you."

Curtis shrugged. "Yeah. Well. Maybe they couldn't afford it."

"Wake up, Curtis," Mary said.

The chief and his deputy took a step back and motioned to the cruiser.

"Wait. Please," Mary said, reaching out to them. The chief stopped again with a near sigh. "Do you remember their names? The people who lived here?"

The chief shook his head. "Sorry, ma'am. Don't believe that I do."

Mary turned back to Curtis. "The realtor. Mr. Deckers.

Maybe he has the records. An old mortgage or deed or something."

"The past is the past, Mary," Curtis said, walking away. "I have work to do."

Mary approached the two officers, confiding in them. "I'm not trying to pry, Chief. I just want answers. Are my husband and I in any danger?"

The chief thought to himself. "No ma'am. I don't believe so. Like I said before, that was a long time ago—"

"That's what everyone keeps telling me," she interjected, then paused for a moment before cautiously asking her next question. "Do either of you believe in the supernatural?"

Chief Riley looked down with a sheepish grin as Deputy Ramirez nodded slightly. "My wife... She used to dabble in that stuff all the time," the chief said. He suddenly switched to a more serious tone. "But you shouldn't worry about it. There are no ghosts here. Just a nice, friendly town." He smiled, exposing two rows of pearly-white teeth.

"Have a good day, ma'am," Ramirez said as they turned away and walked back to the cruiser. A police star was painted along the passenger side, with Redwood Police Department written in big letters. She thanked them for coming out and stood there as the chief started the car and drove off, leaving a faint trail of exhaust as she contemplated her next move.

* * *

Mary woke up the next morning to find Curtis up and almost out the door in a pair of slacks and a dress shirt. They hadn't said much to each other the rest of the day prior, and now he was leaving without even telling her. Something was up.

"Where are you going?" she said, rubbing her eyes.

He stopped at the door and turned with a faint smile.

"It's Monday," he said. "Got to go to work."

Mary rose from the bed, tossing the covers to the side. "What are you talking about?"

Curtis walked back to the bed with his sarcastic smirk. "I may not have an office, or an assistant, but I've got to start somewhere." He strolled toward the bed and leaned against one of the end posts. "Don't you agree?"

Mary looked around, assessing the vastness of the space, just within their master bedroom alone. "Why not just open an office in one of the rooms? We've got plenty of them."

"I need to be out there," he said, pointing out the window. "Out in the public. I plan to look into office space today."

Downstairs, they both had separate studies—Curtis with his oak desk, legal books, and computer, and Mary with her drawing table, tablet, and artwork hanging on the walls. Her office was her studio workspace, whereas Curtis worked outside the home, and with one car between them, she was pretty much stuck there throughout the day.

"The electrician should be here later today to look at that bad wiring in the kitchen," Curtis continued.

"Okay," Mary said, getting out of bed with a stretch. "Good luck today." She wrapped her arms around him and hugged him. "I'm sorry again about yesterday."

"Stop apologizing. Please," he said, hugging her back.

"I'll tell Pastor Phil what happened."

"Don't worry. I'll talk to him soon," Curtis said. He looked into her eyes and told her quietly, "I've been doing some thinking... Obviously I want all of this to work, but if you have real concerns about this house..." He then paused, shaking his head, and then said something so touching she wanted to cry. "If you're uncomfortable here, we can always move somewhere else."

His willingness to compromise so completely came as a

shock, and her mouth nearly dropped to the floor. "You're serious?"

"Of course I am. I moved us here, and if this doesn't work out it falls completely on me."

"No..." she said. "I want to give this a chance."

"And I want to help," he said, taking her hand. "I'm here for you. You know that, right?"

"Of course I do," she said.

He then glanced at his watch and stood up to leave. She couldn't believe he had nearly snuck out of the room while she was still sleeping. "I'll call someone to repaint the door too."

Mary waved him off. "No, that's all right. There's some paint in the garage. I'll take care of that today."

"If you'd like," he said with a quick hug and kiss on her forehead. "Call me if you need anything."

"What time will you be home?" she asked.

He went to the nightstand and grabbed his wallet. "Later this afternoon. I can't believe I almost forgot this." Distracted, he then turned to her. "We'll work out this car situation too. No mass transit here, that's for sure."

"We don't have the money for another car," she said.

He stopped at the door, hand against the frame and spoke with reassuring calm. "We'll figure something out. Love you."

"Love you too," she said.

He was out the door in a flash as she stood there in her gray Hanes T-shirt and underwear. Their heavy curtains blocked most of the sunlight, and the room was still somewhat dark. A glance at the alarm clock on the stand next to her bed said ten past nine. She had the entire mansion to herself and the entire day to do whatever she wanted. Though she knew the most important thing was to begin the illustrations for the next children's book. And take care of the door.

She slipped into a pair of sweat-pants and walked out of the room in her slippers. She felt like jogging that morning, needing a jumpstart. No such routine had been established yet at their new home. This was the first day she had been in the house alone, and the surreal strangeness of her quiet surroundings was undeniable.

She walked down the empty hallway toward the staircase, past rooms still empty, with their doors halfway open. The house seemed peaceful and undisturbed, but as she descended the staircase, she heard a faint ticking noise.

She could still hear the ticking downstairs, following it to the grand foyer where a vintage grandfather clock stood. Its oak exterior was elaborately carved in a leaf-cluster ornamentation. She stopped dead in her tracks. She could swear that she had never seen the clock before.

Where did it come from?

When did they put it there, and when?

Am I losing my mind?

Behind thick glass, a golden pendulum swung back and forth, weights hanging from two chains as the clock's mechanics ticked inside. Two long clock hands were displayed over the clock face, indicating the time as eleven past nine.

She stood in awe of the impossible idea of the great clock appearing out of nowhere, and was ready to retrieve her phone upstairs and call Curtis. She turned toward the stairs, when the clock suddenly chimed, loudly and abruptly, startling her. She grabbed the railing and flew up the stairs as the clock continued clanging, like a warning bell.

She hurried down the hall and into her room where her cell phone rested on the TV stand, plugged in to a nearby outlet. From downstairs the clock went quiet just as suddenly as it had begun chiming. The silence that followed made the hairs on her arms stand up. She held her phone, listening. She swiped the screen and made the call. After three rings, Curtis answered on the car speaker phone.

"Hey. What's up?"

"Hey," she said. "Just a quick question. When did we get a grandfather clock?"

"A what?" he asked.

"A grandfather clock. You know the big antique clock in our foyer. Where on earth did it come from?"

There was silence on the other end as she waited for a response.

"Honey. I don't know what to tell you. What clock are you talking about? We don't own a grandfather clock."

"Of course we do," she said with certainty as she made her way back down the hall and towards the stairs. "It's in the foyer. I was standing right in front of it a moment ago."

"You got me," Curtis said. *"Maybe one of the movers..."*

"What?" she asked. "Placed it there by mistake?"

"I don't know, Mary. I'll look at it when I get home. Makes no sense to me."

She went back down the stairs, prepared to describe every detail of the clock, but by the time she reached the bottom step, the clock was gone.

"Impossible..." she said softly.

"What's wrong?" he asked, detecting the fear in her tone. Her eyes darted around the room, trying to find the clock, as if it might have moved somewhere. After a stunned pause, she spoke. "Nothing. I-I'm sorry I bothered you. Have a good day."

"Okay, honey. You too."

She hung up and held the phone at her side, staring ahead. There was no way she could have imagined it. The clock was real. She had seen it with her own two eyes. She had heard it. Its loud tolling was unmistakable. She shuddered to think that it was a figment of her imagination.

She hadn't had any visions since last weekend, when she saw the figure of a man standing in a window on the second floor. She had begun to feel more comfortable, but the grandfather clock was bringing it all back. Perhaps the house only spoke to her when it wanted to. Perhaps she wasn't in control of anything.

"What do you want from me?" she said, her voice echoing through the halls.

She waited patiently, hearing nothing, not even the slightest pin drop.

"This is pointless," she called out, looking around and pacing the foyer and living room. "We're not moving. My husband wouldn't agree to it, even if I asked him, despite what he told me earlier. So if you're trying to scare us into leaving, it's not going to work." She paused and began a slow stroll to the kitchen, feeling defiant against whatever forces were at play.

ENCOUNTERS

When asking questions of the house, Mary didn't know who she was supposed to be communicating with. She wasn't a paranormal expert by any means. She knew, however, that she had a gift. A gift she had kept hidden away since childhood, and visions of things not of this world were a big part of it.

The house, however, was stimulating her power, whether she wanted it to or not. There were so many signs and signals she was being urged to pursue, too many to ignore. She wanted to learn more about Julie and, at the least, figure out who may have killed her and her family.

She could remember the sounds of the infant crying, the unseen man's voice who spoke to her while she was in the bathroom. The inverted cross on the door was another strange sign, and then, that Monday morning, a grandfather clock she had never seen before.

She walked through the dining room, past a modest, four-seater table, and approached the kitchen, feeling a strange sense of something lurking in the darkness. Fearless, she continued on, ready to face whatever the house had in store for her. She flipped the switch, and the fluorescent lights above flickered on. She stood just outside the kitchen, scanning its freshly painted walls, the hanging dish towels, the clean countertops. There was nobody there and nothing out of the ordinary beyond some dirty plates in the sink. They must have been left there by Curtis.

She was up for the challenge and determined to unearth the truth behind the mansion's gory history, using everything at her disposal. The books, the diary, and copied newspaper articles were all sitting on the desk in her office, and she was ready to dive in. All she needed first was a bagel and a cup of coffee.

A few rooms down from the kitchen, Mary sat at the desk of her studio, a sketch pad and drawing pencils at her elbow. She sipped from her coffee mug and typed away on her laptop, responding to a deluge of work emails accumulated over the past few days. She had a deadline to finish the rough sketches to present to the publisher, and she hadn't drawn a single thing.

A stack of library books rested on the corner of her desk, just within reach. The diary was secured in her desk drawer, next to her Smith & Wesson .38 caliber pistol, a weapon she always kept nearby because of years of living in the city. Classical music played from her laptop as she went into full work mode. It made her feel good to be somewhat settled in and returning from a lengthy hiatus. Her cell phone was in view, with its screen reflecting the sunlight that beamed in the room from the open window behind her. She could feel a light breeze and heard the rustling of trees and the calls chirping of birds outside.

With the clock episode behind her, she felt ready to begin her first sketches for the week. She needed to create the simple picture outline of a family at home wherein a five-year-old boy, Tommy, is being told by his mother at the dinner table to never talk to strangers. It was a simple-enough scene, and Mary swiveled her chair around to the easel behind her, taking her drawing pencil and beginning to sketch over a thin sheet of paper.

Her drawing motions came naturally as she envisioned the family: the father, mother, daughter, and three boys. She sketched with quick, measured lines while entering a strange trance where her artwork took a life of its own.

After several minutes of focused work, she opened her eyes and lowered her pencil, shocked by what she had drawn. There on the paper was a rough sketch of a family, but not the one she had intended to draw. The nicely dressed mother, father, and children lay on their backs, riddled with gunshot wounds and resting in thick pools of blood. She had drawn Xs over their eyes. Their mouths were agape in horror. She backed her chair away, stunned by the image, dropping the pencil to the ground.

She pulled the top drawer open, and grabbed the small, crinkled diary hidden inside. She placed it on her desk, pushing her keyboard to the side, and stared down at its faded, leather exterior. She then opened a document on her computer, a typed transcript of the legible pages in the diary, which she had entered soon after finding it. She flipped the book open to a page in the middle, which she had marked.

I don't know what's happening. I'm scared. I heard Mother and Father quietly discussing death threats. For weeks we've received dozens of unmarked letters in unrecognizable handwriting. They won't even let me go into town anymore. Or to school. Or to the park. Or even in the woods behind our house. I have a private tutor now. Her name is Mrs. Dempsey. She's fifty-two years old and very stern. I asked Mother last night who would want to hurt us. She told me not to worry about it. But I am worried about it. How can I not be?

Mary flipped to the next page, reading.

Mother fired Mrs. Dempsey today after an argument. What it was about, she wouldn't tell me. This is the fifth person they've fired in the past week. Our gardener, butler, mechanic, and swim coach. All of them gone. Now I feel lonelier than ever.

Mary paused, looking up. "Swim coach?" she said. Did the mansion once have a pool? There was nothing in the backyard but solid ground, with plenty of trees and underbrush. She looked back down and continued reading as the girl's next words in anticipation.

Pastor Phil visited the house tonight. He's about the only person Mother talks to anymore. He too expressed concern for our safety but said that God would protect us as long as we had faith in Him and each other. My parents were never really religious people. Though lately, that's all changed.

Mary closed the diary and set it to the side and reached for the copied newspaper articles. She flipped through the copies, frantic, eyes darting along the lines of story. In several different articles, the history of the Bechdel mansion was recapped, picked up and repeated from previous generic content. The estate was at least a hundred years old and had been a part of the Bechdel family for generations.

One article caught her interest by including a few new facts. She discovered that by the turn of the 20th Century, the Bechdel family tree had extended quite considerably, but by 1967, however, their bloodline had been completely wiped out.

She placed the articles to the side and grabbed the library travelogue book. Her mind didn't waver. She gave no notice of time passing or attention to her phone or how many emails piled in her inbox. She opened the first book, *A Brief History of Redwood*. It was a short book, maybe sixty pages long, and there were plenty of old photographs, which showed the progression from a backwoods settlement to a full-fledged town. She flipped through the pages, letting her instincts guide her as she came across a small newspaper clipping, stuck between two pages. She carefully took the clipping out and unfolded it, reading the headline with dread.

Ukrainian Heir Flees Redwood Mansion after Series of Unexplained Events

The article continued: "In the summer of June, 1992, the rural town of Redwood welcomed one of its most prestigious newcomers, wealthy business heir Boris Sokolov and his large family. Since moving to the town, Sokolov made several boastful promises to invest in Redwood, and help to create what he called a town for the modern age. But two weeks later, Sokolov, the self-proclaimed 'savior of Redwood,' fled his new home, the infamous Bechdel estate, without a word, taking his family back to Ukraine, where they were never seen or heard from again."

Mary stopped there and went back to the books, taking in each and everything she could about the town and its history. Her fingers stopped between the pages of another book, detailing Redwood municipal history and Dover County, which surrounded it. Inside, there was another newspaper clipping, folded as before.

This time she found an article about the most recent family to have lived in the mansion, dating back only to 2006. The story said that the family had moved away after the father, Eugene Garland, a wealthy Manhattan land developer, died in his sleep, just three weeks after moving in. She continued reading the article, immersed in the details and mystery surrounding Garland's death, when she felt a sudden and overwhelming fatigue. Her eyes became heavy beyond control and she began drifting away into a slumber that did not seem her own.

A startling vision came over her, real and lifelike. She was in the downstairs ballroom of the mansion., fully furnished and crowded with people. There were servers in tuxedos holding trays with finger foods and champagne glasses and men and women in fancy suits and dresses as jazz music played from a nearby record player.

As the vision continued, she ascended the winding staircase, watching the party from above as three masked men stormed into the house, brandishing rifles and shotguns and shouting at the dinner guests, terrifying and rounding them up into a tight and terrified cluster. Moments later, the party guests and everyone else was blasted away, riddled with bullets as gunfire tore them apart and sent clumps of flesh onto the polished wood floors in an orgy of blood.

The vision then took Mary along the hallway and into the first bedroom on the right, a child's room, the room of a young girl. Now Mary was seeing the mansion through someone else's eyes, perhaps Julie. She came to a window overlooking the darkened courtyard just as a man began banging on her bedroom door. She climbed onto the window sill, closed her eyes in fear and forced herself to jump into the bushes and moist grass below, then getting up and running off in a panic, gasping for air, overcome with the joy of having escaped. She then ran into a man.

Mary could see his face as he pointed the barrel of his rifle at her head: lean cheekbones, stubble, a scar on his left cheek, and a thick head of straight, reddish hair that grew down past his ears. A blast and a white flash of light, when suddenly Mary woke up.

The grandfather clock jarred her out of her deep sleep, bells tolling in sync, and woke her to a darkened office. Her head rose up from the desk, with a newspaper clipping stuck to her cheek. She felt an uncomfortable crick in her neck and, for a moment, didn't know where she was.

She spun her chair around, gasping. The passage of time was unreal. She backed up and stared at her desk, long and hard. Books were strewn open all along its surface, with newspaper articles lying everywhere.

Her blank laptop screen had long gone into sleep mode. She looked at her cell phone and saw that it was a little after 8:00 p.m. "Impossible..." She had found herself saying that word a lot as of late.

She turned back around, looking out the window into the dark sky and listening to the distant chirping of crickets coming from the blackened forest. Fear crept into her heart when she realized that she had read every book and every copied article on the desk. If only she could remember half of what she had apparently read.

She swiped her phone screen and saw some missed calls from her mother, her agent, and from Curtis. She called him first, but his number went straight to voice mail. She still found herself in a state of disbelief.

"Just checking in with you. I'd thought you'd be home now. Call me back," she said into the phone.

She hung up, curious as to his whereabouts, and then rose from her chair, legs stiff and sore. The empty plate on her desk with the crumbs of an eaten bagel, along with her growling stomach, indicated as much. She walked past the desk and out of the room toward the kitchen to make some dinner.

She turned on the hall light and thoughts of the grandfather clock rushed back. She flipped the kitchen lights on, carrying her empty plate to the sink, when the fluorescent lights above flickered and then went out completely. She stood in the darkness, astonished and frustrated, but grateful for a faint glow from the single light above the sink that stayed on.

She placed her plate into the sink and turned around,

looking into the darkness. After a few steps, she felt something slick and slippery on the tile floor below her slippers. She looked down and saw red streaks on the floor. She took another careful step forward and heard a distant moan that caused the hairs to stand up on the back of her neck.

Just past the counter, she saw a figure slowly moving across the floor. She gasped and covered her mouth, trembling. A few feet ahead of her crawled a man on his stomach, with a large hole blasted in his back. His black suit was tattered, torn, and soaked with blood. His organs were hanging out, his intestines dragging behind him on the floor. She could only see the back of his head as he pulled one arm in front of the other with feeble, shaking movements.

She reached for her cell phone, frightened as the man slowly crawled toward her, moaning in agony. Her legs had locked into place, paralyzed with fear. Her cell phone fell from her hand and smacked onto the floor, landing in a puddle of blood.

She crouched down to grab her blood-soaked phone, but it slipped out of her hand and slid across the tile, just out of reach. Then, as if an earthquake had shaken the ground and everything on it, the kitchen came alive with one explosive and sweeping gust of wind that forced every cabinet open a loud, deafening burst. Mary reeled to the slippery ground in terror.

Plates crashed and shattered into pieces. Pots flew into the wall. The refrigerator flew open, sending its contents smashing onto the ground. A dizzying white flash followed, as Mary tried to stand, trying to resist an unseen force pushing her down. Her forehead smacked against the tile, and she felt blood trickling down her face.

She screamed and struggled again to get up as the disorienting cacophony of pots, pans, plates, and glasses crashed all around her. After one final heave, she made it to her feet and vaulted out of the kitchen, slipping on blood and staggering down the hall, not looking back.

Her screams echoed through the house as she stormed down the hall past rooms where doors slammed shut like sideways guillotines hoping to snare her in. By the time she made it to the staircase, she was greeted with the sight of the grandfather clock across the room, chiming louder than ever with blood bubbling, top to bottom. Both chairs suddenly flew toward her like guided missiles.

She jumped out of the way and slid across the hardwood floor as as furniture crashed into the wall in a splintering bang. She looked up to see the chandelier swaying wildly, with bulbs wildly flashing. Doors slammed shut in unison all around her. Moaning continued. A barrage of cockroaches infested the walls around her. Hanging pictures crashed to the ground. In the distance, the kitchen table flew across the dining room and pummeled into the wall.

Mary slipped and fell to her knees, feeling trapped and pinned to the ground. Thick blood spewed from the grandfather clock like a geyser, soaking the ceiling in its red flow and dripping back onto the floor.

"*What do you want?*" she screamed.

A loud bang suddenly came against the front door, startling her further. Her head whipped around, and she stared at the exit and tried to build up the nerve to run. *Was this it for her? Had the house finally come alive to take her away?*

As she crouched down with her palms flat against the floor, sweat ran down her forehead, creating a puddle below. She looked up to see a blinding white light at the end of the staircase. Within that light, she saw the shape of a young girl. Her face was hollow and pale, with her cheeks sunken in and black pupils within her mist-like form, barefoot and dressed in a nightgown. Mary recognized her from the pictures in the paper. It was Julie.

"Don't be afraid," she said, her voice a distant echo. "I've made them stop. You have to help us."

Mary pushed herself up from the ground with her heart racing. "Julie? Julie, is it really you?"

Julie's form flickered like the dying flame on a candle. "There is a darkness in this town. You have to stop it for us to be at rest."

"Tell me what I have to do," Mary said as moans persisted throughout the house, sending a shiver down her spine.

"Our killers," Julie said. "They must be brought to justice."

Mary looked around the grand foyer in shock at the tumbled-over furniture and broken glass covering the floor. "Why are you destroying our home?"

"The others are angry and vengeful, but don't worry about them," she said in a distant, haunting voice. "You're our only hope."

"Who killed your family?" Mary asked.

"They wore masks," Julie said. "That is all I know. One man had a scar on the left cheek. That was my last memory before crossing over."

Mary approached Julie's fading image with tears in her eyes. "I don't know what to do. I'm trying, but I can't do it on my own."

"You won't have to," Julie said.

"Julie, I'm so sorry," Mary said as Julie wavered above the staircase, a transparent shape of light of eternal unrest.

"You can help, Mary. I believe in you. Your daughter's fate is also tied to this house."

"Daughter?" Mary asked. "What are you talking about?"

Julie quickly turned to look behind her and then nervously whipped her head around to face Mary. "That is all I can say…" She then vanished in a blink of an eye as Mary called to her again.

"Julie?" Mary cried out. "Julie!" But she was gone. With

Julie's disappearance, an unseen force threw Mary flat on her stomach as her own body weight tripled and pushed her to the ground. Another flash of white, and she felt a sharp pain in her jaw from smacking against the floor. The other spirits returned with a vengeance, and they weren't going to let her go anywhere. She had to muster enough energy to escape before they drained her of all essence, leaving her a hollow vessel and doomed to join them on the other side.

MONDAY OCTOBER 17, 2016

Monday October 17, 2016
Redwood, Indiana

The pounding on the door continued. The house shook at its very foundation, like the aftershock of an earthquake. Mary wasn't sure if she'd make it out alive, but with one fresh gasp of air, she flew forward onto her feet and hurtled toward the front door. A grandfather clock tipped over and crashed in front of the door, blocking her and pouring human organs and limbs from its top across the foyer.

Mary jumped over the clock without a second glance and smacked hard against the front door as the pounding continued. Her knees and back ached. Her frequent dizziness returned to her with full force, making it nearly impossible to clutch the door handle and push it open. She rose up as heat engulfed her as if from an unseen fire. Her hands went to the door handle and yanked it open as moonlight hit her face. She ran outside, screaming for help, and then collided into a man standing at the base of her steps.

"Hey, there! Listen to me. Calm down..." he said.

She twisted about, but couldn't shake the man's grip. "Let me go!" she said repeatedly.

"Mary, please listen to me," the man pleaded.

Mary looked up trembling and saw Pastor Phil's face watching her with concern. She didn't know what to say.

"Goodness, Mary. What happened?" he asked, releasing her.

Too stunned to respond, she slowly walked toward the front door looked and inside the house. There was no grandfather clock, no blood, and no body parts scattered across the hardwood floor. *Was it all in my head?* she thought with growing doubt in her sanity.

"The house..." she began. "It... it came alive. Julie spoke to me!"

The spirit of Julie Bechdel, the youngest Bechdel child, murdered forty years prior, had reached out to Mary as the house went amok. Her deceased family wanted Mary's help, Julie had said. Their killers were still out there, and they needed to be brought to justice.

Pastor Phil took a step back and shook his head. "The secrets of the Bechdel mansion must stay buried for Redwood to survive," Phil said. "That's just the way it is. That's the way it's always been."

"I don't understand," Mary said, exhausted and shaken. "What secrets?" She suddenly looked up at him with suspicion. "And what are you doing here?"

"Forgive me, Mary," he answered. "I came here to talk—to help, actually."

She closed the front door, turned, and then approached Phil. "I-I don't know what to make of it. The house... it came alive." She paused and hung her head down, staring at the concrete. "*I saw Julie.* She... she *appeared* to me." She paused again and looked up at Phil. "I'm not crazy."

Phil stepped forward and placed a sympathetic hand on her shoulder. "Of course you're not, Mary. You have a gift. I know that they're in there. They've always been in there, but I cannot see them."

Mary turned away, still shaken, and entered the courtyard where she began to pace around. "Why me?" she asked. "I don't know what any of it means."

"It is proof of life after death," he said. "A secret of the afterlife that must stay within these walls. Human beings cannot comprehend the powers beyond our existence. Sometimes, however, there are some, like you, who can catch a glimpse of it."

Mary hung her arms down at her sides, staring Pastor Phil down. "So you've known that this mansion has been haunted the entire time? Why didn't you tell us?"

"I can only get so involved," he said. "This house does not take well to outsiders, or men of the faith, like myself. The dead resent the living. Those restless souls in there want their eternal connection with God, but they're being denied."

"A warning would have been nice. An anonymous tip. Anything!" Mary said.

"I tried to deliver you and Curtis a warning," Phil said, confusing Mary even more. "The Bechdel family bloodline has been cursed for generations. Part of that curse has kept the spirits of their deceased in constant turmoil. Releasing those spirits is and always has been an eternal struggle between good and evil. Matter and spirit."

Mary shook her head, not wholly prepared for a sermon just yet. "I want to help Julie, I really do, but we can't live here any longer."

"There is no escape," Phil said. "Rarely has anyone ever been able to do so."

Mary laughed in disbelief, wiping her eyes. "They can try

me." She walked forward, prepared to blow past Phil, but failed, as he put his hands up and urged her to remain.

"Listen to me. I'll do my best to explain what I know, what I've pieced together all these years about this house and this town." He paused with a deep breath as Mary slowed her charge. Phil suddenly stood aside and beckoned her with an outstretched arm. "Please. Walk with me."

He walked through the courtyard, and Mary reluctantly followed. "I suppose you're wondering about the inverted cross painted on your door. Jerry Hadley, the church landscaper, did that at my behest."

Mary stopped in her tracks, stunned. "*That* was your warning?"

"The spirits have to be contained. I've experimented with other measures before, and the red mark of Saint Peter seems to have been the most effective."

"But you said they would follow me wherever I go," Mary said.

"Yes," he said. "A part of this house will always be with you now."

Frustrated, she could barely wrap her head around half of what he was saying. "How do you know so much about this? What's your involvement?"

Pastor Phil explained that unseen forces had been searching for a "chosen one" for some time.

"I knew the Bechdels well. They were an eccentric bunch. Julie, however, was as sweet as can be. She volunteered at the church and always had a smile on her face. What happened to that poor girl was an appalling act. A young girl's life, cut short for nothing." He continued walking as they neared the empty fountain in the middle of the courtyard. "Her brothers were nice young men. I liked them all." His voice suddenly took a somber tone. "But there is something here, and I'm close, myself, to figuring it out."

Mary studied Pastor Phil under the glow of moonlight—a sharp contrast to the chaos she had escaped from inside.

"Julie mentioned my daughter," Mary said. "I..." Her voice dropped, and she looked on the verge of tears. "But I don't have one."

Phil turned to her with an understanding nod. His white hair was the most visible part of him under the night sky. "These spirits can sense and see things about yourself that you may not know. It could be a sign of things to come in the future."

"How could they possibly know that?" she asked in disbelief. "I'm not pregnant!" She then steadily recalled an evening of the week prior. She and Curtis had made love after an evening of celebrating a new chapter in their lives.

Phil looked prepared to elaborate, when suddenly headlights emerged from the long driveway leading from the gate. His car was nowhere to be seen. He pulled a piece of a paper from his jacket pocket and handed it to Mary.

"Here," he said. "Meet me at this address tomorrow afternoon, and I'll explain everything the best I can." He then leaned in closer, speaking with a stern tone. "You can't tell anyone anything about what happened tonight. Not even your husband."

"But I have to," she began.

"No," he said, raising his hand. "Not yet. Trust me." He rushed off into the nearby woods just as the headlamps of their Ford Expedition bathed her in light. Mary stood there with little understanding of everything that had just happened. She had no idea where Curtis had been all evening or why he was coming home so late. How would she even begin to explain the condition of the house?

Their SUV skidded to a halt ten feet away from her. She felt her body clenching up. Pastor Phil had sworn her to secrecy, while implying the existence of a daughter in the near future. His comments resonated with her, and without warning, images from the past few months flashed through her mind like pictures in a photo album.

DARK FORCES

The Redwood Massacre: Ten Years Later
By Stephen Collins, Staff Writer, Dover Press
June 25, 1985

The vacant Bechdel Mansion has been a site of fascination for crime buffs and journalists for years now. Ten years ago, the affluent family who resided within the rural outskirts of Redwood, Indiana, were brutally murdered along with nine guests in their home one evening during a dinner party.

Also in attendance were the Drakes, another wealthy family, who were celebrating the engagement of their promising daughter, Katelyn, to the eldest Bechdel son, Travis. It was a time of good cheer and new beginnings, a proud moment for both George and Anabelle Bechdel and Victor and Holly Drake. The bond between the families had only strengthened their mutual land-development enterprises, and George Bechdel was also running for mayor of Redwood—his first foray into politics. The future looked bright for the two families and all of their respective endeavors.

Their bright futures, however, ended abruptly that evening when unidentified gunmen stormed into the home, assembled the guests together, and reportedly held them at gunpoint, judging from the way the bodies were gathered in the downstairs grand foyer. What must have seemed like a routine hold-up soon evolved into something more as each and every guest was gunned down and killed, turning the elegant ballroom into the scene of a sickening bloodbath.

Perhaps most shocking of all was the murder of the young Julie Bechdel. The eleven-year-old honor-roll student wasn't spared among the victims. The unspeakable and horrific murder of a defenseless child further propelled the infamy of the crime and brutality of the killers to a horrified public.

True evil had come through Redwood, and no one seemed to understand why. The mansion had been ransacked, a few items were stolen, but to this day, no clear motive has been established. The unsolved nature of the case has led to the public's continuing interest in this dark saga. Many have found it unconscionable that such a crime would appear to be without motive or resolution.

A lengthy investigation yielded no suspects, and the case went cold one year after. The FBI was even involved at one point but were unable to produce enough evidence to convict a single suspect. Afterward, public speculation grew, and conspiracy theories raged like wildfire. One theory was that the murders were an ordered hit by business competitors of both families. Another theory stated that the murders were carried out by escaped convicts from out of town, following a break from the Hartfield Correctional Institute, twenty miles outside of Redwood. Those convicts were eventually captured, but there was no evidence to place them at the scene of the crime, not as if the county didn't try.

The sheer audaciousness of the Bechdel massacre was

made all the more startling when law enforcement and investigative agencies came up empty. The questions were asked repeatedly:

How could a case of this magnitude go unsolved?

How could the murder of two prestigious families go cold?

The massacre, some said, exposed sinister forces at work in an otherwise idyllic and harmonious small town. Many claimed that the town would never be the same. Ten years later, there is still a sense of loss within the community, a loss that endures long after the fading of the town-square memorial and the flowers posted at the gates of the Bechdel estate. Many residents believe that the dark cloud present on that tragic evening still persists in some places, notably in the estate itself. Redwood officials have implemented strict protocols to prevent travelers fascinated with the case from trespassing or squatting around the premises.

For now, the vacant mansion remains tied up in probate litigation as the bank, which owns a substantial share of the property, decides what to do with it. The passage of ten years has not made the property any more attractive to prospective buyers, since memories are long. Most recently, the mayor of Redwood, Frederick Taylor, proposed that the town acquire the property as a tribute to "two of Redwood's finest families."

The ten-year anniversary of the Bechdel massacre has brought travelers from all over the country, taking pictures of the ghostlike mansion covered in winding vines from top to bottom and shielded by bare, leafless trees on cool autumn days. Beyond the gates stands the once-glamorous home of a prosperous family, now a former shell of itself.

Its grand, yet dilapidated, appearance is what ghost stories are made of, and tucked away as it is, the mansion almost seems as though it is trying to spare onlookers its sad and haunting sight. No Trespassing signs are affixed to the fences, and small pieces of faded police tape still cling to the bars of the rusted gate. Will another family purchase and renovate the home one day, eliminating all vestiges of mayhem from its grimy walls? Or will the mansion stand as a relic of enduring folklore? Only time will tell.

REFUGE

Curtis and Mary Malone moved from Chicago and purchased the Bechdel mansion for next to nothing in a town called Redwood, Indiana. From the initial renovation, Mary had sensed that something was off about the house. She saw things. Heard things. But she had always had a sixth sense, a power in seeing things in a way that she had never quite understood.

She soon learned of the unsolved murders forty years before and was intrigued but also incredibly disturbed. How could they live in a place with such a history? But the ink was already dry and the Bechdel estate was theirs.

From their first week there, strange noises and troubling visions began to disturb their quietude. The occurrences were random and subtle. A noise here. A flash there. But on the third Monday of October, with Mary home alone, the house erupted in a cacophony of rage that sent her reeling from a menacing presence.

September 12, 2016
Chicago, Illinois

A month and a half before Mary faced definitive proof of the supernatural, she had awakened in her hospital bed with a deep feeling of dread. It wasn't the miscarriage, it was something else. From the second-story window, she could hear ambulances wailing into the night air. She could see the Chicago skyline, buildings symmetrically aligned and lit up like a million Christmas trees. She looked away as rain began to trickle across the window.

She was the only patient in the small, dimly lit room. A needle was lodged in her wrist, leading to a nearby IV bag. here was a band on her other wrist with a thin cable attached to a pulse monitor. Despite her recovery, inside, she felt completely devastated.

She looked to the empty chair at the side of her bed, where Curtis had been sitting, and wondered where he had gone. Feeling cold, she slid her right hand underneath her hospital gown and across her stomach, where she could feel the outline of stitches under the thick gauze wrapped around her. Like a bad dream it all started to come back. She wanted to cry but could barely find the energy. She didn't understand why things had turned out the way that they had. What did she do wrong? She wanted to make sense of things, but after the miscarriage, nothing much seemed to matter anymore.

The door opened slowly as Curtis walked inside with a coffee in one hand and his briefcase in the other. His button-down dress shirt was untucked, his sleeves rolled up, and his tie missing. His dark, disheveled hair and thick five o'clock shadow made it look as if he hadn't slept in days.

Mary sat up in her bed, her blonde hair tied back in a ponytail, her tired face free of makeup. She could barely find the will to eat, and Curtis had expressed concern about her thinness. At thirty-three, she had hoped to be reaching a new milestone, to be a mother, but fate had taken that dream away. he and Curtis had been married for two wonderful year, but as she lay in bed, she had never felt so hopeless.

Curtis's gloomy face brightened as he saw that she was awake. She tried her best to smile back, but it all felt so fake.

"How are you feeling?" he asked.

"Okay," she said. "Think my appetite is coming back."

He took a seat in the chair next to her and leaned closer. "That's great to hear," he said.

"I'm sorry that you have to spend all this time away from the office," she said, pointing to his briefcase.

"Mary, please," he said. He then took her left hand in his, squeezing. "I told you not to worry about that. My place is here with you now." Curtis looked around the room, hesitant. "But I do want to show you something when you get better."

Mary nodded. "I'm getting there. Show me now."

His smile widened. That was clearly what he wanted her to say, and he was prepared. He set his briefcase on his lap and clicked it open, slowly reaching inside and sliding out a thick manila folder. From the folder, he pulled a sheet of paper and handed it to Mary. She took the paper without a clue of what he was getting at. Her eyes scanned the page. It was a color printout from a realtor's website, displaying a massively sized Victorian mansion.

"What is this?" she asked.

"I've been doing some thinking, Mary, and I think it's time for a change." He looked at her with earnest conviction. "That house is our refuge from all of this."

Her eyes scanned the house exterior, under which details were printed in bold caps: FIVE THOUSAND SQUARE FOOT, FIFTEEN-ROOM, FOUR-BATHROOM HOME with COURTYARD, FOUNTAIN, FOUR-CAR GARAGE, on TEN ACRES of BEAUTIFUL WILDERNESS.

She held the paper up, noticing the price at the top in large, bold numbers.

"Fifty thousand dollars? For what?"

"For the entire property," Curtis said, his face beaming with excitement. "Just think about it. A new life in a small town, just the two of us starting over again."

Mary handed the paper back and looked up at the ceiling. "I don't know, Curtis. Seems like a pretty big step. What would we do with all that space?"

"Whatever we wanted," he answered.

"That can't be the real price," she said in a groggy voice.

"I talked with Lazaro Keely," Curtis said. "A buddy of mine in real estate. He got the lead on the place, and put me in touch with this guy, Bob Deckers, out there in Redwood. He told me all about it." Curtis paused and sat down at direct level with Mary. "The town… you really have to see this place."

Mary felt her eyelids growing heavy. "Can we talk about this later?"

Curtis stood back up, concerned. "Sure thing, honey. Whenever you want. I just ask that you consider it." He closed his briefcase and then sighed. Mary noticed the despondent look on his face and asked him what was wrong.

"Nothing," he said. "I'll tell you later. Let's just worry about you right now."

"Curtis," she said. "I can see it in your eyes. Talk to me."

He shifted in his chair, clearly uncomfortable with delving into the matter any further. But he couldn't hold himself back, and blurted: "I'm out at Jacobs and Maine. Let go. Staff cuts, they called it."

Mary's face sank. "But I thought they were going to make you a partner. You've been there *three* years."

Curtis shrugged and took a sip of coffee. "They lied." He

then leaned forward and took her hand again. "I don't need them. I can start my own practice. I just need your support."

"Of course." Mary nodded with a smile as he caressed her hand. "You're a great lawyer. They have no right—"

"We're going to be fine," he said, leaning back. "Don't worry."

The door opened, and their doctor walked in, a tall, balding man in a long white coat and black slacks. He looked up at them from his thick, square-framed glasses, clipboard in hand.

"Oh good, you're up, Mrs. Malone. I just came by to check on you."

Curtis turned to the doctor with a newly-formed smile and an extended hand. "Dr. Conley. So nice to see you."

The doctor stepped closer to the bed and shook Curtis's hand. "And how are we doing?" he asked, looking down at Mary.

"A little better," she said. There was some relief that he came in when he did, interrupting in a way, but she felt that things were far from over with Curtis.

Dr. Conley flipped through his clipboard, running his finger along the chart. "Your vitals and everything else look good. Your status definitely appears to be improving."

"That's great," Curtis said.

The doctor's smile slowly morphed into a more solemn expression as his tone turned serious. "I am sorry about your loss. You've shown amazing resilience so far. I truly wish both of you the best."

"Thanks, Doctor," Curtis said with a pat on the shoulder of his white coat.

Mary began to drift back to sleep as the doctor's words faded. The mansion entered her thoughts, the picture of it as familiar to her as her childhood school-yard. There was something about the place that intrigued her, though she had no inclination of actually moving there.

September 15, 2016
Chicago, Illinois

A few days after being discharged from the hospital, Mary returned to their apartment only to find it ransacked, pilfered, and violated to a shocking degree. She couldn't understand it. Their quaint apartment had been broken into. Tables had been flipped, drawers thrown out, their contents scattered across the floor. Their television, among other electronics, was missing. It was hard to tell what else had been taken with the rooms trashed the way they were. Their home was in ruins.

Curtis pulled out his cell phone. "Wait here while I check the bedrooms," he said. His eyes were steely and focused.

Mary scanned the living room and adjacent kitchen from the foyer. Papers were everywhere. Drawers and shelves were emptied and raided. The front door was intact without damage. The intruders must have gotten in through somewhere else.

Curtis spoke with urgency as he walked through the hallway and in and out of the rooms. "Hello, nine-one-one? I'd like to report a break-in."

Their three-bedroom apartment was on the first floor, but they lived in a decent neighborhood, and their complex had good security. Though, at that moment, none of those assurances seemed to be true.

As Curtis's voice drifted down the hall, Mary clutched her chest, worrying about what might have been stolen. She had everything important on her computer and hoped that it was still there. Anything and everything, personal and work-related, could be gone. She walked around the mess in their living room, sickened with anxiety.

There were holes in the walls and broken glass everywhere, adding to her fears. She neared her office, fearful of what had been stolen.

Curtis stepped out of their bedroom, phone against his ear. "No, sir. I don't believe they're here, but they really did a number on our home. Please send someone as soon as you can."

She entered her office and sighed with relief, finding her desk intact and her drawing tablet and computer still there. Several items from a nearby bookcase had been tossed on the ground, but nothing appeared to be missing. She felt a light breeze and looked to the open window behind her desk where the burglar must have entered. The glass was smashed out and lying in shards on the carpet below, sending a chill down her spine. A thin white curtain swayed in the breeze on both sides of the window.

Mary met Curtis in their bedroom as he paced the room talking with the insurance company, ready to file a claim. The queen-sized mattress had been flipped. Their dresser drawers were lying on the floor, contents scattered. Clothes were everywhere. The television was gone. A few holes had been punched into the wall, the same as in the other rooms.

She stood in the middle of the room, devastated. Their apartment was in shambles, Curtis had been laid off, and most troubling of all, their newly purchased infant crib, fresh out of the box, was lying in pieces in the corner—a horrible reminder of the worst of their recent losses.

October 8, 2016

Nearly a month later, Mary sat on the living-room couch of their apartment, staring at the pile of packed boxes before her. She couldn't believe that it had come to this. They were actually moving. Chicago had been their home for years. But now everything had changed. They had often discussed moving to a small town where they could raise a family, but never in circumstances like this.

They had purchased the property in Redwood with their remaining savings. Curtis had convinced Mary, after all, that Redwood would offer hopes of turning their lives around. But there were things about the oddly inexpensive mansion that bothered her. Things she could not look past.

She could picture its vacant, dilapidated interiors without ever having stepped inside. She could sense its troubled history and was well aware of the additional expense of its necessary renovation. None of that had happened yet, and their hasty move seemed rash, with little regard being given for what they were getting into. Ultimately, however, she trusted Curtis and also believed that their prospects could only go up, not down, and that their current circumstances would surely improve.

As Mary scanned the empty walls of their apartment and packed boxes stacked in the living room, she felt a growing sadness. Curtis was in the kitchen, on the phone with the movers, who were scheduled to arrive within the hour. The moving truck was then supposed to follow them to their new home in Redwood.

They were really doing it. She tried to suppress her doubts and focus on the future with optimism. Though she held a troubling secret known only to herself. Sometimes, her visions of things to come were disturbingly real, and she had little control of them.

Weeks before her hospital stay, she had had a dream about the miscarriage. Every detail had played out exactly as she had envisioned it, right down to the doctor's sullen expression as he informed her that their daughter, Sophie, was stillborn. Before the terrifying dream turned to reality, she had insisted to herself that it was all in her head.

"What is wrong with me?" she had once asked her mother as a child.

"You have the gift of foresight," her mother had told her. "And you can one day use it for good." Old memories of Pittsburgh, where she grew up, came to her as she sat quietly in their apartment living room.

"Movers should be here soon," Curtis said from the kitchen.

"Okay," she said, staring at the barren walls and the nail holes where pictures used to hang.

Curtis walked into the living room in his favorite hat, T-shirt, and shorts, bursting with energy.

"Hey... Are you okay?" he asked, noticing her quietness.

"Yeah," she said, nodding.

Not convinced, Curtis walked over and sat on the couch next to her and took her hand. "I know you have your doubts, Mary, but we can do this."

She looked over at him with a faint smile.

"This is an exciting day," he continued with a squeeze of her hand. "A new beginning for both of us."

Mary tugged at her sterling-silver necklace, which she liked to wear with her pink button-down shirt. This was, after all, an important occasion. It was early Sunday morning, and they had a long drive ahead. They had spent all of Friday and Saturday packing. She had never moved from a place so quickly.

She looked at Curtis and tried to mask her uncertainty but to no avail. "Just a little nervous about it all," she said.

"So am I," he added. "We'd be crazy not to be. But isn't this exciting?"

Mary pulled her hand away and rose from the couch,

thinking to herself as she retrieved her glass of water from the kitchen bar.

Curtis continued with his thought about Redwood. "The town is beautiful. You really have to see it to appreciate it."

Mary bit her lip. "I didn't want to bring this up because of everything that's going on, but I did some research the other day. A family was murdered in that house in 1975. Did you know that?"

Curtis glanced down, unresponsive. He then looked up at her with a hint of shame. "I'm sorry, honey. That was over forty years ago, and I didn't want to spook you."

Arms crossed, Mary rocked her head back and sighed. "Did you not think that I would find out? Anything else I should know?"

Before Curtis could answer, a large truck roared up outside and honked its horn. Curtis rose from the couch and carefully inched his way out of the living room with his hands clasped together. "Please. We'll talk about this later."

Mary shook her head in disbelief. "This isn't over."

"I know," he said. "I'll make it right. I promise."

Curtis turned and left the living room in an obvious hurry. He was out the front door before Mary could say another word. She closed her eyes, trying to withstand the growing feeling of dread building within. Maybe Curtis was right. Maybe it wasn't a big deal. Her instincts, however, told her differently.

Their new home was, in fact, the site of an infamous mass murder, and she could feel its sinister aura without even being there. She took a deep breath, prepared to put her foot down, when Curtis entered the house with two burly men dressed in identical green polo shirts.

She froze as the name of someone she did not know came to her, and she found herself saying it just above a whisper. "Julie…"

WELCOME TO REDWOOD

Mary and Curtis arrived in Redwood on the Saturday of October Eighth, on the late afternoon of a quiet autumn day. She found the quaint town endearing with its shops and corner stores, historic downtown layered in brick road, parks and fresh-water bay, antique Victorian homes, and small-town ambiance.

They drove slowly down Main Street, which was full of parked cars on both sides of the road. Families and couples of all ages strolled past picturesque buildings and vendor stations where banners hung from lampposts, promoting Redwood's annual Autumn Festival. They passed the town hall, an old two-story building with a clock tower and an American flag waving in the air from a long pole.

There was an old-style theater with a marquee in the front, several craft stores, a grocer, and a park, all enclosed within the same few blocks. Everything seemed untouched and preserved from simpler times. There was surprise to the appeal of a town like Redwood, especially for city dwellers.

Mary felt as though something had brought them out here, something beyond fate, and even beyond her own judgment. As they continued down Main Street, heads turned and glanced at their white Ford Expedition and the large moving truck trailing behind them. Redwood's newest residents had arrived.

Their new home was in a rural area on the outskirts of town. Beyond the wide gate and fence surrounding the property were trees and bushes, blocking most of the house from view. Mary and Curtis drove slowly through the open entrance gate and onto a long path leading to the house. Overgrown grass on both sides reached at least four feet high.

The two-story mansion with graying stone walls was surrounded by deep forest, without another home around for miles. Once past the gate, they soon reached a stone-paved courtyard with a large fountain in the center full of dead branches and leaves. The enormous house, in view behind the fountain, was exactly as Mary had envisioned it, even before seeing the pictures.

Its wide symmetrical exterior had an array of tall windows on both floors and an upper balcony that overlooked the courtyard below. The opulent façade had Greek pillars reaching the barrel-shingled roof that arched upward, directly in the middle. Two chimneys reached out on both ends of the roof.

The outside of the house was faded, with vines running up the sides of the house, almost completely consuming it. The estate was a relic of another time, concealed by overgrowth and years of neglect. There was a lot of work ahead of them.

Monday October 17, 2016

After Pastor Phil had run off into the nearby woods, wanting to avoid any further conversation with Mary or Curtis, headlights advanced down the driveway then past a slight curve. They shined on Mary as she stood in the courtyard, stunned by everything that had just happened.

Had Julie actually reached out and talked to her? It felt real enough, but Curtis would never believe her. Would the disorder waiting inside be enough? Surely the flipped furniture, broken glass, and the state of their kitchen was definitive proof of paranormal existence within the house, and Mary was ready to make her case.

Curtis turned the headlights off and engine. He opened the door and stepped out, confused and concerned to see Mary standing outside with her head down and arms crossed in deep thought.

"Mary?" he asked, quickly approaching her. "Are you all right?" Receiving no response, he raced against the cobblestone ground along the way. "

Mary turned to him, deciding where to start. She opened her mouth to speak, but nothing came out. Curtis placed his hands on her shoulders as she raised her head, hair hanging in her face.

"My God, you're trembling. Mary. You have to tell me what happened."

She raised her arm and pointed to the house. "Julie... she spoke to me."

Curtis turned and stared at the open walkway. The front-porch light flickered, though there wasn't a single light on inside. He then pulled her closer, rubbing her bare arms. "You're freezing. Now please, tell me what happened?"

"Where have you been?" she asked straight-forward.

Curtis paused for a moment and looked down. "I'm sorry. I lost track of time. I was at dinner with Bob Deckers, the realtor. He was introducing me around. Trying to get some clients. I just didn't realize it had gotten so late."

"You could have at least answered your phone," she said, backing away.

"I'm sorry," he repeated, touching her arms.

Mary shook her head, struggling for the right words. "I-I was in the kitchen, and everything just… came apart. I don't know how to explain it. Furniture flew across the room. The kitchen cabinets blew open. Pots and pans were everywhere. I ran to the living room as furniture slid across the room. It was terrifying." She paused, catching her breath. "Then I saw her… Julie Bechdel appeared to me. She wants our help."

Curtis's mouth went agape as he leaned forward in shock. "*Who?*"

Mary turned and held her hands out toward the mansions looming walls. "There are spirits in there. I'm certain of it now. They want justice against their killers." She then turned to Curtis, unbridled conviction on her face. "We have to do something, Curtis. We have to find out who killed the Bechdels."

Curtis stared ahead with astounded skepticism, tired after a long day and growing annoyed. "I don't know what to make of this. I'm very concerned about you, Mary."

She threw her arms down in frustration. "*Why?*"

Curtis sighed and stomped past her to the front door. "I'm going in."

Mary reached for him with panic. "Wait!"

Curtis swung around. "What you're telling me is crazy. I want to know what's going on. Now come inside."

Mary hesitated to elaborate, wondering how she could possibly reach him. She could see what he did not see. They were different in that regard, though there was no denying the state of their home inside. "I told you," she said. "An undeniable paranormal phenomenon is at work. I've been seeing bits and pieces of it throughout the week, and tonight it came out in full force."

Curtis pulled out his cell phone and continued walking to the front door. "If it's really as bad as you say it is in there, I'm calling the police."

"No, not yet," Mary said. "You have to believe me."

Curtis paused with a sigh and turned to her, deeply conflicted. "Fine, let's look at the house together and you can tell me how it happened."

"I woke up to the chiming of the grandfather clock," she began. "That's when it all started."

"Mary…" he said slowly. "I told you earlier today that we don't own a grandfather clock."

"Don't you think I know that?" she said. "It came and went. Another vision, just like everything else."

Curtis stood by the door, silent, trying to make sense of her story.

"Then," she continued, "I was in the kitchen, where I saw the body of a man who had been shot crawling on the floor. It was horrifying. He must have been one of the victims."

Curtis appeared less than convinced. "If they want our help, why are they trashing the house? How about just telling us who killed them, so we can go to the police and end this thing?" He must have thought he had figured it all out, but Mary was far from conceding.

"It's more complicated than that. I don't have all the answers, but I know what I saw and heard. It's real, Curtis. Everything I'm telling you." She stepped forward, entering the house. "Dishes, pots, and pans flew at me all at once. The doors slammed, one by one. They are angered and growing in power with us here."

"*They?*" Curtis ran a hand down his face, clearly perplexed. He followed her inside and flipped on the foyer light and stopped behind her at the adjacent ball room, stunned by what he saw: flipped tables and furniture, paint on a nearby wall chipped where a sofa had crashed into it, and shattered glass from a broken lamp.

Curtis stormed past Mary and then turned around in complete disarray. "You're saying that *ghosts* did this?"

"I don't know, but something did, and they'll do it again." She hadn't mentioned Pastor Phil's unexpected visit and didn't plan to. At least for the time being. The important thing was convincing Curtis that they were now part of something larger than themselves. Their new life in the country had taken a steep, unexpected turn that even she couldn't completely comprehend.

Curtis looked up, his hands fisted. "Whoever did this, show yourself, you cowards!"

Mary moved to his side, pulling his left arm down. "Don't taunt them," she said.

He moved away from her and walked quickly toward the hallway leading to the dining room, passing several closed doors along the way. The chandeliers were no longer swinging back and forth as they had been. The house had become still and quiet, as though nothing had happened beyond the apparent vandalism before them. Mary couldn't understand it. She followed Curtis and stopped at her office, opening the door with caution. Her library books were still on her desk, undisturbed, with newspaper clippings lying about. Everything was just as she had left it.

Curtis entered the kitchen ahead of her, flicking the light switch. "Why are all the lights off, anyway?" he asked.

"I don't know," Mary answered. "All the lights went out at the same time."

"Unbelievable," she heard him mutter.

She continued toward the dining room all the chairs had been moved in separate corners. She could hear the crunching of glass under Curtis's feet from the kitchen as he groaned in disbelief. "It's a disaster area in here."

She entered the kitchen to find Curtis standing by a counter, looking around in shock. All the cabinets were open, as they had been before. Pots and pans were everywhere with plates broken to pieces on the floor. Mary stepped around the broken glass as she approached Curtis.

Drawers had been tossed around, with silverware scattered all over the tile floor. The kitchen was in disarray, ransacked in a way similar to their burglarized apartment in Chicago. It was an eerie, devastating sight. Curtis was livid.

"You fell asleep, right?" he asked. "Isn't that what you told me?" He leaned closer, choosing his words carefully. "Now I want you to consider, just consider, the fact that someone came in here and vandalized our home while you were in a deep, dream-state. You're a very heavy sleeper, Mary. You've always been."

Mary crossed her arms and stared back with defiance. "I was wide awake. Everything happened exactly as I told you. There's no doubt in my mind."

Curtis huffed and sighed, trying to grapple with what made sense and what didn't. "It's just... What you're telling me is impossible!"

She moved inches from his face. "It was right here where I heard moaning, and when I turned, I saw a man crawling across the floor." Curtis remained quiet, a serious look on his face, as Mary continued. "He had a gunshot wound in his back. Looked like a shotgun blast. He was wearing a tuxedo, Curtis."

Curtis shook his head.

"He was clearly the apparition of one of the victims."

Curtis closed his eyes with a sigh.

"Listen to me," she continued. "All of this is very possible. Now you look me in the eyes and tell me that you don't believe me. Tell me that I *dreamt* this."

Curtis looked up reluctantly, wearing a deep frown.

"You're asking me to believe in ghosts. Whatever happened here, I'm sure there's a perfectly reasonable explanation."

"Yes there is. The spirits in this house are communicating with us. Julie Bechdel, the youngest child, seems to be trying to overpower the negativity and rage of the others and tell us what we need to do."

"*Why?*" he demanded, his tone raised.

"So that they can be at rest," Mary said. "At least, that's the best explanation I can come up with now."

The kitchen went quiet as the light above them flickered. Mary took a step back, avoiding more broken glass. She looked to the far corner near the stove and noticed the refrigerator door open, its contents spilled everywhere. The bulb had blown out, and the interior was dark inside. She was surprised, actually, that bulbs throughout the house hadn't suffered the same fate, but most were intact. Could it be that the spirits just weren't powerful enough?

"Oh no..." she said under her breath, staring ahead. "The fridge." She moved past Curtis and closed the refrigerator as he pulled out his cell phone again.

"I'm calling the police now, and that's final," he said.

"Please don't," she said, grabbing a broom and dustpan, unsure where to start.

Curtis clutched his phone, angered. "Someone is playing games with us. I don't know how, but I do know they're very real. Flesh and blood. This is vandalism." He paused, waving his arm across the destruction.

Mary began sweeping up some glass. "I don't know what more I can say to convince you."

"I believe *you* think that's what happened, but this is a matter for the police," he said.

"Do you trust me?" she asked, staring at him point-blank.

"Of course I do," he answered.

"Then stop doubting me right now and listen," she said.

"Our kitchen is in shambles, Mary. I'm just trying to make some sense of this. We have jobs. *Lives*. I want to put an end to this right now."

Curtis prepared to dial as he looked up and noticed her glare. "At least file a report," he said. Mary stared back in stern protest. "Please don't. I don't want anyone else in this house tonight. Let's just sleep on it."

Mary stared back sternly. "I don't want anyone else in this house tonight. I don't know who we can trust. Let's just sleep on it." It was close to eleven, and she felt strangely tired even after having spent hours earlier passed out in a dreamlike state.

Curtis lowered his phone with an astonished laugh. "*Sleep on it*? After what happened here tonight? Are you crazy?" He noticed the sudden hurt on her face and then attempted to backtrack. "I'm sorry. I didn't mean it like that."

"Negative energy isn't going to help our situation," she said. She then leaned her broom against the counter and solemnly approached Curtis. "I can't do this without you, Curtis. That's the honest truth."

He took her hands in his and nodded, unable to completely mask his frustration. Curtis had always been skeptical about her abilities, even before they were married. But then again, so had she.

May stood quietly waiting. She pondered the recent events with a realization of what her mother, many years ago, and now Pastor Phil, had referred to as, "her gift." But she was an amateur. A layman. Perhaps they needed to contact a professional. Or maybe Pastor Phil will provide the answers she needed. There were so many options, but as she saw it, so little time. The house was getting more powerful by the day.

Curtis stuck the phone back in his pocket and looked to

her for answers. "So now what do we do? Just go about like this never happened? Not tell anyone about this?"

"We need to hire a professional psychic medium. Someone we can trust, and someone who can be out here tomorrow," she said.

Curtis looked down expressing clear discomfort. "Are those people for real?"

"Am *I* for real?" she said forcefully.

"What about Pastor Phil?" Curtis asked.

"I plan to talk with him tomorrow as well," she said.

Curtis looked even more irritated than before. She knew that this was the last thing he wanted to deal with. He was on the path to starting his own law practice. He needed clients. He needed work. And all of this was a tremendous distraction.

They had moved to Redwood to find peace and tranquility, a fresh start. Now, it seemed, negative forces were following them wherever they went.

"It's late," he said with noticeably heavy eyes. "You want to get some psychic out here tomorrow, fine. I'll take the day off, and we'll look into it." He cut across the air with his hand. "But that's as far as I'm willing to go with this stuff right now."

"Thank you," Mary said.

She gave him a hug as they momentarily ignored the mess around them. Ahead was a busy day for them both. She then thought of Pastor Phil and his adamant direction that she come alone. "At some point, I also need to take the car into town and do some shopping. Looks like we're out of food," she said with a slight laugh. Not a lie, just an evasion, she told herself.

"Okay," he said, rubbing her back. "We'll figure something out. I hope."

THE MORNING AFTER

After a restless night, Mary woke in the dim light of the early-morning sunrise. She moved her arm to the other side of the bed and felt a bare space, only then discovering that Curtis wasn't there. She raised her head from her pillow and looked across the room, curious. There were no sounds coming from the bathroom, and she noticed their bedroom door slightly ajar.

She turned over and looked at her alarm clock to see that it was ten past seven. The secret meeting with Pastor Phil came to mind, but so did something else, much more urgent, and she felt a sudden need to put her concerns about a possible pregnancy to rest. She couldn't face it yet. First on her list: She needed to see Pastor Phil by herself. Her mind raced with thoughts—intense and foreboding. She wanted to know everything about the Bechdels, and the rest of the town for that matter.

She had fallen into a trance the day before, and a deep sleep kept her from her research. It was hard to understand why. She sat up in her nightgown, feeling alert, and got out of bed, determined to get to the bottom of everything. As she walked to her dresser to get some clothes, she heard Curtis's voice. It sounded as though he was downstairs talking to someone.

She slipped on some jeans and a T-shirt and walked quietly out of the room to investigate. She crept toward the staircase, where she could hear other voices below. She peeked around the corner and saw that Curtis was talking with the police.

She recognized the officers. There was Chief Riley, a tall silver-haired man who carried himself with a quiet disposition, and his younger partner, Deputy Ramirez, whose boyish looks and trimmed black hair matched his unassuming politeness. Feeling betrayed, Mary couldn't believe Curtis had gone ahead and called them.

"We came home last night from dinner, and the kitchen was just trashed," she heard Curtis say.

Holding a clipboard, Deputy Ramirez jotted along, filling out the report as Chief Riley scanned the room.

"And there were no signs of forced entry?" Riley asked, approaching the foyer windows.

"Not that I have seen," Curtis said. "I checked all the rooms, and all windows and doors were locked."

Ramirez looked up. "They had to get in somehow."

Curtis shrugged. "Your guess is as good as mine."

Mary continued to listen in secret.

"They really did a number on your kitchen there," Chief Riley said, turning toward Curtis and Deputy Ramirez.

"You said they messed up your furniture too?" Ramirez asked, looking up.

"That's correct. I straightened it up some. One of our sofa chairs had been flipped. Several couches were moved and misaligned."

"Anything missing?" Riley asked, adjusting his belt where his pistol and radio were holstered.

"Not that I know of yet," Curtis said. "Looks like they came in just to trash the place with special attention toward our kitchen."

Ramirez continued to jot while nodding. Chief Riley took a step back and looked up to the second floor, almost spotting Mary. She moved back against the wall to avoid his gaze and continued listening.

Curtis moved in closer and spoke softly as if in confidence. "Look, Officers. My wife and I are very concerned. We simply don't feel safe with these guys out there. The vandalism to our door was one thing, but this is much worse." He paused in thought then continued. "What I'm trying to say is that we need you to find these vandals. Their fingerprints *have* to be somewhere. There *has* to be evidence here to find out who did this and lock them up."

Mary peeked around the corner again, watching as Chief Riley nodded in understanding. "We'll get Forensics out here." He then turned to Ramirez. "Deputy, go to the trunk and get my fingerprint duster kit."

Curtis raised his hand, stopping the officers, and looked up the stairs with concern. Mary again ducked behind the corner to avoid being seen.

"Later," he said in a more quiet voice than before. "If you don't mind, I don't want to startle Mary with all this commotion early in the morning. Can you come back later?"

The chief studied Curtis, almost suspiciously, and shook his head. "We're not a cable company, Mr. Malone."

Ramirez stood to the side, prepared to go out to the car and waiting on the final call as Curtis continued, "I understand that, but—"

"I'll tell you what," Chief Riley said. "We'll go back to the station, make the report, and give you some time." He paused and raised a finger at Curtis. "As long as you don't mess with the scene."

"Of course not," Curtis said as though he would never even consider the idea.

"Then we'd be fine with it," he said.

Curtis suddenly snapped his fingers, excited. "Did you check the hardware store about any recent paint purchases following the vandalism on our door?"

"I did," Deputy Ramirez said. "Turns out a purchase was made about two weeks ago."

Curtis's eyes widened with anticipation. "Really? Then who are we talking about here?"

Ramirez smiled and shook his head. "Kind of a dead end."

Curtis's smile drooped. "What do you mean?"

"I mean that the last person to purchase red paint was our own Pastor Phil. I went out and talked to him the other day and found him painting his barn."

Chief Riley stepped forward, adding to the conversation. "And seeing as he was hosting the barbecue when your door was vandalized, we really didn't have much to go on."

Curtis waved them off. "No, no. Pastor Phil had nothing to do with that. Maybe some punk kids stole some paint. How hard could it be?" Sensing there was no more to be said, he extended his arm, shaking the hands of the chief and his deputy, thanking them for coming so early in the morning.

"Not a problem," said Chief Riley. "We're gonna grab some breakfast, and then we'll be back later to dust for prints."

"Sounds great," Curtis said. "Thanks for everything."

He walked the officers out and opened the front door as Mary watched, ready to confront him. Curtis closed and locked the door, then turned back to the foyer and headed for the stairs. He was wearing slacks and a polo shirt, seemingly ready for the day.

Mary stepped into view as he reached the top of the stairs. "You're up," he said, trying to mask his surprise.

"You called them?" she said. "Why would you do that after all we discussed last night?"

He took a few careful steps toward her with his hand in the air. "Mary, I just want to explain—"

"Did you really think I wouldn't find out?" she said, interrupting him. "You still don't believe your own wife?"

"Listen," he said, walking closer. "I slept on it, okay. I just wanted to make the report, okay? For insurance purposes. I can't very well claim any of this with your version of things."

Mary crossed her arms. "I see..."

Curtis looked around with noticeable ambivalence. "I *do* believe you. And of course I trust you."

"It doesn't seem like it," she said.

He approached her, speaking calmly and with caution. "I can't even begin to understand what is going on just yet. I'm weighing all of our options here."

Mary nodded, not wanting to argue any longer. His persistent skepticism wore on her, but she knew it was important to get on with the day. "I'm going into town today. You can dust the entire place for prints for all I care, but I've got some business to attend to."

Curtis looked at his wristwatch. "But, honey, we have an appointment with Bob Deckers this morning."

"About what?" she asked.

"About this house," he said.

Mary paused to consider Deckers's involvement. As a realtor, he *had* to know something about the house and its history. Perhaps it wasn't such a bad idea after all.

"Fine," she said. "We'll go together, but I have errands to run."

Curtis nodded with a conciliatory smile. "That's fine. You can go off and do your thing. That'll give me some time to look at office space downtown. "

"Great. I'll get ready now," Mary said, turning away.

"Wait," Curtis said.

Mary stopped and turned.

"We'll look into this psychic-medium thing today as well. I just want you to know that I don't discount what you said happened."

"I understand," Mary said.

"See, I told you small-town life could be interesting. Exciting even," he said with a smile.

Mary smiled back, feeling a little more at ease than the night before. Her day was now about getting answers. Mary had discovered a young girl's diary a week prior, and though the girl never mentioned herself by name, Mary believed her to be Julie.

Mary kept the diary in her thoughts throughout the day—her gateway into the mind of a young girl from an odd, though wealthy family. She planned to take the diary with her to show Pastor Phil.

"I'll be ready in ten," she said, turning down the hall and walking back to their bedroom.

"Okay, twenty minutes," he said from downstairs.

"Very funny," she called out.

She entered their bathroom and closed the door. She then looked into the mirror, staring at her reflection. Her greenish-blue eyes were full of drive, and her blonde hair was tousled. She wasn't going to allow herself to be afraid anymore. Not of what had happened to her in the past or of what was happening now. There was nothing left to do but to push forward and try to figure out the mystery before them, one step at a time.

Dressed and ready for the day, Mary walked down the stairs dressed in a light long-sleeved shirt, dark pants, and sandals, her hair in a ponytail. Curtis was in the downstairs ballroom, moving some of the furniture back in place. The overall damage to their house was minimal beyond the broken dishes in the kitchen. A walk-through of each room the night before showed no new signs of paranormal movement. Again, Mary noticed activity in only a few areas of the house. What did it all mean?

Curtis went to the foyer closet and grabbed his jacket, turning with Mary's approach. "Hey. You about ready?"

"Yeah," she said, purse on her shoulder. She patted its side to ensure that she had remembered Julie's diary. "I could have helped with the furniture."

Curtis waved her off. "It's no big deal. I got it."

There were streaks all over their hardwood floors from the moving furniture. There was definitely something more to the damage than simple vandalism, but for Curtis to acknowledge anything more was to accept the impossible. On the other hand, to deny Mary's story would be to question her sanity. He was indeed stuck.

* * *

By midmorning, Curtis and Mary were headed downtown in their white Ford Expedition SUV. There were only two gas stations in all of Redwood, and in both cases, the prices per gallon were steadily rising. As they passed one of the two, right before Main Street, Curtis suggested perhaps purchasing another vehicle.

"Can we afford it?" Mary asked. "I mean, with everything tied up in that house, I don't see how we can think about making any major purchases right now."

"We can always trade this one in and see what we can get for it. I talked to a guy at a car dealership right in town. Lance Carver. He's got some great deals. Real nice guy too."

Mary turned to Curtis with an arched brow. "Well, you've

certainly gotten around this past week. What else are you up to?"

Curtis laughed, stopping at a stop sign at an empty intersection. "Meeting people, that's all. Need to order some new business cards among other things. I've got to be ready."

"Why do you want to sell the SUV?" she asked.

Curtis shook his head and pressed on the gas. "I don't know. We've had it for about six years now. I want to get something smaller."

"This coming from someone who moved us into a fifteen-room mansion," she said.

Main Street was two blocks ahead. They passed cars parked on both sides of the historical-district street, with its attractive shops, eateries, and pubs. People filled the sidewalk, strolling casually through town even on a busy Monday morning.

Curtis said, "Hey, it's not that I want to sell the SUV, I'm just thinking differently now, okay? A small-town lawyer from the city, like me, needs the right kind of car."

"And what kind is that?" she asked.

Curtis thought to himself and then answered, barely audibly. "A Mercedes..."

"*What?*" she said, laughing.

They turned down Hartford Avenue, where more shops went along both sides of the block. Curtis turned right into the parking lot behind Bob's office, where a sign hung from the side of the building saying, Deckers's Realty. For Mary, it would be her first time actually meeting him. Curtis had discussed him a few times over the past week, and his name had come up more times than she could remember over the past month, so she felt she knew him a bit.

She had seen him from afar during their last stroll through town. He was a tall, distinguished-looking man with trim white hair and a near-bronze complexion. Of course, there were plenty of benches throughout town displaying his smiling face and phone number.

Mary had nearly talked herself out of even going to the meeting. She had pressing matters of her own waiting, but she didn't want to rouse Curtis's suspicion or make it appear as though she were abandoning him. She had been pretty tough on him the past few weeks and realized that much.

Curtis parked a few spaces from the red brick building that housed Bob's office, among many others. As he shut the engine off and grabbed his sunglasses, he seemed upbeat and determined, a sight Mary was glad to see.

"Here we are," he said, opening the door. "Won't take long. I just want to have a few words with him."

"No problem," she said, stepping out of the SUV and onto the pavement. She grabbed her sunglasses as well and closed the door just as Curtis approached, and, out of the blue, kissed her on the forehead.

"Ready?" he asked.

"Sure," she said.

They walked hand in hand to Bob's corner office as vehicles zipped by in both directions on the adjacent street. It felt nice to return to civilization every now and then. The mansion seemed to be located in a world all its own.

She walked with Curtis to the glass door with Bob's name and branch inscribed in black, script lettering, with an *Open* sign hanging below. Curtis pulled the door open, heard a bell ringing, and held the door open for Mary. She stepped inside onto the gray carpet and stood still for a moment as her eyes adjusted to the low lighting inside. Ahead, there were several unmanned desks just beyond a small waiting area. Mary could see an office in the back, behind a glass partition. A man rose from his desk, and as he walked into the lobby, Mary recognized him as Bob Deckers.

He smiled as he approached, looking friendly and

informal in a dress-shirt with rolled-up sleeves and a red tie. "Curtis! So nice to see you." He then extended his hand for Mary to shake and introduced himself. "I'm Bob, and you must be Mary. At last we meet!"

Mary said hello and thanked him for helping with the purchase of their new home.

"My pleasure, Mary," Bob said, flashing a perfect white smile. He then shook Curtis's hand vigorously, adding a just-between-us laugh. "Too bad you had to leave us last night. We were just getting started!"

Curtis looked down with a sheepish grin. "Uh... yeah. Too bad."

Bob looked at Mary, apologetic. "Not that we were up to no good. I hope I didn't keep him out too late, though."

"It's fine," Mary said, trying her hardest to be cordial and relaxed. Bob knew things. She could see it in his eyes. Perhaps he could shed additional light on the Bechdels before her meeting with Pastor Phil.

Bob turned, led them down the hallway, and held his arm out for them to pass. "Please, step into my office. Curtis told me on the phone that you had some concerns about your new home."

"That's correct," Mary said, walking past him.

"I certainly hope you're happy with it," he said, smacking Curtis lightly on the shoulder. "I think your husband has a great career ahead of him out here. I've already talked to at least three people this past week who are looking into his services."

"That's great," Curtis said. "I can't wait to start working again."

They ventured into Bob's well-lit office, but Mary couldn't help wondering about the empty desks they passed on the way there. Maybe Bob ran the office all by himself. She didn't feel comfortable inquiring further.

"Please, have a seat," Bob said, and they each sat in one of the two chairs in front of his oak desk. There were papers scattered on its surface and a blinking office phone sitting under a green desk lamp. Behind his desk were several plaques and certificates naming Deckers Realty as the number-one-voted realtor in Redwood. Mary wondered if that was because he was the *only* realtor in town.

He further rolled up his sleeves and sat down at his desk, belting out a satisfied sigh. He leaned forward with his arms folded on top of the desk and a steely focus in his eyes. "I really do hope everything is going well with the place. Everyone seems taken with Curtis and would love to get to know you as well, Mary."

Mary smiled and nodded. "Yes. I appreciate that."

"So let's start at the start," Bob said, pushing a notepad and pencil in front of him on the cluttered desk. "What can I help you with? Ask away."

Wanting to first see how her husband might put it, Mary turned to Curtis, nodding for him to begin. "Well, Bob," Curtis said, hesitating between his words, "You see... the thing is... we love the place. We really do. It's a dream come true for us. I mean, I know we've only been here a little over a week, but I'm taken with the place, as is Mary." He glanced at her for backup, and she gave him a smile.

Bob nodded, pencil in hand, as Curtis lowered his tone, a sign that the couple's real reasons were soon to come. "It's just..." He paused. "Let's be real here. A horrible murder was committed in that house some forty years ago. To your credit, you informed me of that from the beginning." Curtis paused and folded his hands over, knitting his fingers. "It's just that in a very short span of time, we've noticed some strange things happening."

Bob raised his eyebrows expectantly, waiting for Curtis to get to the real issue.

"Last night..." Curtis continued. "An incident happened at the house like nothing I've ever witnessed. I wasn't there, but Mary was. We're talking some insane, impossible things. Cabinets flying open. Chairs sliding across the floor. Marks on the wall. I'm talking real property damage. Now Mary is convinced that it has something to do with the murders that took place there. She's convinced that it's spirits of the dead communicating with us." Curtis paused, and turned to Mary, his face flushed, either in anger or embarrassment, she couldn't be sure, as they made eye contact. "And more and more, I'm getting inclined to believe her." Of course, that meant that he hadn't quite believed her before, and he supportively reached over and touched her arm.

Bob cupped his chin, thinking to himself, under the low hum of the air conditioner above him. He dropped his pencil suddenly and leaned back as though this was the last thing he had expected to hear. He moved his chair up closer, placed his palms on the desk, and looked at them with an expression of concern and understanding. "Mark my word, I would never have sold you that house under those circumstances. There have been no reports of anything wrong with it in that regard."

"Why was it marked down in price so much?" Mary asked, stepping in. "I was suspicious of that from the start."

"Frankly, it's a pretty bad market out there right now. The percentage your property was marked down was no greater than the markdowns on half the homes around here, or throughout the state, for that matter." He sighed in despair for all those unfortunate sellers. "Indiana is going through a temporary market crisis. Bad for sellers, but great for buyers."

Curtis suddenly cut in. "The thing is, Bob, we don't want to move." He then paused and took Mary's hand. "I can't, however, have my wife being attacked by chairs and appliances while I'm away. I don't know if it's dead spirits or not, but I do know that it's getting worse, and I won't have her living in that kind of environment."

With his quiet demeanor, Bob seemed to understand. He held up a finger, a pause, and leaned down, searching in one of his bottom drawers. Curtis looked at Mary with a smile as she feigned one of her own.

"There's no doubt in my mind," she said to Bob as he was ducked behind his desk. "That house is haunted."

He emerged with several business cards in his hand and began flipping through them. "This is what I can do." He held out a business card for Curtis to take. "Some of these psychic types are scam-artists, but this guy's legit. He's got an office out in Columbus that specializes in cases like yours."

Curtis took the card and examined it. "Cases like ours?" Mary leaned over to get a look at it too.

"His name's Theodore Stone," Bob continued. "He's a paranormal investigator."

"A what?" Curtis said.

"Believe it or not, southern Indiana has quite a track record for that kind of stuff. I can't explain it. It's a phenomenon, really."

Curtis handed Mary the card, and she examined it closely. Mr. Stone's name, office location, phone number, and email address were printed professionally on an otherwise simple black card with white lettering.

"What's wrong?" Bob asked, noticing Curtis's skeptical expression.

"You can vouch for this guy?" Curtis asked. "I was going to do my own research and find someone who wouldn't try to scam us."

Bob pointed to the card. "You're not going to find anyone better in the field. No one near here anyway."

Mary looked up. "How do you know so much about him?"

Bob seemed taken off guard but attempted to answer the best he could. "Last year, Evelyn Chambers, one of our oldest residents, was concerned that her dead husband was haunting her. Well, apparently one of her kids knew about this Stone guy, and he was able to not only verify Evelyn's claims, but he extinguished her husband's presence."

"Why would anyone want to do that to their dead husband?" Mary asked.

"Because she's the one who killed him," Bob said. He laughed at the utter shock on their faces. "Relax. It was fifty years ago. She shot him in self-defense after he beat her in a drunken rage."

Mary gasped, covering her mouth. "That's terrible."

"Sorry. I didn't mean to upset you," Bob said. "But that's what happened."

Mary fingered the smooth, glossy surface of the supposed paranormal investigator's business card. "So this investigator... you met him personally?"

"Once," Bob said. "I met him then, and he gave me his card. Really seemed to know what he was doing." He paused, scratching the side of his ear. "I figure if he helped Evelyn with her situation, he can maybe fix your jam too, and keep you in that house."

"Just what is a paranormal investigator?" Curtis asked drily.

"I think the common term is psychic," Bob answered.

Curious, Curtis looked at Mary. "Well, hon. What do you think?"

Mary leaned forward, looking at Bob. "What do you know about the families that were murdered in that house, the Bechdels and the Drakes?"

"Only what I've read in the papers," Bob said, arms on the

side of his chair. He then looked up at the ceiling, thinking. "I must have been… ten years old at the time. I lived in New Hampshire at the time. Only moved here about twelve years ago."

Mary felt disappointed at Bob's revelation. She had hoped he could tell her something beyond what she already knew. "Do you think we can get him out here today?" she asked, holding the card. "I'd like to have him examine the house immediately."

"Sure," Bob nodded. "We can try. His office is a few hours north, but we can call him up and see."

"I'll handle that," Curtis said, pulling out his cell phone. He turned to Mary and placed a hand on her back. "Why don't you go run your errands while I take care of this? Bob and I have to discuss office space too."

Mary handed Curtis the card and rose from her chair, purse in hand. Bob shook her hand, a gesture accompanied by another wide smile, the habit of a man she knew she couldn't completely trust. Something felt off, not only about him, but about many of the other people she had met in town. She gave Curtis a kiss and left the men to their business. A psychic at their house or not, she had personal legwork to do before she felt satisfied enough to return to their home—a home where anything seemed possible.

CONSPIRACY

Mary turned down Main Street and passed the glistening fountain outside of the town hall. The old, domed two-story building looked to be about fifty years old and was easily the largest building in town. A few blocks down, she parked in a small side lot next to the general store, which also had a pharmacy.

Redwood certainly had its limitations when compared to Chicago. There was only one grocery store, for starters, and a few clothing and specialty stores that all had a local flair. There was no Walmart or outlet store within twenty miles of town. People came to Redwood to escape those kinds of things. Mary could get used to that, but the main thing she couldn't overlook was the secrets buried underneath the quaint town's rosy façade.

Her purse sat on the passenger seat next to her, with Julie's diary tucked inside it. She fully intended to share it with Pastor Phil with hopes that he could elaborate on its origins and content. It was chilly that morning, causing Mary to wear her blue windbreaker. She was glad to have it when she grabbed her purse and stepped outside their white Ford

Expedition covered in a thick layer of dust from driving between their rural neighborhood and town.

A few other cars were parked in the small parking lot. She watched an old couple across the street walk arm in arm to a bus stop and sit on the bench. A steady line of morning commuters drove past her, just as an interesting sight near town hall caught her eye. Two black SUVs pulled to the curb, at the foot of the marble steps leading to the front entrance, which was situated between two large Greek columns. An entourage of men in suits suddenly descended from the building, carrying themselves with a noticeable aura of importance.

Two drivers stood at the sides of their vehicles and opened the doors for the entourage as they climbed in. One man, in particular, caught Mary's eye. He was a tall and bulky man with slicked-back gray hair and a pale, aging face. She had seen his rehearsed smile and poised stance before. His bleached-white teeth had beamed from the Redwood brochure Curtis had shown her weeks ago. He was the mayor of Redwood, Frederick Taylor.

Most importantly, she remembered his brief speech at the Sunday barbecue only a few days ago. He was dressed-down then, but not today, and had spoken with boisterous cheer. She remembered him as coming across as both laid-back and polished at the same time. He was your typical politician, and coming from a city like Chicago, famous for its corrupt officials, Mary knew one when she saw one. That morning, he seemed to be in a hurry. He wore dark sunglasses similar to those hiding the eyes of the apparent security detail surrounding him.

All the fuss around the SUVs seemed a bit much for a small-town mayor. Then Mary remembered something she had read about the town's history and its early settlement as a refuge for some of the wealthiest, most preeminent families in the country. Mayor Taylor looked as if he came from money, and he carried himself as a man of importance equal to that of any big-city mayor.

The Taylors, Mary recalled, had been entrenched in politics for decades. Mayor Taylor was obviously growing older, no matter how much makeup he applied in his photo, and was serving his tenth consecutive term. Once loaded, the security convoy sped off down the street past Mary as she stood in the parking lot watching. Her eyes followed them up the road as they faded from view near the library and fire department.

Mary turned back toward the general store, its hanging wooden sign waving in the slight breeze, and wondered why the mayor had caught and kept her attention for so long. Was she so easily distracted? Maybe purposefully. She had almost forgotten why she had come to the store in the first place but then recalled the unwelcome task before her.

She pulled the glass door open and walked inside the well-lit store as the bell jingled. There was no one inside except a store clerk at the front counter and a stocker filling in the gaps in one of the five aisles just past the display cases. The general store had a little bit of everything.

Redwood had one movie theater, one grocery store, one hair salon, an art gallery, a music store, and several other stores owned and operated by locals, or so it seemed. Mary had hardly seen everything the town had to offer. Most of the first week had been spent at the property, settling in. Now she was faced with a task more consuming than anything she could imagine.

She walked down the aisle with health and beauty aids, past soaps and shampoos, and came to the women's care section. Light pop music played on the intercom speakers above, and she felt comfortable enough to browse the pregnancy test products of which there were only three brands.

She grabbed the First Response brand, promising one-minute results, and tossed it into her red shopping basket. Self-consciously, she looked around as the front bell jingled and a woman walked in. She looked to be in her late fifties, with dyed-auburn hair done up in a near beehive. She wore a long-sleeved black top with leopard-print cuffs, tight black pants, and high heels that clicked on the tiles.

Mary remembered her as one of the haughty socialites from the church barbecue. The woman had barely said two words to Mary then, but Mary had understood. Now they were unexpectedly meeting again, and Mary was in a hurry.

She grabbed a package of soap and a tube of toothpaste from the shelf next to her. She turned the other way and walked down a far aisle, trying to make it to the front checkout without crossing the woman's path. A friendly-faced male clerk awaited her at the front counter. He set his magazine down to ring her up.

"And how are you doing this morning, ma'am?" he asked, sweeping the three items across the scanner.

"Just fine," she said. "Thank you."

The clerk smiled and bagged her items. The lenses of his circular-framed glasses reflected the fluorescent light above. He told her the total, and Mary swiped her card just as she felt the presence of someone directly behind her.

"Excuse me, Steven. Do you have any of those honeysuckle-scented candles in stock?"

Mary turned slightly to see the woman standing closer than she was comfortable with. She grabbed her shopping bag as the clerk told the woman he'd have to look in the back for the candles. Mary took her receipt, thanked the clerk, and walked off, feeling the stare of the woman. She was almost out the door when the woman's voice called to her.

"Mary Malone?"

Mary stopped and slowly turned to face the woman, shopping bag in hand. "Yes?"

"I thought that was you," the woman said, squinting. "We met at the church barbecue."

"Oh yes," Mary said with a smile. "I'm sorry, I can't remember your name…"

"Beatrice," the woman said. "Beatrice Thaxton."

"Nice to see you again, Beatrice," Mary said, turning back to the door. "Have a nice day."

"How's life at the Bechdel mansion?" the woman asked.

Mary turned around more quickly than she intended, taken aback by the question. "Fine…" she answered. "Just getting settled in."

"No ghost hauntings or anything of the sort?" Beatrice asked with a slight laugh.

"Nope," Mary said, trying to feign a smile. "It's been great."

Not content to end it there, Beatrice continued. "They say that place has been haunted for as long as anyone can remember."

Steven suddenly emerged holding a large scented candle. Beatrice turned to him, leaving Mary standing there dumbfounded. "Oh, thank you, Steven," Beatrice told him, seeming to forget all about Mary.

Mary turned and left the store, feeling slighted in some way she couldn't pinpoint. Perhaps it was the woman's tone and demeanor, her abrupt and impolite comments. Mary got back in the car and slammed the door shut. She set her purse and shopping bag on the passenger seat and then fished through her purse for something of importance. She pulled out a slip of paper, the one given to her by Pastor Phil, and looked at the address: 1715 Seneca Lane.

She put the address into her phone GPS and waited for a signal. She was twenty minutes away from what she assumed to be his house. Pastor Phil had not been upfront about the details of their planned meeting or why he wanted her to keep it a secret. One thing she was sure of, however: He knew more than she did about the town and was her best hope of figuring everything out within reason.

* * *

Mary traveled fifteen miles to the rural outskirts of Redwood, the road running alongside pastures and deep forest. Morning radio news discussed the governor's controversial proposal to provide mortgage relief across Indiana. With the money they had invested into the Bechdel mansion and its subsequent renovation, she figured they could use all the help they could get.

Pastor Phil had chosen a remote meeting spot, to say the least. She assumed the address he had given her was his house, but now she was doubtful; there was no telling what to expect out here. They were meeting in secret, and the question was: Why? And whom did Pastor Phil not want to know about it?

She slowed at a railroad crossing covered in weeds. There was a rusty yellow caution sign to her right, but it didn't look as if a train had come through in decades. As she continued over the tracks, her GPS signal went away, causing Mary to panic. She was in the middle of nowhere, without a house in sight. She gripped the wheel and continued down the cracked pavement of a dusty road, trying to stay focused on the meeting at hand. The GPS directions re-appeared, much to her relief, indicating a right turn in three miles.

She was eager to talk to Phil and get to the bottom of everything, starting with: What was he doing at her house last night? What purpose did the inverted cross on their door serve? Why had the so-called spirits "chosen her," as he put it? She had dozens of other questions too, and a yearning for answers that might bring normalcy back to her life. The road curved, and the shopping bag shifted in the passenger seat, an unwelcome reminder of uncertainty. It was too early to take the pregnancy test, but she wanted to be sure when the time came.

A dirt road came into view on her right between gated pastures of grazing cows. There was a mailbox at the end with the numbers 1715 posted above. She slowed and turned onto the road, causing the SUV to shake and rattle down the bumpy terrain. Forest appeared on both sides of the long road, with no house in sight. About a half mile later, she still didn't see anything. Of course, meeting at a coffee shop was out of the question. They just *had* to meet out here in farm country where there wasn't a soul around. And what of Pastor Phil? Did he have a family? Who was he?

Ahead, she saw an old-fashioned two-story house with a front porch and wooden railing that ran along the entire house. The dirt road veered off to the side, where a blue station wagon was parked next to a round, stone well, with a pitch-roof canopy above it. To the right of the house was an open red barn with stacks of hay visible inside. Farther in the distance was an old silo, higher than the trees around it. Mary didn't remember the last time she had been on a farm. Not since she was a child, at least.

There were some small vegetable crops to the left of the house and several livestock pens with roaming chickens and pigs. Mary looked around, taking everything in while keeping her eyes open for Phil. She parked next to the station wagon, where the grass was at its thinnest, and shut the ignition off. The front porch door swung open, and Phil emerged wearing dirty overalls and a T-shirt underneath—the first time she had seen him so dressed down. He adjusted his glasses and squinted ahead, placing one hand on a porch rail near the steps.

Mary opened her door and grabbed her keys and purse, stepping outside as Phil walked down the steps and across the yard to meet her.

"Welcome. So glad you could make it," he said, appearing exhausted but attempting a smile.

"I wouldn't miss it. Not after what you told me last night," Mary said, studying him, with eyes hidden behind sunglasses.

They stopped a few feet from each other with an awkward silence between them. Phil pulled a rag from his front pocket and wiped his forehead. He then motioned back toward the house. "Can I get you a glass of water or anything? Tea? Coffee?"

"No, thanks. I'm fine," Mary said, not wanting to stall their meeting.

Phil turned to the house, looking around. "Well… how about we go for a walk, then? It's a nice day. What do you think?"

"Sounds good to me," Mary said.

Phil led the way as they walked through the yard and around the right side of the house toward the barn. Pebbles crunched under her sandals as they trod along a dirt path into the backyard. She looked up, looking for the source of a faint, squeaking sound, and saw a weather vane on top of the roof, spinning around, with the silhouette of a black rooster perched on top, above the directional letters. She didn't want to seem too nosy but was curious to learn more about the pastor, who had been in Redwood for so many years.

"Do you live out here all by yourself?" she asked.

Walking beside her, he turned away slightly, with an apparent reluctance to delve into personal details. "I do now," he answered.

Noticing his reserved tone, Mary continued, "You seem to know so much about me. It's only fair, don't you think, that I know a little about you?"

"Sure," Phil said. "I don't mean to sound cryptic. I have a son, and a daughter. My wife passed some years ago."

Mary was stunned. "I'm so sorry," she said.

"My son lives in California with his family, and my daughter lives in Florida with hers. All I can say is that this place isn't for everyone."

"Well," Mary said. "I'm sure that you miss them."

Phil kept an optimistic demeanor and tone as they neared the hay barn. "The wounds have long healed. I'm very happy here. I've always been."

"It's a beautiful house, don't get me wrong," Mary said, "but you're way out here all by yourself."

They continued to follow the trail past the barn, as Phil shrugged, as though the thought had never crossed his mind. "I've never tired of it. This is my home. This is where I belong."

The cloudy sky above provided some shade, and the cool air enhanced Mary's senses. The faint clucking of chickens and snorting of pigs could be heard from the animal pens on the other side of the house.

Mary lifted her sunglasses up to the top of her head and steered the conversation toward the answers she was there to get. "Last night, you spoke of secrets in this town tied to something sinister. Wouldn't that be a reason to move away?"

"There are secrets," Phil answered. "Can't blame the town for that. We certainly can't blame this beautiful countryside that surrounds us."

"I suppose you're right," Mary said as she examined the silo ahead. They passed a garden that stretched half the length of his backyard and was surrounded by chicken wire. There were several plants sprouting from the soil, supported by thin brackets and appearing to have developed nicely.

"There's my garden," Phil said, noticing where her attention was. "Harvest is coming in just nice."

"It's lovely," she said.

"The farm has been a part of my family far beyond my time," he said as they neared the silo, which was a good distance away from the house.

Mary turned to him. "You were born here?"

Phil smiled. "Sure was. Lived here until I was about sixteen. Ran away from home. Went through a real rough patch until I found the faith. Then I came back with a wife and kids in tow, just before my parents passed."

Mary didn't know what to say. There were obviously gaps in his brief summary, but she didn't want to pry beyond what was necessary. Pastor Phil looked to be in his late fifties, early sixties. His kind blue eyes could turn serious at times, as they had the night before, when he showed up at her doorstep without warning. Her main question was whether or not she could trust him.

"Any siblings?" Mary asked.

"Yeppers," Phil answered. "Three brothers and two sisters."

"And where do they live?" she asked.

Phil turned to her and shook his head. "Far away. Country life wasn't for them. Now it's just me and my livestock." Phil suddenly stopped, as they came to a clearing into the forest, leading to a trail that Mary wasn't sure she wanted to explore. Phil didn't scare her—she actually felt pretty safe around him, as if he were a father figure—but the bits and pieces of his story hadn't added up yet, and she wasn't ready to dive in.

Phil said, "For the longest time, there was talk of a curse in this town. Sounds ridiculous, I know." He paused with a sigh. "But I've given my complete devotion and trust onto the Lord, He is my guiding light."

"Is your last name Evans?" Mary asked. She didn't know exactly where the question was coming from.

Phil looked at her, surprised, then glanced up as a flock of birds flew overhead.

"Relax," she said. "I found a newspaper article from 1975 that had your name and picture. It was right after the Bechdel murders."

"I've tried my best to dissociate myself with that particular surname," Phil said. "It seems to have brought nothing but trouble in my life. Like I said, the only family I belong to is with my Lord and Savior. I've dedicated my life to the church, and it's brought me much happiness." He paused, turning toward the farmhouse, admiring it in a way. "You probably look around here and see a lonely old man." He then lowered his arms, making direct eye contact with her. "But I'm not lonely, my dear. I can feel Him all around."

Not being particularly religious, Mary couldn't help being skeptical herself, though she didn't doubt his sincerity.

"Pastor Phil," she began. "I do feel like I can trust you. At first, I didn't know. It seemed like you had this weird interest in me. You knew my name before I had even met you. You knew about Curtis too." She paused, trying to get her thoughts together. "What I'm trying to get at is that there is a lot you haven't told me, and I'm here now, at your request, to find out more."

Phil crossed his arms and leaned back, stretching. "I'm telling you what you need to know. I just ask for your patience."

She was trying the best she could, but her mind was going in a million different places at once. *What did she need to do about the house? Or was it too late?*

"Who killed the Bechdels?" she asked pointblank.

Phil stared at her for a moment and then responded. "I don't know. No one knows for sure. The few police chiefs who've come and gone through the years couldn't figure it out. The FBI even spearheaded the investigation in the seventies and came up short."

"I keep seeing things," she continued. "Scenes of the murder. All the blood and mayhem. The house is trying to tell me something."

"Of course it is," Phil said. "It wants you to avenge their murders."

Mary stared back, shocked that Phil would even indulge such a suggestion. "So you believe in the supernatural? Spirits? Psychic extrasensory perception? All of that stuff?"

"Not all of it," Phil replied. "I believe in what I know and what I see. Like I said, the Lord works in mysterious ways."

"Are we in any danger?" Mary asked, concern evident in her eyes.

"You were in danger the minute you drove into town," Phil said.

Mary stepped forward, incensed now. "I need specifics. What is wrong with that house? What is wrong with this town? And what is this about my *daughter*?"

Phil looked down and then raised his head with a sigh, signaling to the woods behind his house. "Walk with me."

At that point, Mary felt like she had no choice. She walked alongside him as they continued down the trail into the cover of the forest. "Several affluent families reside in Redwood and have for generations. The town itself represents a kind of last stand between the old and the new, and some residents have fought hard to keep it that way. The old way, I mean. Long before my time, there are rumors of different families fighting for power and influence. In the old days, things like duels and other means of public combat were practiced to settle feuds, but that all soon changed."

Mary cut in, nearly laughing. "Duels?"

"Exactly," Phil said as they walked together. "Then a darkness came to this town in the form of black-magic rituals. The occult. Envy, spite, vengeance nearly consumed the town, and at the turn of the twentieth century, Redwood fell under the influence of this evil. There was talk of witches and covens and all the stuff of folklore. The First Christ Church of Redwood was established only a few decades ago, after several churches that preceded it were mysteriously burnt to the ground. It was constructed in defiance toward those burnings and as a force for good."

Mary was intrigued to learn about Redwood's sketchy history, though Phil still hadn't explained what her role in everything was. "What changed?" Mary asked.

Phil turned to her with a solemn expression. "Things got better."

"*What?*" she said, mouth agape. "What do you mean by that?"

"I mean that after they died, the town has never been more in harmony or more at peace in its entire history. The wealthiest families around here have gotten even wealthier as tourism has peaked year after year. Things, more or less, have been perfect."

"But what's the connection?" Mary asked.

Phil answered with a vagueness that Mary found increasingly deliberate. "Consider the fact that the only thing that hasn't been at peace is that house. And it never will be until the spirits are laid to rest."

"How am I supposed to do that? By finding their killers?" Mary asked in disbelief. "The FBI couldn't even do that. Do I look like some kind of special agent to you?"

"Other families have moved into that house, attracted by the same financial lure and prestige you were," Phil continued. "None of them have lasted long, as their short stays always resulted in tragedy." He paused, stopping along the trail and pointing at her. "But you. You have a gift, and they know it."

"Is there, perhaps, any substantive information you can provide?" Mary asked, growing impatient but understanding of Phil's meticulous nature.

"You're the key," Phil said. "As the new owner of that house, it's up to you." He moved closer to her, speaking in confidence even though there wasn't another soul around. "But I want to help."

"What else can you tell me?" Mary asked flat-out.

"Before the murders," he began, "George Bechdel was planning to run for mayor of Redwood. And you want to know who he was running against? None other than Redwood's own Mayor Taylor."

Mary's mouth dropped. "You mean to tell me that Mayor Taylor had the Bechdels killed?"

"I can't say that with certainty," Phil said. "But I can say he was definitely involved somehow. The town. The unseen elite. They conspired to do it, and believe me, I did my fair share of investigating. I talked to the local paper. I searched around, just like you're doing now..." His tone dropped as he looked down in sadness. "And it was around that time when I lost everything."

Mary took a step back in disbelief. "What are you trying to say? Have people come after you?"

"It's best if I didn't go into any details at the moment. I've spent years reading about the supernatural. The spirits in the house will remain until the truth is exposed.

"Like some kind of purgatory?" Mary asked, astonished.

Phil stepped forward and gently took Mary's hand in his. She remained still, calmed by the look in his fading eyes. "I understand this is a lot for you to take in, but let's be smart about this. We can't make any waves until we know for certain who to go after. I do have a theory about your predicament, however."

Mary shook her head, exhausted by his fantastical explanations for everything. "Might as well get it all out."

"I'm pretty sure that you've been here before. Not just in this town, but in that mansion."

"*What?*" she nearly shouted out.

"Hear me out," said Phil, taking a step back. "I don't know when or how—maybe when you were too young to remember. The house brought you back. It was never your husband or the price, the great deal you got on the place, or any other factors. It was always meant to be, and it's not going to allow you to go anywhere until the spirits are freed."

Mary ran her hand across her forehead and squeezed her eyes shut. "No. No, that can't be the case. There has to be some other explanation."

"I had the inverted red cross painted on your door to serve as a warning, to let you know that it wasn't all in your head."

"Why inverted?" she asked.

"Because the house is unworthy to display a real cross. At least in the condition it is now. Ultimately, I was trying to keep the spirits at bay, which I've been doing for forty years now."

Stunned into silence, Mary stared ahead into the forest until Phil placed a hand on her shoulder, startling her. "The answers will come to you. For now, you must go back, and we can talk about this later."

"Later?" she said, now desperate. "But Julie needs our help. We can't wait any longer."

"She'll be okay for now," he said, giving her shoulder a light squeeze. "Julie, I believe, is the strongest spirit of them all."

Mary laughed nervously as a tear rolled down her cheek. "How would you know that?"

"Just a hunch," he answered.

Mary nodded and then reached into her purse as if just remembering something. She pulled out the small, leather-bound diary and handed it to Phil. "Here," she said. "I found this."

Curious, Phil took the diary and carefully opened it. His face nearly turned white as his eyes zeroed in on the tiny cursive writing on each faded, dusty page. After a few moments, he looked up at Mary with a smile. She was surprised to see tears forming in his eyes as well. "It's her..." he said. "She was such a sweet little girl." He handed the diary back to Mary and told her it was time to go.

"But there's so much more I need to know," Mary said. "I don't even know where to begin."

"You've begun already." Phil placed a hand over his heart in an exhausted gesture. "I'm just an old man who has lost everything but his farm and his parish. And it seems like this whole time, I've been waiting for you to return."

As they walked back to the house, Mary pressed him to elaborate, but he would say no more. Instead, he made small talk about the nice overcast sky and cool weather as she returned to her vehicle, filled with thoughts of new directions. They planned to speak the next morning with hopes of involving Curtis next time. When she started the engine, she saw that it was well past three in the afternoon. *Had they really spent that much time talking?*

She backed out and glanced in her rearview mirror. Phil was on his front porch watching her. He raised his hand up with a wave and she honked in return. She noticed her cell phone resting on the middle console. She had completely forgotten about it and had several missed calls from Curtis.

Great, she thought. *Now I'm the one in trouble*

She continued the drive in silence, her mind racing with all the things that had been revealed. Pastor Phil couldn't possibly know all that he claimed to be true, but for some reason she did not doubt him. Their meeting posed more questions than it had answered. She took a deep breath and continued home, feeling like a crazy person in a crazy place.

Strangely, she felt better about their old mansion, now that she had some idea of what might be going on. The house wasn't trying to hurt her, Phil had explained. It wanted her help. She suddenly received a text message from Curtis telling her that he was already home and that she didn't need to pick him up. She texted him back, asking how he got home. His answer: Theodore Stone, the paranormal investigator, was in town and had given him a ride. She couldn't believe it. She forewent downtown and maintained the rural route home, relieved to not have to drive in the busy afternoon traffic of Main Street.

About twenty minutes later, she pulled into the rusty gates of their home, eager to meet the so-called psychic Curtis had employed. The conspiracy Pastor Phil had spoken of lingered in her mind as she entered the courtyard and saw a two-door maroon Oldsmobile parked nearby and a man in dark clothes and a fedora talking with Curtis. They both looked up as she pulled in, and Curtis waved to her. Now things had gotten really interesting.

THE PROFESSIONAL

"Honey, meet Theodore Stone," Curtis said as she stepped out and approached them.

"Call me Theo," the psychic said with a warm smile, shaking her hand.

He had a dark, trim beard and hazel eyes. He looked youngish, probably in his thirties, and wore a rumpled black jean jacket, blue jeans, and a tucked-in white, button-down shirt with a collar. The creased fedora on his head played well into his "psychic detective" image.

Curtis stood back with a look of admiration on his face. "In the presence of two psychics. How exciting!"

Mary turned to Curtis with a mocking smile. "Very funny."

"I'm serious!" he contended.

Theo seemed intrigued. "So Curtis tells me that you have certain 'abilities' as well."

Mary waved him off. "Hardly. But I've seen things. Visions of the future which sometimes seem to happen."

"She sure seems certain that this place is haunted though," Curtis added.

"I'm glad you called me," Theo said. "Luckily I wasn't too far from town."

Curtis turned to Mary. "Turns out he was only a few towns over, and when I mentioned the Bechdel mansion, he made it a priority to be here."

"I have to admit, I've always had a fascination with this place. I've been to Redwood before. About a year ago."

"We heard that," Curtis added. "You helped an old widow with a husband who was haunting her from the grave." Curtis laughed as though Theo was in on the joke.

Theo, however, kept his reserved demeanor. "So you've heard. That was a real fiasco," he said.

Mary studied their psychic, trying to get a sense of his authenticity. She had been on the fence about her own abilities through her entire life, and now she had to decide whether being a psychic was a real thing, and if he was worth the money.

"How much do you generally charge for your services?" she asked him.

Theo glanced up, looking as though costs were the least of his concerns. "Well," he began. "I was telling your husband that, given the job, the rates vary. But generally, I charge twenty-five per hour."

"I told him that was pretty reasonable," Curtis added, as though Mary needed convincing. "Just want to get to the bottom of this once and for all."

Theo turned and looked at the mansion, taking in its sheer size. "I'm surprised this place is still here, actually."

"Why's that?" Mary asked.

"Because it's sat dormant for years. Who in their right mind would willingly live in a haunted house?" he asked, followed by a laugh. "The papers back then called it, *The Socialite Slaughter.*" He turned to the couple and spoke in a confiding tone. "You've since purchased this mansion, renovated it, and now the question remains, is it haunted?"

"I'm not sure," Curtis said. "But there's definitely something wrong. Mary can tell you more."

"We need your help," Mary said.

"Okay," Theo said. "Where should we start?"

"I'd say the kitchen first," Curtis said. "That's where it all started, right, Mary?"

"Yes," she said, turning to Theo. "Did Curtis tell you what happened last night?"

"He did," Theo said. "It sounds like you were put through a pretty traumatic experience." He then clasped his hands together, ready to go inside. "I say we go in and take a look around."

Mary watched as both Theo and Curtis walked toward the front steps. She remembered her shopping bag still on the passenger seat. She didn't feel like telling Curtis just yet about any pregnancy now or in the future, since nothing had been verified. She was playing it safe.

Pastor Phil's words about her past suddenly came back to her. She had no memory of ever being in Redwood at any point in her life. What made him so sure? How did he seem to know what the house's motivations were? She was eager to talk with him some more to find out. Curtis called to her from the house as she stood in the courtyard, staring ahead.

"I'll be in in a minute," she said, going back to the car. She grabbed her purse and put the contents of the shopping bag inside. She closed the door and walked back toward the house, looking up at its walls, determined to uncover its secrets. Inside, she found Theo and Curtis heading toward the kitchen. She set her purse down on a table in the foyer and followed them. Her footsteps across the hardwood floor echoed down the hall as she caught up.

"The worst of it happened in here," Curtis said as they neared the kitchen.

He flicked the switch, bringing to light the broken glass, pots, pans, and dishes smashed and strewn across the floor. Theo let out a low whistle.

Mary placed her hands on the counter and looked around, absorbing it all once again. Theo was busy, crouching down to inspect the debris more closely, then standing to examine the cabinets, but not touching anything.

"Sense anything, Mr. Stone?" Curtis asked him.

"Please. Call me Theo," he said, turning around from the kitchen sink. "It's hard to say just yet," he said. "Need to see all the rooms before I can make any true determination."

"I was standing right here," Mary said, pointing to the counter in front of her, "when the kitchen just... came alive. The cabinets flew open. Drawers flew out. Plates flew out and shattered on the floor. Silverware scattered everywhere, all within a split second." She stepped forward with steely conviction, stopping just inches from Theo's bearded face. "And this was right after I saw a man in a tuxedo crawling on the floor with a shotgun blast in his back."

Theo scratched his beard. "Interesting..."

"And you don't sense anything?" Mary asked, her eyes unblinking.

"Do you?" Theo asked her in a playful manner.

"How about we check out the rest of the house?" Curtis suggested as he motioned to the hall.

Mary sighed in frustration as Theo walked away as though nothing strange had happened in the kitchen. "I'm not crazy," she said as they left.

"No one is saying that," Curtis said from the hall.

She looked around the kitchen in wonder. *It really happened, hadn't it?* Curtis followed their psychic through different rooms as they made their way into her office. She left the kitchen and met up with them, lost in her own thoughts.

If only there was some way to make their new life in Redwood work. According to Pastor Phil, saving their house would mean ruffling some feathers in town. Whoever was behind the Bechdel murders was still out there, and while she had the mayor fingered as a prime suspect, Phil had explained to her that it was more complex than that.

Theo glanced at her desk, where the stack of library books and copies of newspaper clippings rested.

"Mary loves research," Curtis said.

Theo turned to her with a hint of admiration. "Planning on writing a book about Redwood?"

"Just looking for answers," she said. "There are secrets to this town, buried for generations."

"Now that, I'm sure of," Theo said, looking up at the wall and admiring Mary's nature artwork.

"I told her she should just write a book. She can even add some illustrations to it," Curtis said.

Mary stormed forward, blocking her desk from further scrutiny. "I was sitting right here yesterday evening. It must have been nine or ten at night. I had been sleeping. But it was no normal sleep. I was in some kind of trance." She paused and began shuffling around the clipping copies, finding the actual clippings that she had found in one of the books. "Things started to make sense. Just a little piece of the puzzle. Next thing I knew, I was woken up by the chimes of a grandfather clock that doesn't exist."

"And at that point," Curtis interjected, "the house apparently went berserk, tossing tables and furniture everywhere."

"That's what happened," she said. "We've been over this again and again."

"I know. I know," Curtis said with a shake of his head.

Theo nodded and then took his fedora off, revealing a

thick mat of short dark hair, slightly graying on the sides. "I think it's pretty clear that the house is trying to communicate with you." He turned and exited the room without saying another word, which Mary found odd. Curtis followed him out the door as Mary looked at her desk and grabbed a college-ruled notebook and pen. She then left the room to join Curtis and a man she was growing increasingly skeptical of.

They continued their journey room by room, many of them still empty. "Lots of space," he said as they made their way upstairs.

"It sure is," Curtis said. "Growing up with a family of five in a small apartment in Philadelphia certainly makes you appreciate the space."

"What do you do? If you don't mind me asking," Theo said.

"Lawyer," Curtis was quick to say. "I'm trying to set up a practice here in town."

They continued to search each room, with Mary's hopeful expectation that Theo would soon *sense* the spirits' presence and affirm that she had been right all along. But after each room, his response was always the same: There was a slight, lingering paranormal presence within the house, but it was hard to determine exactly what they were dealing with.

"Perhaps the worst of it is over," he said with confidence.

"I want to believe it but can't," she responded. "Julie Bechdel spoke to me. She's suffering within these walls, she and her family, and they need our help."

They went upstairs and walked through each room only to find what Theo described as a "the fading residue of paranormal activity."

They checked the attic, the garage, and even toured the

backyard, walking past old sculptures, the trimmed bushes, the lilies that festooned the cobblestone walkway.

After the lengthy tour, they convened in the dining room to discuss what options they had left. Mary wasn't very impressed with their psychic's abilities thus far. He seemed to come up with more reasons to dismiss what she had seen and experienced rather than verify what she knew to be true.

As they gathered, Theo took a seat at the head of the table between Mary and Curtis. A large brass chandelier lit the room in an elegant fashion, prompting thoughts of long-ago social gatherings.

Mary set her notebook down with Julie's diary sealed in a Zip-Lock bag. She leaned forward with her arms folded on the table as Theo flipped through his own pocket-sized notebook. Curtis sat back in his chair with an air of satisfaction, crossing his arms. Mary could tell he just wanted the whole thing to be over with. He must have felt that the time was near. There was no real evidence of anything out of the ordinary, except what she had seen and heard.

Theo shifted in his seat and lowered his notebook as Mary prepared to make her case. "You have a beautiful home here," he began. "And thank you for the tour."

"You're quite welcome," Curtis said. His hand went to the five o'clock shadow on his normally clean-shaven face, which made him look as tired as Mary felt. "So what do you think?"

She remained quiet, interested in Theo's findings, if any, while also preparing to present some of her own from the past week.

Theo glanced at them and spoke as though he were giving a deposition. "I sense a disturbing history to this house. There is definitely an aura of unrest permeating every room, more so in the grand foyer and gallery, where I believe the murders took place."

Curtis leaned closer with his hands folded, looking troubled, as if this was not what he wanted to hear. "What exactly did you see to bring you to that conclusion?"

Theo raised a calming hand. "I'll get to that in one moment, if you don't mind."

"Of course. Please go on," Curtis said, leaning back.

"This house has been vacant for many years. Decades, I'm guessing. Your presence has, for lack of a better term, *awoken,* the dominant spirits that exist within these walls." He then turned to Mary. "I believe that considering Mary's latest episode, the spirits sensed her own powers and wanted to reach out and communicate with her. What you probably saw there, Mary, was them at their most powerful, and I would guess that it would probably be another ten to fifteen years before they grew the strength to do something like that again."

Skeptical, Mary was quick to respond. "And why is that?"

"Sometimes it's hard to explain the subtleties of telekinetic energy, but suffice it to say, the paranormal presence within these walls is fading fast."

Curtis seemed pleased at the news as he cut in. "Earlier, my wife and I had discussed the possibility of an exorcism." He then laughed at the thought. "Is that what it's going to take?"

Theo scratched his bearded cheek, considering the question. "It certainly wouldn't hurt. Perhaps a good, old-fashioned exorcism would give you some peace of mind."

Curtis laughed again. "I wouldn't even know where to begin. Can you find exorcists on the Internet?"

Theo shrugged. "Sure. Just make sure they're certified."

Curtis rolled his eyes, clearly not convinced of any of it, but Mary was not prepared to let things go that easily. "So what you're saying is that we don't have much to worry about?" she asked, clearly intending to put Theo on the spot.

He placed his palms flat on the table and closed his eyes, tilting his head back slightly. His methods remained a mystery to her, even as he opened his eyes to answer.

"What happened in this house will always be a part of it. From what I sense, there will always be a presence, but it is growing weak and will soon vanish."

"Well, there you go," Curtis said with enthusiasm.

Mary shook her head and casually flipped open her notebook, pen in hand, and began reading from a list. "Saturday evening, October ninth, candles erupted during an argument with Curtis. Monday morning, October tenth, heard a man's voice outside bathroom that asked me 'What are you so afraid of?' That same evening, heard faint cries from an infant, coming from all over the house.

"I saw what looked like a raccoon with a demonic face in the living room. I don't even know if it was real or not. It made unnatural, monstrous noises and scurried into the wall, where the pest control men found this..." She paused and pushed the wrapped diary toward Theo as he looked down, confused. "Go ahead and open it. Take a look," she said. "But be gentle with it. It's a very old diary, written by Julie."

Theo stared at the diary sealed in its bag like an artifact or police evidence. He touched the plastic and then looked at Mary. "You found this here?"

"Yes. There are several missing pages, and I haven't read the whole thing yet. What I do know is that Julie considered her parents very domineering. She also, more times than once, refers to her parents' *enemies*, of which there seem to have been many."

"Fascinating..." Theo said, pulling the diary out and carefully thumbing through it.

Mary looked down at her timeline, continuing. "On our first visit to downtown, an elderly woman half out of her mind on the street seems to know who I am and that we recently moved into the Bechdel property. I run into a man, a pastor at the local church, who also seems to know who I am without even being introduced."

Mary paused to take a breath and then continued reading as Theo flipped through the diary, deeply focused. "Sunday afternoon, October sixteenth. Arrive home with Curtis to find an inverted cross painted in red over front door. Monday morning, October seventeenth. Heard chimes of a grandfather clock. Clock disappeared and reappeared throughout the day." Mary paused, reaching the end of her list.

She looked directly at Theo and continued. "And that brings us to last night, when the kitchen blew apart. When the spirits exposed themselves in a fiery rage, howling, slamming doors and moving furniture, casting bleeding body parts from the top of the grandfather clock."

She stood up and pointed down the hall toward the stairs. "Then a force pinned me to the ground so that I could not move. I was right over there when the ghost of Julie appeared and made everything better. She said that she needed my help."

"What kind of help does Julie want?" Theo asked.

"As she put it, to find her killers so that the spirts of the victims can rest."

Mary leaned against the table, searching their faces for reactions. Theo looked deep in thought and was still holding the diary in his hands. Curtis sat back with an embarrassed look on his face.

Theo lowered the diary and cleared his throat. "That's all very detailed and intriguing, Mary, but I'm just not sensing much here now. It could all be just a passing phase. A last hurrah."

"A phase?" she said. "I'm sorry, I don't think so."

Theo looked over at Curtis, and a nervous laugh escaped. "I've been doing this a long time, and I think I know a paranormal entity when I see one. The energy just isn't here any longer."

Curtis suddenly cut in. "I don't understand, Mary. This is good news. We should be so lucky."

"It proves nothing," she said. She then leaned over and took the diary from Theo's hands and placed it back into the bag. "You should also know that Mr. Stone's findings completely contradict everything Pastor Phil told me about this place."

"Pastor Phil?" Curtis said, surprised. "What did he tell you?"

"He's been living in Redwood longer than we've been alive, and he knows that there's something seriously wrong with this house."

"Is that where you were today?" Curtis asked. "You guys friends now?"

"If I may," Theo said, standing up. "It's perfectly reasonable to have doubts about my findings, Mary. If my initial diagnosis isn't adequate, I'd be happy to stay overnight and monitor the house."

"I don't know if that's necessary," Curtis said, stretching. "I think we're good."

"*No. We*'re not," Mary said.

Curtis looked at her, upset. "The man gave us his diagnosis. His business is done here. Now we can go back to our lives and put all this nonsense behind us."

"Mr. Stone, with all due respect, I don't think you get it."

"Please, call me, Theo," he said.

Mary was getting closer to revealing more of what she had been told, beginning with the pregnancy claim, but she was beginning to feel increasingly paranoid at the same time.

Suddenly, the chandelier swayed and creaked as though a

powerful gust of wind had just blown through the house. They looked up in unison, just in time to see the chandelier swing hard and fast like a pendulum, and then an unseen hand seemed to rip it from the ceiling, as plaster gave way and wires dangled and sparked with electricity, and plaster and pieces of wood began falling.

"Look out!" Mary shouted, as she fell back against the wall.

Curtis and Theo both jumped to the side and hit the floor just as the chandelier crashed down onto the dining-room table, exploding with a tremendous blast of shattered bulbs and bronze fragments. The oak table cracked down the middle but was still able to withstand the crash. Mary crawled, dazed and ears ringing, to a place in the corner where the diary had landed after being launched into the air.

"What in the holy hell was that?" Curtis shouted from the floor on the other side of the table.

Theo rose from the ground a few feet away from the ruined chandelier. His hat had fallen off, and he appeared just as shocked as Curtis. As Mary neared the diary, she noticed lights flickering down the hall. She was certain that the presence was upon them. The house was coming alive again.

CONTACT

From the ballroom came a cacophony of discordant and startling sounds: whistles, drums, bells, and harps. Curtis and Theo stood over the fallen chandelier split in pieces on top of the dining room table, where they were seated only moments ago. Mary grabbed the diary in a frantic lunge, while feeling the unmistakable mark of the spirits having returned. She felt vindicated but also frightened. One door slammed shut, followed by another.

Mary guided herself toward the hallway, pressing up against the wall in an attempt to avoid the risk of being struck by a flying object or an entire piece of furniture. If the spirits of the dead wanted her help, they certainly didn't act like it. Her head swung to the side, where Curtis still stood in shock at the dining-room table. Theo, however, was occupied examining the hanging wires with which the chandelier was still attached above. He appeared to have a certain understanding of what was going on.

"You were saying something about the spirits being gone?" Mary said, leaving the room as if being guided by some force.

They both turned to her, and Curtis gestured for her to come back. "Mary! Where are you going?"

More doors slammed, in unison this time. In the ballroom, the furniture scraped against the hardwood floor, screeching and sliding across the room.

"Theo, what's happening?" Curtis asked, turning to him.

Behind his serious expression, Theo looked pale. "I don't know, Curtis. But your wife is probably on to something."

"No," Curtis said. He looked up, pointing at the ceiling. "Faulty electronics and wiring. That's it." He continued with this point, despite having to shout above all the noises coming from all the cardinal points of the house.

Mary shuddered to think of their kitchen bursting into chaos once again. She had reached the hallway, striding confidently with the diary in her hand.

Theo backed away from the table and started to follow, as Curtis spun around, shouting.

"Hey! Are we going to talk about this, or what? This is not the time to be running off." Seeing that they were ignoring him and moving on, Curtis attempted to catch up, breathing hard and calling their names, imploring them to stop.

Mary moved away from the walls and walked fearlessly down the hall as Theo reached her and Curtis trailed close behind.

"Where are you going?" Theo asked.

"She wants to talk to me again. Julie."

"You're right, Mary," Theo said.

"What?" she said, turning her head to look at him, confused.

"I could sense it the minute I walked in, but..."

"But what?" Mary said with an arched brow.

"But I downplayed it, and for that I'm sorry."

Was he lying then, or now? she wondered.

From a distance, they watched a lampshade fly across the

room and crash into the wall. Curtis jumped as the lights above flickered. Doors to all the rooms along their path were slammed shut. Curtis tried one of the handles, but it wouldn't budge. Mary slowed as they entered the ballroom, where a sofa and chair had been flipped upside-down. Fortunately, the room was minimally furnished.

A low rumbling flowed throughout the house, followed by a creaking of every post and beam and header and floorboard, as though they were on an old ship at sea. Mary felt eager yet apprehensive as she approached the staircase, hoping to find Julie waiting for her. But the house was all sound and fury.

"Julie, speak to me," Mary said, holding up the diary. "We need more clues!"

Curtis walked up beside her and took her arm. "Mary, please. This house is dangerous. We should leave."

"Hold on," Mary said as she pulled away and approached the stairs with caution. "Julie?"

Suddenly, the house went still and quiet. The chandeliers stopped swaying, and for a moment, everything seemed safe.

"All right," Curtis said calmly. "Now let's all take a walk outside and talk about this."

A split second later, a deafening crash erupted upstairs, sending all three of them to the floor for cover. Mary screamed as Curtis threw himself across her back, shielding her.

Theo remained lying on his stomach, looking up as a chandelier swayed precariously from side to side. "I think Curtis has the right idea," he said, reaching for his hat, which rested on the floor beside him. Light tremors shook the floor like an aftershock.

Curtis helped Mary up as she held the diary against her chest. Theo pushed himself up and began to make his way carefully to the door, when an unseen voice hissed and echoed throughout the room, followed by a strange and faint ringing in the air.

"Bring them to us..."

Mary scanned the room frantically, then looked at Curtis with fear in her eyes.

"What?" he asked from near the front door.

"Did you hear that?" she asked him.

Theo approached Mary, deep in thought. "I did."

"What are you two talking about?" Curtis asked.

"Where's Julie?" Mary asked, looking up.

"She isn't here. You will talk to us now..." An overlay of witch-like voices murmured from the walls surrounding them.

"What do you want?" Mary shouted. Theo walked up behind her, looking around as though he could hear them too.

"Who are you talking to?" Curtis asked, fearful now. He tugged on Mary's arm, but she wasn't going anywhere.

"You know what we want. Bring them to us, or we'll take what is ours..."

Suddenly there was silence. The faint, high-pitched ringing vanished. The house went still again, and Mary felt that their latest paranormal encounter was over. She leaned over, light-headed and out of breath.

Curtis held her up and rubbed her back, concerned. "My God, Mary. Are you all right? Let me help you."

"I'm fine..." she answered. "Just need to sit."

Curtis led her over to the nearest flipped-over sofa chair and righted it, helping her take a seat. Theo paced around the room, deep in his investigation. Mary rested back, feeling her forehead. Her heart raced with worry. The voices, which she was sure Julie wasn't a part of, referenced what she had feared the most, that she was indeed pregnant.

"It's too soon..." she said under her breath in a pained

voice.

Curtis leaned closer. "What are you talking about?" He rose up from his knees and looked around the room in panic. "Can someone please tell me what's going on here?"

Theo walked over to Curtis, with his hands in his pockets, looking slightly ashamed. "I received an anonymous call from someone today. I don't know who it was, but they made me an offer."

Curtis looked at Theo, bewildered, but with a faint idea of where he might be going.

"They offered me one thousand dollars to convince you and Mary that nothing was wrong with the place. I don't know why, but that's what they offered."

Mary leaned forward in the chair, eyes narrowing. "I wonder if Bob Deckers had anything to do with this. He originally gave us your card."

"Oh, Mary. Come on. That's ridiculous," Curtis said, throwing his arms in the air.

Mary stood in defiance, despite her apparent light-headedness. "Why? How long have you known Bob? How well do you really know him?" She paused and looked up at the ceiling as a stillness came over the room.

Too frustrated to respond, Curtis read the scribbled marking on the cashier's check Theo held out. There was no maker's name or signature. "One thousand dollars?" he said. "Why would anyone care if we stayed or left?"

Theo shrugged. "I don't know, but I'm sorry for deceiving you both. They told me to expect a call from you within an hour... and then you called."

Curtis looked up at Theo, his face red with anger. "I want you to tell me what this is about, Mr. Stone. No more games."

Mary glanced over at them as Theo looked at Curtis with a nervous look on his face. He removed his fedora and brushed back his hair with a panicky sigh. "Maybe we should talk outside." He then glanced up at the chandelier no longer swaying above them. "Don't want another close call with one of these things crashing down."

"Talk," Mary said, rising from the chair. "No more stalling."

Theo scratched his beard with another sigh and then waved his hat around, as though to speak further would be painful. Curtis crossed his arms and stared at Theo, not having to say another word, because his face said it all. Their psychic, it seemed, wasn't all he was cracked up to be.

Theo said, "I can sense what this house wants. The time is nearing. I've often thought about this place, but part of me has always been afraid to come here." And then his eyes clouded over. "You see, my mother disappeared investigating the Bechdel murders twenty-eight years ago. I've been looking for her ever since."

"Excuse me?" Curtis said.

"I know this sounds like a pathetic excuse, but business has been pretty rough. In fact, you're my first clients in a long time." Theo took a step back, scanning the high ceilings above, clearly reluctant about elaborating further. But he had said too much already and couldn't end there. "I needed the money so that one day I can find out what happened to her."

Curtis and Mary looked at each other, astonished.

Theo waved to them feebly, turned, and walked to the front door, past a lamp lying in pieces and more flipped-over tables and chairs.

"Sorry for wasting your time and misleading you," Theo said. He spun around, offering his parting words. "Mary is right about this house. There *are* powerful forces here, and they're not going to stop. I'm sorry again." He turned back around, opened the door, and walked out.

"Wait!" Mary called. "Where are you going?"

"I've got to hit the road," he said. "That's where I belong

anyway."

Mary looked at Curtis, desperate, but he was too occupied with surveying the destruction in the room. She followed Theo out, and Curtis called to her not to bother, but she was on a mission.

Mary ran down the front steps and through the courtyard to Theo's Oldsmobile, and stood with him there, pleading. "But we're trying to solve the same case," Mary said. "You can't go!"

"I'm sorry, Mary, but I prefer to work alone," Theo said. He paused and looked around. "This house is bad business. All I sense here is a bunch of angry spirits, save for that little girl you're trying to talk to. She seems to be the only one at peace. It's sad, really."

Curtis stood at the doorway with his arms crossed. "Let him go, Mary. We'll find someone else."

Mary moved to the side of Theo's car, blocking the driver's-side door. "You're not going anywhere." She then turned to Curtis. "We need him."

Car keys in hand, Theo huffed and looked at Mary with frustration. "Best of luck to you, Mary."

Mary continued to block his path, unwavering. "You could have lied to us and kept that money, and that you didn't, matters to me. I can't do this all on my own. We share something, Theo, and you know it."

Theo backed away and tilted his head, looking into the sky. The afternoon sky was awash in blue streaks, with thin, scattered clouds shielding the sun.

"I'd like to help, but I wouldn't even know where to start. Plus, I have my own methods. The best thing you can do is move, and even that may not help you."

"We'll pay you. You can stay with us here as our guest, and we can solve this thing together."

Theo sighed and looked down, conflicted. "I don't

think so."

Curtis approached them and stopped at the hood of Theo's automobile. His shoulders sagged and he was noticeably pale, looking as if this was the last thing he wanted to deal with, or could deal with, that day.

"I know how you feel, Theo," Mary continued. "I've spent so much of my life denying these visions, suppressing them, but it's time to embrace what we have and work together."

Theo looked up with a look of consideration. "I'd like to."

"Then do it," Mary said.

Theo glanced over at Curtis as Curtis shrugged, too exhausted to fight. "I could stay an extra day or two and see what happens."

"Thank you. We have plenty of space," Mary said with a smile.

"What exactly does the house or these *spirits* want?" Curtis said, pacing around the front of the car with his hands out like a lawyer in a courtroom.

"It's hard to say," Mary began. "Julie has tried to reach out to me. That poor girl… she must be terrified."

"Vengeance," Theo answered. "She's doing her best to quell them, but they're growing more powerful and resistant."

"Vengeance against whom?" Curtis asked, vacillating again, as though the entire conversation was absurd.

"The murderers," Mary said. "Who else?"

"Exactly," Theo said.

Mary glanced at him, satisfied that they seemed to be on the same page. She then walked over to Curtis with her hands folded in front of her. "I think we're in great danger. I talked with Pastor Phil today. He admitted to having the inverted cross painted on our door."

Curtis's eyes widened with anger. His Adam's apple dipped with a swallow. "*What?*"

Mary put a calming hand on his shoulder. "He said he did it for our benefit. To warn us, protect us, possibly."

Curtis shook his head in doubt. "This is crazy. *We can't even trust the town pastor?*"

Mary talked almost in a whisper. "Forget about the door and listen to me." She then paused, hesitant for a moment to continue. "We have to do this. Pastor Phil explained it to me. There's no escape."

Curtis stepped forward, his face a litany of stunned expressions. "Are you serious? How the hell would he know?"

Theo stood back, leaning against his car, not saying a word.

"I don't know," Mary said. "But he told me that these *vengeful spirits* would claim *someone* one way or the other."

Curtis threw his arms down, laughing. "I'll believe that our home is haunted by spirits of the dead, but that one sounds a little too far-fetched to me."

"Tit for tat," Theo said casually from the side of his car. "Sometimes netherworld spirits will make a demand of living hosts. They already resent you enough for being alive, and they'll take all that is precious from you if you don't serve them accordingly."

Mary looked back at Curtis as he slumped forward and caught himself on the maroon hood of Theo's car.

"Are you okay?" Mary asked, wrapping her arms around him.

"Yeah…" he said in a daze. "I just felt like I had the wind knocked out of me."

They couldn't explain how, but it seemed that, for Curtis, everything finally seemed to have sunken in.

* * *

Mary and Theo set up in the den, laying out all of Mary's

books and newspaper clippings on a center table in the otherwise unfurnished room. After they cleaned up the latest destruction caused by the unseen forces, Curtis checked the rest of the house for damage, examining every nook and cranny. He also looked as though he was finally starting to realize that their dream home was too good to be true after all.

That evening, Mary led Theo up the stairs and showed him the guest bedroom where he would be staying. It was a quaint room with a twin bed, dresser, and not much more in regard to furnishing.

"This is the only other room we have with a bed at the moment," Mary said, showing Theo in.

"Quite all right," Theo answered.

Mary glanced at the shoulder bag Theo was carrying. "You always bring an overnight bag?"

Theo nodded and smiled. "For whatever reason, I had a feeling that I would be staying here for more than a day, not necessarily in this house of course."

"If I hadn't chased after you, it looks like you would have packed it for nothing," Mary said.

Theo walked to the bed and set his bag down. "I suppose you're right." He turned to her, with sincerity in his tired eyes. "Thank you for this. The opportunity, I mean. I hope I don't let you down."

Mary crossed her arms. "Hey, I just want to go back to my quiet life of drawing and sipping tea."

"I hear you," Theo said. He took his fedora off and placed it on the bed next to his bag. Mary didn't ask, but she was pretty sure they were around the same age. She felt a connection with him beyond their psychic traits.

"What month were you born?" she asked.

Theo froze in the middle of pulling off his jacket. "Month? I'm a Gemini, if that's what you're asking."

"Me too," Mary said, surprised.

"I figured as much."

Mary cocked her head. "What makes you say that?"

"Just a hunch," he said, flashing another smile.

Mary placed her hand on the door, halfway out. "Well, I have to go talk to Curtis and see how he's doing. How about we meet downstairs in about twenty?"

Theo tossed his jacket on the bed. "Sounds good."

Mary nodded and closed the door. She felt in good company, at least for the time being.

Wearing his night T-shirt and plaid pants, Curtis sat leaning against the headboard, his laptop propped on a pillow. He peered down through his glasses at the glowing screen and barely noticed Mary as she walked in.

"What're you up to?" she asked, making her way over to the bed.

"Just surfing the Internet, looking at all these paranormal videos," he said, typing. "I had no idea this stuff was so popular. Some of these videos have over two million hits."

"Curtis, this is serious," she said, leaning against the bedpost.

"I know," he said without looking up.

Mary paused, astonished by his impulsive decision to watch Internet videos at a critical time such as this. "And we have to understand that there is no escape from this. We have no choice but to find out who murdered those two families. They are not going to let up."

Curtis looked up at her with the glare of his laptop screen reflecting from his glasses. "Let's talk reasonably. How do we know any of that is true?"

"I don't know," Mary said, shaking her head. "But I can feel something pulling at me, whether we move back to Chicago or not."

"I don't doubt you at all. I simply have reservations about some of the ghosts and spirits. Who is telling you this, for instance?"

"Pastor Phil made it very clear. Why don't you go with me tomorrow, and he'll explain."

Curtis slowly shut his laptop screen and set it to the side with an exhausted breath. "Aside from him vandalizing our front door, we barely know him. Think about it, Mary. We've been here two weeks."

"We have to trust him," she said, stepping back from the bed. "How else can we make sense of any of this?"

Curtis simply scoffed and lay down. Mary looked over to the nightstand where her purse rested. She then walked past him to the door. "Theo is downstairs, and we have a lot of things to discuss."

Curtis stared up at the ceiling in a vacant stare. "You do what you have to do. I've got to sort some stuff out." He feigned a smile, but it was clear that the day's events had rattled him. "I still don't know what's going on, but I do know that you were right. Either that, or we're both completely insane."

Mary laughed a little to herself. For a moment, she found the entire matter humorous.

Downstairs, the furniture had been turned right-side up and the room cleaned up as much as they could. The chandelier was still in pieces on the dining-room table, evidence of the impossible destruction they had seen with their own eyes. So far, there only seemed to be certain rooms or areas throughout the mansion where paranormal activity flourished—the kitchen, dining room, and ballroom.

The occurrences seemed random in nature but were growing in power each time. Mary didn't know how much time they had left. She wanted more than anything to communicate with Julie directly. For now, the spirit of the little girl was absent, with something much more ominous in her place.

She found Theo in the den, standing over a table with a lamp shade hanging above. Her library books were spread across the table's mahogany surface along with all the newspaper clippings she had acquired. In the center of it all was Julie's diary, sealed in the plastic bag. Theo asked her where Curtis was.

"He's still reeling from all this, I think," she said.

"Understood," Theo said. "It's one hell of a blow." He pulled a paper flier from his jacket and handed it to Mary. It was a printed advertisement for psychic medium services with an address, number, and website listed. "For all your investigative needs," he said with a tinge of sarcasm.

Mary examined the flier as Theo took one of the travelogue books from the table and flipped through it. "You know, before my foray into the psychic business, I was simply a private investigator."

"Really?" Mary said, laying the flier on the table.

"Had a good run, but I needed something more. I needed a gimmick. Something that would make me stand out." He turned to her, snapping his fingers. "So I became a paranormal investigator. And as you can see by my business card, it's totally legit."

Mary laughed as she took Julie's diary out and carefully turned through the pages. There was a gradual progression of Julie's entries expressing concern for her and her family's safety. She reviewed some of what she had read earlier.

September 02: My parents won't let me attend school this year. They told me that I'll be taught at home "for my safety."

September 15: They won't even let me have anyone over at the house. I can't see my friends anymore. Mother and Father don't care.

September 23: I haven't been able to leave the house for weeks. I can't stand it! My older brother told me that we're in danger. He tells me this stuff just to scare me. Why is he so mean?.

Mary lowered the diary, feeling a deep sense of sadness for Julie. The girl was denied a childhood. Her young life was cut short, needlessly. Mary vowed, if anything, to find the killers for Julie's sake and bring her closure. The murders were initially reported as a home invasion, a robbery of sorts. And although the house had been ransacked, there were few things stolen, leading police, at the time, to other possible motives.

How the case had still gone unsolved decades later baffled Mary. Was it purposeful? Was there a cover-up? It seemed fairly obvious to her that the individuals responsible were town locals with an axe to grind. Perhaps that was the conspiracy. The town was in on it.

"So who are our suspects?" Theo asked, circling the table. "Isn't that the main thing we need to find out?"

"The town pastor has extensive knowledge of Redwood. Or at least he claims to," Mary said. "He told me that George Bechdel was running for mayor against Frederick Taylor, the current mayor."

"I had read about that," Theo said. "And Taylor has been Mayor since then."

"If that's the case," Mary said, "he's our prime suspect."

Theo grabbed some newspaper clippings, examining them. "So they never brought Taylor in for questioning back then?"

"I don't know," Mary said.

"Hard to believe that they wouldn't." Theo resumed his thinking and began circling the table. "It's unlikely that the perpetrator or perpetrators were outsiders, and while it's certainly a possibility, this whole thing reeks of a local cover-up."

"I can see the investigators asking themselves the same questions we're asking back then as well," Mary said.

"Who runs the police department now?" Theo said, stopping in his tracks.

Mary thought to herself for a moment. "Police Chief Riley and his partner, Deputy Ramirez."

"That's it?" Theo asked, astonished. "That's the entire police force?"

Mary shrugged. "Sure seems like it."

Theo ran his hands through his hair with a groan. "We're going to need ten more detectives and psychics to punch through this one."

"According to Pastor Phil, the conspiracy extends beyond the mayor. Taylor is just the tip of the iceberg."

"Wonderful," Theo said. "Now if we could just bring everyone here for questioning..." He then paused, as though a lightbulb had lit up in his head. "Why don't you have a housewarming party here and invite everyone from town? You've definitely got the room," he said, teasing.

Mary nodded, considering the idea. "But first things first; we have to meet up with Pastor Phil tomorrow. Are you in?"

Theo glanced at his wristwatch. "I think I can pencil it in."

Mary smiled and studied Theo's worn but spirited face. He had shifted from his cockier, less-authentic manner to someone who genuinely seemed interested in what he was doing. He was gradually gaining her trust back.

"Why did you change your mind?" she asked him.

"About what?"

"Why did you decide to help us?"

Theo thought to himself and then took Julie's diary in hand. "I'm on a mission of my own, Mary. My mother, she was young. Disappeared at twenty-five along with my uncle. I was just an infant."

Mary stopped with her mouth agape. "I'm sorry, I had no idea."

"It's fine," Theo said, lightly scratching his chest. "That was a long time ago. 1985."

Mary leaned in closer. "What about your abilities? Weren't they able to help you *see* what happened?"

Theo shook his head. "It's almost as if what happened is being blocked from me. Nothing but a blank screen, and I can't figure out why."

"There's still hope for her, right? I mean, if there was never a body," Mary began.

"It wasn't just her," Theo added. "She was with some friends, a team of psychics. Apparently they got in over their heads. They all disappeared." He then paused with a deep sigh. "I don't want to alarm you, but some of her last notes discuss investigating your house. She called it The Bechdel Project."

"Is there any evidence that she's been in this house before?" Mary asked.

"The last anyone saw of them was just before they went on a road trip through Indiana, but there's no evidence that they ever specifically stopped here."

Mary touched his shoulder. "Again, I'm very sorry."

Theo nodded and continued in a vacant tone. "I've nearly given up on it all. I even had my doubts about this house, but I don't remember the last time I felt as exhilarated as when that chandelier crashed down on the table." He quietly laughed to himself. "This is the kind of stuff I live for."

"Well, I'm glad you stayed," Mary said. She paused suddenly, when the lights began to flicker, and a faint humming surged through the room. Theo froze in place, listening. In the silence, the lights returned to normal and the humming ceased. "Going to be one long night," he said.

DISARRAY

Mary woke the next morning to find Curtis lying next to her. This was the first time in days that he hadn't been up and dressed when Mary woke up. She had slept only a few hours, and it was already daylight out. Theo was in the guest room next door. At least she hoped he would still be there, as his actions were anything but predictable.

She'd had a dream about Pastor Phil the night before that she could only vaguely remember. In the dream, she was back on his farm, searching for answers, but couldn't find him anywhere. She approached his barn and saw him in the distance, walking toward the woods in his backyard. She ran, calling out to him as he entered the woods and disappeared. She couldn't remember what had happened after that.

She removed her covers and climbed out of bed under the dim morning light glowing through the curtains. She had been up pretty late with Theo, trying to tally a list of suspects. She didn't know many people in town, and those she had met at the Sunday barbecue, so many names and faces at once, were blurry images in her mind. There was no denying that, for now, Pastor Phil was their sole source for information.

Until they made a breakthrough, her life was on hold. The house itself embodied an ever-changing series of daily moods and veiled supernatural activity that might explode at any moment. In the end, who would believe them, except Pastor Phil? Curtis, it seemed, was finally coming around, but as Mary walked barefoot to her closet in a T-shirt and underwear, she felt strangely alone. She opened her walk-in closet door and flipped on the light to see a line of clothes she hated hanging along the entire right side of the closet.

"Julie..." she said softly. "If you're there, talk to me."

The air was still and quiet. She didn't know why she had called out for Julie. Like Julie, Mary was beginning to feel like a prisoner of the mansion.

"Everything okay, Mary?" Curtis's dry voice called out from the bed, sounding tired.

She quickly grabbed a pair of jeans and a blue short-sleeved top from the hangers and walked out. Curtis was seated upright in bed, awake and looking alert. He reached for a glass of water on his nightstand and swigged it back in one long gulp. He lowered the glass and took a deep breath, watching Mary as she approached. "When did you go to bed?"

"Not too late," she answered. "A little after midnight."

Curtis tossed the covers to the side and stepped out of bed. "I still don't completely trust that guy. Tried to play us for a bunch of fools. Could still be at it."

Mary made a quick motion with her hand, her voice just above a whisper. "He's in the next room. Quiet down. And besides, you were more than happy with him before the truth came out."

Curtis scoffed. "I don't care. He's shady."

"He's the best hope we have right now," she said.

Curtis turned away and reached for his cell phone on the nightstand. "I'm calling Pastor Phil so we can get to the bottom of this."

Mary tossed her jeans on the bed and moved quickly over to him. "Give it time. Phil wants to talk with us, but he's a very cautious man."

Curtis held the phone up, prepared to dial but hesitated. "So am I."

"We'll speak with him today. I promise," she said.

Curtis lowered the phone, conceding, and then lifted his head, as though another thought had just entered his mind. "So what else is on the agenda today?" he asked.

"We start building a case. You can help us with that."

Curtis slumped his head back down on the pillow. "I want to set up a video camera down stairs. We need to begin documenting this stuff." He ran his hand through his hair, yawning. "I can't believe it. A haunted house..."

Mary walked past him and toward the bathroom. "We need to focus and prepare ourselves. Gather our strength and concentrate." She then closed the door, hearing Curtis sigh.

She went to the shower, hoping that a smooth rush of warm water would help get her mind straight. The water hit her face, soaking her hair instantly as her mind drifted to the hundred options before them. They could run away and start over again. After all, where was the proof that the curse of the Bechdel mansion was tied to them? The more she delved into it, the more unanswered questions arose, more than she knew what to do with. And time, she felt, was running out. They'd been warned. Their lives were at risk.

Mary brought the bar of soap down her chest and over her stomach as water trickled down her bare, smooth skin. Listening to the gentle sound of the running water, thoughts of Julie entered as familiar as a summer breeze.

Mary emerged from the steamy bathroom feeling refreshed, wrapped in her bathrobe and wearing a towel around her head. Curtis was sitting on the bed with his laptop open, typing away. She was surprised to see him beaming with excitement when he looked up at her.

"Mary," he said excitedly, "I think I've got the answer!"

She stopped a few feet from the bed and removed the towel, letting her hair drop to her shoulders. "What's going on?"

Curtis flew from the bed as though he could hardly contain himself. "Hear me out. It's so simple." He paused for dramatic effect as Mary waited patiently for him to continue.

"We have definitive proof of paranormal existence here, right in our house." He smiled broadly. "And I have a brilliant idea about how to turn this to our advantage."

Mary nodded without comment, a reserved expression on her face. Curtis walked over to her and put his arm around her shoulders, pulling her closer. "This could be it, Mary. A genuine haunted mansion and it's all ours. Do you know how many millions of people would travel from all over the world to visit here? Do you have any idea how big this can be?" He went back over to his laptop and scrolled down the screen, continuing his pitch. "I've been looking up all sorts of famous *haunted* landmarks throughout the country. We can really pull this off." He looked at Mary with anticipation, disappointed in her reserved demeanor.

"Curtis..." she began. "We can't trivialize what happened to these people." She turned to the window, pointing. "Their murderers are probably still out there."

"I know," Curtis said. "I've thought about that. We can reignite interest in the case this way. Bring more attention to it. More than we could even imagine."

Mary spoke with quick candor. "We need to stay on track here. That's what's important."

Curtis grabbed his cellphone, which was sitting next to the laptop, and picked it up, undeterred. "There's no reason we can't do both."

"Curtis..."

He held the phone to his ear after dialing. "At the very least, I'm going to give Bob Deckers a call and see what he thinks."

Mary gave up and walked back to the steam-filled bathroom and wiped a clear streak across the mirror, studying her face for a moment. She looked thinner, drained almost. It was very subtly different from a few weeks ago, but she could see it. She heard Curtis talking on the phone, loud and boisterous at first, and then his tone changed to one of utter shock.

"No..." Curtis said softly. "How did he die? What happened?"

Mary's heart seized, and she dropped her hairbrush in the sink. She rushed out of the bathroom just as Curtis got off the phone.

Curtis turned around to face her, holding his phone at his side, his expression vacant. "I can't believe it..."

"Did you just say that someone died?" Mary asked.

"I'm... I'm in shock..."

Mary froze, seeing the despondent look in his eyes. "Curtis? Talk to me. What happened?"

Curtis rubbed his face and sighed. "Pastor Phil..."

"What about him?" Mary asked.

"Bob Deckers just told me a minute ago."

With panic in her heart, Mary approached Curtis, deeply concerned. "*Told you what?*"

"I don't even know how to say it, Mary. Apparently, he was found dead this morning."

"*What?*" Mary shouted. The words made no sense to her.

"Found dead? That's impossible. How?" She could feel her legs shaking, and she hoped that it was all a bad dream.

Curtis continued in a shocked tone. "It's the strangest thing. I was just going to ask Bob if he had Pastor Phil's number."

"Who found him?" Mary asked.

"Some woman from the church went to his house this morning to make him breakfast or something and found him lying in bed. Bob said he died in his sleep."

Mary began pacing the room, short of breath. "There's no way." She turned to Curtis, upset. "There's no way!"

"That's what Bob told me," he said.

"Get him on the phone," Mary said, walking toward Curtis with her hand out, ready to take the phone.

Curtis held the phone behind his back and put one arm around Mary, pulling her closer in a hug. "I'm sorry, Mary..."

"Just doesn't make any sense," she said. "We were supposed to talk to him today." She felt completely in denial, even as a sick feeling rose in her gut. She hadn't known him long but felt a certain kinship with Pastor Phil. He seemed like a good man. He also hadn't appeared in ill health, which immediately made her suspicious.

"I can't believe he's really gone," Curtis said, rubbing her back. "Just unreal."

"Something isn't right," Mary said. She suddenly remembered her dream from last night, in which Pastor Phil had walked away from her and disappeared into the woods. There had to be a meaning to it, clues that could help her figure out what had really happened to him.

Curtis backed away with a serious expression. "For now, we're just going to have to accept it."

Mary shook her head. "I can't." She went to the bed and grabbed her jeans. "We're going to his house."

"Now?" Curtis asked, surprised.

"Yes, now," she said, putting her blue, short-sleeved top on.

"It just seems inappropriate," Curtis said.

"I wouldn't suggest it if I didn't think it was necessary. There are answers there. I had a dream about him last night. He was walking through the backyard."

"But there'll be cops there. Paramedics. Does he have a family?"

Mary shook her head, with sadness clearly evident on her face. "He did at one point."

"What happened to them?"

"They're gone," Mary said. "His wife passed away years ago. His children... well, I'm not sure where they are."

Curtis stepped forward, arms crossed. "Just what do you expect to find out there?"

"Like I said, answers." Dressed, she went to the bedroom door and opened it, walking outside to find Theo down the hall, heading toward the stairs, barefoot and in jeans and a T-shirt.

"Theo!" she called out.

He turned around with an empty coffee mug in his hands. "Good morning," he said with a slight smile, which dropped as she quickly approached him with a look of dread.

"Did you dream last night?"

"Dream?" he asked, confused. He looked up thinking. "Yeah. I think so. I've had problems remembering dreams as of late."

"I have bad news. We were informed that Pastor Phil passed away last night."

Theo's eyes widened. "No way."

She touched his arm, her eyes serious. "I dreamt about him last night. We're going out there to see if there's a connection."

"Where?"

"To his house," Mary said.

Theo crossed him arms, assuming the posture of a studious professor. "Didn't you call him our lifeline last night?"

"Yes. He knew everything about this town, and we were supposed to talk to him today."

"Well, that's certainly an odd coincidence," Theo said.

"It wasn't. There's foul play involved, I can feel it."

Theo moved past her and headed back toward the guest bedroom. "Let me grab my hat and shoes, and I'll be right down."

Mary thanked him and went down the stairs, her mind racing with a hundred possibilities. She wasn't willing to accept Phil's death as being from natural causes. She had to trust her instincts. She felt that she owed it to him to investigate.

They drove out to Pastor Phil's farm under the morning sun and a blue sky. Mary sat on the passenger side, with Curtis at the wheel and Theo sitting in back, scrolling the screen of his cell phone. Mary couldn't deny that showing up at the house was somewhat invasive.

"Before we left, I set up my video camera downstairs," Curtis said.

"Is that what was taking you so long?" Mary asked.

"Hey, someone has to capture this stuff," he replied. "Surprised I didn't think of this earlier."

"Fair warning, you might find the camera in pieces when we return," Theo said, leaning forward. "The supernatural are generally adverse to such exposure."

"Not in any movie I've ever seen," Curtis said.

Intrigued, Mary turned to Theo. "Is that true?"

Theo nodded. "In most cases, a spirit will either remain unseen on camera or destroy the equipment altogether. When they are captured on film or video, which *does* happen sometimes, it's generally carelessness on the part of the entity."

Curtis struck the steering wheel with his clenched fist. "Hey, those *spirits* dropped a chandelier right on the table. They could have killed us."

"We don't know their intentions yet," Mary said. "All I know is that Julie asked for our help, and that's who we're doing this for."

"Just be careful," Theo said. "Unless you don't mind your cameras being destroyed."

"You both worry too much," Curtis said.

They reached the railroad crossing near Phil's house that Mary remembered from before. She felt anxious at what they would find. They couldn't very well just waltz into Phil's home and begin searching the place, but they had to do something. As they neared Phil's dirt road, Mary decided on their plan.

"When the authorities approach us, we haven't heard anything about Phil's passing," she said. "So look shocked and dismayed when they tell us. I will be inconsolable, and then say I need to walk it off. Something like that."

Curtis turned onto the dirt road at Mary's request.

"Good plan," Theo said.

"Thank you," she said.

"He really is way out here, isn't he?" Curtis said, driving slow and steady as the car vibrated over the bumpy terrain.

"Hard to believe I was just here talking with him." She was quick to wipe her eyes as they watered.

"Why didn't you tell me you were coming out here yesterday?" Curtis asked.

She turned to him with a hint of remorse. “I’m sorry. He swore me to secrecy at first. I didn’t want to betray his trust.”

They neared the end of the dirt road, which stopped at the old-fashioned white fence at the front yard of his property. His two-story house was in view, partly obscured by an array of vehicles and flashing lights from several first responders. There were two ambulances, one police car, and a long red fire engine, all parked in front, shielding Phil’s blue station wagon on the side of the house. Mary could see a few paramedics huddled by one of the ambulances.

Chief Riley was in view on the front porch, with Deputy Ramirez and what appeared to be a distraught, gray-haired lady. Mary assumed she was the woman who had supposedly discovered Phil. What exactly was she doing there in the first place? To fix breakfast, really? Mary had her suspicions but didn’t want to be too distrusting of the townspeople. That, to her, wasn’t going to help anything. She was the stranger in town. Not them.

“Hope everyone’s ready,” Curtis said. Heads turned their way as soon as he parked alongside the white fence. Mary took a deep breath and prepared to open the car door. Through the window, Theo quickly took a picture of the scene with his phone and then slipped it inside his pocket. He put his hat on and got ready.

CRIME SCENE

"I never met Pastor Phil, or any of these people for that matter. Won't they be suspicious of me?" Theo asked.

"You're our friend from out of town," Mary said.

Curtis turned the ignition off as those already on the scene turned, with unfriendly, questioning faces, to stare at them. Mary stepped out and immediately approached the house with concern, as Theo and Curtis met up at the back of the SUV and then followed her.

"This is crazy," Curtis said softly to Theo, who nodded in response.

Mary passed the front gate and walked into the yard visibly distraught, her eyes widened. Her feelings were honest, despite the ruse she was about to commit. "What happened?" she asked the three male paramedics. They all looked to be in their early thirties and wore identical polo shirts and slacks. Their expressions were both sympathetic and businesslike.

"Mr. Evans... he passed away, ma'am. Are you family?" the tallest of the men asked.

Mary cupped her mouth as though in shock. "We're

friends of his," she said, lowering her hand. "He was our pastor."

"What's going on, honey?" Curtis asked, approaching with Theo.

Mary spun around, shaken. "It's Pastor Phil, they said he passed away."

"Oh no," Curtis said, putting his arm around her. "I can't believe it."

"Pastor Phil?" Theo said, stepping forward. "What happened?"

"We really can't say at the moment, sir," the paramedic said. The handheld radio on his belt crackled with the voice of a dispatcher asking them their status. He grabbed the radio and nodded at Mary along with his sympathetic co-workers. "I'm very sorry, ma'am."

The paramedics walked to the other side of the ambulance, leaving Mary, Curtis, and Theo with the news. Chief Riley was already coming down the steps of the front porch with Deputy Ramirez at his side, approaching them.

"Is it really true?" Mary asked.

The chief stopped a few feet in front of her and removed his dark aviator glasses. "'Fraid it is, Mrs. Malone. Real shame too. Everyone loved Pastor Phil. Can't think of a bigger loss to the community."

"I don't understand," she said, wiping her eyes. "I didn't know that he suffered from any health problems. He couldn't have been any older than fifty."

"He was sixty-five," Deputy Ramirez said. "All signs at the moment point to natural causes. House was secure. No signs of forced entry, and he was found by Grace here. Looks like he passed in his sleep."

The woman, Grace, approached them curiously, sizing them up. "Can we help you?" she asked. Her suspicious expression changed as she recognized them. "Oh, yes. You're that new couple in town, the Malones."

"Yes," Curtis said. He then turned to Theo. "This is a friend of ours from out of town, Theo Clark."

"Nice to meet you all," Theo said. The chief and his deputy glanced at Theo, narrowing their eyes. He was definitely the stranger among them, but Theo knew what they might be thinking and tried his best to stay calm. "I just can't believe this. It's terrible."

"What are you doing here?" Grace asked them, looking at Mary.

Mary took a deep breath and wiped her eyes again. "We were supposed to meet Phil for breakfast. He invited us over." She then planted her face in her hands. "So unreal… he was such a good man." She meant every word of it, but had to add a little theatrics to further convince them.

"But *we* were supposed to have breakfast," Grace said, tugging at the pocket of the summer dress that went down to her ankles. "He never mentioned anything about other guests."

"He invited us yesterday," Mary said.

Grace thought to herself and then turned away, shielding her face and sobbing. "I just can't believe he's really gone," she muttered.

Deputy Ramirez put his arm around Grace.

"A real shock," Chief Riley said, as he looked up into the sky.

Mary stepped forward. "Who was the last person to see him?"

Chief Riley seemed taken aback by her question and looked at her, thinking. "Not really sure of that at the moment. When he wasn't at church, Pastor Phil led what could be called a solitary, private life."

"I just think we need to consider everything," Mary said. She then looked to Curtis. "Don't you think?"

"Yes, of course," he nodded. For a moment, he seemed to consider her questions out of line, glancing at the chief to see his reaction, but then added, "Until otherwise proven, we should consider the possibility of foul play."

Curious, Chief Riley scratched his chin. "You suggesting that he was murdered?"

Mary answered for him, saying, "The whole thing is suspicious to me."

Grace's sobs turned into a full cry as Deputy Ramirez continued trying to console her.

"Where is his body?" Mary asked.

Chief Riley pointed to the ambulance nearest to them. "Right in there. They're taking him to the coroner in a few."

"Treat this as a homicide, Chief. I implore you," Mary said.

Clearly rattled by the suggestion, the chief shuffled in place. "Who in their right mind would do something to Pastor Phil? He didn't have any enemies as far as I'm concerned."

Theo stepped forward with his own explanation. "All you need is a motive," he said. "Happens all the time to people just like Pastor Phil."

Chief Riley nodded, but his annoyance showed. "Well, we'll certainly look into it. In the meantime, I ask that you go about your business and let us do our job. I'll keep you posted."

Mary turned away. "I think I need to walk a bit, clear my head. It's just too much." She immediately pivoted and moved toward the house, followed by Theo.

Chief Riley called out to her, and Curtis told him that she just needed a minute. Mary continued her quick pace, head down, passing Phil's blue station wagon.

"Where are you going?" Theo said quietly.

She moved around to the side of the house and into the backyard, out of view of the chief and the paramedics. "I'm retracing his steps from my dream," she said. "It's all I have to go on."

They could hear the clucking of chickens and grunting of pigs in their fenced-in pens. There was a sadness to it all. What was going to happen to all of his livestock? Mary continued her journey through the backyard and toward the adjacent forest, hoping for any hint of Phil's presence. It was hard enough to believe that he was dead, even harder to consider that his spirit was somehow watching them.

"You sense anything?" she asked Theo.

"Nothing yet. Nicely kept house. He lived out here all alone?"

"That's what he told me. His wife passed some years ago. His children live out of state. I sensed some real sadness in him yesterday. I don't even know if he talks to them anymore or why that would be the case."

"That is sad," Theo said. He seemed oddly choked up all of a sudden, as though the news had just hit him hard.

"Are you okay?" she asked as he lagged behind.

He looked over at her and straightened up a bit. "Yeah… it's just… I really wish something would come to us. I'm sick of drifting around and looking for answers."

Mary slowed and moved closer to him, concerned. "Now's not the time to feel like that. Pastor Phil may have been murdered, and we have to be on top of things."

Theo stared ahead with a quiet chuckle. "Maybe I'm losing my touch. Haven't had a successful paranormal outing since Evelyn Chambers."

"We're going to figure this out," Mary said, offering her reassurances. "I don't believe in coincidences. Not where this town is concerned. Did you ever think that maybe we were brought here for a reason?"

"Sure," Theo said. "I've been drawn to this town ever since my learning about my mother's disappearance." He swung at the air in frustration. "I just wish I could find a clue. A sign. *Something*!"

"We can solve this," Mary said. She then continued walking toward the woods, scanning the ground for any clues no matter how small. The grass was mere inches high, with sticks and leaves lying about from nearby trees, but nothing of substance. "This is where Phil was in my dream. I was by the barn and called out to him, but he kept walking."

Theo stopped. "Hold on."

Mary turned around, inches from where the forest began. "What is it?"

He held his hands halfway out at his sides. "We're close to something." He looked ahead, pointing to a small branch, split and hanging low from a pine tree. It looked unnatural as if damaged by human hands. "This way," he said, entering a narrow path into the forest. There were more signs along the way, indentations in the grass resembling footprints, several broken twigs, and disturbed ground.

Mary moved to Theo's side, noticing something ahead lying among the leaves on the ground. It was small and black, like a sock or glove. "There's something there."

They moved quickly, crouching to avoid branches in their path. Mary leaned down and retrieved the item with an anxious heart. "It's a glove."

"Wow..." Theo said, examining it. "Wonder where the other one is?"

Mary caressed the tips of the glove, sensing disarray in the pit of her stomach. She was short of breath, with a powerful force pressing down on her, and felt panic and despair all at once. As she closed her eyes, she saw a faint, shadowy figure hovering over her, covering her mouth and pressing down on her with its whole body weight. She gasped, and was caught by Theo as she fell back.

"Hey! Are you all right?" he said.

She snapped out of her trance, surprised to find herself in his arms. "What happened?"

"You zoned out. Sort of teetered back and forth for a little bit, then you gasped like you were having a heart attack and fell back."

"Phil was murdered, and whoever did it left this glove," she said with certainty.

"Through carelessness or what?" Theo asked.

Mary turned to him, still holding the glove. "I don't know, but we need to keep this between you, me, and Curtis for now."

"You don't trust the cops?"

Mary shrugged. "Chief Riley and Deputy Ramirez seem like good people, but we can never be too careful."

The forest beyond their narrow path got thicker, with no indication of where the suspect had gone from there. Mary turned back to the house, pushing the glove into the side pocket of her jeans. "We should head back now," she said, prompting Theo.

He agreed, and they journeyed back the way they had come, with an idea of what caused Phil's death. From the backyard, they passed Phil's vegetable garden, another somber reminder of his absence. The farm felt ghostlike now, and Mary was curious whom the property would go to. "I'd be interested in seeing Phil's will," she said to Theo.

"Definitely," he said. "What do you think of Grace? Anything's possible, right?"

Mary grimaced and shook her head. "Very doubtful she had anything to do with it. I think she's just as shocked as all of us." As they came around the house, she heard Curtis asking Chief Riley about their own supposed break-in.

"I mean, vandalism is one thing, but who breaks into your home just to trash your kitchen and leave?"

The chief nodded and then responded, "Stranger things have happened."

Deputy Ramirez and Grace were back on the porch, talking together. They looked up as Mary and Theo walked by.

"Any suspects yet?" Curtis asked the chief.

"Not a one," he replied. "Natural causes means the suspect might be a heart attack."

Mary and Theo approached, as Curtis huffed in frustration. "Are you okay?" he asked Mary.

"I'm fine," she said. "I think we'd better go now."

"Very well," Curtis said. He turned to Chief Riley and shook his hand, thanking him. "Guess we'll be on our way now."

"You folks try to enjoy your day, despite all this unpleasantness," the chief said. An ambulance engine started as two firefighters emerged from the house. Despite their efforts they still looked cool and professional in their short-sleeved button-down shirts, which were neatly tucked into their blue slacks. Mary stood in front of Chief Riley with a serious, pleading look in her eyes. "Please make sure they check for any signs of struggle on Phil's body."

"If something happened to the good pastor, the coroner's office will find it. Mark my words," the chief said, sounding irritated.

"Did Phil leave a will?" she asked.

"I'm sure he did. I'll have to contact Steve Atwood at the courthouse. Deals in probate law."

Curtis's eyes widened. "Really? That's an area I've always considered. I'll have to talk to him."

Mary especially liked the idea, thinking Curtis clever for it. Perhaps they were on the same page, or maybe Curtis just wanted to network. Either way, getting a look at the will could help put some of her theories to rest, or to the test, even adding to them.

Chief Riley dug into his pocket and pulled out some business cards, handing one to Curtis. "This is him here, Atwood."

Curtis thanked the chief as Mary and Theo shook his hand and said their goodbyes. As the three left, Mary quietly remarked that she wished they had gone inside.

"We can always come back," Theo said.

They all got into the SUV and took another look at Phil's house, with lights of the police and rescue vehicles flashing out front. The sight was as sad as anything Mary had witnessed in a long time. Gone, along with Phil, were all his secrets about the town and any further elaboration on who might have killed the Bechdels and why.

"It's a damn shame," Curtis said, turning the ignition.

Mary reached into her pocket and pulled out the glove. "We found this back there."

Curtis glanced down, intrigued. "A glove?"

"It was in the woods behind his house," she said. "Looked like it was recently dropped there, no leaves or debris on top of it."

"Well, *that's* interesting," Curtis said.

Theo leaned forward from the backseat and cut in. "We think that our suspect might have left it there when he escaped."

Curtis hit the brakes, stopping the car just as they entered the dirt road. "Wait a minute. Are you saying that you took evidence from a potential crime scene?" He turned to Mary, surprised. "You need to give that to the police, especially if this killer is still out there."

"What are they going to do with it?" she asked. "File it away in the evidence room and sit on it for another forty years?"

"They need to know," he said. "Mary, this is serious."

"I know that, Curtis. I need you to trust me on this. I could sense something just by holding it. The vision was blurry, but I'm getting closer."

At the wheel, Curtis sighed and squeezed the bridge of his nose, squinting in frustration. "Coming here was one thing, interfering with an investigation is another thing altogether."

"Mary has had a pretty good track record about things so far," Theo said from the back. He then leaned back as Curtis glanced up at him in the rearview mirror. "But hey, I'm just an observer here."

Curtis shook his head and then put the car into drive. "This isn't right. You're both taking this thing too far."

Despite his objections, Curtis kept driving as they continued down the dirt road, Pastor Phil's house fading in the distance. Mary believed there was more at stake than ever now. If they could get to Phil, they could get to anyone. No one was safe. On their way home, she wondered when she was going to make the Enemies List of the powers that be. The time, it seemed, was quickly approaching.

FUNERAL

Nearly the entire town was present for Pastor Phil's memorial, taking place at the same church he helped establish and grow. It had been two days after his death, and in that time there had been no evidence of foul play discovered. Mary wasn't surprised. She sat in one of the pews farthest back with Curtis and Theo at her side. The pews ahead were packed with men and women in their Sunday best. Only they weren't there to listen to another of Phil's sermons.

With his arms folded over his chest, his body was dressed in a gray suit and lay peacefully in a shiny empire-blue casket. The surreal sight sent tears to Mary's eyes. His placid face and closed eyelids looked almost as if he were only sleeping.

There was a framed picture of Phil on display next to his casket. In it, he was standing in front of his garden with a woman at his side, at least ten years younger, vibrant and full of life. His children, oddly enough, weren't present. His wife, Alisha, was mentioned during the eulogy presented by the pastor's assistant, a man named Cliff Bronson.

He was a short, pudgy man in his early twenties who

Mary had seen at the Sunday barbecue. He had seemed eager and friendly. He was noticeably sweaty at the podium and slightly nervous, but he did his best to offer a proper closing to the sudden death of a beloved town resident.

"Philip is now with his wife, Alisha, who left this world much too early from a tragic brain aneurysm. During this remarkably difficult time, Phil's faith never wavered. He did not lament his plight and curse God for his circumstances—he trudged on and offered guidance, support, and the word of our Lord to so many of our town's residents.

"He was a selfless man who always seemed to bring out the best in people. We know that he led a life of stunning loss all around him, but he always stayed on the path of the righteous."

Cliff paused and looked up from his notes and dabbed at his forehead with a handkerchief. A large black metallic cross hung on the otherwise bare wall behind him. Large floral arrangements had been set up on both sides of Phil's casket, a dim spotlight providing a glow from above. A woman sat at the church organ in the front corner, not currently playing.

The entire room was filled with the sound of quiet sobbing, and there didn't appear to be a dry eye in the house. "Redwood will never be the same without the thoughtful guidance of Pastor Phil. I can guarantee that I'll never be the same. Phil was a friend and mentor to me as he was to many of you. Even those who don't regularly attend his services can attest to his goodness to others.

"He leaves behind an important legacy that we must continue in his honor." Cliff paused again and shuffled through his notes as a man in the audience coughed loudly. Cliff looked up and quickly extended his arm to the front left pew. Seeming flustered, he said, "Here with us is Mayor Taylor, who would like to say something about his friend and ours, Pastor Phil..."

A man in a dark suit rose from the pew, and Mary recognized him immediately from his gray, slicked-back hair. He slowly made his way to the podium, walking with a slight limp. Cliff left the podium as the mayor lurched over to the microphone and looked into the crowd with his piercing gray eyes. He appeared somber, a striking contrast from when Mary had briefly seen him speak at the church barbecue.

"Thank you, Cliff. And thanks to all you good people for paying your respects to one of Redwood's most cherished residents." He paused and took a deep breath, wiping his eyes and his wrinkled face.

Who was Mayor Taylor, and what did he want? Most importantly, did he have a hand in Phil's death? Mary believed there had to be a connection. Mayor Taylor said, "Like Phil, I suffered some loss in my life as well." He signaled toward the front pew, where several suited men, both young and old, sat in a line, listening attentively.

"My boys are all grown up today, and they'd make their mother proud. When she passed in a car accident, we didn't think we'd ever be able to go on as a family, but with Phil's guidance, his excellent sermons, and his utter compassion, he pulled my family from the depths, and I will be eternally thankful for that. Not a day goes by when I don't think of Delia, but I know that she, Phil, and Alisha are smiling down on us, at peace." Taylor paused and coughed into his balled fist. He then looked up with watering eyes. "My brothers are also here from out of town to pay their respects to the man who brought so much joy to this community. I'd like to introduce Liam, Garret, and Jeffery, all fine men who I'm honored to have here. And my sons, who you all know."

The three older men turned slightly to nod at the crowd. They were old, but well built, with full heads of gray and white hair, just like the mayor. Mary squinted, trying to make out their faces. The one in the middle, named Garret, she believed, caught her immediate attention. He had a noticeable scar on his left cheek that sent shivers down her spine. Julie had shown her a man with a scar in the last memory of her sad, short life. Mary had said she no longer believed in coincidences, especially where Redwood was concerned. This moment and that scar were no exception.

She grabbed Curtis's arm. "What is it?" he whispered.

"The Taylor brothers," she said in a hushed tone. "I think they might have been involved in the Bechdel murders."

He looked at her, slightly put-off. "Mary, please. We're at a funeral."

Looking rather bored, Theo wondered what they were whispering about as Mary turned to him. "Get a good look at their faces," she said, pointing.

From the pew, she could also see the elderly socialite who had so bluntly addressed her in the store the other day. Bob Deckers sat a few rows ahead of them as well. There were many faces she recognized, but still she felt at a loss. She didn't actually *know* any of them. Pastor Phil was the only person in town she could have called a friend.

Theo leaned forward, zeroing in on the Taylor brothers. Women who appeared to be their wives sat among Mayor Taylor's sons. Theo's face froze the minute he narrowed in on the middle Taylor brother, Garett, right before he turned back around.

Mary noticed the disturbed look on Theo's face. "What is it?" she whispered, but Theo didn't answer. Mary shook his arm, but he continued to stare ahead without acknowledging her, as Mayor Taylor continued talking at the podium.

"This is a little off the subject, and I hope you'll forgive me," he was saying, "but I hope to see everyone here at the annual Autumn Festival this weekend. My family will be in attendance as well. There will be a special song and dedication to Pastor Phil and all his life's works that will kick off the festival."

Mayor Taylor leaned back and looked over the crowd. He looked older than the picture Mary had seen in the Redwood brochure. The skin on his aged, spotty face sagged, especially under his dark eyes. He walked slowly from the podium as the organist played a low, melancholy tune.

Theo glanced at Mary with a look of newfound realization evident on his face. "I saw my mother," he said. "For the first time since she disappeared, I saw her, in the room of a vacant house, *your house,* with my uncle and the others from the college."

Mary turned to him, stunned. "Just now?" she asked.

"Yes," he replied. "The mayor and his brothers were there too."

She was shocked at the revelation, but it confirmed what she had been feeling. The idea of a conspiracy was taking shape quickly before their eyes. Already a shady character, Mayor Taylor appeared to be even more connected than she had originally believed him to be. Though, Phil had urged her to look beyond the town's power players. There were others, he explained, murderers who were just as responsible as the Taylor family seemed to be. Mary sat there as the memorial service continued, feeling a slight pain in her stomach.

After the service ended, she walked with Theo and Curtis to the front of the First Christ Church of Redwood and stood in line to view Phil's casket. They made their way forward slowly, as quiet chatter and sobbing continued throughout the room, while in the background, organ music played softly. Mary said little as she noticed Theo looking around the room like the detective he was. He certainly wasn't being subtle about it.

Curtis squeezed her hand, and she looked at him and smiled. "Now I feel bad for being mad at him about the door," he said softly.

"It's okay," she said. "None of us could have seen this coming." She thought about all the information that died with Pastor Phil, the names of people he never gave her. A strange thought occurred to her: Would she be able to see Phil, now that he had passed? It was a sad thing to consider. It could also prove helpful.

They finally made their way past a flower arrangement and close to Phil's casket, where there was a small group praying. Mary tried to peer over a man's shoulders and could see Phil lying peacefully in his casket, a light white powder applied to his face. She could feel the tears coming.

Suddenly, the man in front of her turned around and collided with her. She was still looking at Phil when his shoulder hit her.

"Pardon me, ma'am," he said.

They made eye contact, and she froze, realizing it was Mayor Taylor, and for a moment she felt fearful that he had read her mind, but quickly pushed the thought away. He looked at her strangely and then put a finger to his chin.

"Oh. You're that couple who moved into the old Bechdel Mansion. Welcome to Redwood," he said, extending his hand.

She shook his hand, feeling a near jolt of energy travel through her. She pulled her hand away, trying to keep her composure.

"Nice to meet you."

Satisfied, the mayor turned and rejoined his family as they walked away from the casket. She felt light-headed and out of breath.

"Mary, are you all right?" Curtis said from behind her. She turned to face him but fell into his arms, passing out before she could answer. Some of the people in line gasped as he caught her.

"Mary!" his muffled voice called out.

The organ music began to fade as her mind drifted to other places, with visions of the future striking in tiny fragments and then disappearing. Then everything went black.

A vision of a gloved hand entered her mind, a hand that was pressing down upon Phil's open mouth as he struggled to breathe. A hand belonging to a masked man who stood over Phil's bed in the darkness and reached for a nearby pillow with his other hand. "Doesn't have to be this way. Just tell me where it is," the man was saying.

With watering, widened eyes, Phil shook his head and tried to grab his attacker, resisting, only to be pinned down furiously. The pillow slammed down over his face with suffocating force. Phil thrashed and thrashed about, tossing his head, kicking his legs, but his attacker's weight managed to hold him down. Phil writhed and twisted for long, deadly minutes before his body seized, gasped, and collapsed into deadly stillness.

The man removed the pillow from Phil's face, breathing heavily himself, and then backed away from the bed. He pulled a cell phone from his pocket, making a call as he walked into the living room. He was tall, slim, and completely dressed in black

As he stepped into the living-room light, he pulled off his ski mask and Mary could see his face. It was clean-shaven with a bronze tan. He also had short, graying hair, looking eerily similar to Bob Deckers, the realtor. He held the phone to his ear and spoke in a low, hushed tone.

"I've looked everywhere, and I can't find it!"

A woman who looked familiar to Mary appeared in her mind. She was on the phone in bed and wearing a nightgown, her auburn hair in curlers. Mary remembered her name from their store run-in, Beatrice Thaxton.

"Keep looking!" she hissed. "Do you have any idea what will happen to us if you don't find it?"

"You don't have to remind me, damn it," Deckers said over the phone. "The pastor… it's not looking good for him."

"What did you do, Bob?" she asked.

After a lengthy pause, his voice shot back, "Nothing! We'll talk later. Gotta go."

"Wait!" Beatrice said. "Have you checked the backyard? Phil might have buried it out there."

Bob sighed into the phone. "No. It's pitch-black out there, and I don't have all evening."

"If you don't find it, that damn Taylor family will. Now quit stalling and get me some results!"

She could see Curtis, Bob Deckers, and three other men, all wearing suits, sitting in a dimly lit pub, eating and drinking into the evening. Curtis took a sip of beer and glanced at his watch. "Well, I've got to head back to the ol' homestead. My wife is probably worried sick."

Bob waved him off and then held four fingers in the air. "Can we get another round of shots, Bethany?" he called out to a frumpy female bartender with short, curly blonde hair.

"No, I'm fine," Curtis said, holding up his keys. "Still have to drive."

"Come on!" Bob said. "What's the rush?"

Another one of the men with dark, slicked-back hair, cut in. "Yeah, Curtis. Don't go running out on us now."

Curtis stood and shook his head. "Sorry guys. Don't want to leave my wife in our huge mansion all alone."

"Oh, you poor baby," the other man said as everyone laughed.

"Seriously," Curtis said. "Mary is just convinced there's

something wrong with the place. She's all into the supernatural."

"Really?" Bob said, leaning in. "What has her so convinced?"

Curtis shrugged. "Things that go bump in the night. Things like that. I mean it *is* a little creepy. People *were* murdered there."

Bob stretched back as Bethany arrived with the shots, placing them on the table. "Curtis, the only thing wrong with that house is the guilt you're going to feel living like a king for next to nothing."

One of them grabbed his shot and held it up in a toast. "To ridiculous extravagance!"

All the men, save Curtis, threw their shots back and slapped the table.

Mary was in a room that resembled her living room, but completely unfurnished and the hardwood floors covered in dust and debris. The room was dark except for the flashlights of three armed men, shining against a young woman and three other men, being held against their will in the mansion.

The woman and her companions recoiled against the wall as the three men waved their rifles, taunting the group. Suddenly, another man in a heavy trench coat entered the room, smoking a cigar, as rain poured outside the window.

"You're trespassing on private property," the man said, removing his rain-soaked hat. He stepped past one of his men, and Mary could see his face clearly. It was Mayor Taylor.

"There'll be a steep price to pay for that, unfortunately. A steep price, indeed," he continued.

"Let us go!" the young petite woman shouted.

The mayor nodded and looked to one of his brothers next

to him, aiming a rifle at the young and frightened group. "Garret, I think you know what to do."

Suddenly, things shifted back to real time as Mary awoke from her trance. Theo and Curtis were at her side as she was being carried down the aisle.

"Make way," Curtis said. "Please."

They moved quickly as her head rose up as her consciousness returned. She wasn't entirely sure what she had just envisioned, troubling as it was. There was far more to the puzzle. Everyone was a suspect, and time was running out.

The Taylor brothers watched them suspiciously as they hurriedly left the church, trying to get Mary out of the crowd and into the fresh air. She could feel Theo trembling and was equally shaken by the clear understanding that there was no going back from any of it now.

OUTSIDERS

Redwood, Indiana. June 25, 1985

The ten-year anniversary of the Bechdel massacre brought Elizabeth Stone to the rusty gates of a vacant mansion, keen on discovering the secrets inside. The Bechdel mansion, ghostlike in its grand and dilapidated appearance, had ceased being an attraction to curious onlookers who were swiftly ejected from the premises following vigilant measures implemented by the town mayor. The mansion grounds were strictly off limits to the public, and the message was clear enough: outsiders not welcome.

The estate had long been stuck in probate limbo, for every time someone purchased the land, they would soon flee the mansion, hastily and without explanation. There were many who believed the mansion was haunted, cursed even, and fascination with it only grew with the passage of time. The murder of the Bechdel family and their dinner party guests unleashed something unspeakable on that quiet autumn evening, and the unsolved nature of the crime only fueled speculation of a grand conspiracy, either of silence or collusion.

There were rumors of the supernatural, an ominous force that still resided within the mansion's faded walls.

On the night of the murders, investigators found bodies riddled with bullets, piled in a bloody heap. Next to the bodies were bullet casings scattered on the floor throughout the ballroom. The front door had been busted open, and tables and furniture were tossed and turned, and perhaps most tragically, a young girl was lying dead outside the mansion in a courtyard, shot point-blank.

After a lengthy investigation, authorities were unable to find the killers due to a "lack of evidence," though the public remained increasingly skeptical of this claim. Many believed the clues were there, buried somewhere inside or outside the mansion.

On the evening of June 25, 1985, Elizabeth Stone found herself at the mansion's front gate, determined to get to the bottom of the most heinous crime in Redwood's history.

She stood in the darkness of the long-abandoned site where fallen trees, looming weeds, and an abundance of overgrowth consumed the front yard, concealing the Bechdel mansion from view. No Trespassing signs were posted on all sides of the gates, and there were still tattered strips of police tape hanging from parts of the iron bars, a reminder of the terrible crime committed only ten years prior.

Accompanied by her brother, Ben, and their two friends Adam and Scott, Elizabeth had arrived at the premises with a purpose. The friends possessed a unique gift—a telepathic ability between them that they had gradually harnessed over the years when they met in college. The hoped, some day, to establish a practice as professional investigators. But not just any investigators—their gifts lay in the world of the paranormal.

They could see things, stark visions of the past or future. Eager to discover the truth behind the murders, the group had traveled far to see the Bechdel mansion in person with hopes of unlocking its darkest secrets.

That evening, they all wore black and carried backpacks full of supplies on their shoulders. From where they stood, they could barely see the Bechdel house beyond the overgrowth and neglect surrounding the premises. Their hike from town had taken them five miles through forest, and they were careful not to draw attention to themselves.

They were aware of the visitor ban on the property, but it had been so long since the murders, they didn't see why anyone would notice or even care. Pockets of white light flashed in the distance. A storm was approaching. And the time of night was closer to the hours of the massacre, and by design, ten years to the day.

With his hair tucked under a skullcap, Ben leaned against the gate railing and gripped it with his gloved hands. Elizabeth stood next to him, her hair tied in a bun, scanning the area ahead with a pair of night-vision binoculars. Adam, short and pudgy, with his shaggy hair tucked under a dark baseball cap, stood across the road, keeping watch for approaching vehicles. Scott, tall and skinny, with his shaggy hair tucked into a backwards hat, approached the gate and looked up, examining the arrow-like points at the top of the gate twelve feet above him. With a pair of bolt cutters in hand, he walked along the gate and approached the main entrance, chained shut with multiple padlocks.

"Someone's coming!" Adam said nervously.

The group froze as Ben whipped around. Farther down the road, nothing could be seen. "Where? I don't see a thing," he said quietly but intensely.

Adam stared ahead some more, squinting his eyes. "I-I don't know. I thought I saw someone."

"No more false alarms," Ben said. He then turned back to his sister, Elizabeth, and asked her how the place looked.

"It's clear," she said. "As far as I can tell."

"All right. Let's get in there," Ben said, clasping his hands together. He signaled to Scott to use his bolt cutters, but Scott was barely able to see where to cut. "I could use some light here."

Elizabeth looked at Ben, concerned. "Keep flashlight usage to a minimum. We could be spotted."

Ben nodded and pulled his flashlight from his bag. "I'll be careful."

He then approached Scott and knelt down, cupping the light with his hands, just enough for Scott to see several rusty padlocks over the thick chains around the gate. He cut the first lock, squeezing with all his might. It snapped off the chain, with links much thicker than the padlocks. He then went to the next one and did the same, and soon they were in.

The cracked concrete walkway took them through an underpass of spreading tree branches that seemed to reach out for them. Ahead, beyond the bushes and ankle-high weeds, they could see the shape of a fountain, wrapped in vines, with weeds sprouting at its base. They entered a courtyard with grass growing between cracks in its foundation.

"We're close," Ben said as they continued forward under a dark sky.

The looming, shadowed shape of a massive structure lay ahead. Ben turned on his flashlight, exposing the gritty surface of a two-story mansion, windows boarded up with old plywood. He approached the steps and turned off his flashlight as everyone gathered around.

"All right, folks. We brought crowbars for a reason."

He paused and glanced at the seemingly impenetrable fortress before them, its roof arch forming a tremendous summit, high like a steeple. The night air was quiet beyond the distant chirping of crickets.

"Look, I think there's a side door here," Adam called out from a canopied entryway leading to a vast three-door garage to the side. "It's all boarded up, but I'm pretty sure it's a side door."

He slipped off his backpack and pulled out a crowbar. The others approached the garage as Adam jammed the crowbar behind the plywood and heaved, gritting his teeth. The wood began to crack, pulling away from the side framing.

Adam and Scott stepped forward with their crowbars to assist. Working together, they tore the plywood from the entrance, revealing a door with exotic engravings and layers of chipped paint. They were getting close.

"All right, stand back," Scott said, his arm extended, as if pushing them back. He stuck his crowbar into the tiny gap near the deadbolt and then kicked at the door with full force, splintering it open with a resounding crack. He stumbled forward and grabbed the frame, brandishing his flashlight and shining it into the garage while catching his breath.

"Good work," Ben said from behind him.

Scott nodded. "It's a mess in here," he said, squinting ahead. The massive garage was full of boxes and cobwebs hanging from the walls. Inside, the air was dry and stale. The group walked in, scanning the room with their flashlights.

"What's in all the boxes?" Adam asked, looking around.

"Who the hell knows," Scott answered.

Excited, Adam continued. "We should open them and see what's inside."

"Not now," Ben said from the front of the line. "We need to find the ballroom where the murders took place. It's almost time."

“Fine,” Adam said, brushing his shaggy hair to the side. His ball cap had fallen off some time ago.

They reached the end of the carport, where they found another door leading inside. Ben turned the brass knob, but the door was locked. Elizabeth brushed the cobwebs off her clothing as Adam scratched his head in a panic. “They're in my hair!” he said.

“Calm down,” Elizabeth said, lightly brushing her hand across his hair. “You're okay.”

Ben stuck his crowbar into the side of the door and kicked it open. Once inside, he shined his flashlight around the room, only to see an old, empty kitchen before them. Some empty pots lay scattered across the dusty countertops. The lack of airflow and the smell of warped wood and mildew made it feel as though they had entered a tomb.

The group continued past the kitchen to a dark, narrow hall with stained walls and debris strewn along the cracked tile floor. Chandeliers hung from the high, vaulted ceilings, covered in cobwebs. They entered a large room that resembled an open bay or reception area. Elizabeth looked around at its encompassing walls and identified it as the ballroom.

“We're here,” she said. “This is where it happened.”

There were a few tables and chairs stacked in the far right corner of the room. She approached the pile and pulled at a small, dusty table, dragging it across the room. “This should do nicely. Let's go ahead and get started.”

They littered the dusty ballroom with glow sticks from their backpacks, illuminating the center of the room, where they pulled together chairs, setting them around the table. There were several more rooms to explore, but none as important as the one in which they stood. Adam pulled out a tape recorder from his pack, as Scott unzipped the bag containing their bulky camcorder. Such definitive proof of the supernatural was sure to make a name for themselves.

Heavy winds grew outside, beating against the house as thunder rumbled in the distance. A storm was approaching, and its foreboding presence only heightened their sense of urgency and anticipation of things to come.

Adam prepared the tape recorder as Scott mounted their RCA VHS camcorder onto its tripod. He switched on the mounted camera light, testing it as a bright beam flowed across the dusty table and chairs. Distant thunder crackled outside. The chandeliers suddenly began to sway with a subtle creaking.

Adam looked up, spooked. "It's getting weird in here, guys. Maybe we should just hurry this up."

"Agreed," Elizabeth said.

The group gathered around the table under the beam of the camera light and faint illumination from the glow sticks strewn about the floor. A blast of lightning startled them as the impending storm intensified. Static buzzed from the sound recorder as the red camcorder light blinked.

"All right, group," Ben said, seated now like the others. "We've traveled a long way to be here. Let's get started."

Elizabeth held her hands out and tilted her head. "I can feel the negative energy in this room. It's growing by the minute."

"I can definitely feel a presence too," Scott said.

"Lots of rage," Adam added with his eyes closed.

Another booming crash of thunder erupted outside, sending tremors through the house. The creaking sway of the chandeliers intensified as faint, indistinguishable sounds echoed from all over the house, from above, and from both halls leading from the vast foyer. With the windows boarded up, the inside of the house was a strange, pitch black, beyond any artificial light provided by the group. One look into the surrounding darkness was a reminder of how alone they were in that house, but as the group settled in, they felt not only the presence of each other, but also that of forces beyond their control.

"Everyone just stay calm," Ben said from the head of the table.

The group closed their eyes, breathed in, and exhaled in unison. Even in the stale air of the sealed house, they felt a rush of cold air pass through. Their hands lay flat on the table as their heads tilted upward and the chill in the air slowly increased.

With a steady, calm voice, Ben continued. "We are here on the night of June twenty-fifth, 1985, as agents of the paranormal. Our psychic connection is pure and just, and with it we intend to do good by uncovering what occurred in this house ten years ago to the date." Another boom of thunder sounded outside, and droplets of water began to rain down on the house.

Ben continued his oration, his voice rising over the increasing threat of the storm. "I am reaching out to the Bechdel family as a vessel from our world to theirs."

Elizabeth jumped in her seat and opened her eyes, startled. "I felt someone touch me." She looked around to see that everyone's hands were still on the table.

"Just stay calm. We'll reach them in due time," Ben said, eyes still closed.

"I am calm," she said.

"I saw something," Scott said with excitement, pointing ahead. "An apparition by the staircase!"

They turned their heads to look, but saw nothing in the darkness.

Ben resumed his otherworldly communication. "We are here to help you find peace, to discover the truth behind your deaths. Tell us the identity of your killers. Speak and be at rest!"

"There!" Elizabeth said, pointing to the other side of the room.

Everyone turned again to see the faint white glow in the corner. Stunned to silence, the group stared ahead as the white orb drew closer, forming the shape of a little girl in a nightgown. Rendered speechless at its approach, the group froze in the light of the camera. Her tiny bare feet floated above the floor, and her cherubic face was slightly sunken in, with bulging black eyes and her face framed with long, curly locks down to her shoulder.

"Oh my God..." Scott said, jumping out of his chair. He moved to the camera and immediately swung it around to capture images of the girl.

"Sit down, Scott," Elizabeth said in a panic, but the girl had vanished.

Ben, Elizabeth, and Adam sat at the table, glaring at Scott in disbelief.

"You didn't..." Ben said. "Please tell me that you didn't just lose her."

"I'm sorry!" Scott said.

Ben swung his head around, scanning the room. "Julie? Julie, are you there?" He paused as rain continued to descend on the house in a relentless downpour. "Julie? Can you talk to us? We're only here to help."

Suddenly, the camera light exploded, sending sparks into the air. Scott stumbled back with a scream and covered his face. The glow sticks on the floor flickered out, one by one, slowly turning the room dark. Their heads rose to see the chandelier directly above them light up, with the bulbs bright yellow.

"Focus, everyone," Ben said, urging calm. "We came here for a reason, remember?"

"How long has this place been without power?" Adam asked, mouth agape.

"Ten years, I imagine," Scott answered.

"Don't be frightened," Elizabeth said, watching the chandelier in wonder with everyone else. "They're reaching out to us. Everything is going as planned." The words had barely left her mouth when the flashing bulbs of the chandelier faded out, plunging the room back into darkness.

"*Escape...*" a faint, unseen voice whispered, freezing them to their seats. "*Run...*"

MEMORIES

Redwood, Indiana, October 2016

Curtis flew down the road in their Ford Expedition, with Mary in the passenger seat and a concerned Theo in the back. Pastor Phil's memorial service hadn't gone exactly as planned. Mary had had her most significant psychic episode yet, being inundated with fragments of the past. The experience had exhausted her, leaving her barely conscious, with several stunned attendees watching her leave the First Church of Redwood in haste with Curtis and Theo at her side.

The key, it seemed, was Mayor Taylor. Long suspicious of his involvement in the Bechdel murders, Mary had bumped into the mayor as they were nearing Phil's open casket. The shake of his hand had sent her into an unexpected semiconscious state in which she saw things, clues that pointed to a conspiracy larger than she could have ever imagined.

"What happened back there, Mary?" Curtis said, gripping the wheel. "Are you all right?"

"Where are we going?" she asked, her eyelids heavy.

"The hospital," Curtis said. "This has gone far enough."

"Why?" Mary said, rubbing her head.

Curtis swerved through a curve in the road and glanced at her with surprise. "Look at yourself. You nearly passed out back there again. We're going to find out why."

Theo leaned forward, carefully interjecting. "These visions... sometimes they take their toll on a subject."

Curtis glanced in the rearview mirror, not particularly happy. "Theo, with all due respect, I've been going along with all of your explanations since you got here. We're going to have her checked out, and that is final."

Mary snapped out of her daze, more alert than ever. "I'm fine, Curtis. I promise." But she could already see the hospital in view.

"I don't care," Curtis said, keeping his eyes forward.

"Stop the car," Mary said.

Curtis ignored her while increasing his speed.

"Stop the car!" she repeated.

Curtis shook his head and slowed down, veering onto the shoulder of the road.

"The Taylor family," Theo said from the back. "I know they're involved with all of this."

"It's worse than you think," Mary said, looking back and forth between Curtis and Theo, deeply worried. "It's just like Pastor Phil told me; the conspiracy goes beyond the Taylors. There are others involved, like our realtor, Bob Deckers."

Curtis turned his head to her, deeply skeptical. "What are you talking about?"

"I saw him, Curtis," Mary said, her voice strained. She rubbed her forehead again and sighed.

The car idled, and Curtis turned back onto the road, shaking his head. "You saw him? What, like in a dream?" he asked.

"Mayor Taylor *is* the link," she answered. "I shook his

hand and instantly felt this kinetic energy that unleashed these visions."

"You were pretty out of it for a moment there," Theo added.

Curtis huffed and shifted the car into gear. "Okay, time to get you checked out."

"Please," Mary said, gripping his arm. "Just... give me a moment."

Curtis looked agitated but tried to remain patient. "I don't want to take any chances, okay? This is serious, and I'm very concerned about you."

A semi-truck roared past them, shaking the windows and leaving a burst of air in its wake.

"I'm fine, Curtis. You have to believe me," she said. "Bob Deckers murdered Phil, suffocated him with his own pillow. But that's not all. He was looking for something."

"What else did you see?" Theo asked, urging her on.

Curtis turned and looked out his window, shaking his head. "That's impossible."

"He's not who he seems," Mary added. "The mayor wanted us to move into that house, and Deckers worked with him to make it happen."

"But... why?" Curtis asked. She could see the stunned conflict in his eyes.

"I don't know why just yet," she answered. "But it all fits some kind of pattern."

Curtis glanced into the rearview mirror, feeling a hint of paranoia as Theo leaned forward. "During the service," Theo began, "I saw a vision of my mother in your house, many years ago. She was there with my uncle and their two friends." He smacked the seat next to him. "They were there!"

Mary opened the glove compartment and pulled out the dirty black glove they had found outside Pastor Phil's house. She handed it to Curtis with conviction in her eyes. "This belonged to Bob Deckers. We should go ahead and take it to the police chief and tell him we found it outside Phil's house."

"Are you sure we can trust him?" Theo asked.

Mary turned her head back, took the glove from Curtis, and handed it to Theo, who began examining it.

"That's what we're going to find out," she answered. "Judging by Bob's reaction to the glove, we'll know where he stands."

"Maybe Deckers had to get out of there in a hurry," Theo said, enthusiasm building in his eyes. "We should go to Phil's and investigate. I'm sure more will start coming back to you."

Mary nodded. "It's still a little hazy, but you're probably right." She waved both her hands, fanning her face.

"I want to nail those Taylor bastards," Theo said, clenching his fist.

"Enough. Both of you," Curtis said, reaching for the mysterious glove in Theo's hands. He then took the glove and sighed. "Let's not get too carried away. One thing at a time. First, we have Mary checked out. Second, if you really think Bob Deckers had something to do with this, let *me* talk to him first. I won't let him know anything, but I can read people pretty well." He paused and held one finger in the air like a stern father. "Lastly, I want you both to slow it down, and don't get yourselves in any trouble."

Mary quickly interjected. "All we want to do is have a quick look at Pastor Phil's place. We won't be there long."

"Yeah. We'll be in and out of there in no time," Theo added.

Curtis opened the center console and placed the glove inside, looking up at the eager faces before him. "I'm not a psychic," he began. "I'm just a lawyer with one client." After a short breath, he conceded. "There's something going on in this town, and I want to get to the bottom of it just as much as you. But let's do this smart. We can't run around town making wild accusations."

Theo nodded. "I'll tell you one thing, we definitely have the Taylor brothers' attention now," he said.

"What do you mean?" Curtis asked.

"I think they were hired to take out the Bechdels," Theo said with certainty. "And they're back in town now for a reason."

"And if we're not careful, we could be next," Mary added.

Curtis whipped his head around, confused. "*What?*"

"Julie told me that their killers must be brought to the mansion to lift the curse," Mary said. "We *have* to do something."

Curtis then massaged his temples with a sigh. "I've got to be out of my mind to go along with this."

Mary turned to him, wanting to gain his support. "We need you." She then turned to Theo. "We need each other. We can finally bring peace to that house and justice for its victims."

Curtis thought to himself with the SUV still idling. The overcast sky gradually shifted from blue to a looming gray. "Why would officials of this town conspire to get us into the house in the first place?" he asked, scratching his chin.

"That's what we hope to find out," Mary said.

"And what happened to my mother and uncle," Theo said.

Curtis looked forward, placing both hands on the wheel with a sigh. "All right. I'm on board. Hospital first, then we'll look into this."

Mary agreed as he drove off, hitting the gas a little harder and, a half mile down the road, turning into the Dover County hospital, a large two-story building that looked to be undergoing renovation with sheets covering some of the windows above and railed platform surfaces surrounding the building. However, the full parking lot indicated business as usual.

Mary's mind drifted to her earlier research. She recalled that Mayor Taylor had many relatives working for the county who lived in other towns throughout the area. The Taylors were everywhere. His wealth and influence had spread after the Bechdel murders, beginning with his first successful mayoral election against an already deceased George Bechdel —a position that, forty years later, he still retained.

It was hard to believe that anyone would hold a single office that long without trying to move up the political ladder. Why stay in one place for forty years?

For Mary, the key was in finding out the root of Mayor Taylor's power, how he had acquired it, and how much more he had accumulated over the years. The names most prominent were clear enough: Mayor Taylor and his brothers—Garret, Liam, and Jeffery —Bob Deckers, Pastor Phil, and socialite Beatrice Thaxton. What was the connection? What did they want so badly from Pastor Phil that they had killed him? Or had they?

Mary scoured her mind for the answers, trying to make sense of what she had seen after shaking Mayor Taylor's hand at the funeral. Perhaps Julie's diary would shed more light on her inquiries.

Mary sat atop an examination table with its vinyl cushioning and paper covering, waiting for the doctor to come back. Medical posters hung from the walls around her, and long, fluorescent lights buzzed above. The doctor had run some tests, took her blood, and checked her pulse and vitals. Two hours had passed since they first arrived.

So much for a quick visit, she thought.

The hours lost, she believed, would have been better

spent investigating. Though she was a children's book illustrator and the furthest thing from a detective, Theo's arrival had revealed elements of her abilities she had never known to be present. She could learn from him. She could harness the psychic energy she was certain existed inside her and use it for good.

She waited anxiously for the doctor to return as Curtis and Theo sat in the waiting room, most likely bored out of their minds. Theo was still on the payroll, but that didn't even seem to matter to him anymore. He had grown invested and heavily determined to find out what had happened to his mother.

As Mary began to learn of Redwood's strange record of unsolved crimes, and then considered who was running the town, the list of unsolved cases came as no surprise. She had met the chief of police, Chief Riley, and Deputy Ramirez, a few times, and had liked them and felt as if she could trust them. She did wonder: could they possibly be in on the conspiracy too? She hoped that wasn't the case and was confident that Curtis could get to the bottom of it. Her mind raced as the doctor entered with a chart in hand.

He wore a green polo shirt, an ID card dangling from a lanyard around his neck, black slacks, and black dress shoes. He was Indian, with thick, dark hair and square-framed glasses. He was clean-shaven and polite and spoke to Mary with a methodical calmness that put her at ease.

"Everything looks good so far, Mrs. Malone. But I'm still very concerned about these panic seizures your husband talked about."

Mary waved him off. "It's hard to explain, but it almost feels like that's coming from another part of me." She moved her hands in a circle around her face and head. "Like some kind of aura that can't be physically measured. My mother told me that I was unique when I was younger. That what I had, a psychic awareness, sometimes skipped generations. She said that my great aunt was known to possess psychic abilities. Do you believe in that kind of stuff, Doctor?"

The doctor smiled with nervous laughter while flipping through the pages on his clipboard. "I'm sure the possibilities for all conditions exist out there." He then looked up, almost as though he was holding something back. "I…" he began with a pause.

Mary moved her head forward, wide eyed. "*Yes?*"

"I'm not aware if you already knew this or not, but you're… uh, pregnant."

The words smacked her across the face, leaving a faint tingling. She'd long had her suspicions, especially after what Phil had told her, but she had showed no signs yet and felt it was still too early to tell.

"How many weeks?" she asked, barely above a whisper. She wiped at the tears streaming down her cheeks.

"Looks like you're still in the first trimester. Congratulations!" His tone changed when he saw the sadness and worry on her face. "Is… is this a planned pregnancy?"

"Yes and no," Mary said, shaking her head. She wiped at her tears and stood up, trying to hold in her emotions. "It's just… so much is going on right now, and I'm very worried."

"I understand," the doctor said. "If it makes you feel any better, you're in very good health."

"Thank you, Doctor," she said, feeling slightly nauseous.

Julie had mentioned something about the pregnancy, which Mary had dismissed. The spirits in the house were well aware, it seemed, of what she had been denying. She wondered what that meant and why they seemed interested in the first place.

A child, she thought. *A child so soon after the...*

She moved her hand across her stomach, unable to even

think of what had happened only a few short months ago. She didn't want to go through something like that again.

"Thanks again," she said, looking up.

"Don't worry," he said, clearly noticing her troubled demeanor. "I have a feeling that you and your husband are going to be very happy." He smiled and opened the door for her, walking her out to the lobby, where she found Curtis sitting in one of the chairs with one leg resting on his knee and his head down as he scrolled through his phone. The doctor told him that Mary's vitals were good but to come back immediately if she suffered another "fatigue episode."

The doctor then offered his parting words. "Congratulations!" he said, shaking Curtis's hand. Curtis stood up, confused, as the doctor walked away with a smile.

"Congratulations?" he asked Mary. "What is he talking about?" His face looked even more perplexed when he noticed Mary's watering eyes.

"Oh," she said nervously. "It's true, Curtis. I really am pregnant."

"*What?*" he said loudly while holding his chest. "Are you sure?"

Mary reached out for him, helping him regain his composure. She noticed people in the lobby watching them. "Yes, but keep your voice down."

Theo approached with a can of soda, unsure of what had just transpired.

"You guys okay?" he asked.

"We're fine," Mary said.

"Mary is pregnant," Curtis said. He hugged her tightly, and she could feel his warmth against her body.

"Um… Congratulations," Theo said, sipping his soda. "I'll give you guys a minute here and go check out the snack bar."

Theo walked away as Curtis released Mary and backed away, his shock all too apparent. "This is big, Mary. I mean, you told me you thought you were pregnant before… but with what Pastor Phil had said and everything…I just…I didn't know what to think."

He pulled her closer for another hug.

"This is a blessing," he said softly into her ear.

"I know," she said with her voice trailing. "I hope so."

TRESPASS

Redwood, Indiana, June 25, 1985

Decades before Curtis and Mary had made the Bechdel home theirs, an incident had occurred there, never to be discovered. Four amateur paranormal investigators were eager to discover the secrets within the mansion, only to face an entity far more dangerous than what they could have imagined.

"Run..." the whispery voice had warned them. But it was too late.

The group huddled together quietly, waiting in heightened anticipation, when suddenly a startling pounding shook the front door.

"Holy shit," Adam said.

"Everyone just stay calm," Ben said. They could barely see a hand in front of their faces as another pounding, this one even louder, caused them to jump.

"Who's out there?" Adam asked, shifting in his seat and calling out in a panicked tone. "Someone's out there! Who is it?" Another heavy rap followed and the doorframe groaned, as though a SWAT team was trying to break their way in.

Elizabeth stood up, palms flat on the table, ready to run. "We need to get out of here."

Both Scott and Adam rose in haste, grabbing their backpacks. Their chairs squeaked against the dirty tile floor and nearly fell back. Another resounding strike rattled the door on its loosening hinges as its thick wooden panels began to separate from one another.

Adam held his crowbar up like a baseball bat as Scott took the camera off the tripod. Ben switched his flashlight on and pointed it toward the foyer, where the banging continued.

"Did you hear those voices?" Elizabeth said, backpack over her shoulder, ready to make a break for it.

For the first time that evening, a collective fear came over the generally fearless group. After a brief silence, the foyer erupted with a blast and several large people stormed into the house, with lights mounted to their rifles shining throughout the room. Adam was the first to bolt, sprinting toward the kitchen in a fury. Elizabeth shielded her face from the weapon lights, squinting. The silhouettes of men emerged, taking positions around the room and closing in on the stunned group.

"Who are these people?" Scott cried out. "Ben, talk to me."

"I don't know..." Ben said, his face pale with worry and fear.

Lights shined into their faces from all sides as rain continued to pour outside.

"Don't move!" a man's voice shouted. Their group's hands went immediately into the air as unseen hands grabbed the backs of their shirts and yanked them away from table.

The armed men threw them against the wall by the staircase. Ben, Scott, and Elizabeth stood there shaking as the weapon lights continued to blind them.

Adam screamed from afar, emerging into the room with two armed men at his side.

"Found this one trying to escape out of the garage," one of the men said to a tall, shadowy figure who had been standing back, watching the proceedings like a detached observer.

"Easy, assholes!" Adam shouted as he spun around, enraged.

"What is this all about?" Ben asked the men calmly.

The group's eyes adjusted to see that they were surrounded by six men, their faces largely concealed under the shadow of their baseball caps. Having burst into the house from outside, they were wet from the rain. Their apparent leader, with big, broad shoulders and a square jaw of stubble, stepped forward and lit a cigar, blowing smoke in the direction of the group.

The red glow of his cigar revealed piercing eyes and thick eyebrows arched downward with contempt. A few puffs later, he moved closer to the group and offered them an amiable smile.

"I don't believe any of you are from around here, are you?" he asked in a low, gravelly voice. He puffed on his cigar long and hard as the group looked at each other, backs against the wall, still reeling from the shock of it all.

"Who are you?" Ben asked, speaking up first.

"Now, now," the man said, blowing out a long stream of smoke. "Let's start with you first."

Elizabeth watched as the men confiscated both the audio recorder and video camera, shoving them into bags.

"My name is Ben Stone, and these are my friends from the University of Cincinnati. We're..."

"You're trespassing," the man said, cutting him off. "That's what you're doing."

"We're investigating," Ben said with defiance.

"Please, sir," Elizabeth said, stepping forward. "I'm sure this is all one big misunderstanding."

"I don't doubt it," the man said, turning to her, inches from her face. She could smell the cigar smoke as it drifted down in a haze around them.

"Are you the police?" Elizabeth asked, confused and disoriented.

The cigar man paced from one end of the group to the other, puffing away. "You mentioned something about a misunderstanding," he began. "So let me see if I got this right. You traveled from afar to break into a house clearly marked off-limits." He paused, examining the confiscated video and audio equipment. "I suppose you came here to capture ghosts or something like that. Did you find anything?"

No one answered as the cigar man continued. "You've trespassed onto a historical site of great importance to our fair town. You've violated this space with your utter disregard for the sacred ground before you."

"Sir, if I could…" Ben began.

"I'm not finished!" the man said, halting. He then resumed his pacing as silence fell over the frightened group. "I want IDs first. Then we'll get to the bottom of this."

In unison, the men pointed their rifles at the group.

"You heard the man. Let's see those wallets!" another man shouted.

The group nervously dug into their pockets and pulled out their wallets, searching for their driver's licenses. The men rounded them up and handed them over to the cigar man, who flipped through them, clearly amused. "Cincinnati, eh? Well, you're a little ways from home." He pocketed the licenses, perplexing the group further as he turned to them with a friendlier tone. "I'm Frederick Taylor, mayor of Redwood. My police department received a call about a disturbance at the old Bechdel estate. We don't take such offenses lightly, especially from folks looking to desecrate the home of one of Redwood's most cherished families."

"That wasn't our intent, sir—" Ben tried to add.

"Quiet!" the mayor seethed, pivoting around. He paused, allowing for calm. "I especially don't like being pulled out of bed at this time of the evening, especially with a storm like this raging outside." He looked at the group, seemingly ready to wrap things up, or so they hoped.

"We're incredibly sorry," Elizabeth said. "This is a part of a project of ours. An investigative documentary."

The mayor leaned closer to her with great interest. "Oh? You don't say! A school project?" Suddenly, one of his men tugged on the side of his coat, showing him the video camera. He then looked through the viewfinder with one eye as his face went from amusement to starkly serious.

"What is it?" Scott said abruptly. "What do you see?"

The mayor backed away from the camera slowly and handed it back to his man. He then scanned the room up and down with a new look of worry and dread on his face. "Gentlemen, it's about time we leave this place." He backed toward the door, signaling to his men. "It's not safe here."

"What about them?" one of the men asked, rifle pointed at the group.

The mayor stopped and thought to himself. "Well... do what needs to be done, Clayton. Take 'em out in the woods and finish it."

The group could hardly believe their ears. "What did he say?" Scott asked, stepping forward, astonished. "What the hell did you just say?"

A blow to his head sent him crashing to the ground. Elizabeth opened her mouth to scream, but found herself too shocked to make a sound. Scott struggled slowly to his feet as Ben helped him up. Adam started to step forward, but Scott mouthed, "I'm OK." Pointing their rifles, the men herded Adam, Ben, Scott, and Elizabeth into a tight circle.

Their legs moved forward as the men pushed them to the rear of the house, then out toward the backyard, with the barrels of rifles and shotguns against their backs.

They're just trying to scare us, right? That's all. Just send us a message?

Elizabeth closed her eyes and searched for guidance from the spirits, anything that would let her know what to do and how to escape what seemed to be their awful fate.

ENCOUNTERS

Mary woke the next morning with Julie's diary resting on her lap. She had neared the end of it, surprised by the level of detail written in its small, faded pages. Julie had chronicled a troubling time for her family, leading up to their infamous murder. The fate of the Bechdels was a story of intrigue, suspicion, and increasing paranoia. The family had something of great value hidden in the house, and there were plenty of characters from town trying to get it.

Julie herself knew little about it, but she often spoke of a secret underground room somewhere in the house, well-hidden from rogue outsiders—a place where her parents stored a vast fortune dating back generations. Of course, as Julie stated in her diary, she had never seen the supposed room and was beginning to doubt its existence.

She wrote: "Travis told me again today about this treasure room, but when I asked him to show me where it was, he refused. I told him that I didn't believe that it was even real, that it was just something he and John and Alex made up to mess with me. He said, 'Suit yourself,' and walked off. I don't even know why I bother sometimes.

"Mother and Father haven't let me out of the house for weeks. WEEKS! I'm a prisoner. They let me go in the backyard sometimes, but that's about it. They pulled me from school, won't let me see my friends, and worst of all, they forgot my birthday last week. Can you believe that? Who forgets their daughter's birthday? Mother apologized the next day, over and over again, and said that they've been so busy, they missed it. She promised me a big birthday party, which hasn't happened yet.

"I told her that it was okay and that turning eleven was no big deal. She was pretty nice to me the rest of the day, and I could tell she felt really bad. I just wish I had someone to talk to. Father says things will get better soon, right after the election. I don't know why he had to run for mayor. The guy who is running against my dad is a real jerk. I think my parents are afraid of him.

"His name is Mr. Taylor, and he showed up here the other day to talk to my dad. Apparently, it didn't go well and there was shouting and all sorts of threats. I don't know what to think about it anymore. Just seems like there's a black cloud over our house that won't go away. I hope things get better. I really do."

Mary took a deep breath, feeling the delicate texture of the signed passage, and turning to the next page. Though there were many pages torn and missing from the diary, Mary was able to piece together the fragmented history of a trying time for the Bechdels, as seen through the eyes of their young daughter.

Julie's parting words projected a deep apprehension about the dinner party soon to come. She spoke of a rushed engagement between her oldest brother, Travis, and his high school sweetheart, Katelyn Drake. Julie vowed to uncover the secrecy surrounding her parents' mysterious fortune, their interest in the Drake family, and her father's decision to join the mayoral race. Through all of this, there had been several references to a Mr. Taylor, who had worked for her parents at one point years prior as a landscaper, but was let go for undisclosed reasons.

Mary considered these tidbits to be engrossing, but she was no closer to discovering the killers than before, though her main suspect, Mayor Taylor, was looking more likely by the day. She lowered the diary and looked around the room, hoping for any signs of Julie. Mary had yet to figure out what triggered the spirits to action, but nonetheless, she always felt as though she was being watched.

She looked down, knowing that she was nearing the last of Julie's entries. She wished there were more to draw from. She wished Julie would simply appear, spirit form and all, and explain to her what happened on that horrible evening of June 25, 1975.

Mary began reading: "During breakfast, Father yelled at Travis and sent him away after Travis expressed, for like the fifth time, doubts about getting married. I'd never seen Father so angry. Well, not in a while. My parents both seem stressed and on edge. This stupid mayor election is close, but it looks as if Father has a good chance.

"I heard my parents talking in the lounge the other evening. It sounded like they were arguing. Father revealed to Mother that Mr. Taylor tried to pay him to drop out of the race. Father refused the money, which I admired him for. Mother seemed upset, though. She said that the Taylors were bad people, and that Father was playing with fire. I don't know. It's all so ridiculous. Why can't we be a normal family? Why are there so many secrets among us? Why did my parents forget my birthday? So many questions.

"Mother is running around this morning with the cooks and servers like a madwoman. So much is riding on this dinner party, she says. Why are they so concerned with impressing the Drakes? They're people just like us, right? Travis told me that sometimes he feels like he's being used. He really likes Katelyn. She's beautiful, and they've been together for two years. But, it's like, my parents want to join the families just so we can be even more rich and powerful, or something like that. And with this secret room, now I don't know what to think.

"I can already hear everyone downstairs, running around. It's going to be a long day. I just wish I had someone I could share all these thoughts with, all these worries. On a day of such celebration and so many people, I've never felt so alone. I'm going to find out what my parents are up to, and I'm going to find out about the Drakes, mark my words. Detective Julie is on the case."

Mary stared at the last page as a single tear dropped from each of her eyes. She closed the diary, holding it close, and stepped out of bed, unsure where Curtis was. She was fairly certain that Julie's room was close, though she hadn't yet identified which room belonged to which sibling. She and Curtis were in the master bedroom, which she was certain once belonged to George and Anabelle Bechdel. The question was, which room had Julie slept in?

What room had she been forced to run into as her parents and their party guests were being massacred? From what window did she climb out, trying to escape, only to be found and executed without mercy? Anger rose in Mary's gut as she pushed open her bedroom door and walked down the hall past a row of rooms to her right, many of them still empty. She could hear Curtis pacing around downstairs. His voice was upbeat and chipper.

"It's in the earliest stages, but the doctor confirmed that she's pregnant," he said. "I know, isn't it amazing?"

There was a pause as Mary crept forward, wondering who he was talking to.

"She's sleeping right now, Mom, but I'll be sure to have her call you once she's up and ready."

With her question answered, Mary stopped at the fourth room to her left and slowly pushed the door open. Inside, its floors were barren. Sunlight beamed in through a grand window, and within this space she could feel Julie's presence.

This was her room, Mary thought, imagining it decorated with Julie's things: her bed, toys, and books.

She stepped inside with her bare feet touching the ground. Her hair was down at her shoulders, and she was wearing a T-shirt and plaid pajama pants that she couldn't remember changing into the night before. When did she fall asleep? Why hadn't Curtis woken her?

Sunlight hit her face as she approached the window and stared outside into the courtyard below. Their Ford Expedition was parked next to the empty fountain and Theo's Oldsmobile. She was relieved to see that Theo was still here. He seemed genuine and trustworthy enough, but Mary found herself worried each morning that he would be gone, and she couldn't understand why. Perhaps because Theo was a loner and the case before them was already spiraling out of control. Just as Theo crossed her mind, his voice sounded behind her.

"Morning, Mary," he said.

She whipped around, startled to see him leaning in the doorway. She said hello and asked if he had slept well.

He was already dressed for the day in his collared shirt, jeans, and beige jacket. His beard had grown thicker on his youthful face. He held onto his creased fedora, which he had been wearing less and less. Mary wondered if the hat was, overall, just part of his image as a paranormal investigator. Around her, it seemed, he could be more himself.

"Tossed and turned for a little bit," he admitted. "Just couldn't get this image of my mother out of my mind."

"I understand," Mary said, clutching the diary. She held it out for him to see. "Julie wrote about the Taylors in her diary."

Theo's eyes widened. "What did she say?"

"Apparently there were some real issues between the Bechdels and the Taylors. Julie's mother warned her father not to 'play with fire,' as she put it."

Theo shook his head in disbelief. "How is it possible that the authorities never made that connection? How is Mayor Taylor even on the street today?"

Mary turned back to the window, envisioning Julie's frantic escape. She could feel the girl's fear, desperation, and primal urge to survive. She placed a hand against the wall, balancing herself as she looked down, hair covering her face.

"You okay?" Theo asked, stepping forward.

"Yeah… I'm fine," she answered, raising her head. "Some politicians think that they're above the law, and in Mayor Taylor's case, he clearly is." She then stood up straight and turned around, conviction shining in her eyes. "But we're going to change that."

Theo and Mary later joined Curtis at the breakfast table, where he had bagels and coffee waiting for them. He was alert and energetic, and Mary could sense that his mind was in a hundred different places at once as he jumped from one point to another. "I want you to take it easy, Mary," he said, taking a sip from his coffee mug. "Have Theo investigate for all I care. Things are different now."

He looked off in another direction as Mary sat still across from him, feeling defensive. Theo wisely stayed out of it and picked at his blueberry bagel with a steaming cup of coffee at his elbow.

"Nothing changes, Curtis," Mary said.

Curtis's stern expression of concern remained unwavering. "We can't take any chances this time." He then turned to Theo. "Can't you go out to Phil's yourself? I'd prefer Mary to cut out some of this activity."

Mary rose from her chair, pushing it out behind her. "I'm going, and that's all there is to it." Curtis started to say something, only to be cut off. "I appreciate your concern, but I'm not sitting this one out and letting the Taylor family get away with murder."

With little recourse available, Curtis backed down, only to offer a point of contention. "One day, Mary. One day of playing detective, and that's it." He cut the air with his hand as if delivering the final word. "We'd be better off getting out of this town completely, if you ask me."

Mary had never heard him talk that way before. The mansion and the town had been a dream come true for Curtis and until now, he had not disparaged the idea. The situation, it seemed, was getting to him, especially since hearing about her pregnancy.

Surprising Mary, he set the mysterious glove recovered at Phil's on the table, and next to the glove, he placed a Ziploc bag. He sealed the glove inside as they watched quietly. "I'm actually curious what Bob will say about all of this," he said, switching gears.

Theo took a sip of coffee and cut in. "You're not actually going to accuse him of murder right away, are you?"

Curtis scoffed. "I think my years practicing law might just afford me some tact in these matters."

Theo raised his hands apologetically. "Sorry, I didn't mean it like that."

Curtis waved him off with a laugh. "I know you didn't. Now, can we please wrap this thing up today and be done with it?"

He rose from the table as Mary placed her hand on his arm, causing him to pause. She looked up at him with unease. "This is serious, Curtis. The Taylor family could come after us just like they did the Bechdels."

Curtis moved his hands up and rubbed his temples. "Which is why we're going to the police," he responded.

"The same police who have let the Taylors rule over this town unchallenged?" Mary asked as Theo again kept to himself.

"Okay!" Curtis said, holding up the glove. "I'll confront Bob and see what he knows." Already sensing Mary's concern, he added, "I'll be careful."

"Thank you," she said.

Suddenly, her cell phone rang on the kitchen counter where it had been charging. She walked into the kitchen and grabbed her phone, looking at the screen. It was an unknown number, and she hesitated for a moment before answering. "Hello?" she said, softly.

"Mrs. Malone?" a man's voice said.

She backed toward the sink, elbow resting on her other hand with the phone against her ear.

"Yes... this is she."

"Yes, Mrs. Malone. This is Dr. Patel."

She knew she recognized his voice and felt instant relief, though she didn't pause to think of why he would be calling her first thing in the morning. "Yes, Dr. Patel. How can I help you?"

His first words, "I don't want to alarm you," did the exact opposite. Mary could already feel her heart rate increasing. He continued: "I was looking at some of your test results, and I'm a little concerned." There was a slight pause as he continued. "Nothing major. I just think you should come by as soon as you can."

Even as the warm morning sun radiated through the window above the sink, she felt light-headed, at a loss for words. "What is it, Doctor?"

"Just a precaution," he said. "It's been a little difficult to pinpoint your current trimester with this pregnancy because… your fetus. It belongs to…"

"The fetus?" she said. "What are you talking about?."

He paused again and then spoke in a low hissing tone Mary had yet to hear from him. "It belongs to us."

Mary lowered her phone and looked around the kitchen as the lights flickered, chilling her to the bone. "Julie," she whispered, closing her eyes and balling her fists. "Where are you? How did you know about this? Tell me what's going on."

There was nothing there—no apparition or visions. She felt strangely alone even with Curtis and Theo in the next room. There was a pause in her thoughts when suddenly, the cabinets above her blew open again without warning, launching plates and dishes into the air, inches from Mary's face.

She frantically ducked, falling to the ground just as the dishes smashed into the wall behind her, a cacophonous riot of sound jolting her sensibilities. She heard Curtis call out to her and rush toward the kitchen, but the door slammed shut in his face, locking him out.

"Mary!" he shouted, banging on the door to no avail. "Mary!"

She slowly rose to her feet, shielding her face from projectiles. The cabinet doors slowly swayed as dishes settled on the floor around her in pieces. Mary stared forward, defiant and without fear. Both Curtis and Theo were still at the door, pounding and yelling, trying to break in, but the barrier was impenetrable.

"Where's Julie?" Mary demanded. She felt a slight chill, a presence, brushing against her shoulders. She stared ahead and saw a faint orb-like glow that formed into the image of a woman. At least half of a woman. Her pupils were completely black, and there was anger across her sunken face as her features contorted into a demonic look.

"You'll not see Julie," the figure hissed. "You will talk to me."

"Mrs. Bechdel…?" Mary said, gripping the counter behind her.

"Quiet!" the figure said as coldness consumed the room, causing Mary to shiver. "Enough of your stalling. You have one day or we'll claim the child as our own."

Mary stepped forward, incensed. "How dare you threaten me!"

Suddenly, a gust of hot air flew into her face, followed by a deafening roar. For a moment, everything went black, and Mary found herself sitting on the floor, dazed, just as Curtis kicked the kitchen door open and rushed inside. With Theo following, they found Mary on the floor next to the sink with dishes surrounding her.

"What in the hell just happened?" Curtis asked, helping her up.

"I don't know," Mary said. "But we need to figure this thing out or escape before it's too late."

INVESTIGATION

They fled the house, shaken and disturbed, with the weeks blurring together. Julie's diary, the spirits, the Bechdels, the Taylors, Pastor Phil, Bob Deckers, and the town of Redwood—everything, it seemed, was connected. Mary was eager to discover the patterns that existed, buried within decades of deceit. The plan was clear enough for the time being. Mary and Theo would go to Pastor Phil's house. Curtis would handle Bob Deckers. In the interim, they weren't sure what hung in the balance.

There was no telling how close they were going to get with so much on the line. Mary was confident, however, that the conspiracy came down to a political hit job against a family considered a threat to the powers that be.

They drove into town that morning, surprised to see Main Street full of celebration as cars and residents clogged the streets. It was the day of the much-heralded Redwood Annual Autumn Festival. Mary had forgotten all about it.

A large banner hung over the street reading: 50th Annual Redwood Autumn Festival. There were vendor booths along the sidewalks, offering homemade pumpkin cupcakes, pumpkin-scented candles, and handicrafts.

Stacks of hay and carved pumpkins and stuffed scarecrows marked all corners of the street. In the town square, a large stage had been erected, with a bluegrass band entertaining an enthusiastic crowd. Families were everywhere, strolling through the park and along the storefronts. Children with painted faces carried balloons as couples walked hand-in-hand under a vibrant blue sky with just enough puffy clouds to shield the sun.

Festival-goers looked too preoccupied to care what Mary, Curtis, and Theo were up to. Curtis slowed the car, frustrated with the traffic, as they neared the business district where Bob Deckers's real estate office awaited. He turned left at an intersection, taking another detour to avoid the blocked-off roads. Mary looked out her window and caught a glimpse of several police officers patrolling the streets on foot. The town's chief of police, Chief Riley, and his partner, Deputy Ramirez, were the only police Mary had seen since moving there. Apparently on that day, a bigger presence had been employed.

Mary envied the townspeople who seemed content in their obliviousness. But she was on an important mission. Peace would come soon enough...she hoped. As they turned right onto an empty side street, Mary's eyes were peeled, keeping watch for the mayor or his brothers. She believed that, for the most part, the mayor's sons were not involved in his criminal enterprise.

They never entered her mind. His brothers, however, were another story. They were dangerous, deadly people. She gripped the armrest as their SUV approached Deckers Realty on the corner at the end of the block. His bottom-floor office was housed with several others in the vintage five-story brick building. It was only a couple of days ago that Mary and Curtis had been in his office, receiving assurances from Bob that nothing was wrong with the house. Mary believed him to be a liar and a snake.

Curtis pulled to the side and parked next to a meter. He sat for a moment as the vehicle idled, gathering his thoughts. Mary looked out her window, trying to see inside the office through the glass-door entrance, but it was tinted too dark. The building looked ominous, and a change of plans suddenly came to her. She turned to Curtis as he pulled the black glove from the middle console, still sealed in its Ziploc bag.

"Why don't we just stick together?" she said. "We'd be a lot safer that way."

Curtis shrugged. "Relax. I can handle Bob."

Theo placed his hand on the back of Curtis's seat and leaned forward. "I think Mary has a point there, Curtis. I wouldn't trust that guy as far as you could throw him."

Curtis sighed. "You don't think that I know that?"

"Of course we do," Mary said as air from the dashboard vents cooled her face. "I just don't want anything to happen."

Curtis opened his door. "Okay," he said sarcastically. "Let's all go and talk to him. I'm sure that won't make him suspicious or anything."

Mary turned to Theo, searching for the answers. Curtis was right. If they were all to approach Deckers at once, he would probably be more reluctant to talk. Bob and Curtis knew each other, had had drinks together, and at the outset had appeared to be friends. Perhaps it was better for Curtis to go alone after all. Mary opened her door and stepped out of the car as Curtis met her on the sidewalk.

"We could wait for you here," she said. "How about that?"

Curtis slipped the glove into his front jacket pocket and then touched her shoulders. "I don't even know if he's here. I called his office and told him that I was going to swing by but didn't say when."

Mary felt uneasy about the call. She had wanted to surprise Deckers, not give him notice of their visit. Sensing her worry, Curtis kissed her lightly on the cheek and backed away. "I'll be fine. I'm sure whatever he's into, he's not going to get away with it."

"Thanks for doing this," she said, offering a parting hug. "I'm sorry."

"For what?" Curtis asked, surprised.

"For getting you wrapped up in this."

Curtis looked at her with a steady, dignified expression. He wouldn't have it. "Someone has played us, Mary, and I'm going to find out who and why." He paused, with a reassuring hand on her arm. "But I'm not going to announce anything to Bob, or make any accusations. I just want to read him, see how he comes off. Just like in a courtroom."

Mary told him to be careful as he waved and walked toward the building. She looked around, feeling as though she was being watched, but the street was mainly empty. Curtis went to the door and pulled on it, but it was locked. He cupped his hands and tried to look through the glass and then knocked. He turned back to Mary with his hands out.

"Not here yet," he said. He knocked again, waiting patiently, but no one came. He backed away from the door and walked toward Mary while pointing across the street. "Think I'll just hang out in the coffee shop until he gets here."

Despite not wanting to split up, Mary knew that she and Theo couldn't wait around much longer. "Okay," she said. "We'll head out to Phil's then, while the festival is still going on."

She walked around to the driver's side as Curtis followed. The street was strangely quiet, except for the faint echo of bluegrass music and random cheering echoing in the air. It was more than likely that Bob himself was at the festival, but something told Mary that he would be returning soon. She climbed into the SUV as Theo opened the rear-passenger door, stepped out, and got into the front seat. Mary brought her window down and Curtis leaned in, looking at them through the shade of his sunglasses.

"You two be careful, okay?" he said.

"We'll do our best," Mary said, "and hopefully not come back empty-handed."

Curtis tapped his fingers above the door. "I'll call you when Bob shows up. Certainly don't want to spend all day waiting in a coffee shop." He gave her a quick kiss and told them good luck. Mary rolled her window up as Curtis headed toward the modest coffee shop across the street. Its sign above the door read "Ben's Roasted Coffee House" in big green letters.

"Well, we've accomplished nothing so far," Theo said, pulling his fedora off his head and tossing it in the back seat.

Mary watched Curtis entering the coffee shop and turned to Bob's building. *Where was he?* Maybe he got the hint and fled town, an option Mary was seriously considering.

Pastor Phil's words came back to haunt her. *"They will follow you wherever you go,"* he had once said. She wondered if he was referring to the living or the dead.

They drove to the next stop light, leaving Curtis at the coffee shop. Pastor Phil's house wasn't too far, but they didn't have much time. Mary felt trapped, but she wasn't afraid. She pushed all her doubts aside with a singular focus on finding out the truth. "We can do this," she said to Theo. "We have to."

Theo nodded without reply and then about halfway down the street, he laughed to himself.

"What?" Mary asked.

"Nothing," he said. "You're so into this. It's inspiring."

Mary smiled. It was a compliment, she supposed. Perhaps she was more confident than before. If that was the case, she'd need every last ounce.

* * *

Phil's farmhouse looked empty, and that was good news. Mary parked in the front alongside the wooden fence surrounding the property. Phil's blue station wagon was still parked in the driveway leading to the front porch. The lonely sight filled her with sadness. The two-story house already looked deserted. She was still concerned about the livestock —chickens, pigs, and cows—Phil had in backyard pens. What would become of them and Phil's garden and his modest crops? What would happen to the house itself?

She recalled that on the day of Phil's death, Chief Riley had mentioned a will and ownership of the farm tied up in legal proceedings. Phil had children, a son and a daughter, but she had never met them. They hadn't even attended their father's funeral. Mary wondered if they even knew that he had passed. If they did, she found it unconscionable that they wouldn't have gone to his memorial, but she tried not to judge.

Mary turned the ignition off, and Theo urged her to wait. He then held up a small pair of binoculars, then slowly scanned the house and adjacent barn. Just because it looked as if no one was there didn't make it so. Mary surveyed the house herself, on alert for anything out of the ordinary.

"I suppose we better have a look around," Theo said, lowering his binoculars.

Mary held her hand on the door handle, hesitant. "I have to admit, I don't really like the idea of breaking into his house. It feels so… disrespectful."

Theo reached back and grabbed his fedora, putting it on.

"Phil would understand, I'm sure. We are, after all, trying to solve his murder."

For the first time, the prospect that Phil might not have been murdered entered Mary's mind. She had seen Bob Deckers suffocating Phil in her mind and then saw him searching the house for something of apparent value. The vision had left her short of breath and dizzy during Phil's memorial service. She had nearly collapsed, but the vision was clear enough.

Deckers had walked away empty handed, but not before leaving Phil's corpse in the bedroom. Whatever he was looking for, Bob Deckers didn't find it. Mary suspected that the Taylors were somehow linked and was certain that she'd find evidence of their presence in the house.

She stepped out of the SUV and onto the pebbled path leading to the front yard. The quiet stillness, broken only by a cool breeze rustling the trees, was comforting in some ways, ominous in others. She continued past the fence and up the dirt driveway with Theo at her side.

Brown leaves were strewn across the lawn, many already covering the roof of Phil's old station wagon. Two empty chairs sat on the front porch, rocking faintly. Instead of trying the front door, Theo veered off to the side of the house, and Mary followed. Her mind raced, baffled by the whereabouts of Phil's mystery item, something so important that he had lost his life over it. Mary's visions of Phil's murder were one piece; she now needed her abilities to lead her one step further to find whatever Deckers was after.

They reached the open backyard, and Mary was stunned to see a multitude of empty pens, their doors flung open, swaying on their hinges. All the animals were gone. She stopped and looked around, mystified.

Theo halted near some steps that led to an elevated cedar

deck and turned to Mary, noticing the troubled expression on her face. "What is it?" he asked.

"Phil's livestock," she said. "They're all gone…"

Theo looked out into the backyard from over Mary's shoulder. "Well. That's good. Someone came and got them. Moved them to another farm maybe. Better than them starving to death."

Strangely enough, Mary felt more troubled than relieved. Something wasn't right.

"Come on," Theo said, walking up the steps. "Help me find a way in."

Mary turned and followed, her eyes on the barn next to them. She could smell the hay stored inside and watched as a black cat scurried inside between the double doors. She reached the top of the deck as Theo pulled at the sliding glass door to no avail.

"Damn," he said, moving to a nearby kitchen window.

Mary peered inside, looking beyond the glass's glare, and what she saw shocked her. Phil's furniture had been flipped and his living room ransacked. A bookshelf lay collapsed on the floor, books everywhere and papers lying in an alarming disarray, scattered and in small heaps. A sofa and love seat lay on their sides, torn open and gutted, with foam hanging out like innards. The entire scene was reminiscent of Mary and Curtis's apartment in Chicago. Their break-in had been one of the primary reasons for their moving to Redwood in the first place.

Mary stared into the living room in disbelief. She then turned to Theo, who had just removed the screen over the kitchen window, opening it. It looked as though he hadn't even noticed anything yet. They were certainly not the first people to have visited Phil's place in the past few hours. That much she was sure of. Whoever had broken inside had been looking for something as well.

"Theo, come here," she said with a whisper. Theo set the screen down, walked over to Mary, and glanced through the sliding glass door, freezing in place.

"Holy shit. How did I miss that?"

"That's what I was wondering," Mary said. "Someone beat us here."

Theo pressed his face against the glass, looking in. "This is insane."

"Whatever they were looking for, I don't think they found it," Mary said with confidence.

Theo backed away and turned to her, thinking. "What makes you so sure?"

"Because the job looks so disorganized and hasty, almost like they took their frustration out on the furniture." Mary took a deep breath while pressing her hands against the glass. "We need to get in there and start looking."

"I'm on it," Theo said, moving back toward the open kitchen window. He climbed in as Mary waited, casting nervous glances behind and around her. She heard the clinking of dishes and silverware hitting the floor as Theo hopped off the kitchen counter. He then entered the living room, carefully moving around the hazards in his path.

Mary wondered how the intruders before them had gotten in. The search and subsequent trashing of the house looked disrupted, as though something had alerted the culprits to flee. Mary could feel the lingering presence of more than one individual. Theo unlocked the sliding glass door and pulled it open for Mary as she walked inside, thanking him with a pat on the arm.

"So what do you think?" he asked her.

"I'm not sure," she said. "We need to check the entire house."

Theo leaned closer, his tone confidential. "What about that woman we saw here the morning of Phil's death, Grace?

Think she had anything to do with this? She did have a key to the house, remember?"

Mary laughed softly. "I don't think so. I have the feeling we're dealing with three men," she said.

"The Taylor brothers?"

Mary nodded while carefully examining the room.

"Well… they were going to be my second guess," Theo said with mock confidence.

Mary smiled, looking past the hall, alert. "Let's check the rest of the house."

They moved around a fallen bookcase and into the hallway, across from an adjacent office. Inside, papers were lying everywhere. Drawers had been pulled out from a large desk, their contents poured onto the floor. They continued down the hallway, passing more rooms, all in similar disarray. Nothing of value, it seemed, had been stolen; computers and other electronics remained. It was no ordinary burglary. Mary was sure of it.

"Sense anything yet?" she asked Theo.

Theo examined the startling holes in the wall next to him. Shattered glass from a broken picture frame lay at his feet. "It's hard to say, but I think you're on to something here. I don't think that our perpetrators found what they were looking for."

Picking their way across the hardwood floors, they emerged from the office hallway and entered the front of the house and a large family room. It was situated at the bottom of a wide, old-fashioned staircase with stained-wood risers. The family room, like all the others, was trashed—couch flipped over and gutted, lamps thrown, and desk drawers lying about and emptied. There were even holes in the wall.

"What a horrible thing to do to a pastor's home," Mary said as they reached the bottom of the staircase.

Theo motioned for her to go upstairs with him when she

noticed something peculiar on a small, undisturbed coffee table near the foyer. She walked past Theo and approached the table, her misgivings intensified. On the coffee table lay a .45 caliber pistol.

Theo was already halfway up the stairs when she called him back.

"What is it?" he asked, rushing down the stairs, approaching her.

"Look," she said and pointed to the pistol.

Theo was stunned; they both knew the pistol did not belong to Phil. He reached for it when suddenly a black Bronco with large wheels and tinted windows came down the road and pulled up directly behind Mary's SUV. Panic gripped her chest as the Bronco skidded to a halt and the doors swung open and three men jumped out. A fourth was in the driver's seat. Theo snatched the pistol and took Mary's arm.

"Come on. We have to get out of here."

"Where are we going to go?" she asked. "They know we're here."

She stared out the window near the foyer. Its thin white curtain barely concealed her as the men surrounded her SUV, looking inside and taking down the license plate number. She could see them better. The man on the right side of her vehicle was none other than Garret Taylor, scar visible on his cheek even from a distance, and his brothers. After realizing that no one was inside the SUV, Garret whipped his head around and glared toward the house. Theo pulled Mary down as they ducked out of sight.

"One of them must have forgotten this!" Theo said, holding the pistol. "We need to get out of here or hide."

Mary rose slightly as her breathing increased with her growing panic. The Taylor brothers ran toward the house and up the front lawn with their pistols drawn and their eyes steely. They were wasting no time.

"Run!" Theo said, pulling Mary up. "Let's go!"

With a sudden jolting kick to the front door, the men were only a few feet away. Mary sprinted off with Theo back down the hall just as Taylor brothers stormed inside.

To avoid being seen, Theo yanked Mary inside the first room to their left, where they took refuge in the corner of the room, hunched down and hiding on the other side of a bed. As Mary crouched down lower, she knew they had made a mistake in trying to hide. They were trapped, with their only escape being a nearby window that was closed with the blinds drawn. Footsteps sounded down the hall. They had company.

Curtis watched Bob Deckers's office from afar, sipping warm green tea in a corner booth of the coffee shop. He had been waiting for nearly thirty minutes while growing more doubtful that Deckers would indeed turn up. His cell phone lay flat on the table as he scrolled through the screen, feeling hopeful that Bob would either call or show. He could hear the faint sounds of the festival blocks away. There was no one in the dimly lit coffee shop, save for a twenty-something female barista and an elderly man at the counter. Curtis sat in one of the five booths at the front window, staring out.

The longer he sat waiting, the more he began to doubt the entire operation. Was he expecting Bob Deckers to simply confess to the murder of Pastor Phil? Curtis thought long and hard about what he was to do. They should have gotten the police involved from the beginning, he believed, but Mary didn't currently trust the police—or most people in town, for that matter.

He finished his second cup of tea and turned back to the building across the street, surprised to see a man walking toward it. He was carrying a briefcase and wearing slacks, a button-down shirt with the sleeves rolled up, and a tie swaying around his neck. His slicked-back gray hair shifted in the breeze and he had a slight five o'clock shadow on his tan face.

It was Bob Deckers. Curtis could recognize his hurried walk anywhere. Curtis rose from the booth and tossed a five on the table. He grabbed his cell phone and jacket, waved to the barista, and walked out of the coffee shop, watching Bob unlock his front office door and slip inside. Curtis gave it a moment. He certainly didn't want to come barging in moments after Bob's arrival. He wanted Bob to settle in and get comfortable—then he would confront him.

He leaned against one of the pillars holding up the canopy above the front door and waited. For the first time that day, Curtis began to feel a little nervous. He would be confronting Bob Deckers for the first time since Mary had accused the man of murdering Pastor Phil.

Curtis pulled his cell phone out and sent Mary a text message telling her Bob had just arrived at his office and that he was going in. After waiting a minute or so, and getting no response, he wondered what she was doing.

Had they found anything, or was the entire thing a wild goose chase?

Curtis looked at his phone again. It was ten after two. The downtown festival was kicking into high gear. He could smell barbecue in the air, which made his stomach growl, but could stall no longer. He still hadn't heard back from Mary and decided to call her. Several rings later, the call went to her voice mail.

"Just calling to get a status," he said after the beep. "Our guy just walked in, and I'm going to have a talk with him. Call me back as soon as you can. Love you, bye."

He hung up and put the phone back in his pocket. He walked toward the road and looked both ways. There were no cars going in either direction. The block resembled a ghost town. Curtis crossed the four empty lanes and made his way to the other side, where old buildings lined the street. There was little doubt that Bob could see him coming if he was anywhere near his window. Most windows along the first floor of the buildings were heavily tinted. Next to Bob's corner office, there was an empty parking lot to one side and a pizza joint on the other called "Bricklayers Pizza." Curtis hadn't eaten there yet, but the aroma he had smelled last time had been tempting. This time, however, Bricklayers was closed, like many of the shops on the block.

He thought of knocking on Bob's door, but then decided to be bold, just walk in if possible, maybe take him off guard and gain the upper hand. He pushed against the door carefully, fully expecting it to be locked, but it wasn't. He opened it only as far as necessary and slipped inside the darkened lobby that had empty desks at both sides of the room, like some telemarketing office, closed for the day.

The blinds were all shut, and Curtis realized that he had been safe from exposure the entire time—unless of course, Bob had been peering outside through them like some paranoid nut job. So far, that didn't seem to be the case.

A lone light illuminated the office, coming from Bob's private office at the end of the room. His was separated by glass and a door, while every other desk sat out in the open. Curtis, to that day, hadn't seen a single other Realtor in the office, and had thought it too invasive to ask.

He walked across the gray carpet, between the lines of desks on both sides, and approached the lone office at the end where Bob sat, head looking down and scribbling onto some papers, seemingly unaware of Curtis's advancing presence.

Curtis approached the open door and gave it a knock. Bob's head jolted up.

"Curtis!" he said, startled and clutching his chest. "I didn't even hear you come in…" He set his pen down and was quick to cover his notebook. On his forehead were beads of sweat, and he looked exhausted. His surprised expression faded easily as he smiled at Curtis and welcomed him in. "Yes, I'm sorry. You called me earlier and told me you'd be stopping by. It's just, a lot is going on right now, and I forgot."

"No problem," Curtis said, entering the office. He took a seat in one of the two green vinyl chairs in front of Bob's desk.

Bob closed his notebook, and then looked back at Curtis with heightened enthusiasm. "Oh. I talked to that leasing office downtown, and they're willing to let that unit on Sixth Street go at a great rate."

"Wonderful," Curtis said with a smile while clasping his hands together. Under normal circumstances, he would be ecstatic hearing such news, but he was far too distracted to talk business. Despite this, Curtis kept his tone and demeanor friendly and receptive. Bob's worn face, thin five o'clock shadow, and wild eyes showed a man already on edge. Curtis didn't want to push him.

Bob leaned back in his chair in a confident manner with his head cocked back and proceeded to get on with their meeting. "I figured you and Mary would be at the festival today. What can I do for you today, Curtis?"

Curtis looked down, laughing to himself. "Yeah…Mary's out and about. We're planning to spend the rest of the day out in the crowd."

"Sure is a nice day for it," Bob said. He opened the briefcase resting on his desk and looked inside as if checking the contents, but didn't take anything out.

"Are you planning to join the festivities?" Curtis asked. "I hope to catch that band again later today."

In response, Bob pulled a flask and two Dixie cups from

the briefcase resting atop his desk. He quickly poured an amber liquid into the cups and looked at Curtis with a devilish smirk. "How about something to get the party started?"

Curtis fanned his hand and politely declined.

"What? Oh, come on, Curtis. Let it go. It's the weekend." He held Curtis's cup up, his eyes gleaming. "You can't turn down Irish Whisky. It's against the law. You should know that."

A thought suddenly came to Curtis, something about the old adage: loose lips sink ships.

"Sure, Bob," he said, taking the cup. "Why not?"

He tipped the drink back, swigging the warm whiskey, which burned his throat and sent his eyes watering. It was pretty strong stuff. Bob tipped his back as well and exhaled with satisfaction. He was already pouring his second cup before Curtis had even set his down. He seemed distracted and antsy, and Curtis could definitely tell that something was on his mind.

"Are you all right?" Curtis asked.

Bob paused for a moment, cup in hand, feigning surprise at the question. "Yes. Yes, of course. Just long hours, you know?"

Curtis turned his head and glanced at all the empty desks outside Bob's office. "You should outsource some work to your staff," he said with a chuckle. He turned back just as Bob took a sip from his cup.

"Yeah. What staff?" he said, eyes watering from the drink.

Curtis laughed. "I just assumed they've been on sabbatical."

Bob nodded with a vacant stare, looking beyond Curtis's shoulder. "That's nice of you to say, Curtis. Truth is, I had to downsize a few months ago. Economy has been in the crapper, real estate has taken a hit, and we all have to do our part."

Curtis leaned forward with a serious expression and spoke with an equally serious tone. "I wanted to ask you a few questions, Bob. If you don't mind."

Bob looked up, beaming with intrigue. "Oh yeah? Like what?"

"Nothing really work related, but I was hoping we could talk about my house."

Bob's enthusiastic expression faded with his sigh. "Great, I knew it," he said, smacking his hands together. "You want to put it back on the market, don't you?" Curtis tried to speak, but Bob cut him off. "It's okay. You wouldn't be the first."

"We don't want to move," Curtis said curtly. "This is about something else."

Bob cocked his head, confused. "Well... what then? Spit it out."

The familiar hum of the air conditioner sounded overhead as Curtis gathered his thoughts. It was strange to think of all the activity taking place only a few blocks away as they sat in the nearly vacant Realtor's office, staring at each other.

"I want to know if you're really being honest with us," Curtis began.

He noticed Bob's friendly demeanor immediately change to something guarded and suspicious.

"You assured us that nothing is wrong with that house, but that has not been the case. You know me, Bob. I'm a practical, literal person. I don't put any stock in curses and ghosts and psychics, but I believe you know plenty more about the Bechdel property than you say you do. And I want to know your involvement."

A silence fell over the two men as Bob shifted in his chair; he placed his palms flat on the desk and eyed Curtis intently. "Involvement with what?" he asked in a slow, quiet tone. His eyes narrowed, and for the first time, Curtis could sense a sinister side in Bob that he hadn't seen before.

"With everything," he answered, with his arms held out in an all-encompassing way.

Bob laughed to himself, looking down, and took another sip of whiskey. "Looks like that shot went straight to your head there, Curtis, because I have no idea what you're talking about."

"How well did you know Pastor Phil?" Curtis asked, searching for any nervous giveaways in Bob's movements or statements. Bob was already acting strangely enough for Curtis to at least point the authorities in Bob's direction. He could make an anonymous tip or just go to the police himself. Or was he being carried away, going overboard? He needed more than just a hunch. He wanted to see how convincing a liar Bob fancied himself to be.

Bob answered his question about Phil with little hesitation. "I knew him well enough. Everyone did. Heck, he was the town pastor."

Curtis folded his hands together as Bob poured more whiskey into his cup. Curtis declined again, this time meaning it.

"Suit yourself," Bob said.

"I understand that many people *knew* Pastor Phil, but I'm more curious about you. Were you friends?"

Bob's confident posture and steely, attentive focus suddenly diminished as his hands gripped the front of his desk, fingers tapping, his voice with an edge now. "Sure. We were friends. What's your point?"

Curtis took a long breath, knowing that the moment of truth was nearing. Bob already appeared shaken, and Curtis wasn't certain how far he could go without blowing his intent. "My point is that there is clearly something wrong with our house. No past owners have stayed in the house more than a few weeks. Some of them even died, I heard. You never told that to me or Mary."

Bob finished his cup off and sighed again while growing increasingly agitated. "What is this, Curtis?" he snapped. "You're all over the place. First, it's Pastor Phil, then it's your haunted house. Where are you going with all of this?"

Curtis could already see two important signs. Bob was being evasive and deliberately ill-informed. It wouldn't take much to rile him up further, but Curtis knew he'd have to be careful. "Trust me, there's a connection," he said. "Pastor Phil came to our house the other night when I wasn't there. In fact, I was with you and those other guys at the pub. Apparently, he came to warn Mary of a dark, supernatural presence in our home."

Bob looked at Curtis blankly, then his face twitched and his lips moved upward into an uncontrollable smile. "Are you serious?" he said with a guffaw.

"That's what she told me," Curtis answered. "She also told me that she had a dream about you. Apparently, you were with Phil the night he passed away." Curtis pulled the glove from his front pocket and held the bag up for Bob to see. "We also found this on Phil's property. Looks a little too big for Phil's hand. Do you know who this might belong to?" He expected more evasiveness from Bob, maybe a nervous laugh or some half-baked excuse, but what Bob did next truly shocked him. He reached into his briefcase and pulled a 9mm pistol out, aiming it at Curtis.

"What are you doing?" Curtis asked, frozen to his chair.

"Quiet," Bob said. "I've heard about enough from you, Curtis. Now toss that over here."

Curtis tossed him the bagged glove, saying nothing more. He wondered if the pistol was really loaded, and if so, would Bob actually shoot him in the back if he tried to flee?

Bob continued, full of hostility. "Here's what's going to

happen. Call Mary and tell her to meet us here. I want to hear about these dreams she's having."

Curtis looked around the office and then behind him on the off chance that someone might walk in and help save him. "I… My cell phone is on the fritz. I haven't been able to make any calls this entire day."

"Bullshit," Bob said, on his feet and approaching Curtis. "You get her here in the next five minutes, or I'm going shoot you where it hurts."

As the pistol got closer to his face, Curtis resisted the urge to flinch. He had never seen this side of Bob before, and it became suddenly clear to him that Mary was right all along. Bob undoubtedly had something to do with Phil's death. He could have been the main bad actor all along.

As Curtis sat in Bob's office, pistol aimed at his face, he knew that he perhaps had said too much. He had expected a reaction from Bob, probably outright denial, but he hadn't expected this.

"You'd really shoot me?" Curtis asked in disbelief.

"That all depends, Curtis. I get no satisfaction out of this, but you've left me no choice. And now… I want to know what your wife knows too."

"I'm not calling her," Curtis said, defiantly. "So I guess you're going to have to shoot me." He briefly glimpsed rage on Bob's reddened face before it subsided as he smiled instead in a slightly menacing way.

"A proud man to the end. Careful now, Curtis. Pride before the fall."

"Why us?" Curtis said. "You could have gotten plenty of others into that house."

"You seemed like a nice couple," Bob said. "The mayor vetted you personally and gave the green light."

"Vetted? Green light? What is your relationship with the

mayor, anyway?" Curtis asked with near contempt. "Do you work for him? Did he pay you to murder Pastor Phil?"

Bob suddenly vaulted up out of his chair and slammed his fist on the table, taking Curtis by surprise. "*Where the hell do you get off asking questions like that*?" he shouted. "You come to our town and think that you know everything?" He paused, leaning forward, his eyes narrowed in disgust. "You're nothing but outsiders here, Curtis, so I'd watch yourself. Now call your wife before I really start to get pissed."

Curtis knew he had no choice and pulled his cell phone out from his side pocket, holding it up. "If I call her, the only thing I'm going to tell her is to call the police, so you can drop that shit right now." He slipped the phone back into his pocket, hoping Bob wouldn't demand turning it over. If he got the chance, he could call 9-1-1.

Bob exhaled loudly and stretched his neck, as though deciding what to do about Curtis's threat. He slowly moved back from the desk and made his way around to Curtis, pressing the pistol against his temple, causing him to flinch.

"I'm not in the mood for games," he said. "I could shoot you right here and find your wife myself. So, by all means, keep being difficult."

Without warning, Curtis grabbed Bob's arm, gripping him by the wrist, and jumped up, ready to charge him. The pistol fired a deafening blast into the air, shattering the glass of Bob's office window.

Bob slammed against his desk and tried to regain his balance as Curtis charged toward him, but Bob, still holding the gun, drew his arm back and smashed Curtis in the face with the thick metal barrel of the hot pistol. Another white flash and Curtis was on his knees, dazed and face throbbing.

"You crazy son of a bitch!" Bob shouted. "You trying to get shot?"

Curtis looked up, ready to launch into his adversary, but

Bob was too quick. He brought the handle of his pistol down in one swift crack against Curtis's skull. As Curtis collapsed, part of him wondered why Bob didn't just shoot him. His head throbbed with pain and he expected another blow as he struggled to stand, but couldn't. He felt the heel of Bob's shoe kicking him in the ribs. He was fast losing consciousness, and there was nothing he could do but drift into the darkness, in a moment of peace.

* * *

Mary lay low, peeking under the bed, with Theo breathing heavily next to her with the stolen.45 caliber pistol in-hand. The Taylor brothers were inside, fired up and searching for them. One of the men was taunting, calling: "Come out, little kitty. Nice little kitty. Nobody's going to hurt you. We just want to say hello."

She tried to keep her body still. Theo lay on his side, his arm extended under the bed, pistol aimed. Footsteps sounded on the wood floors from all around the house. Escape seemed impossible. Even if they made it outside and into the SUV, the Taylors would most likely follow them wherever they went, even if they did get away, which wasn't likely. No, that wouldn't do. Their best bet would be to flee the house and escape on foot.

"Where are they?" she heard one of the Taylors shout. "Search every last inch of this house!"

"Here, kitty, kitty."

There were only so many rooms in the house, and Mary knew it to be only a matter of time before they were discovered.

"What do we do?" she whispered to Theo as footsteps clomped around upstairs.

His head turned toward her slightly as he gripped the

pistol, holding it up. "We try to escape, but in the meantime, be ready for anything."

The thought of being in the middle of a firefight terrified her, but it would seem that they had little choice but to defend themselves. Would the Taylor brothers really shoot upon finding them? Were they really the murderers she thought them to be? Perhaps the entire thing was one big misunderstanding. However, as their voices carried down the hall, she concluded they were very much capable of what she feared.

"You find 'em, don't hesitate to put 'em down," one of the Taylors said in a quiet voice, coming from right outside the room. "But leave one alive so we can find out what they're doing nosing around here."

Mary heard the door to the room they were hiding in creak open wider as she lay on her chest, hoping to remain concealed.

This is it, Mary thought with a shudder. *They're going to find us, and they're going to kill us.*

Not going to happen, she heard Theo say, but he hadn't actually spoken. For the first time, she could actually hear his thoughts. It was a revelation.

Mary, listen to me. We're going to be okay, he continued.

Oh my God. You can actually hear my thoughts? she said. *And I can hear yours?*

Your abilities are getting stronger. A man is getting closer—I can see him. I want you to shield your face and cover your ears. Then we run.

Okay, she said as her body trembled with anticipation.

The footsteps got closer and closer, and she prepared for the deafening blast of a .45 caliber pistol. Just then, one of the other brothers shouted from the stairwell, "Hey! Y'all come up here. I think I found something. Could be exactly what we're looking for!"

The footsteps stopped and changed direction, fading away, and Mary could breathe again.

"That was a close one," she whispered to Theo.

"You said it. Now let's make a run for it. Now or never."

The Taylor boys, it seemed, had assembled upstairs, where they could be heard moving around above them. Theo rose from behind the bed and walked with cautious steps to the door and into the hall as Mary followed. They turned right toward the trashed living room where the sliding glass door was in view—the most practical exit.

From there, Mary wasn't sure where they'd run, but she knew they had to get as far away from the Phil's house as possible. She felt disappointed that they hadn't found the coveted item they had come looking for, the hidden element that had drawn nefarious forces to the house in the first place. But for now, survival took precedence.

"This way," Theo motioned as he walked toward the living room. Mary followed, and they stepped around the papers, glass, and tables in their path. Theo slowly pulled the sliding glass door open just as they heard footsteps trample down the staircase.

Mary's heart seized. "Hurry!" she said. "They're coming."

"I know that," Theo said, pulling the door open enough for them to slip through. "I can hear too."

Mary nearly pushed her way out as Theo squeezed past the sliding glass door and onto the deck. The brisk air was a welcome feeling, but they were still in great danger. Mary pulled the door shut and turned to Theo just as he raced down the stairs.

Mary followed and as they reached the bottom, she glanced at the barn again. Something, a presence, attracted her, and she could swear something of value lay within.

"In the barn," she said, pulling Theo's arm.

"What?" he asked as though she were mad. He clearly was

prepared to run into the woods and get as far from the house as they could, but Mary insisted.

"Follow me," she said, rushing past him and toward the big red barn that, for now, offered a different kind of refuge for Mary.

SHOWDOWN

Curtis woke up on the floor of Bob's office, head throbbing. Long fluorescent bulbs flickered on the ceiling, and he could hear rustling coming from Bob's desk in addition to a faint second voice, shouting on the other end of a phone.

Bob was whispering, "I had no choice, I told you that. He knows too much!" Bob rose as Curtis shut his eyes after hearing the squeaking of Bob's chair. He could sense Bob's approach and searched for some way to turn the tables and possibly escape. For the moment, he was safe. Bob was distracted, but that would soon change.

Bob said, "We're getting out of here. This place is too hot. I'll call you when I get to the mansion."

Curtis opened one eye halfway and saw Bob's pant leg inches from his face. He gazed upward and saw Bob's silhouette standing over him, pistol still in hand and phone to his ear.

"I've got it under control right now. Don't worry." He paused as though he was receiving an earful from the other end of the line. "I told you not to worry! I'll call you later." He hung up with a long sigh and then stared down.

Curtis could feel the surging adrenaline beyond the pain in his head. If he was going to do something, now was the time. He opened his eyes and grabbed Bob's leg, hammering his knee as Bob howled and bent forward. Curtis punched him as hard as he could in the side. Bob screamed in pain as his knees buckled and he hunched downward, catching a punch to his right cheek.

Curtis felt a pop of cheek bone against his knuckles and then rolled to his side, pushing himself up and fully level with Bob, who had managed to get back on his feet, leaning now against the corner of the desk. He held his face with one hand, grunting, and gripped his pistol with the other.

Bob stumbled back as Curtis prepared to charge him, knowing it was a risky move, with Bob still being armed.

Bob's muffled cries of pain only energized Curtis further. He found his footing and then charged at Bob with all the strength he could muster. Inches from tackling Bob, Curtis felt a blunt, shocking blow to his head as Bob swung the pistol and knocked him down on his side. As he lay on Bob's gray carpet, panting, he could feel warm blood oozing down his forehead. The blow had left a deep gash. But it wasn't the second pistol-whipping that surprised Curtis. It was why Bob just didn't shoot him.

Curtis brought his hand to his head, struggling to get up as his vision blurred. He felt disoriented and near shock. Bob's voice echoed as he paced around Curtis, admonishing him.

"I really didn't want it to come to this, Curtis. I don't know why you have to be so difficult." He stopped at Curtis's side and knelt while talking just above a whisper. "You think that you're going to fight your way through this? Be a hero? Not happening, my friend." Bob rose again, smoothing his hair. He walked to his desk and began rifling through his drawers while talking to Curtis in a nervous and distracted tone. "I'm sorry about this, I really am. I wish you hadn't come in here making accusations at me."

Curtis wiped the blood from his forehead with his sleeve and attempted to stand tall again while pushing his weight against the desk. Bob slammed one of the drawers shut and stuffed some papers into his briefcase, seemingly indifferent to Curtis, as though he were certain that Curtis had been subdued.

"I don't know how I got wrapped up in all of this," he continued. "You have to forgive me, Curtis. I'm only doing what is necessary. I'm bankrupt, okay? I'm divorced. I've got nothing." He suddenly paused, took a deep breath, and then shouted, "I'm a desperate man!"

"What the hell is it that you want?" Curtis managed to mutter in his state of semi-consciousness.

Bob grabbed his briefcase and approached him, kneeling down again and talking softly. "I'm glad you asked. What I want at the moment is pretty simple. I've asked you to call your wife here, which you won't do without jeopardizing me. So you leave me with no choice but for us to go back to your place. And wait. Got it?"

"No," Curtis said, leaning against the front of Bob's desk. "I mean, what do you want with all of this? Why'd you kill Phil?"

Bob chuckled in a mean way. "There you go again with the wild accusations." He stood up, pointing the gun at Curtis. "Come on, let's go."

Curtis looked up at Bob's uncompromising face and realized he had little choice. Desperate people did desperate things, and Bob was on edge. His arms and legs were shaking, and Curtis knew that the next time, Bob might not hesitate to pull the trigger. He couldn't do that to Mary. He wouldn't do that. As long as he was still alive, there was hope. He pushed himself up as Bob backed away, not wavering with his aim.

"Just put that damn gun down, will ya'?" Curtis asked, rising from the floor and holding the desk for balance.

"No, thanks," Bob said. He motioned toward the empty lobby ahead. He pulled a tissue from his pocket and tossed it to Curtis. "Might want to clean up first."

Curtis wiped the blood from his forehead, carefully dabbing. He couldn't tell how large the gash was, but it hurt to touch. He then limped out of the office with Bob following him. Curtis said little as they continued through the lobby and toward the exit, where daylight streamed through the tinted windows. Once they were outside, Curtis believed Bob wouldn't get very far. Someone would notice what was happening. They had to.

"Where are you parked?" Bob asked as they reached the door.

Curtis turned his head slightly, his hands still up. "Mary has the car."

Bob smiled. "Perfect. Well, then, looks like you'll be driving my Volvo. I parked about a block up the street."

"Driving?" Curtis said.

Bob lowered his pistol slightly and shook his head. "Curtis, you don't really expect *me* to drive, do you? How would that work exactly?"

"How do you know I won't just crash us into a brick wall?"

Bob laughed, almost too hard, and then slapped Curtis on the back. "What? And leave Mary a widow? I don't think so, but nice try." He then told Curtis to quit stalling and open the door. Curtis pushed the glass door open. There was a sign hanging on the inside of it that read Closed. Curtis stepped outside and felt a cool breeze.

The sidewalk was empty. Music could be heard in the distance from the festival on Main Street. It was more than likely that Bob was going to want to avoid the crowds and would want Curtis to take an alternate route on the back roads. He turned to see that Bob was hiding the pistol under a suit coat draped over his arm.

With his sleeves rolled up, tie swaying, and briefcase in hand, Bob looked to be a normal businessman. No one would suspect a thing unless Curtis gave them reason to. Curtis glanced over to the coffee shop across the street, where only ten minutes ago he had been sitting safely inside.

He had expected deception from Bob, maybe anger when he was confronted, but Curtis never expected things to turn out as they had. Mary's warning that they stick together came back to him. He'd never hear the end of it. He hoped to have the opportunity to eat crow.

"That's right," Bob said, staying carefully behind him. "Up this way. It's the blue Volvo ahead, right next to that mailbox."

Curtis looked up the street where several cars lined the sidewalk, the Volvo the first among them. He heard Bob shuffle in his pocket for the keys and found the scenario almost humorous. Almost. He'd never driven anywhere at gunpoint before. They reached the front of the car as Bob pressed the automatic key and the locks clicked open. "Okay, Curtis. We can make this simple. Avoid the busy roads and get us to your house. I'll tell you how."

Curtis said nothing. He went around to the driver's side door just as a man on a motorcycle raced down the road and jetted past them. There wasn't much sense in flagging him down, or trying to "play hero" as Bob had put it. There would be other opportunities, plus in the end, Curtis didn't think Bob was going to make it.

He was a nervous wreck, sweaty and agitated. Curtis

could play it to his advantage, but he would have to be careful. There were other players involved beyond Bob. Whomever Bob had been talking to on the phone seemed to be in on it too.

"Get in," said Bob, nudging him with the pistol.

Curtis opened the door and sat inside, leaning against the warm fabric of the driver's seat. Bob came around the front and heaved himself into the passenger's seat, the pistol in his lap pointed at Curtis but still concealed by his suit coat.

He handed the keys to Curtis. "Go ahead and start the engine there, buddy," Bob said, resting his cell phone on the dashboard. "Let's move!"

Curtis turned the ignition, wishing he could talk to Mary somehow. He wasn't sure what he would tell her. He'd deliver a warning somehow without Bob's knowledge, though Bob was watching him like a hawk. Curtis drove forward, leaving the parking spot and getting onto the road ahead. He followed Bob's directions and stuck to the back roads. Part of him wanted to drive the car into a wall just as he had mentioned, but Bob was right. He wasn't going to put his own life at risk, and he had a responsibility to Mary.

Bob rubbed his forehead, exhausted, and then put on a pair of dark shades. His tiredness was showing, and Curtis wondered if he had even slept the night prior. He was stunned to think how long it had taken him to realize Bob's shadiness. All those weeks, all those friendly meetings that had taken place between them. It had taken Mary time to figure it out, for her to tell him who Bob really was. Curtis regretted not believing her. How could he have been so blind?

As they got farther away from downtown, Bob's mood seemed to brighten as he offered Curtis some empty-sounding assurances. "Don't you worry, Curtis. I like you and

Mary, and I don't want anything to happen to either of you. Just play along, and you'll both come out of this thing just fine."

Curtis nodded, not saying a word as they continued down a two-lane rural road about five miles from the Bechdel estate. It was an absurd statement coming from a man who had recently pistol-whipped him twice and threatened to shoot him.

Silence soon fell between them. Bob seemed tired of talking and actually rested his head back for a moment. Behind the wheel, Curtis was limited in his ability to fight back, even with the pistol resting inches from his grasp. For a moment, he thought that Bob might even doze off. That'd be all he would need to make a move.

Such thoughts filled his mind when suddenly Curtis noticed lights in his rearview mirror. A police car was trailing them, flashing its lights with intent to pull them over. Or so it seemed. Bob's eyes opened and he flew forward in a panic. It seemed as though the police cruiser had come from nowhere.

Curtis signaled to the right and slowed down.

"What the fuck are you doing?" Bob shouted.

Angered, Curtis whipped his head around. "What do you want me to do, go on a high-speed chase?"

Bob swore and pounded the dashboard. "Okay, okay. Go ahead and pull over, but don't say a word to him or I'll shoot both of you. I don't even care." He then punched the dashboard again in frustration. Curtis felt blanketed by relief. There was no way Bob was going to get away with any of this. He slowed to a stop on the shoulder of the barren road, even more relieved as the cruiser followed and halted behind them, lights flashing.

"Not a word," Bob said, exposing his pistol. "Be smart."

Curtis shut the engine off and glanced into the rearview mirror. The lights continued flashing and a young officer stepped out, a man Curtis recognized immediately. It was Deputy Ramirez. There was a chance Curtis could send him a signal, or something else that could get him out of this without getting himself killed. He rolled down the window while pulling out his wallet. Bob opened the glove compartment, pulled a sheet of paper out, and tossed it in Curtis's lap.

"That's the registration. Remember what I said."

"Ten-four," Curtis said as Deputy Ramirez approached.

"Afternoon, Deputy," Curtis said.

"Good afternoon, sir," Ramirez said, seemingly not recognizing him at first. Curtis felt immediately safe, prepared to tell the deputy everything, but he hesitated. An ominous premonition seized him, a warning of something horrible about to happen. There was no going back now for Bob or any of them, and Curtis knew it.

Deputy Ramirez, however, had just interfered with something beyond his understanding. Curtis maintained a friendly smile and cautious demeanor, despite Bob glaring at him. With a pistol aimed at his side, Curtis felt powerless to do anything, and as Ramirez appeared at the driver's side window, he took a deep breath and hoped for the best.

Mary and Theo ran to Pastor Phil's barn and slipped inside its open, red double doors. The dryness and smell of hay in the air was overpowering. Theo pulled the wooden doors shut behind them and then struggled to place a two-by-four board behind the cross-braces on the back of the doors, sealing them shut.

"Won't that raise suspicion?" Mary asked. "I'm sure they noticed that the doors were open last time they were here."

"It buys us some time," Theo said. "You're the one who insisted that we run in here."

She admitted as much, but something else was bothering her. "Were we really reading each other's minds back there?" she asked excitedly. "You could hear me?"

Theo seemed just as amazed and in doubt. "I think so. I thought I could hear you, but I wondered if it was just my mind playing tricks on me."

Mary's heart pounded with her excitement. They had reached a new threshold in their abilities, but for the time being, they had to concentrate on survival.

Mary scanned the barn, which was lit only by light streaming in through cracks in the siding. There was a ladder ahead of them, leading to the second floor of the barn. Haystacks were piled on all sides and on the second floor. There was a nearby wall with a pitchfork, shovel, and rake mounted on pegs.

Phil seemed to have been an efficient farmer, but finding that out wasn't the reason Mary's instincts had led them into the barn. Since they couldn't leave, she did her best to figure out why she had felt the need to be there. Theo kept a careful eye on the door with the .45 poised and ready to fire.

Mary slowly paced toward the wooden ladder, thinking out loud. "What if no one has found this secret thing Phil has hidden because they're looking in the wrong place?"

Distracted, Theo leaned closer to the door and peeked through one of the slits. He kept a careful eye on the house as Mary placed her hands on the ladder and looked up into the rays of sunlight that leaked into the barn from open slits between the wooden above them. She felt exhausted and unnerved but also purposeful. This was where they belonged.

If not for her last-second impulse to head for the barn, naturally, she and Theo would have fled into the forest, where there were plenty of places to hide. But not now. They had chosen the barn for a reason. She paused and looked around at all the haystacks. The needle was there somewhere, she was sure of it. If only she had a better idea of what they were looking for.

"What would Phil have that was so important that he would be killed for it?" Mary said out loud.

"I don't know, but one of the Taylor brothers just walked outside." Theo turned and rushed toward the ladder, urging Mary to climb up it. "Come on. We're safer up there."

Mary climbed the ladder, making it shake and wobble. She felt the approaching presence of the Taylor brothers as she made it to the platform, where straw lay scattered on the floor and bundles of hay surrounded them. There was certainly no shortage of hiding spots.

She walked along the second floor, peering down as Theo pulled the ladder up and placed it flat on the second-level platform. He covered his mouth, trying to shield a cough. "It's so dusty up here," he said, quietly sneezing. "But at least we're hidden." Of course the door, boarded from the inside, was a giveaway.

"What if they torch the place?" he asked. "With all these hay bales, we wouldn't have a chance."

"They won't if they think what they're looking for is hidden here," she said with false bravado.

Mary crept past some haystacks and approached an octagon-shaped window overlooking Phil's backyard. Two Taylor brothers were in view below, minus Garret, the one with the scar. She had learned their names at Phil's memorial. The other brothers, Jeffery and Liam, were tall and lean, like Garret, with full heads of gray hair—their skin pale and ghost-like. Jeffery was clean-shaven with trimmed hair and wore blue jeans, boots, a jean jacket, and dark Aviator shades.

Liam, on the other hand, had long wispy hair down to his shoulders and a thick handlebar mustache. He had noticeable cuts on his cheeks and forehead, like markings caused by glass in a car accident. All three brothers were menacing in their own way, as though they were programmed to harm others without care or reason.

Jeffery and Liam walked past Phil's garden, searching through the backyard with deft precision. Jeffery had his pistol drawn as he scanned the woods ahead. Liam split off, approaching the forest from the other side, empty-handed. Mary assumed that it was Liam's pistol, carelessly left behind, that Theo had taken.

She heard Theo's footsteps creak behind her as he snuck over to the small, dirty window to get a better look.

"Looks like they're not interested in the barn," he said. "Not yet anyway."

"Fingers crossed," Mary said.

As they watched the brothers move farther away from the barn and into the forest, a new worry suddenly overcame her. What if the Taylor brothers decided not to leave? What if they decided to set up camp for the next few days or even weeks? What if they called others to join them in a wide search of the entire property, including the barn?

She moved away from the window and pulled her cell phone from her pocket, prepared to call Curtis. There were several missed calls from him, a text asking her status, and a voice mail, and she decided to just call him back. After several rings, the phone went to voice mail.

"Curtis, call me back, please, as soon as you get this message." She hung up while weighing her next option: whether or not to alert the police.

It was clear that their lives were in danger and that things could get much worse. Theo was at the window, keeping a careful eye on the Taylor brothers. Mary asked him about Chief Riley. "What do you think? He gave me his card. I can at least let him know what's going on out here."

"At this point, we don't know who's in on this thing and who isn't. Can we trust the police?" he asked, still looking out the window.

"I don't know," Mary said. "He seemed like a straight-up person. What choice do we have? How long can we hide in this barn before they find us?" She was aware that her fear and uncertainty were beginning to show, despite how confident she had been when they had first run into the barn. She didn't want anyone to get hurt—not her or Theo, or the Taylor brothers for that matter. "I could make an anonymous call," she said. "Report a break-in at Phil's. At least that'd get them out here. Or maybe they have caller ID.

Theo finally turned his head to her with a look of understanding. "Whatever you feel is necessary. Either way, it doesn't look like we're going anywhere for a while."

Mary looked at her phone, trying to decide the best course of action. It seemed there was little choice but to alert the authorities. If anything, it would at least put the Taylor brothers in an awkward position.

"You see anything?" they heard Jeffery yell from one side of the backyard.

"Nah… You?" Liam shouted from the other.

The nearness of their voices was enough to push Mary toward calling the police. She held up Chief Riley's card and began to dial when she felt a jolt of electricity as a strange glitch turned her screen black. Her fingers continued to move across the screen as she stared in disbelief, waiting for it to come back on. Desperation coupled with fear grew inside her along with increasing frustration.

"What the hell?" she said.

"What happened?" Theo asked. His head was turned back on window patrol.

"My phone... it just died." She pressed the side power button to no avail. "Oh, please, please, come on."

Concerned, Theo turned back to her and pulled his phone from his pocket. He glanced at the screen and then handed it to Mary. "Here. Try this."

She shook her head and put her phone away, still confused, and took his. "Thank you."

She swiped the screen and was immediately met with another static shock, startling her.

"You okay?" Theo asked after hearing her say "ow!"

"Yeah..." she said, staring at the blank screen. "Your phone died too."

Theo swung his head around, eyes narrowed. "What?" He yanked the phone from her hand. "What are you talking about?" He tried various methods of getting it to power back on to no avail. For a moment, nothing made sense—another unexplained phenomenon. Through the confusion, however, Mary had a moment of clarity. She walked past Theo as he remained preoccupied with his phone. Something was leading her, providing the assistance she had hoped for since arriving at Phil's house. The barn held secrets after all. She had brought Theo inside here for a reason.

Mary spun around, eyes brimming with conviction. "There's something hidden here," she said. "Something of great value."

Theo looked up, holding his phone. His head turned like an oscillating fan, surveying the barn in all its vastness, looking in all directions. "Where do we start?"

"Anywhere," she said. "Just keep looking until we sense it. There's a needle somewhere, and it's up to us to find it."

Theo took a last glance outside the window. The Taylor brothers were heading back into the house. "We better hurry then," he said. "They're going to focus on this barn soon enough."

Mary agreed and climbed down the ladder first as Theo began his search upstairs. She'd hoped that it would come to her, whatever it was they were looking for. Another piece of a conspiracy puzzle she still hadn't yet solved.

AGAINST THE WALL

Deputy Ramirez stood outside the car window, taking a glance inside Bob's Volvo. At first, the deputy didn't seem to recognize either men. He simply examined the car from behind his Oakleys. He smelled of aftershave, and his neatly trimmed high fade looked recent. The hand mic clipped to his shoulder crackled with static. He held a notepad in one hand and kept his other hand near the holstered pistol on his side.

After his own generic greeting, Curtis's friendly tone seemed foreign to himself as though he were listening to someone else speak.

Ramirez took a closer look and smiled in recognition. "Mr. Malone, hello! Almost didn't recognized you for a minute there."

Bob leaned forward, making himself known as well. He was sweaty and seemed on edge despite his wide-eyed smile. Curtis hoped that Ramirez would be remain oblivious, for his own sake. Deckers was growing more erratic by the minute.

"Deputy Ramirez, good to see you!" Bob said with a wave, his pistol still concealed under his suit coat.

Ramirez took his glasses off and waved back. "Mr. Deckers. Nice to see you." He then did a double take, realizing something was out of the ordinary. He placed a tan hand on the door and leaned in. "Isn't this your car, Mr. Deckers?" he asked.

"Why, yes," Bob said, growing increasingly nervous. "Ol' Curtis wanted to take it for a drive. I'm thinking of selling it to him."

Ramirez nodded while looking down at his notepad. "I see. Well, you might want to replace that left taillight before you put her on the market."

Curtis stared ahead, not saying a word. The cuts and bruises to his face were on his right side, concealed from Ramirez's view, but as he sat there, he could feel a warm line of blood trickling down his forehead.

"Taillight?" Bob said, surprised. He turned around, looking out his back window. "Gee, I had no idea. Thanks for letting me know, Deputy."

Deputy Ramirez nodded again and then scratched his head, in anticipation of an awkward follow-up. "Yes, but according to our records, you were informed about this deficiency two weeks ago and given a warning. It's in the system."

Bob paused, thinking to himself, and his smile dropped. Curtis could see the tiny beads of sweat dripping down his forehead. He opened his mouth, appearing to be combative, when his shoulders slumped and he smacked himself on the forehead. "Gee... you know, Deputy. Now I remember." He paused, shaking his head. "It was during the Labor Day festival. Seems like forever ago." His face then bounced up, smiling. "I'm sorry, I completely forgot. I promise to get that replaced today."

Ramirez continued scribbling on his pad. "I understand that, Mr. Deckers, but it's official policy. I'm going to have give you a ticket this time."

Curtis glanced at Bob through his peripheral vision and could see that he was doing his best to mask his irritation.

Ramirez continued. "So I'm going to have to see both your licenses and registration, please."

Bob turned his head, glaring out the window. "Deputy Ramirez, please. I'll change the light today. Can't we just let this one go? We're in a very big hurry."

Ramirez shook his head. "I'm sorry, Bob. I'd like to, but this time I've got to give you the citations. Those are the rules."

He said no more and seemed to expect their compliance without further issue. Curtis fished through his wallet and pulled his license out, handing it to the deputy. Bob, however, was increasingly agitated. He bit his lip and reached for the glove compartment, opening it. Why didn't he do what he was told as quickly as he could and get rid of the deputy as fast as possible? After all, it was only a minor traffic ticket.

Curtis was careful not to turn his head toward the window, lest Deputy Ramirez inquire about the injuries. He wiped the thin trail of blood from his forehead as Bob handed over his license and registration. For a moment, they sat in silence as Ramirez looked through everything. Curtis glanced at the bulge on Bob's arm hidden under a gray suit coat.

"How's everything going at your place, Mr. Malone?" Ramirez asked Curtis as he handed the licenses back to him. "Any other *strange* occurrences?" He laughed as Curtis smiled sheepishly.

"It's been quiet. Still hoping you guys can catch those vandals," he said.

Ramirez nodded as he filled out a citation. "I've got my eye on some teenagers in the area. One of them, Scott Landis, may just be responsible for a string of incidents, along with his little buddies." He tore the citation from his book and leaned in, handing it to Bob, who snatched the ticket away. Ramirez said, "I think they're the same ones behind a cemetery vandalism last week."

"That's terrible," Curtis said. "Hope you catch them."

Deputy Ramirez rested his arm on the door again and leaned in to offer his parting words. Curtis had a patch of gauze on his forehead given to him by Deckers that had managed to stop most of the bleeding, but it was steadily slipping out of place, and he was already thinking of what excuse he would give for it.

"Redwood is a nice community. A safe community, and that's how we like it," the deputy said with inherent pride. "But just like anywhere else, you've got your troublemakers."

"Ain't that the truth," Curtis said.

Bob remained stoically quiet, clutching the ticket in one hand and hiding his pistol in the other. Ramirez looked into the car again, as if something was bothering him. There was clearly tension in the air, and it seemed as though the deputy was beginning to take notice. "You guys all right?" he asked.

Bob quickly turned his head, putting on a clueless expression. "Yeah, of course. Just in a rush, like I said."

"Oh yeah," Ramirez asked. "Where to?"

"My place," Curtis said, cutting in. "We're hoping to surprise Mary with dinner before she gets home."

"And where's Mary at today?" he asked, in his seemingly endless sea of questions.

"Still at the fair," Curtis and Bob said in unison.

"Ah," he said, patting the side of the door. For a moment, it seemed as if the deputy just wanted to make small talk. Curtis had never seen Bob so anxious. His knee was shaking, and he was constantly wiping the sweat from his face with a pocket square.

"Really sorry about having to give you that ticket, Mr. Deckers. Don't worry, I went with the lowest fine allowed, ten dollars."

"That's fine," Bob said curtly.

Curtis placed his hands on the steering wheel, deeply conflicted. The time to put a stop to everything was nearing an end. Deputy Ramirez's unexpected appearance was a godsend, and Curtis felt it was his only chance to stop Bob before it was too late.

Could he mouth the word "help!" Would the deputy understand if he did?

He knew that once they got to the Bechdel mansion, Bob would be in complete control. He and Mary could be easily disposed of in complete privacy.

"Well... I guess I'll let you gentlemen get on your way then." Curtis readied to turn the ignition when Ramirez's hand mic crackled with chatter. *"Bravo Six, this is Alpha Twenty. What's your status?"*

"Go!" Bob seethed with his teeth gritted.

Curtis's hand gripped the keys, ready to turn on the engine, but the deputy's arm was still resting on the door as he answered the radio. During the time they had been pulled over, the blue autumn sky had gradually transitioned from something bright and inviting to gray and foreboding. There was a storm rising, and Curtis couldn't help but wonder if the weather itself was mirroring the trajectory of their descent.

"I can't!" he whispered forcibly to Bob from the side of his mouth. "You want suspicious? *That's* gonna look suspicious."

"I'm here at a traffic stop, over by the Bechdel property," Ramirez said into the mic. Curtis recognized the voice on the radio as that of Chief Riley himself. As partners, the two officers made a good pair, in Curtis's opinion. When Mary raised suspicion that the police chief and deputy were in on the conspiracy, Curtis couldn't imagine it.

Bob suddenly pulled his gun out from under his coat, fingering the trigger. His bulging eyes were fixated on Ramirez as the chatter on the radio continued. They could faintly hear the chief talking but couldn't make out what he was saying.

"Roger that," Chief Riley told the deputy. *"I'm at the fair with a county detail. Keep your eyes peeled, Deputy. Spoke with Anna, who runs the little coffee shop there on Michigan. She reported two men taking off in a blue Volvo. Said one of the men looked pretty beat up and the other one had a gun."*

Ramirez froze without responding. His eyes darted back to the car, examining it inside and out. The connection was meaningless to the deputy. He knew both Bob and Curtis and knew them to be friends and associates. If anything, his expression showed an acknowledgment of a freakish coincidence.

"I'll keep an eye out," he said into the mic. "Over and out."

Curtis felt a deep sigh of relief, but when he quickly glanced in Bob's direction, he could see the pale, panicked face of a man about to make an abhorrent mistake.

Ramirez tapped on the door again and then caught a glimpse of Curtis's beat-up face, previously concealed. He suddenly straightened his posture and gripped the handle of his holstered pistol. "What the hell happened to your face, Curtis?" A stark realization came over his face as he backed away from the Volvo, taking in the blue color and once again noting the strange and low-key demeanor of its passengers.

"What are you two up to?" he asked as though it was impossible for either of them to do something wrong. Ramirez should have known better.

Just as Curtis opened his mouth to offer assurances, the

barrel of the pistol entered his view and blasted two deafening shots into Deputy Ramirez's head, dropping him instantly. Curtis flinched and felt the hot singe of an ammo casing striking his cheek.

There was a loud ringing in his ears, and for a moment, he thought that it was he who had been shot. As if to prevent any resistance, Bob jammed the pistol into Curtis's temple, shouting at the top of his lungs, "Get the hell out of the car, now!" Feeling as though he were on autopilot, Curtis placed his hand on the door handle and pushed the door open.

He didn't understand why Bob was yelling or what had just happened. But as he stepped out of the car in a daze, he saw Deputy Ramirez's motionless body lying flat on the ground, face-up, with blood oozing from his skull and forming a thick puddle on the pavement.

Curtis felt his knees buckle and his stomach twisting in knots. The shock was too great. He vomited on the side of the road, inches from the deputy's body. As he straightened up, choking in the air, Bob rushed around the car, shouting to him to help drag Ramirez into the brush unless he wanted to join him.

"Get it together, Curtis! You don't have much time." He was already at Ramirez's arms, pulling him to the side and into the grass. "Grab his legs. Come on! Hurry up!"

Curtis mustered the will to make it over to where Bob waited panting, pistol in hand. Everything felt surreal. He thought of nothing else while grabbing Ramirez's legs and carrying his heavy body into the nearby forest. None of it felt real—not in the slightest.

* * *

Mary moved around the floor of the barn with intense concentration. She didn't fully understand why Phil would hide something in the barn as opposed to the house, only that it would be less likely to be found. She called out to Phil in her mind, hoping for guidance, but nothing tangible came through. She still felt shaken to have shared a moment of genuine telepathy with Theo.

They seemed to be linked somehow, beyond just possessing similar psychic abilities. Mary believed that whatever they were looking for held answers to many of her questions—starting with the claim that she had been to Redwood as a child. She didn't know why she had such expectations beyond a premonition of things to come. Straw floated down from the second-story platform as Theo moved haystacks around, scouring the wooden floor for clues. In Mary's mind, she saw a small hole or compartment under the floorboards. She had shared this with Theo, much to his relief. She asked him repeatedly if he had seen anything yet. He told her that he hadn't and hypothesized that the visions weren't being shared with him for a reason he couldn't pinpoint beyond his being an outsider.

"So am I," she had told him.

As Theo continued his search upstairs, Mary grabbed the pitchfork from the wall and began moving aside haystacks as quietly as she could.

Mary scraped against the dusty floorboards. It seemed a hopeless search, save for tearing the place apart. She rested the pitchfork against the wall and stood for a moment, scanning the area. It was exhausting work. Theo's footsteps continued above as Mary pondered the whereabouts of their mystery items.

If they failed to find anything in the barn, she knew they'd have to revert to searching the house—which had many rooms and endless possibilities. And if they failed to find anything there, she had to consider his acres of property and all that would be entailed in that. The search was beginning to feel hopeless. Theo said as much as he leaned on the upstairs railing and called to her in a quiet voice.

"I mean, really. It could be anywhere," he said, looking as dirty and exhausted as she felt.

"Doesn't look like we're going anywhere soon," she responded. "So, might as well keep looking."

Theo nodded with a vacant stare on his face and then walked to the ladder and climbed down. Mary began to lightly tap the floorboards around her, listening and feeling the area out. There were still plenty of haystacks to be moved. For all she knew, the mystery item could be stuffed in one of those perfectly symmetrical square blocks of hay, which looked nearly impossible to sift through.

"Maybe Phil never wanted it to be found. Whatever it is," Theo said, approaching her.

Mary gazed at the floor. "I don't know. Something tells me he was planning to share everything with me. He just wanted a couple more days." She turned and looked at Theo, her expression serious. "He was a very cautious man. I think that's how he stayed under the radar for so long."

A beam of sunlight crept into the barn through a small window high above them at the front of the barn. Mary followed the shadow cast by the pitchfork to a corner of the room where two columns of hay were stacked neatly. It seemed almost as though the pitchfork were pointing to something. Theo continued his own search, systematically mapping and looking but also thinking again and again about their earlier telepathic episode.

"I can't believe it. Speaking to each other like that. Have you ever experienced anything like that with anyone?"

"No..." she said, still following the shadow deep into the far corner.

"Why don't we try it again?" he said. "This could be a real breakthrough."

Mary stopped and tried her best, telling Theo that their mystery item was close, but he didn't seem in a receptive state.

"Are you trying?" he asked.

"Yes," she said quietly.

"Maybe we have to be under duress or something like that. What I want to do is figure out how we did it."

"Me too," she said, continuing her careful advance to the corner. She remained alert, but not so much to what Theo was saying. After a few more comments about their breakthrough, he finally realized she might be on the brink of a major discovery.

She arrived at the corner and stood in front of the haystacks without moving and closed her eyes. Her mind felt free of burden. No longer was she thinking of the Taylor brothers or the town conspiracy or Beatrice Thaxton, the elderly socialite who had toyed with her the other day in the corner store, or anything not related to the mission at hand. The only thing she could focus on was whatever was hidden beneath the floorboards.

"What is it?" Theo asked, approaching her. He then stopped and listened carefully to the sounds outside the barn. The Taylor brothers were nowhere to be heard. Were the brothers silently stalking them, preparing an ambush? He turned back to Mary. "I think it's only a matter of time until we're made. Whatever we're looking for, we need to find it fast or get out."

"I think we already have found it," she said, kneeling down. "Phil… I think he's guiding me." She rubbed her hands across the surface of the floor in a circular motion, dirtying them with hay and dust.

"I don't sense a thing," Theo said. "I can't hear your thoughts. Nothing." It sounded strange to hear Theo even say such a thing. No one would believe them if they made such a claim, especially Curtis. Their earlier telepathy may have been a fluke or a collective figment of their imaginations.

Mary suddenly stopped gliding her hands along the surface of the floor and turned to Theo, pointing toward the other end of the barn where tools were hanging.

"Grab that shovel and saw."

Theo spun around, noticeably thrilled, but with questions of his own. "Is it here? Are you certain?"

"No," Mary said. "But I've got one heck of a hunch."

Theo wasted no more time and dashed over to grab the tools. Mary stood up and pushed part of one haystack column aside, followed by the other. The effort made her lightheaded. The blocks hit the ground with a soft thud when suddenly a voice entered her mind—not Theo's, but someone else's.

"Enough running around. You're going to have a child, remember? Stop this nonsense."

Mary froze, wondering if it was her own thoughts, but she had no control of them.

"Who are you?" she asked, the words not leaving her mouth. *"Why are you in my mind?"*

"Do you recognize my voice?" the man asked.

"No."

"I came into your room the second day you moved into the Bechdel mansion. Do you remember? You were about to get into the shower. I asked you what you were so afraid of."

Mary fell to her knees in shock, and Theo placed a hand on her shoulder. "Mary?" he whispered in a fearful tone. "Are you all right?"

She snapped out of her trance and whipped her head around, a startled look in her eyes filled with questions. "Yes... I... I don't know what happened."

"Your eyes looked like they were about to roll into the

back of your head. You were muttering something, but I couldn't hear it."

"Really?" Mary said, rubbing her forehead. "It's so weird hearing all these voices. Your voice, and now… some stranger."

"You sound like a crazy person," Theo said, gently hovering over her.

Mary laughed softly and then noticed the shovel he was holding. "It couldn't have been Phil. The voice, I mean. He said he spoke to me before. Weeks ago."

Theo motioned with his head. "You also moved those haystacks out of the way and drew a circle."

Mary turned around quickly, verifying Theo's claim. Sure enough, drawn in the thin layer of sand and dust covering the floorboards was a perfect circle, pinpointing the location of their search. Or it was just a circle indicating nothing? Either way, Theo was quick to move.

"Some people draw X's, you draw circles. That's fair." He knelt down and felt around the floorboards, leaving her circle intact. "Yeah. Something's definitely under here." He looked up. "It's giving off some kind of warmness. Kinetic in a way."

Suddenly, they could hear distant voices. The Taylors were back outside.

One of the brothers yelled, "I don't care where they ran off to, we gotta find 'em. Sons of bitches took my gun!"

"Calm down, Liam," another brother said. "We got their license plate info. Now let's get out of here."

The brothers sounded close, as if they were speaking from the back porch. It was strange that none of them had mentioned the barn yet or seemed to have any interest in it.

"Enough of that. Get your shit together," a gruffer voice interjected, which Mary assumed to be Garret's. He carried himself as the leader of their group, so perhaps he was the oldest. Perhaps he was just a natural leader.

Mary thought of her vision a few nights ago, shared, she believed, from the recesses of Julie's memories. A scarred face had stared down at her in the moonlight. She recognized that face the moment she saw Garret at the funeral and trembled at the thought of being near a man who would shoot a child in the face. It made her sick to her stomach.

"Hey..." Theo whispered, not making a move. "Whatever we need to do, we need to do it fast. They're going to check this barn eventually."

She felt that Theo and she were close to a discovery. Just a few more minutes were all they needed. She was sure of it.

Suddenly, Garret continued talking, close by outside the barn. "Listen, you two. We can't piddle around here anymore. We don't know who was here or why. We don't know where they went, and we don't know if they alerted the authorities. So we need to leave before the brass show up."

Mary sighed in relief, but Theo stayed alert, listening. The Taylor brothers said little more and went back inside the house. Was it a setup? Mary wasn't sure.

"All right, let's do this," Theo said, dropping down to a knee. He positioned the saw over one of the floorboards and brought his arm back, prepared to begin.

Mary looked ahead, past Theo, to where she noticed something off about the very board he was about to saw. "Wait," she said, holding her arm out. Just then, they heard the front door to Phil's house open and slam shut and then the sound of movement and voices carrying across his yard. Then the distant chatter between the Taylor brothers faded, followed by the sound of their car doors opening.

"Wait a minute," Jeffery's voice said, laughing. "I got something for these folks."

Mary pondered what he meant by that comment but

found out all too soon when she heard the sound of glass shattering and more laughter.

"Quit screwing around, Jeff, and get your ass in the car," Garret barked.

Their engine roared and car doors slammed. Mary was still suspicious of whether they were actually leaving or not.

"What did they do, smash a window out?" Theo asked.

"Sounded like it," Mary said.

"Bastards..." he said.

"If that's the worst they do to us, we can count ourselves lucky," Mary said. She turned her focus back to the floor where she noticed that the entire floorboard in question was slightly off—it had a brighter color, barely noticeable, yet different from the rest. Mary got up and walked to the wall where the board ended.

"What is it?" Theo asked.

His own abilities had seemed diminished since they entered the barn, as though Mary was the only one privy to Phil's secrets. She pulled up the board and noticed that it wasn't nailed down like the others.

Theo took a step back, surprised, as Mary began lifting it up. He grabbed the midsection and they removed the board from the floor, revealing the tamped earth beneath the barn.

Theo looked into the gap in the floor and saw darkened orange earth with a damp, musty smell. He ran his hands through the clay-like dirt, barely able to contain his excitement. "I can't believe it." He then placed the saw onto the flooring as though it no longer served any purpose. "You did it, Mary."

Mary paced along the gap and waved him off. "We did it, Theo. We're a team, remember?"

"We are?" Theo said. He then looked down, thinking to himself. "Yeah, I guess you're right." He took the shovel in one hand and nudged at the dirt below. "This is about where you drew that circle."

Mary stood across from him and nodded. "We're so close. I just know it."

Theo began digging, pushing the shovel hard into the ground with his boot and then bringing up a shovelful of dirt that he placed to the side. "Although you *did* tell me to grab a saw for no reason. We can't all be right all the time."

"Very funny," she said, brushing her hair out of her face. "Just keep digging."

"Yes, ma'am!" Theo said in a heightened, mocking fashion.

Mary couldn't take her eyes off the hole he was digging. Therein lay all the answers to the secrets that had plagued her since they had arrived in Redwood—or so she believed.

Theo kept digging, and the hole got deeper with more and more dirt piled to the side. Though she had felt guiding forces bringing her to this very spot, she could not envision what lay buried there. That was still a mystery. As was Pastor Phil. Who was he, really? What had happened to his children? His siblings? All she knew for certain was that his wife had passed away some years ago. If only she could have talked with him for a few more days. Her mind stayed on the hole. She paid no attention to the cell phone in her pocket even as it vibrated. Theo heaved and dug the shovel in again and again, growing exhausted.

"Want me to take over?" she asked.

His sweaty face looked up, and he shrugged. "I'm good, thanks. Almost there."

Mary looked into the hole, four feet wide, a few feet deep, and just as she was about to reach into her pocket for her cell phone, Theo hit something. Metal? It had that sound. He stopped immediately, eyes bright with anticipation. He glanced at Mary, and for a moment, neither of them said a word. Theo dug the shovel into the ground again, striking a metallic object buried exactly where Mary had drawn the circle.

"This could be it…" he said. "We're onto something here…"

DESPERATE MEASURES

Bob and Curtis carried Deputy Ramirez's lifeless body into the nearby forest through a sparse path and down a slope covered in layers of leaves. Curtis felt strangely removed from what he was doing, as though his mind had taken refuge in the recesses of his subconsciousness. Ramirez was heavy, and they struggled to carry him.

Holding his ankles, Curtis looked away from the ghost-like face of the deceased deputy, with his eyes rolled back, mouth agape, and a hole in his forehead. Bob said little beyond grunting his demands to move faster as they descended the hill and stumbled toward a narrow gully absent of water that looked like both a ditch and a grave.

They stopped at the edge of the dark crevice, and Bob heaved and pulled Ramirez by the arms, only to face resistance from Curtis, who held his ankles tight.

"What the hell are you doing?" Bob said, sweat running down his forehead and his silver hair a tangled nest.

Curtis straightened his back, defiant. "This man had a family. A wife and children. I'm not going to let you toss him down a hole like this."

Bob smirked in amusement. "No offense, Curtis, but I don't really care what you think at the moment. Now back away."

Curtis gripped Ramirez's ankles tighter and yanked him from Bob's grasp. "You sick son of a bitch. You killed a police officer for nothing. A good man who had done nothing to you." He took a step forward and shouted, his voice echoing through the forest. "What could possibly be worth this man's life? Or Pastor Phil's life? *Have you no soul?* What is wrong with you?"

Bob stared ahead silently, with sunken eyes that said everything there was to say about his state of mind. His pale and worsening appearance were only the visible signs of a man who had embraced the darkest of human tendencies. His moral regression had indeed stunned Curtis, who, before seeing Bob's true nature, had thought him a boastful but affable man—a good man to have in your corner.

Now he could see that there was nothing good left in Bob. It was as though he was possessed—an unrecognizable morally destitute being. There was malice in Bob's frantic eyes, which convinced Curtis that he had never actually known the man.

"I understand you're angry, but spare me the lectures," Bob said. His finger caressed the trigger as he aimed the pistol between Curtis's eyes. "Keep it up, and you'll make this all too easy. I could shoot you here and toss you down the hole with Martinez. I'll get the answers I need from Mary either way."

Curtis flinched with the realization that he could very well suffer the same fate as the murdered deputy lying at his feet.

"I really don't want to make your wife a widow," Bob said. "But don't take that as a weakness. You're alive right now because I respect you, Curtis, and you might be useful to me. Keep it up though, and that could change really quickly."

Silence fell between them, the only sound that of unseen birds cawing in the distance. Mere miles from his house, Curtis had never felt so isolated or helpless. He wanted nothing more than to call Mary, warn her, and tell her to stay as far away from the house as possible. But it didn't seem as if Bob was going to let that happen, not then, anyway.

Curtis glared back at Bob, his eyes watering with rage and his crimson face flushed. "I will *not* allow you to toss his body down there." It would seem he had made his decision, despite his sense of self-preservation. Curtis took a step forward and pointed down at Ramirez. "Leave him be. What does it matter? In the end, there'll be no covering this up, no matter how powerful the Taylor family is."

Bob sighed; he didn't care, and this wasn't worth the fight. "Fine. Drag him over to those bushes, and let's get the hell out of here."

Curtis felt the compromise was as much as he was going to get and pulled Ramirez's body toward an oak tree and into a nearby thicket of elderberry bushes. He vowed to somehow return and ensure that Deputy Ramirez's body was given a proper burial; the shock of it all was still raw in his mind.

"Hurry up!" Bob said as Curtis did his best to place the body carefully within the brush. "We have to hide that cruiser next, so check his pockets for the keys."

A strong cool breeze blew through the woods, causing branches to sway and dead leaves to rustle on the ground. The overcast sky shielded the sun, and Curtis could sense a storm on the horizon. The keys. He had no choice. He felt along Ramirez's pockets and discovered a key chain clipped to his belt. He pulled the keys off, half wanting to toss them in the ditch and watch Bob jump down after them.

He wanted nothing more than to leave that terrible forest

with the hope that this grim ordeal would soon come to an end. As they trudged up the hill, Curtis turned and glanced at the bushes below where Ramirez lay, concealed from the naked eye. Bob walked slightly ahead of him, and Curtis saw that, for the first time, he wasn't being carefully watched by his captor.

For a moment, he felt an opportunity to run from Bob. In his mid-thirties, Curtis was younger and most likely faster than Bob, who looked at least ten years older. Just as they reached the top of the hill, Bob spun around as though he could sense Curtis's plan.

"Don't make me pull this trigger, Curtis. I'm a damn fine shot, and I wouldn't test me if I were you."

Curtis slowly raised his hands. "I don't know what you're talking about."

"Of course you do. Now let's move that cruiser."

They approached Ramirez's abandoned cruiser. Its windows were rolled down, and Curtis could see a notepad in the middle console and a coffee cup wedged in the holder. A police radio mounted below the dashboard crackled with static. There was a shotgun holder affixed to the side of the passenger seat and a closed laptop on the passenger seat.

Bob opened the passenger door and motioned toward Curtis with his pistol. "You've got the keys. Let's start 'er up."

Curtis opened the door and got in. He put the keys in the ignition and started the engine, feeling a growing sickness in his stomach. He felt like an accessory to murder after the fact and was certain Bob would make that claim regardless.

Bob pointed past his Volvo, where a puddle of blood remained on the faded pavement of the two-lane road. "Drive. There's a path ahead."

Curtis reluctantly pulled onto the road and passed the Volvo, continuing for about fifty feet until Bob had him veer to the right and toward a clearing in the woods. They drove over dirt mounds, tree stumps, and bushes lying in their path, reaching a shaded area not visible from the road. Bob seemed pleased enough and told Curtis to park.

"That's good. We've wasted enough time as it is."

Curtis felt his pocket along the bulge of his cell phone. "I need to call Mary. She's probably worried sick by now."

Bob shook his head. "Not yet. You'll call her when we get back to the house. Everything will run smoothly from there."

"She may already be there."

"So be it," Bob said. He then gestured to the forest around them with his pistol—a pistol that Curtis wanted more than anything to grab from him and then put a bullet in his head. "Let's go."

Curtis opened the door and stepped onto soft, leafy ground, staring into the wilderness. Distant thunder rumbled in the sky. The storm was closer than he had thought.

* * *

Theo tossed aside his shovel in a frenzy as Mary stood back, astonished that they had actually come across something. She drew closer as Theo dropped to his knees and lunged toward the hole, unearthing a thick metal box with his eager hands as chunks of dirt fell from its top and corners.

"What is it?" she asked.

Theo carefully balanced the object and set it gently on the ground as Mary stood over it.

"It's got some weight to it," Theo said. He brushed some sand from the front of the box, revealing a combination dial. As he wiped more sand from the surface, he pulled at the carrying handle, but it was locked shut. "It's a safe," he told Mary.

Why would they expect anything less?

Mary crossed her arms, staring down at their discovery. It was an old-model safe with rust covering areas of the bluish metallic surface. "I guess a shoe box just wouldn't have been Phil's style."

"I suppose not," Theo said, smiling. He felt along the surface of the vintage safe—about three cubic feet and seventy pounds—for the combination dial. Their success was bittersweet, since whatever was secured inside was still a mystery, but Mary had a quick suggestion. "If we found the right tools, I'm sure we could get this open."

Theo brushed the dirt from its top surface and glanced at Mary with an arched brow. "You ever crack a safe before?"

"No," she said. "Have you?"

"Nah. But how hard could it be?" he said with a shrug.

"Not too hard. I hope," she said, though she couldn't help but feel increasing skepticism of the plan.

Theo looked around the barn, marveling at the hole before them. "How did you know…?" he asked Mary.

She thought to herself, uncertain of the right answer. "I just… I trusted my instincts, that's all."

Theo shook his head. "No, this is something else. In a property so big, randomly finding this is a one in a million chance, and you led us right to it."

She knew what Theo was getting at. Her abilities, it seemed, were surpassing his. He stated as much as he rose to his feet, brushing sand off his dusty blue jeans. "You're the real deal, Mary. I have to admit it."

She waved him off and turned around to face the barn door. The Taylor brothers had left moments ago, and she didn't think they'd be coming back anytime soon. She envisioned them prowling the town, desperately searching for them or waiting perhaps blocks away. There seemed to be no escape.

Perhaps they had no real business unearthing what was in

the safe beyond protecting it from outside forces. Maybe it was what Phil would have wanted.

Theo rolled the combination dial around, hoping to get lucky, and then looked up at Mary. "He never mentioned this thing?"

Mary turned back and shook her head. "He was going to tell me more. We had barely scratched the surface before he died."

"You think he had a hand in guiding you to this? Perhaps he trusted you more than anyone else."

Mary said nothing as she paced along the floorboards, disturbing the hay scattered about. Whatever Phil had wanted in the end, Mary still felt a responsibility to get to the truth for Julie. Maybe the contents inside were of no use. But what if they were? Things had gotten complicated, however, with the Taylor brothers out there. They were now in serious danger.

"We need to go," she said, and walked to the entryway, lifting the plank locking the barn doors. Theo crouched down and picked up the safe, cradling it like a bowling ball.

"Is it heavy?" she asked.

"Not too bad," Theo said with assurance despite the heave he had given. "Like carrying two bowling balls."

Mary looked around, hesitant. "Let's get this place in order first. Cover our tracks."

Theo sighed and set the safe back down. "Very well."

They set to rearranging the haystacks, filling the hole back up with dirt, and setting the floorboard back in place. Minutes later, they left the barn, feelings satisfied enough that their tracks were covered.

As they cautiously approached Mary's SUV, they noticed glass lying on the ground at the rear. No surprise. They'd heard the attack. A large rock lay in the back seat, launched through the back window by Jeffery Taylor. The Taylors had sent a clear message and could return at any time. Mary was surprised to look down and see her tires intact. Perhaps the Taylor brothers wanted her to drive off. Their search would be over, and it would be easy to ambush them.

She kept a careful eye on their surroundings as Theo set the safe in the back seat, covering it with a towel. Traveling into town seemed risky, but they needed to get the safe open somehow, even if that meant just locating the proper tools.

"Any real ideas on how to get that safe open?" Mary asked as she backed out and drove away.

"I'm thinking," Theo responded, gripping the armrest as they bounced along the uneven dirt road. "I've seen them do it in the movies. All we need is a welder and a crowbar."

Mary laughed to herself, enjoying the shared excitement between them. "Is that it? I guess we're in luck. How about some goggles, a helmet, maybe?"

"Sounds good; I like goggles," he said lightly.

Theo pulled the .45 caliber from his pocket and held it in both hands, examining its shiny surface. His mood changed. "If I find out those Taylor bastards had anything to do with my mother's disappearance, I'll shoot them dead with their own pistol."

They reached a paved two-lane road, and Mary turned left, ten miles from downtown. She was prepared to take the risk.

"We're not killers," she said. "And that's not why I'm doing this. Whoever killed the Bechdel and Drake families and Pastor Phil needs to face justice in a court of law. They need to be held accountable for what they did. Killing them… well, that's just an act of vengeance."

Theo ejected the magazine from the pistol and held it up, inspecting the rounds inside. "You're kind of naive, Mary, but I understand where you're coming from."

"I'm understand your anger," she said. "But let's play it safe for now, okay?"

He slapped the magazine back into the pistol and slipped it inside his jacket. She could sense the inherent risk of walking around downtown, completely exposed. The mayor would most likely have lookouts posted everywhere. The Taylor brothers could be waiting for them nearby, watching their every move. Despite all that, she wasn't going to be afraid. She would face them head on. Everything, she felt, now relied on her determination to do so.

* * *

The autumn festival was in full swing, and Mary felt luckily inconspicuous with all the activity going on around them. The distracted crowd and the entertainment afforded them the perfect opportunity to move through downtown undetected—that was if they hadn't already been seen. Mary took the back roads and detours back to where they had dropped Curtis off.

With Bob Deckers's corner office in view, she felt unease in the pit of her stomach. There was an ominous aura surrounding them, in addition to their unanswered questions, starting with Curtis's silence on the phone. She hadn't heard from him for what seemed like hours.

Staring at Bob's undisturbed office created further distress. He and Bob couldn't possibly still be talking, could they? She called Curtis's number again, frustrated by the fifth ring, and then left a message that couldn't hide her growing worry. "We're outside Bob Deckers's office, and we need to get home as soon as possible. We're going to look for you on foot now. Call me." She hung up with an exhausted sigh.

With his eyes on the gray, five-story building in front of

them, Theo could feel Mary's growing anxiety. "Everything okay? When was the last time you heard from him?"

Mary pulled forward and drove past the building, approaching the adjacent pizza shop. She slowed a bit passing Bob Deckers's tinted windows, and then sped past the pizza place, turning into an alleyway. For the moment, they were out of sight from any passing vehicles. "We haven't spoken since we dropped him off. I've missed a bunch of his calls and text messages, but even those stopped about thirty minutes ago. Now he's not answering the phone."

"What was the last thing he said to you?" Theo asked.

Mary looked at him with deep worry in her strained, blue eyes. "He told me that Deckers had just arrived, and that he was going in to talk to him."

Theo cupped his chin, thinking. "They could just be having a long talk. Your husband is a lawyer, you know," he teased gently.

She nodded and drove slowly toward a large green dumpster, parking directly behind it and concealing her vehicle from view. She felt confident enough that the Taylors wouldn't be searching the alleyways.

If anything, they already knew who she was and were scoping out her home. But she and Curtis had a gate and a newly installed security system. That had to count for something.

She shut off the ignition and told Theo that they'd be on foot, at least until they found Curtis. There was trouble of some kind; it wasn't like Curtis to ignore her calls. She felt drained after fleeing for their lives at Phil's farm and then unearthing the safe.

All of it was so much that her keen foresight wasn't on par with what it usually was. And there were other complications. Theo seemed distracted by the safe sitting in the back, eager to recover its contents. He didn't even want to leave the vehicle, and she couldn't blame him, but finding Curtis was the most important thing.

"Are you sure about this?" he asked. "Maybe we could hide it somewhere for the time being."

Mary stepped out of the car, looking around. "We'll only be gone for a few minutes. Trust me."

Theo reluctantly stepped out of the SUV and closed his door then examined the shattered window in the back. "I don't like this," he said. "Why don't I just wait here?."

"Come on," Mary said, walking fast down the alleyway. "We can't split up. Not with Curtis missing."

Theo huffed but followed, ultimately giving in. They emerged from the alleyway and onto the sidewalk to the distinct sound of folk melodies playing in the town square. There was an endless feeling of cheer permeating the whole of downtown, which Mary couldn't have felt more at odds with. There were a few people on the sidewalks ahead, passing shops and going to their cars, and they paid her little mind. As she passed Bricklayers Pizza, with Bob Deckers's office in view, her anxiety increased. Either they were in there or they weren't. And if they weren't, then where were they?

She envisioned Bob Deckers at the police station giving his confession as Curtis stood hovering behind, watching. She hoped for nothing more than that, but if that were the case, Curtis would have called her by now.

They walked up to the office. The blinds were shut and a "closed" sign hung in the window. Theo pulled at the glass door of Deckers's office, but it wouldn't budge. He tried to look inside as Mary approached, clearly worried.

"Nothing," Theo said. "Not a soul inside."

Mary looked in, finding a gap in the blinds, and saw the familiar empty alignment of desks on both sides of the room, and beyond that, Deckers's office in the back. Something on the floor sparkled, like glass, but there were no lights on and no signs of a single person inside.

"Just great," she said. She held her cell phone up again to see if Curtis had responded to her latest text and call. Again, nothing. She walked past Theo and headed down the sidewalk toward the festival grounds, soon entering a world of face-paintings, pumpkin pies, and autumn cheer.

Under different circumstances, she could see Curtis and her having a wonderful time, but these were far from normal circumstances. Pastor Phil had been murdered, and now Curtis was missing. They passed a few buildings as the music grew louder and more people filtered out into the road in their path.

Mary could see the tops of tents and booths in the distance. She moved quickly around a few barricades with Theo trailing and entered Main Street, slightly disoriented by the blur of faces all around—none being Curtis or Deckers. The stage was roughly a hundred feet ahead of her and past most of the assembled crowd.

There were kids with snow cones and balloons, carnival booths featuring apple bobbing and ring tosses, craft beer tents, and barbecue trucks. There seemed to be a little of something for everyone. Mary moved through the crowd, feeling both inconspicuous and slightly exposed at the same time.

She felt drawn to the stage where a man was strumming his acoustic guitar, his soulful voice accompanied by familiar, folksy chords. She could see a tall, silver-haired man ahead standing near one of the booths with a plastic cup in hand. Didn't she know him? Theo caught up to her just as her pace increased, and they maneuvered around the crowd with stealth-like ease.

When they were five feet from the Bob Deckers look-alike, Chief Riley suddenly entered her line of sight, just as surprised to see her as she was to see him. He halted suddenly and touched her arms to avoid a collision as his Aviator sunglasses nearly flew off his face.

"Careful there, ma'am," he said.

"Chief Riley!" Mary said.

"Ah, Mrs. Malone. So nice to see you."

Mary stood on her toes, looking over the chief's shoulders, only to find her mystery man no longer there. He had disappeared.

She found herself distracted, but with Bob Deckers now only a figment of her imagination, she turned to Chief Riley with her full attention.

"How are you today? A little crowded, eh?" she asked.

The chief moved next to a cotton candy booth where the crowd had thinned out. The singer on stage had just wrapped up his last song as the crowd cheered his fast-strumming finale.

"Yes, ma'am. One of the busiest days of the year. Something about fall time always brings out the celebration gene in people around here."

Mary leaned closer as though she were speaking in confidence. "I'm looking for Curtis. Have you seen him anywhere, Chief?"

Chief looked up and thought to himself. "No, I haven't actually. He's been at the fair?"

"Yes," Mary said. "I dropped him off a while ago at Bob Deckers's office." She paused, already afraid that she had said too much. Theo stood behind her, watching the stage with his hands in his pockets while trying to stay unnoticed by the chief. His eyes were alert and purposeful. Mary knew that, despite his nonchalant stance, he was keeping a lookout for the Taylor brothers. They could be anywhere, plotting their next move. The safe, however, was elsewhere and out of their reach—if that was indeed what they were looking for.

The chief seemed intrigued by the mention of Deckers, but then said that he hadn't seen him either. He then said, "I did receive a call from the coffee shop across the street from the Realtor office. Owner said she saw two men walking to a blue Volvo. Real suspicious-like."

Mary was stunned by the news. "Suspicious-like? What do you mean?"

The chief shrugged. "Like something wasn't right. I'm about to go over and talk to her myself. Just waiting for Deputy Ramirez. Have you seen him anywhere?"

Mary thought to herself. She had seen other police officers, but not him. "No, I'm sorry. I haven't."

"Well, that's just odd," Chief Riley said. "He's been MIA for nearly an hour now."

"This coffee shop call," Mary began with a worried expression. "Did they describe who they saw?"

"Two Caucasian males," he said. "One tall. The other about average height."

"And what were they doing that was so *suspicious*?" Mary asked.

"Going over there to get more details in a minute," he answered, as though he didn't want to elaborate. "She said one man was leading the other to a blue Volvo and holding what looked like a firearm."

Mary's mouth nearly dropped. "Chief Riley, doesn't Bob Deckers own a blue Volvo?"

He turned to her, clearly not making any kind of connection. "What do you mean?"

She was prepared to make a scene right then and there when a new speaker took the festival stage, blaring into the microphone. "Ladies and gentlemen, we hope you've enjoyed the festivities thus far for our annual autumn festival!"

Mary saw that it was Cliff Bronson, Pastor Phil's assistant, speaking on stage. He was wearing a flannel shirt and blue jeans, his mustache trimmed, and his hair cut short on his balding head. Mary, taken aback by his presence, saw that there were more surprises in store.

Bronson said, "I'd like to introduce our own master of ceremonies, the man who has been this town's mayor since before many of us were born… a man who has overseen the growth and expansion of an enclave of tiny buildings and modest surroundings into the vibrant town before us. Ladies and gentlemen, Mayor Taylor!"

The crowd cheered as the mayor emerged on stage, bounding in a lively way from the steps below. He was domineering and stocky, like his brothers, with gray hair and a clean-shaven, though slightly sunken face. Even from a distance, she could see into his soulless dark eyes as he took the microphone and scanned the crowd with respect—or contempt, upon a closer look.

Mayor Taylor raised his arms as the clapping and cheering grew louder and louder. Theo placed his hand on Mary's shoulder, causing her to turn her head.

"We should get out of here," he said with urgency.

She scanned the park, the stage, and the various booths around them and didn't see any sign of the brothers, but he could feel their presence, just as she was sure Theo had.

"Okay," she said. "Chief Riley got a tip about two men going to a Volvo outside Deckers's office. The taller of the men looked like he was brandishing a gun."

Theo's eyes widened as he shifted toward the chief. "Crap. Then what are we waiting for?"

But the chief was fixated on the mayor, as were most people in the crowd.

"I can say that, without a doubt, October is one of my favorite times of the year!" the mayor bellowed to more applause. "And spending this lovely afternoon with the fine folks of Redwood is more than I could ask for. It's something I look forward to each and every time."

The mayor paused, taking in a breath and lowering his arms. He leaned closer to the crowd, grabbing the microphone and talking to them in a more intimate fashion than before.

Mary could see his charisma and his ability to control a crowd—but she also saw a lot more, a man who cared about nothing more than power.

"Before the night's end, I promise a big surprise. So stick around for the big unveiling. That's all of you, okay?"

The crowd applauded, some shouting and whistling. The mayor paused again and pulled an apple from his coat pocket. "You see this delicious morsel? It was grown right here in the apple fields of Redwood. One of our finest homegrown products." He bit off a big chunk from the apple, crunching and chewing it, with an almost vulgar satisfaction evident on his face.

In the middle of the routine, an aide rushed across the stage and took the mayor's arm, speaking into his ear. The mayor stood frozen as his mouth slowly continued chewing. He swallowed and then leaned back into the microphone, distracted and rushed.

"That's all for now, everyone. Relax, have some food, and enjoy the day!" He was rushed off stage to the confusion of the crowd as a musical duo quickly appeared and began playing. In a matter of moments, the mayor disappeared, security detail and all. Mary knew that she and Theo were in trouble, and she knew they needed to make themselves scarce.

Mary glanced at Chief Riley, whose attention was still on the stage. She was ready to confide in him and recruit his assistance when her cell phone suddenly vibrated in her pocket.

Chief Riley had a call too. He walked toward the stage after listening to an APB on his radio mic. He was then gone in a flash. Mary pulled her phone out and knew it was Curtis even before looking at the screen.

"Hello? Curtis, where are you?" she said.

Theo stayed near, keeping watch, as Mary moved between the cotton candy and the ring-toss booths. There was a pause on the line, so she continued. "Damn it, Curtis. Where have you been?"

"Hi, Mary..." his voice said.

"That's all you have to say? I've been worried sick about you."

"I'm at the house... Where are you now?" he asked. His voice sounded strained, suspicious even. She knew something was wrong.

"How'd you get to the house? Where's Bob?"

"He-he dropped me off," Curtis said unconvincingly.

Mary was frantic. "Curtis, you have to tell me what's going on. I'm with Chief Riley right now."

There was another pause, and Mary was certain that she could hear a faint voice in the background. Curtis had sounded distraught, and Mary felt her stomach churning.

"He killed Deputy Ramirez!" Curtis blurted into the phone. *"He's got a gun pointed at me right now!"*

Mary gasped and clutched her chest just as she heard a loud *whack* that was followed by static. "Curtis!" she shouted, causing Theo to turn around and look at her with concern. She held a finger up, telling him to wait as she listened, ear pressed against the phone, her eyes watering. She heard shuffling on the line, and then someone spoke. A voice she was in no way surprised hearing.

"Mary, this is Bob."

"Where's Curtis?" she seethed.

"He's fine... for now. Listen to me, you bitch. You so much as look at Chief Riley or any police officers between now and your journey home, I won't hesitate to put a bullet in your husband's head."

"What do you want?" she asked, trying to control the trembling in her voice.

"I want you to come home. Bring your investigator friend with you. You know, the little rat who betrayed me. I'll be waiting."

Mary looked at Theo with uncertainty. "Theo Stone? He left a few days ago."

"Is that so?" he said.

"I promise," Mary said with conviction.

"Don't screw with me, Mary. Curtis told me all about that hack."

"He's not with me!" she nearly shouted.

There was a pause followed by Bob talking a little more

calmly, like he'd bought it. *"All right... Get over here. No stops. No police. Just you. Do that and you and your husband will live."*

Mary didn't feel right about any of that. She could sense a trap. "How do I know you won't hurt us?"

"Because all I want is information," he said. *"And then you'll never see me again."*

He hung up without saying another word, leaving Mary shaken and holding the phone in a daze. Theo grilled her, speaking softly as the latest folk-rock band continued its lively set on stage. There was no sign of the mayor or his brothers, or Chief Riley for that matter. Mary saw other police in the crowd, but none of whom she recognized. The chief would have been her only bet, and he was gone.

"Bob Deckers has Curtis," she said to Theo. She covered her face suddenly, holding back tears. "Oh my God. I knew we shouldn't have left him. This is all my fault."

Theo held her arms, trying to reassure her as Mary stared at the ground in despair. "No one is to blame here, Mary. We're all trying to do our best with this situation." He paused, looking around, and finding the right moment, he escorted Mary out of the crowd. "I've got a plan," he said, guiding her away. "But let's get out of here first."

Curtis woke to find himself sitting in a darkened room, his hands and legs tied to a chair behind him. He jerked at the rope but was unable to move. He lifted his head, the top of his skull throbbing, and tried to look around, eyes squinting in the dim light of a mysterious room. The white curtains behind him glowed in the afternoon light, streaming in through a bay window. The room was illuminated enough for him to then realize that he was downstairs in the ballroom.

The winding staircase was to his left, roughly fifty feet away, with hallways on both sides of him leading to other rooms. He still couldn't believe the scale of the mansion. His head pounded as recollection of what had happened came rushing back to him: the moments leading up to Bob's assault and everything that had happened before that. He tried to remember the details, to fix the narrative in his mind in a way that made sense. Leaving the office at gunpoint. The senseless murder of Deputy Ramirez. Hiding Deputy Ramirez's police cruiser. Then driving Bob's Volvo to the mansion, being taken inside and told to call Mary.

Curtis had complied and soon realized that he couldn't mislead Mary, whether there was a gun to his head or not. He tried to warn her and then received a quick blow to the head with the barrel of Bob's pistol, knocking him unconscious.

He probably had a concussion, given the number of times Bob had struck him. Still, Bob had not shot him, not yet. This, he believed, meant that Bob needed him alive for some reason. He needed something from him, and their business was far from over.

He could hear Bob walking up and down the hall to his right, which led to the kitchen. And as he heard Bob's dress shoes clacking against the tile floor, he could also hear him talking on the phone, just loud enough for Curtis to decipher some of what he was saying.

"I've got him here, with Mrs. Malone on the way. Yes, everything is in place." There was a pause as his voice faded in the confines of the hall, only to resurface once he drew closer to the ballroom. "Beatrice, just tell them to hurry up. This damn mansion gives me the creeps." He hung up the phone, footsteps growing closer. Curtis bowed his head and closed his eyes just in time to hear a curious swooshing sound of water in a bucket. Before he could react, cold water drenched his face, streaming down from his head, wiping out Curtis's sight and making him howl in protest.

He snapped forward, livid and unable to free himself from the rope tying his hands and ankles behind him. Water dripped from his face as he gasped for air. As his eyes flickered rapidly, he saw a blurry figure pacing in front of him.

"Wake up, buddy. Your wife will be here soon."

Curtis took another deep breath, still in shock from the jolt of cold water thrown into his face. Bob continued in his snide and self-satisfied tone. "Sorry I had to subdue you there, but it's all for your own good. I don't like having to hit you over the head every time you step out of line."

Curtis jerked again at the rope, but it was hopeless. Bob had tied them too tight. "Untie me..." he said.

"Careful now," Bob replied. "You don't want to knock the chair over. You'll be like a turtle on its shell. You ever seen how foolish one of them look, all helpless like that?" Bob laughed to himself as Curtis squinted with malice.

Curtis regretted not stopping Bob when he'd had a chance in the office. He couldn't stand the sight of Bob in his house. It was a violation, much like so many others: their apartment in Chicago being broken into, the inverted cross painted on the mansion's front door, and the kitchen left in shambles by what? Supposed supernatural forces? What did it all mean? Was any of it connected?

Curtis sat helpless in his chair, unable to harm Bob when that was exactly what he wanted to do. Rage burned inside him as he discreetly pulled at the rope around his wrists.

"You haven't explained anything," he said to Bob. "I don't know what the hell you want. I don't know why you killed Pastor Phil. I don't know any of it. All I know is that you are a lying, murdering scumbag."

"Not necessarily," Bob said flippantly. "Once everything falls into place, I'll be greatly rewarded for my steadfast loyalty and belief in the mission." He got within a few feet of Curtis and patted his cheek as though he were a child. "Keep your chin up, and you'll get through this fine."

Curtis jerked his head away, face flushed with his rage. "Don't touch me again, you bastard."

Bob backed away and shook his head in disappointment. "No need to be so angry. You and Mary could come out of this thing on top if you just use your heads." He paused and took his pistol out while glancing down at the screen of the cell phone in his other hand. "Of course, if you refuse, you'll be very sorry in the end. You'll wish that you'd just cooperated."

"Who the hell are you?" Curtis demanded, his loud voice echoing throughout the room. "You shot an innocent man in the head. A family man. A—"

"Shut up," Bob said, waving him off. "Yes, yes. We've been through this before. I know what I did, and it had to be done. You'll see soon enough." He then lowered his pistol and walked toward Curtis, a steely glare on his face.

"You want to talk about family? My wife left me without warning two years ago." He took another looming step toward Curtis, his tone rising with anger. "Took my three daughters and disappeared. Left me a letter. *A letter*! Dear John all the way. I haven't seen her or my children since. It's like she went into hiding. She took everything from me." He paused again and held the pistol up, pressing it into Curtis's forehead. Curtis flinched as Bob continued. "I always fantasized about finding her, about holding the gun against her head just like this and making her pay."

He yanked the pistol away and stepped back as Curtis sighed in relief. "She left me for another man, but I'll find them some day, and when I do, I can't wait to see the look on their faces when I leave them dead on the floor." He slipped the pistol into his front coat pocket and began scrolling through his cell phone as Curtis stared ahead, disgusted.

"You're a monster," Curtis said.

Bob replied, his eyes still on the phone as he typed a message. "Flattery will get you nowhere, my friend. Just you wait until the others arrive. We're going to have one hell of a party." He walked past Curtis toward the bay windows and drew back one of the curtains, looking out.

Curtis stared ahead at the blank wall near the staircase. They still hadn't hung any pictures yet or done other things that would have made the place more homelike. They should have taken two months off, not two weeks. With his hands and ankles bound to a chair, such ideas seemed inconsequential, a pipe dream. Curtis's mind drifted further into the future, to a time when all their misfortunes were long behind them. That was if they could just survive the day.

* * *

Mary raced down Keaton Street, a rural three-mile stretch leading to her house. Theo sat in the passenger seat, holding a bag of tools they had picked up in haste at the hardware store. She had been right. Nobody had disturbed the SUV or the safe, tucked under its blanket in the back seat. Neither of them were experts in picking a safe, but Theo had insisted they at least try.

It seemed he was more obsessed with the contents than she was. Mary couldn't think of much outside of their current situation. With Curtis in peril, she could barely concentrate enough to drive, but when Theo insisted that he drive, Mary wouldn't have it. She was going to get them there. She was going to save Curtis. She was going to see that Bob Deckers paid for his crimes. And if the Taylors showed up, she would see to their justice as well. She felt wild and emboldened, pushed to the brink, and as she floored it down the empty, two-lane road, Theo pointed toward the forest and shouted for her to stop.

She swerved to the shoulder and slammed on the brakes, making the SUV screech to a halt. Their bodies jerked forward, and for a moment they sat in the idling vehicle not saying anything.

"What is it?" Mary said, her fuse nearly lit. Deckers had Curtis, and there was nothing she could do about it. They were already at the house with God knows who else.

"I see something in the woods. Looks like a vehicle," Theo said. His door opened, and he was already stepping out when Mary called out after him. "Theo, we don't have time for this." She paused and slammed her hands on the steering wheel. "Theo!" But he was already halfway there and approaching a gap between two trees that led into the woods.

Mary turned off the ignition and looked around for anything or anyone out of the ordinary. To her, it was very possible that the Taylor brothers were either on their trail or already at the house, waiting for her. She patted her purse, where her loaded .38 special rested, and then stepped out onto the pavement, following after Theo. Even before entering the woods, she could see part of a police light hidden behind leafy branches.

Mary believed Theo had a good eye to have noticed the car from the road. Or something more. He kept charging forward toward the vehicle, removing sticks and branches that had been covering the path. There were tire tracks leading to the vehicle, and it was clear to both of them that something wasn't right. The cruiser wasn't supposed to be there.

"Someone had to have parked this here not even an hour ago," Theo said, trying the doors, though all of them were locked. Mary looked inside through the windshield and observed the undisturbed police equipment lying about inside.

"This looks like Deputy Ramirez's cruiser," she said.

Theo backed away from the rear of the car, horrified. "You don't think that...?"

Mary shook her head, a familiar sickness growing in her stomach. "I don't know. I mean, Chief Riley put out the APB. He told us so. Maybe the deputy saw the blue Volvo, and they..."

Theo stepped forward, irate. "What are you saying, that Bob Deckers had something to do with this? That he killed Deputy Ramirez?" He threw his arms down in frustration. "Who are these people we're dealing with?"

"I don't know! We just moved here," she said defensively.

Theo continued to study the cruiser and the ground around it, flustered while thinking to himself. "Okay... Maybe they took Deputy Ramirez hostage with Curtis," he said, weighing the other possibilities.

"Maybe," Mary said, locked on the police cruiser with a concerned, vacant glare.

Theo walked past her toward the SUV, touching her arm. "Let's go. I've got a plan."

She turned and followed after him with no clear sense of what happened to Deputy Ramirez. She didn't want to admit it, but she could feel a growing unease about the possibility of his fate. The thought sickened her. She emerged from the woods, taking one last look at the cruiser from afar. Her mind was shifting in a hundred different directions.

Theo had made a point in his bewildered outrage. *Who exactly was she dealing with?* She soon came to the conclusion that she had no real idea—corrupt officials, a ruthless family, and a possible murderer, all within this picturesque small town. It was a disturbing scenario.

Once they were seated inside the SUV, Mary started the

engine and sped down the road, getting ever closer to home and ready to confront whatever danger lay ahead. Theo watched the forest slip by while weighing his own options.

"So Bob Deckers thinks that I've split town? Good. Here's an idea. Drop me off about a half mile from the house, and I'll sneak around through the back and put the kibosh on Bob before he knows what hit him."

Mary glanced repeatedly into the rearview mirror. Her lack of response and straight-faced expression indicated her lack of confidence in the plan. "You really think that would work? What if there are others there besides Bob? We could be dealing with the entire Taylor clan. They might even be hiding in the back too. You could get killed."

"So could you," Theo offered in a quick retort.

"I have to do this. You don't."

"Please, Mary. I'm in this just as deep as you now." He turned his head to look at the safe in the back seat. "I can take the safe, put it somewhere they won't find it."

Mary's eyes lit up. "*What*? Absolutely not."

"What if they search your car?" Theo held his hands out as though there were a hundred disastrous possibilities. "Think about it. They get what they want, there's no reason to keep you alive. That safe could be the only leverage you have."

Mary suddenly slammed on the brakes. Theo gripped the dashboard as her tires skidded across the pavement.

"Enough," she said, gripping the steering wheel. "Why don't we just open it now and find out what's in it ourselves? That way, we'll know for sure."

Theo seemed surprised by her suggestion. "But what about Curtis? He's waiting for you." It seemed strange that he was the one bringing it up.

"Don't you think I know that?" Mary asked in frustration. She brought her hands to her face with a sigh, her eyes watering. "I'm not sure what to do." She then slapped her hands down on the steering wheel and pulled onto the shoulder, the car idling. "Bastards!"

"It's okay," Theo said, placing a hand on her shoulder. "You're not alone in this. I only want to help." He reached for the bag of tools they had purchased and set it on his lap. He pulled a crowbar from the bag and held it up. "Let me take a crack at it."

Mary nodded, glanced down the road, and resumed driving. Still miles from the house, she turned onto a back road and drove down it until she found a suitable place to park. She slowed and coasted under the shade of several red maple trees, just off the pavement, their leaves all nearly fallen.

Once they stopped, Theo hopped out, eager to get started. Mary looked at the dashboard clock. It was nearing 5:00 p.m. Theo opened the rear passenger door and reached into the back seat for the safe. Mary opened her door and stepped onto the ground, carpeted in dead leaves.

"I'll pull the hatchback down. Just set it in the back," she said to him. "You'll have room to work."

"Be careful of the broken glass," Theo said.

He wrapped his arms around the safe and heaved, lifting it from the back seat and then carrying it to the rear of the car. Mary went around to the other side and grabbed the bag of tools, pausing for a moment to look around. Birds fluttered above, cawing, as squirrels scurried up the trees around them. The undisturbed nature provided temporary comfort for Mary. She felt safe and at peace. She could almost believe, for a moment, that things hadn't gotten so quickly out of hand. But the truth was unavoidable: she would have to face the Taylors at some point. There was no turning back.

"Little help," Theo called out, expecting the tools. Mary snapped into action and approached Theo, handing him the bag. The safe was seated upright, with its thick metal door facing them, and the large combination dial resting in the center, like a challenge or a dare. Its discolored surface had rusted, and there was a fair amount of dirt and grime covering it.

"Do you know what you're doing?" she asked.

"No," he told her.

Setting the crowbar aside, Theo sifted through the bag, pulling out some metal rods, a power drill, batteries, screwdrivers, files, and a hacksaw. It was clear he had never done anything like this before, but they couldn't find a place open that sold either an electrical circular saw or a welder. This was the best they could do. Theo took the power drill first and pressed it against the safe's door, just above the combination dial.

He turned to her with a faint look of uncertainty. "I'm no expert, but if I can get into the drive cam somehow, I'm pretty sure I can bypass the spindle and then breach the lock."

"I'm not sure what you just said, but please be careful..." Mary told him.

She kept watch as he pulled the trigger and pressed the thick quarter-inch drill bit into the safe, barely making a scratch. He pressed harder as tiny sparks flew, with the drill grinding against the safe's seemingly impenetrable metal surface. Just when it looked as though he'd push through, the drill bit suddenly snapped in half. Frustrated, he lowered the drill and shook his head.

"Looks like it's not going to be that easy. That was our thickest drill bit," he said, grabbing the crowbar.

Mary stood cautiously to the side in deep thought, searching for some alternative. She could sense that something was off. There would be no way to break into the safe with the tools they had. Such thoughts crossed her mind as

Theo plunged the crowbar into the slit where the door was mounted, pushing down with all his might. His efforts seemed futile, and she could sense his increasing anger with every failed attempt.

He took the drill again, replacing the bit with another. Placing the safe flat on its back, he pushed the drill into the small dent he had made the first time and pressed against the metal, again scratching the surface but doing little else.

"Damn it!" he said as the bit snapped in half. He tossed the drill to the side and grabbed the crowbar again as though he was prepared to club the safe into submission.

He raised the crowbar into the air and swung down harder and harder, a loud clang sounding with each spark-inducing blow, barely making a dent. Theo pummeled the safe continually as sweat dripped from his face. Mary jumped at an idea and grabbed his arm before he could take another swing.

Theo paused, looking at her with shock as she managed to hold his crowbar-wielding arm back against his will.

"What?" he said, angered.

"A thought came to me. Let me give it a shot."

Theo looked down at the safe then back to Mary with a nod. "Very well," he said, stepping back. "It's all yours." He tried hard not to smirk.

"In the case of this safe," she said, "none of these tools are going to work. We're going to have to take our chances with this." She reached for the combination dial, spinning it a few times to get a feel for it.

"You're going to guess the combination?" Theo asked, astonished.

"Just think of it like a riddle," Mary said.

"Well," Theo said, scratching his head. "You've gotten us this far."

He backed up as she adjusted the knob, setting it on zero.

She then spun the dial to three times to the left, stopping at the fifteen. "There were fifteen victims in the Bechdel massacre."

She paused and then spun the dial to the right. "And from what we know, there may have been three killers that evening." The dial stopped at three, and Mary hesitated. "One more. What could it be?"

Theo thought to himself, struggling to come up with anything. "How many children did Phil have?" he asked.

The question seemed to click with Mary, and she brought the dial back around to two. She spun it to the left, awaiting a clicking sound with heightened anticipation, but nothing happened.

"It was a noble attempt," Theo said. "Looks like it's back to plan A."

"Wait," she said. "I think that you're on to something. Phil's family. Plus his wife, that makes three."

Theo ran a hand down his face with a sigh. "I don't know. Seems like we're just grasping at straws here."

"We are," Mary said in response.

She repositioned the dial and spun it wildly from fifteen to three to four. She wasn't expecting any miracles, but upon hearing a resounding click, she nearly jumped out of her skin. Theo's eyes widened in disbelief. The crowbar dropped from his hand into the dirt as he stumbled forward.

"Did... Did you just..."

Mary could barely believe it herself as her hand clutched the dial. She pulled a lever near the dial with her other hand and the door began to slowly move, opening quietly as rust fell from the hinges and a sliver of light crept into the opening.

"That's incredible," Theo said.

She held the door half shut and turned to Theo, not fully

ready to see the stored contents inside. "I don't know how to explain it. Seems like pure luck."

Theo laughed. "Luck? Yeah right. You're the real deal, Mary."

Mary blushed. "I don't know, Theo. I never asked for any of this. You know I get headaches, right? Sometimes, I pass out just like that." She slapped her hands together, startling Theo. "I just want to live a normal life somewhere safe where no one can bother me. Is that too much to ask?"

Theo looked to the safe, unable to answer.

"Well, is it?" she asked.

"Not now, Mary," Theo said. "Everything will go back to normal, I promise. But right now we need to focus."

Mary gave him an understanding nod. Theo signaled to the safe and asked her to do the honors. She pulled the door open, revealing a dark interior packed with what looked like thick file folders.

Theo stood over Mary, studying the contents. "It's like some kind of time capsule."

She reached inside and pulled out one dusty folder with a drawstring tying it shut. But that wasn't it. There were other folders inside, including a few trinkets that piqued Mary's curiosity. She pulled a porcelain doll out and set it to the side.

The girl was wearing a Victorian dress, and her long curly locks went down to her knees. Next, Mary found a golden bracelet and carefully set it aside as well next to the doll. When she discovered the next item, Mary's heart nearly sank. She held a framed picture in her hands of Phil and his wife, Alisha, standing in front of their farmhouse with big smiles on their faces. But, like some kind of personal treasure trove, there was more.

She found another framed picture, this one of three teenagers standing around Pastor Phil, all smiling, sticks in hand with marshmallows at the ends. They were in front of a cabin somewhere in the mountains. Phil had never looked happier.

"It's his kids," she said to Theo, who then leaned in closer. "Phil's children."

"Wow…" Theo said. "Maybe he just wanted to protect the items closest to his heart, the things that he cared about the most."

"There's more to it," Mary said with certainty. In addition to the thick file folder, there were three manila folders filled with documents. Most surprising of all were the last items they came across, all sealed in an oversized Ziploc bag. Inside it were bundles of cash secured with rubber bands, and next to the cash were two U.S. passports. Mary fished out the passports, opened them, and saw that they belonged to Pastor Phil and his wife.

"Surprised he didn't have a gun stowed in there too," Theo said. "Who was this guy?"

"I don't know…" Mary said. She set the bag of cash aside, unconcerned about counting it. It looked to be a few thousand dollars, if that. Her main interest was the contents inside the folders. Theo watched patiently as she untied the drawstring around the file folder, its contents nearly spilling out.

Though it was initially overwhelming, it didn't take long for them to figure out what Pastor Phil had been hiding. There were years, decades even, of investigative reports done by Phil—typed documents, written logs, journal entries, and damning black-and-white photographs of all the major players in town.

He had pictures from outside other mansions and people Mary didn't recognize, and others that she did. There were photos of Beatrice Thaxton, Bob Deckers, and most importantly, Mayor Taylor.

She was even more disturbed to find photos taken from outside, through the windows of what appeared to be the mayor's mansion, party guests inside, dressed strangely in cloaks and robes. Many of them were wearing animal masks —pagan-like, with horns and antlers. The pictures got increasingly disturbing as the costume party soon descended into a debauchery of naked bodies converging upon one another in a kind of wild orgy. Mary nearly dropped the pictures in shock.

Theo lifted his head from several documents he was scanning. "This is incredible. It looks like Phil was trying to build a case, not only against the Taylors, but everyone involved in the murder conspiracy."

His eyes widened when Mary handed him the pictures she had just looked at. "What the hell?" he said, grabbing them.

"He was spying on the mayor. For how many years, it's not clear."

She glanced down at an open notebook and read the first part of his written log. It detailed the time and the activity of Mayor Taylor and his entourage. Apparently, the mayor would host extravagant parties for powerful people from everywhere near and far, across the country.

Redwood, it seemed, was a refuge for the upper-crust crazies. They could do anything and not have to worry about exposure or consequences. It was a crooked operation, as Phil explained in his writings, even more so given the certainty of Mayor Taylor's certain alleged involvement in the Bechdel murders.

"I don't understand," Theo said. "Why would he sit on all of this and just let the mayor run things? He could have easily gone to the press."

Mary immediately thought of Phil's wife and kids. Maybe her death and his children's disappearances weren't some unfortunate circumstance after all. "I'm sure he had his reasons."

Theo took the next folder and opened it, taking immediate interest. "Hello, what's this?"

Mary tied the file folder back together and turned to Theo as he thumbed through the next folder, stunned. "I can't believe this," he continued. "This is your house."

"What?" Mary said, leaning toward him.

"It's a bunch of pictures of your house!"

Theo handed Mary a dozen glossy black-and-white photos of all sides of the mansion. The photos looked old, and there was crime scene tape everywhere. She assumed that he had taken the photos not long after the murders. Theo flipped through more photos when a sealed baggie fell from inside the folder and hit the floor of the car. Mary reached for it and saw that it contained an old skeleton key—at least she assumed by its design. Things were certainly getting interesting.

"Mary," Theo said, pulling a large folded sheet from the file, "this looks like a map of your house."

She took the paper and unfolded it, revealing a map of sorts—a blueprint, even. Her eyes trailed over the paper, and she took notice of a path to a lower level of the mansion that neither she nor Curtis knew existed.

Theo set the folder down and read from another paper that had gained his attention. "Here, listen to this." He cleared his throat and began reading. "Dear Phillip, you have been such a wonderful source of guidance for our family. I'll never know how to truly repay you. As you know, there are few people that we can currently trust. Word has gotten out, and our family fortune may soon be gone. The fortune has been passed down the line for generations. I would ask that if anything were to happen to us that you take the role of protector, not only of our home, but also the vast fortune that is hidden below.

"I have not touched a single golden coin, for legend has it that the fortune brought a curse through my ancestors' robbery of a pagan elder. Yes, it is crazy to consider such a fantastical story, but as I write this letter to you in haste, I can sense an end to things coming very soon.

"Once we are all gone, I believe the curse will be lifted, and you can enrich yourself with something my family should never have had in the first place. It is the least I can do. I've provided a map and key to the catacombs below our house, located so deep that not even the most modern excavation team would locate it without this help. Thank you again, Phil. Best wishes to you and your family. Pray for us. Your friend, George Bechdel."

Theo froze with the letter held tightly in both hands. Mary was beside herself, trembling in the silence. Nearby trees rustled from an approaching breeze as she grappled with their new discovery.

"Do you think any of that's true?" Theo asked.

"I don't know, but it would certainly explain what the Taylor brothers were looking for."

Without further hesitation, Mary grabbed the file folder and handed Theo the rest. "Here. You take this half. I'll hold onto this. If this is what it takes to get Curtis back, I'll give them everything."

Theo took the folders and the bag of cash and then stopped Mary. "Hold on, I have an idea." She smiled. "Yes," he said, "another idea."

He set everything down and kneeled, cupping a handful of sand. He then rose and tossed the sand inside the safe.

"What are you doing?" Mary asked.

"We don't have to give them anything. Just the safe. We

fill it up with dirt, you hand it over, and the rest is between them and Phil."

Mary's worried face seemed somewhat unconvinced. "Yes, but what if they demand the rest?"

"There is no 'rest.' They'll think that we couldn't open it." Theo took the file folder from her hand. "I'm going to take it all with me. I'll hide it under your gazebo for the time being. That way, if anything happens to me, you'll know where it is."

Theo's plan made sense, but Mary still had her worries. "I don't know. I feel like we're playing with fire here."

Theo kneeled down and scooped up another handful of sand, tossing it inside the safe. "That's where you're wrong, Mary. They're the ones playing with fire."

A COMPROMISE

Bob Deckers stared out the window through the curtains, eagerly awaiting Mary's arrival, gripping his pistol at his side. He placed his hand on the window and breathed against its surface. The moment he was waiting for was nearing. It was falling together in ways he couldn't ever have planned or imagined. There was a distant rumbling in gray, overcast sky. Soon there would be rain the likes of which they couldn't have imagined.

Curtis sat tied to the chair, facing the opposite direction, trying to maintain his stamina despite his throbbing head and slipping consciousness. Fearing that he would pass out soon, he yanked at the rope around his ankles and wrists repeatedly with all the strength he had left. "Enough of this," he said. "Untie me now!"

Bob turned from the window in response. "Why would I do that? So you can try to attack me again and then get pistol-whipped?" He paused with a laugh. "I'm not sure you can take another hit, Curtis, so I'm going to have to say no."

"Untie me!" Curtis shouted.

Bob watched with quiet amusement as Curtis thrashed

around. "Calm down before you give yourself a heart attack," he said.

"You son of a bitch," Curtis seethed.

Bob slowly approached from behind with his pistol out. "Do we really need to go through this again? I told you that we'd work all of this out once Mary got here. What's the problem?"

"Why us?" Curtis asked. "You or the mayor or anyone else could have taken this house and done whatever you wanted to it. Why involve us in the first place?"

Bob stopped directly behind Curtis and put a hand on his shoulder. "That's a complicated story. I think I'll let the mayor explain that once he gets here."

"The mayor?"

"That's right. He's taken a special interest in you two. Well, more so Mary than you. We did our research. Mary has a gift, and she's going to help us."

"Why on earth would she help the two of you do anything?" Curtis asked.

"She wants to live, doesn't she?" Bob said. "And I'm sure she wants you to live as well."

Curtis shook his head, his short hair sticking out wildly in all directions. He had thick bruises on his face. "So that's it? Threaten us with our lives like a couple of thugs?"

Bob sighed. "Call it what you want. In the end, the mayor is going to get what he wants."

They heard the sound of a vehicle from the courtyard, its tires running across the concrete as its engine hummed. Bob went immediately to the window, peeking out cautiously. Twenty feet from the window sat the Ford Expedition, with Mary at the wheel.

"Excellent," Bob said. "Now we can begin."

* * *

Mary observed Bob's blue Volvo parked outside their home with nervous trepidation. She was relieved to see no other vehicles, for she had little clarity on who was inside the house besides Curtis and Bob. She picked up her cell phone and called Curtis again, fully expecting Bob to answer, which he did after three rings with a simple, *"Hello, Mary."*

"I'm outside," she said.

"I know. I can see you."

She looked at the front windows of the house and could see his figure watching her from the ballroom.

"Who else is in there?"

"Just me for now."

The "for now" struck her as an ominous hint of things to come. "How do I know I'll be safe when I go inside?"

"Nothing will happen to you as long as you cooperate."

"Where's Curtis?" she asked.

"He's right here with me. Come on in. We're both waiting for you."

"Okay," she said, hanging up the phone.

The thought of Curtis in peril upset her beyond words. She took her purse, feeling the weight of her .38 inside, and then opened her door. She thought of Theo and hoped he could sneak into the house undetected and help her subdue Bob.

She didn't have the upper hand just yet and would have to play along. She grabbed her keys and stepped out of the SUV to an eerie silence that permeated the courtyard. Their nearby fountain remained empty, along with dozens of unfinished projects around the house. She wondered if she and Curtis would still live at the Bechdel mansion after everything was over—if it ever was going to be over.

Bob moved away from the window in the distance as she approached the steps to the front door, having little awareness of what the situation was waiting inside. She tried to envision it but could only see empty rooms with an unseen, angered presence gaining momentum. The spirits were back. She could feel them roaming about.

Her hands gripped the elegant handle of their French double doors as she pulled them open. A creaking followed, alerting anyone in the house to her presence. There were no lights on beyond the foyer, and the gray clouds overhead only made things darker. It seemed as though every curtain in the house was drawn, the better to conceal the activity going on.

Mary thought of Chief Riley and how she regretted not calling him the moment they found Deputy Ramirez's car. Curtis's safety, however, was her chief concern. She would not gamble with his life. The chief would know everything soon enough, or so she hoped.

Mary walked through the foyer with caution as the staircase came into view. To her right was the vast space of the ballroom where she saw Curtis sitting in the darkness, tied to a chair, head bobbing down, with Bob nowhere to be seen. She ran to Curtis immediately and fell to her knees in front of him. His battered face shocked and horrified her.

"Curtis, oh my God, what happened to you?"

He lifted his head up with a faint smile as she touched his knees. "I'm okay. Glad to see you..."

"You're not okay," she said, running her hands to his back, where his wrists were tied. "What is this? What has that monster done to you?"

"What I had to," Bob's voice called out from behind her.

She swung her head around to see him standing in the lounge doorway with his pistol aimed at them. "He'll live. Now what I need you to do is sit tight until the other guests arrive, and then we'll iron all of this out."

Mary rose with one hand on Curtis's leg, glaring at Bob

with disgust. "You're a sick man. I'm ashamed we ever trusted you."

Bob waved her off with a shrug. "I'm not that bad. Heck, I'm not even going to tie you up. But if you step out of line, you'll leave me no choice."

"Go to hell," she seethed. "You killed Pastor Phil, didn't you? *Why?*"

He walked toward her, shoes clicking against the floor, and motioned to an empty chair he had placed next to Curtis. "It was nothing personal, and neither is this."

"I saw Deputy Ramirez's cruiser on my way here, all tucked away in the woods. Where is he?"

"I don't know what you're talking about," Bob said matter-of-factly.

"I think you do. Chief Riley said he hadn't heard from the deputy in over an hour, right after putting an APB out on a blue Volvo—*your* blue Volvo."

Bob shrugged. "Not a clue."

"Yes, you do," Curtis said with gritted teeth.

Mary turned to Curtis shocked. "What happened?"

"Sit down and shut up," Bob said, aiming the pistol at her.

Mary stood defiantly, thinking of her .38, but it was no time for a shootout, at least when Bob had a careful eye on both of them.

"I'm only going to ask once," he said.

She moved to Curtis's left side, rubbing his back, and then sat with her eyes locked on Bob.

"Place your purse on the ground in front of you," he said.

"Why?" she asked.

"Call it a precaution," he answered.

"I'm not giving you my purse," she said, gripping it.

Bob pointed the pistol above him and fired a single shot into the ceiling, blasting a hole through it, and small chunks of drywall fluttered down. The cannon-like blare of his .45

nearly knocked Mary out of her chair. Curtis's head jolted up, his eyes wide and discolored face sweating.

"The hell is wrong with you?" Curtis shouted.

"I'm sick of asking your wife a second time to do things." He then pointed the hot barrel directly at Curtis. "The next time she gives me lip, I'll shoot you."

"Okay!" Mary said, slightly trembling. She stood and placed her purse on the floor, just out of reach.

Bob rushed toward Mary's beige purse like a hawk and kicked it away from her, looking up suspiciously as it slid against the wall. "Gee, Mary. I felt a little weight in there. What do you have in there? Are you packing?"

"What are you talking about?" she snapped.

Bob smiled. "Exactly," he said, walking to the purse. For a moment, his back was turned, and Mary thought of slamming his head against the wall just to knock him out. But no such action would happen. He was armed, and they weren't. It was as simple as that.

"I'd appreciate you staying out of my personal belongings, please," she said.

Curtis looked up with similar contempt. "Leave her purse alone."

In response to them both, Bob unzipped the purse and pulled it open with his eyes widening in great interest. "Mary… I'm stunned." He pulled the .38 out and held it out, dangling it by the handle with two fingers. "You're a little badass, aren't you?"

Mary felt crushingly powerless at the sight. "I always carry that on me. We used to live in the city."

Bob stood up and placed the .38 in the back of his pants. "I'm sure you do. For now, I'll hold onto it for safekeeping. At least until our business is done."

"Do you have intentions of keeping us alive?" Mary asked,

her face flushed with anger. "Or do you plan to discard us like Pastor Phil?"

Bob stepped forward, pondering the question as Curtis cut in. "Don't talk to him anymore, Mary."

"To answer your question," Bob loudly interrupted, "it's not entirely up to me. That's the mayor's call."

"The mayor?" Mary said as her eyes narrowed. "I knew it."

"Of course you did," Bob continued. "And the mayor now knows that you know. He's not very happy, having to unexpectedly leave the autumn festival in the middle of a speech so he can come here, but he's been waiting for this moment a long time."

"What are you rambling about?" Mary asked.

"Mary, please," Curtis said. "Just leave it be."

Bob took several assured steps closer, staring them down. "Mary, you were chosen for a reason. You've been here before, right here in this mansion when you were only a child."

Bob's claim shook Mary to her core. She would have dismissed him immediately had Phil not alluded to the same thing during their last conversation.

"Back then," Bob said, "I was just a kid living in Dallas, but apparently, your parents were once interested in purchasing this mansion. The year was 1986, and you were the first person to ever make contact with them."

"Who?" Mary asked.

Bob shook his head. "I think you know who I'm talking about. The mayor found out all about you. He knew then as he knows now that the Bechdel estate was cursed. What he needed was someone who could help him use it to his benefit."

"That's insane," Mary said with her arms out. "I don't remember ever being here before in my entire life."

"Of course you don't. You weren't here long. My predecessor in the realty business showed your parents around. Already, he could see the strange connection you had with the house. You were talking to thin air. At some point, you wandered off and then, much to your parents' horror, you fell down the stairs."

Both Mary and Curtis listened in disbelief. Bob's tall tale had failed to convince her just yet, as there was no evidence of any of it.

"You hit one step on your way down, bumping your head. You could have very easily died that day, but you stopped mid-fall. Your parents rushed to the stairs in hysterics with Jerome, the Realtor, and saw you levitating in the air, unconscious, floating safely to the ground in front of their astounded eyes."

Bob paused, taking a deep breath. "They never purchased the mansion, of course, and the next day, you had no memory of the incident or of the mansion at all."

"How do you know this?" she said in a loud accusatory tone.

"Word gets around. On the day of your parents' tour, the mayor later arrived just to welcome them to town. But he wasn't there to simply welcome them—he wanted to see if they could sense the same thing he did. He wanted to see what the house would do to them, what it could do to them, like every unfortunate owner who has lived here before."

"My parents knew that I moved here. Why would they keep something like that from me?" Mary asked.

Bob shook his head. "Before you moved here, the mayor sent them a very clear message. If they ever wanted to see you again..."

"He *threatened* my parents?" she asked.

"I didn't say that," Bob said.

Curtis remained uncharacteristically quiet, noticeably stunned by Bob's claims as he continued, "Mayor Taylor is a bit of an enigma, himself. He has some weird fascination with the occult. A relationship, he claims, that is responsible for his entire legacy. You're now going to help the mayor maintain that legacy."

Mary remained awestruck, trying to make sense of everything he was saying. She felt along the top right of her forehead, where she'd had a small scar just below her hairline for as long as she could remember. Her mother had always said Mary had gotten it in a fall but never elaborated how.

She shuddered to think of any of it as true, remembering what Pastor Phil had said about coincidences in Redwood: there were none, as everything was somehow connected.

"If this house is so cursed, why come here at all?" she asked.

"Yeah. Why not just bulldoze the place and be done with it?" Curtis added.

Bob thought to himself, finger on his chin, and then addressed the couple. "This is just a payday for me. If you've ever gone through bankruptcy, you know how desperation can rear its ugly little head. Plus the mayor has promised to help me find my ex-wife and children." He then pivoted and began pacing around the couple. "But he'll explain it much better."

Bob paused at the rumbling of vehicles outside and then hurried to the window, pulling back the curtain with excitement. "Ah, the entourage has arrived."

Mary got up from her chair, placing a hand on Curtis's shoulder. Bob's back was to her, with the revolver sticking out from the back of his pants. Knowing that he was distracted, she crept closer to the window and could see two black SUVs pull into the courtyard with the Taylor brothers' Bronco trailing it. Panic settled in upon her realization that she was going to face the mayor and his cronies.

Bob breathed against the window as her hand slowly

reached for the exposed revolver. He suddenly turned, as if sensing her, and pointed his pistol in her face, causing Mary to flinch and back away.

"What in the hell are you doing?" he said, motioning to the chair. "Sit down."

"I wanted to see who was here," she said, innocently with her hands up.

"Sure you were. No more games. I'm not in the mood for it, and neither will the mayor be."

Mary peeked out the window as the vehicles parked and the headlights turned off. She watched as men in suits exited the SUVs and opened the door for the mayor to step out of the first vehicle in the line. He was wearing the same three-piece suit she had seen him in earlier when he was speaking at the festival. As he stepped out, he looked up at the house with a mixture of wonder and contempt.

His brothers hopped out of their Bronco, rifles against their shoulders and taking a keen interest in her Ford Expedition. Jeffery pointed to the broken window in the back and laughed, seemingly amused with his previous antics.

Garret led the way toward the house, stone faced and with a look of grim premonition.

"Why are they armed?" Mary asked. "What is this?"

"Sit back down," Bob said. "Not going to ask again."

"I'm moving!" Mary said, stomping off to her chair.

"Mary…" Curtis said as she sat near him.

She turned to him with pure sadness in her eyes and lightly ran her hand along his bruised face. "I'm so sorry for all of this," she said, trying to hold back tears.

"It's not your fault. Don't say that. Looks like they've been playing us from the beginning."

"They're not going to get away with it," she said, assuredly.

"If we don't make it…" he began with a swallow. "If we

don't… just know that I love you more than anything. I only wanted us to be happy." His voice lowered to a whisper. "They can do anything they want to me, but you have to try to escape. We have a child now. That's all that matters."

Mary felt warm tears streaming down her cheek as she held his face. "I'm not leaving you, and they're not going to win." She paused, looking around the room and hoping for Julie to intervene somehow, some way. "I was supposed to find justice for her," she continued. "And I think we're close to making that happen."

Bob walked toward the foyer at the sound of the doorbell. Mary thought it strange that they would bother at this point. "You two don't go anywhere now," Bob said with a smile. It seemed as though he was taking a certain pleasure in the situation despite his claim that it was all business.

With his brief absence in the foyer, Mary knew she had to act fast. "I'm going to untie you," she said quietly to Curtis. "I can't stand seeing you like this."

"Leave it," Curtis said. "We don't want to piss these people off. Mary, he killed Deputy Ramirez. Shot him in the head like it was nothing."

Mary covered her mouth with a gasp. A sickening pain hit her stomach, and she felt dizzy with shock.

"I can't believe it… Where is he? Where's his…?"

"His body? Bob made me help him drag it into the woods." He clenched his eyes shut as tears gushed out. "So help me God, he'll answer for this. He has to."

Mary rushed to her purse, hoping to get her cell phone in time. If they were truly going to face their demise, as Curtis seemed to suggest, she had to let the chief know about Ramirez. She leapt from her seat and ran to her purse, dropping to one knee, just as the doors opened in the foyer. With precious seconds left, she pulled her phone from her purse, grabbed the chief's card, and dialed as fast as she ever had.

After two rings, her eyes darted to the side where she could hear footsteps growing near and the voices of several men in their midst.

"Chief Riley speaking," his voice said.

"Chief," she whispered in near panic. "Deputy Ramirez. He's dead. Bob Deckers shot him. Blue Volvo. The same vehicle you were looking for."

There was a brief pause on the line before he spoke. "Who is this?"

"It's Mary. Chief, listen. Curtis told me that it's off of Madeline and Antelope. About a mile down the road, you'll find his cruiser…" She paused, fighting back her tears. "And his body is somewhere close. Please. We're in serious trouble."

She hung up the phone, stuffed it in her pocket, and ran back to her chair, breathing heavily. It was unfortunate that she couldn't have talked to him longer, but she had pressed her luck as it was.

Mayor Taylor entered the ballroom flanked by his security detail. His brothers entered the room next, cocky expressions on their faces. Most surprising of all, however, was when Beatrice Thaxton entered. Mary couldn't believe the sight, but then the vision returned to her, as clear as it had been when it entered her mind during Pastor Phil's memorial service: Beatrice talking on the phone with Bob Deckers after he murdered Phil. She was connected with the conspiracy somehow.

Mary's cell phone vibrated in her pocket. She knew that the chief was trying to call her back, but it was too late. He would have to put together the pieces from there. Nonetheless, she trusted that he would spring into action soon enough. He couldn't have been involved in the conspiracy. Like Phil, the chief was trustworthy enough. The main players in the conspiracy, she believed, were now all right before her eyes.

The mayor approached them as his security detail of six husky men in suits took positions throughout the room, some of them watching out the window. His brothers kept their distance and took seats at the staircase, setting their rifles in their laps. Bob Deckers stood with Beatrice near a china hutch, quietly conversing as the mayor exchanged serious, thoughtful looks between Mary and Curtis.

He clasped his hands together and bowed, followed by a friendly tone Mary had been accustomed to hearing in his previous speeches to the town.

"Mr. and Mrs. Malone. I do apologize for the inconvenience, especially on the day of our annual Autumn Festival. I promise not to take too much of your time." He paused, scanning the room, and Mary remained quiet, curious about what else he had to say.

"No doubt Mr. Deckers filled you in a little about why we're here, and I would like to further explain so as to clear everything up. Much of this is just one unfortunate misunderstanding. You see, I do not believe our beloved Pastor Phil was murdered."

He then stopped and glared at Bob, who sheepishly looked away with a hint of embarrassment and fear on his face as the mayor continued.

"Mr. Deckers has a tendency to get carried away while making wild claims that have no place in reality. Just to be clear, I had nothing to do with the tragic deaths of the Bechdels and the Drakes. I was personal friends with both families, and even though George Bechdel was my opponent in the 1975 mayoral election, I respected the man and had nothing but good will toward him and his family."

Mary remained seated, resisting the urge to call him out. She could see that he was lying and that beneath his cordial demeanor was a cold, calculating, and corrupt man. For now, he was masking his intentions, and Mary allowed the charade to proceed.

"I do apologize about what has happened to you and your husband, and I can promise you that we won't be here long." He paused and looked around the ballroom, a hint of nervousness visible on his face and in his movements. "There's a history to this estate that I'd rather not go into at the moment if you don't mind. I'm not exactly comfortable being here for any extended period of time." He then clapped his hands together with vigor. "But be here I must. Believe it or not, Mary—do you mind if I call you Mary?"

She nodded.

"Excellent," he continued. "I know a lot about you and would like to set the record straight. I know of your gift, and I believe that your presence here thirty years ago meant something. That is why I was so eager to have you back." He turned and pivoted as if giving an academic lecture, and spoke like the rehearsed politician he was. "I'm a patient man, Mary. I wasn't going to rush anything. I wasn't going to force you to come back here, for I always knew that someday you would return."

He paused and looked at Curtis. "Your husband saw to that, but in his defense, no one in their right mind would turn down this place at the price on offer. No one at all. Now, I know that you were at Pastor Phil's earlier, probably searching for clues just as my brothers were. They arrived, and you got spooked and hid. I understand that. However, it's now time to reveal to me what you found."

All eyes went to Mary. The last thing she wanted to do was to help him with anything, but having what he wanted gave her immediate comfort. Only she knew that the safe in her SUV was full of sand and nothing else.

Mayor Taylor stood over her, waiting, his red tie hanging

down and the American flag pin shining on his lapel. Mary looked around the room and pointed to Beatrice Thaxton.

"What is she doing here?"

Mayor Taylor turned around. "Ms. Thaxton? Well. She's an intricate part of what we're trying to accomplish today. Some might say a guru of sorts."

"Don't worry about me, dear," Beatrice said, sauntering toward Mary and Curtis in her glittering evening gown and high heels. She carried herself the way a Hollywood starlet might, although well past her prime. She was indifferent to Curtis's injuries and Mary's distress.

"I'm here to ensure that everything goes swimmingly." She placed her arm around the mayor, who then leaned in closer and kissed her on the cheek. "Plus, who else looks after Freddy better than me?"

With his arm around Beatrice, the mayor turned to Mary. "Beatrice has been an advisor of mine for years, offering the comfort I need. She was there for me after my wife's death when everything seemed hopeless."

"We're going to the top," she continued. "For you see, we're in the process of priming the mayor's eldest son, Raymond, for a political career." She paused, patting the mayor's liver-spotted hands. "First we took Redwood, next we'll have the entire state, and possibly more. Our legacy will last generations."

Mary could hardly bear looking at Beatrice's self-satisfied smile and turned her head away with a hidden scowl. She knew all too well about the woman's involvement in Phil's death. What could possibly be worth such an act to her?

Beatrice left the mayor's side and approached closer, speaking in a soft tone. "There was a time I felt bad for you and your husband. You seemed like decent enough people. I even tried to warn you about this place, but you didn't seem to catch on. That was, I believe, because you looked down on us. We're just small-town folk while you're the big-city hotshot."

Beatrice paused, adjusting the pearls around her long, skinny neck. "Well, honey. Today we have the upper hand. You just listen and do what the mayor asks of you, and everything will be okay. Trust me." She then puckered her lips at Mary and blew her a kiss.

Mary narrowed her eyes as Beatrice turned away, telling everyone she had to use the bathroom. She walked off down the hall as the mayor turned back to Mary and Curtis, prepared to continue his explanation of why they were there.

"I know she can seem a bit... unusual, but she's loyal, and in my line of work, that's the most important thing. I hope you can respect that."

Mary felt primed to throw an insult at the mayor and his ridiculous notion of loyalty, but instead she chose to get to the point. "What do you want, Mr. Mayor?" she asked.

"It's simple," he answered. "For starters, I want whatever it is you found at Phil's place, and don't try to convince me otherwise. I know you were there, and I know you were able to find something. You're just that good. I will explain what else I want soon enough, but let's start at Phil's place."

"I found a safe," she said. "It was buried under the floorboards of his barn."

Shocked, the mayor turned to his brothers, seated on the staircase. "Did you hear her? Any of you geniuses think to look there?" He took a step back, shaking his head in disbelief. "What the hell am I paying you for?"

The brothers stood up in unison, scratching their heads as Curtis rocked his seat forward, twisting his arms and trying to free himself.

Curtis looked visibly relieved. "There you have it, Taylor. My wife found what you're looking for. Now take your gang of degenerates and get off of our property." He swung his head around, looking at everyone surrounding them. "Take the safe and leave!"

Mary placed her hand on his leg, trying to calm him, but he wasn't having it.

"Did you not hear me? Get out!"

The mayor gave an understanding nod and continued to speak cordially. "In time, Mr. Malone. I know that you're just an innocent bystander in all of this, and I'd urge you to remain patient with us until our business is over."

"I've done everything I can, Mr. Taylor. Now untie my husband," Mary said. "He has nothing to do with any of this."

From the corner, Bob Deckers snorted with a laugh.

The mayor looked convinced and then turned to Bob. "Can you please oblige the Malones? I

think he's ready to calm down now."

"Yes, Mr. Mayor," Bob said grudgingly as he walked over to the couple, pulling out a pocketknife. He knelt behind Curtis and cut at the rope as Mayor Taylor looked to Mary, holding out his hands as though a deal had been solidified.

"The safe," he began. "Where is it?"

"In the back of our SUV. The same vehicle your brother vandalized," Mary said.

Mayor Taylor glared at his brothers, who then looked away. "Very uncalled for," he said with a chastising tone. He turned back to Mary, sympathetic. "My sincerest apologies. The culprit will gladly reimburse you for the damages." The mayor then shifted back to an authoritative tone as he pointed at his brothers. "Go get the safe, and don't come back unless you have some equipment to open it with."

They nodded and walked toward the foyer, leaving the house. Mary turned to the window, which captured a view of the driveway, watching them approach her vehicle as the mayor continued speaking.

"You *do* understand why this is necessary, right, Mary?

You see, Redwood's treasured Pastor Phil also had a dark side to him. He was a muckraker, gathering phony information on some of Redwood's most influential people, myself included, for the purposes of blackmail. No one was more shocked than I to learn that a man of his stature was so blinded by lies and ambition. I don't hold any ill will against the man, and I still mourn his death."

Mary stood up, unable to hold her tongue any longer. "You're a liar!"

The mayor's security detail reached for their pistols, concealed by their suit coats, but the mayor waved them off dismissively.

"It's okay," he said. Turning back to Mary, he said, "I understand that you see me as something of a villain. But you've been lied to, Mary, even by your own instincts." He put a hand over his heart and stepped forward, once again the practiced fraud. "I'm no *murderer*. I've dedicated my life to public service. If I was as bad as you may think, why would I spend my entire life in Redwood as mayor of this town? Not exactly the most ambitious path, is it?"

Mary moved closer to the mayor, inches from his face. "Maybe what's in this house is holding you back. Maybe your political career has been tainted since the beginning. Maybe Redwood is the only town on this planet that would elect someone like you over and over again."

Curtis urged her to calm down, placing his hand on her arm with a reassuring tap. The mayor seemed unfazed in the silence of the room, maintaining eye contact until Mary took a step back and sat down. This was not the time to push her luck.

The mayor then continued, unabated. "Do you want to know who alerted me to Phil's deception? It was Beatrice, and it wasn't until after his death that we learned of his secrets. In the end, it came down to money. He was broke and on the verge of losing his home and the church. Maybe blackmailing Redwood's wealthiest and most influential leaders was part of his desperate mission to get everything back."

Mary remained quiet, even though she didn't believe a word he was saying. Her biggest question was where she fit in with the mayor's overall plan. She had information on the supposed underground catacombs and the supposed cursed treasure and skeleton key. She doubted the validity of any of it. Of all the far-fetched stories, buried treasure was the most difficult to accept, even more unlikely than the existence of a paranormal presence. But if not for a treasure, why would the mayor keep her or Curtis alive?

"Mr. Mayor," she began. "This thing that you call a 'gift.' I'm afraid it's all a bunch of superstition. I really don't know what more I can do for you. I would kindly ask that you let me and my husband go. You'll never hear from us again. I promise." She wanted to mention Deputy Ramirez but knew that doing so could ruin any chance of their release—as slim as their chances already were.

The mayor scratched his chin and thought to himself. For a moment, she couldn't tell if he was really considering letting them go or simply mocking her. "You've done great work so far, Mary. Of course, you know the precarious situation we both find ourselves in. We both want something from each other. I want to use your gift, you want me to release you and your husband. I get it. Probably the best thing for both of us is to work together. To trust each other and do what's right."

Mary leaned forward. "Can you give me your word that no harm will come to us?" she asked, even though she knew what kind of man he was and that any guarantee was worthless. It didn't hurt to try, however, and the mayor seemed far more malleable when hidden behind his phony charade.

Mayor Taylor paced around the couple, in deep thought or pretending to be, as raindrops began to hit the windows like tiny pellets, building in weight and speed. "I don't want to hurt either of you, understand? I'm perfectly open to compromise, and once our business is done, we can go our separate ways."

"Your associate over there shot Deputy Ramirez point blank in the face," Curtis said, pointing at Bob Deckers, who was standing across the room. "Is that what you would call a compromise?"

Mary felt an immediate shift in the atmosphere, which became instantly more hostile and dangerous. It was out there now, and there'd be no going back, though she was pretty sure Deckers had already informed the mayor of the deputy's death. She squeezed Curtis's leg, urging him to stop, but he didn't seem to want any of it.

The mayor brought a hand to his chin, clearly taken aback, and pondered the accusation as Bob glared at Curtis. "I did not know that," he said, staring back at Bob. "Is this true, Bob?"

Deckers shook his head. "He doesn't know what the hell he's talking about. Just look at that face. Probably suffering from a good amount of delirium or concussion as we speak."

"You're a pitiful liar, Deckers," Curtis said.

The mayor stared at Bob, studying the anger and uncertainty in his face. "Tell me the truth, Bob. Did you shoot one of my deputies?"

Bob turned away from him in anger and stormed down the hall and out of view. "I don't have to listen to this shit. I'm having a smoke."

The mayor remained in place and signaled one of his bodyguards, stopping him from following Bob. "Let him be." He then paused and looked at Curtis. "I can assure you that Mr. Deckers will be dealt with in time."

"Bullshit," Curtis spat.

"Please," Mary said.

Curtis pushed her hand away and stood up. "This entire charade has gone on long enough. Your brothers murdered the Bechdel and Drake families. It was obvious from the beginning. We know it, and you know it, so cut the shit!"

"Curtis, stop!" Mary shouted.

Curtis saw the look of fear on her face and went silent, as though he had just become aware that he was possibly sealing their fate. Mary looked up and saw the mayor seeming to ponder Curtis's words, his expression ambivalent: both disbelieving and amused. "I'm not sure what to say to that, Mr. Malone. It's not the first time I've been accused of having a hand in that massacre. There have been dozens of investigations, and not one has yielded any evidence that suggests what you're accusing my family of. So please, keep your wild conspiracy theories to yourself."

Curtis slowly lowered himself back into his chair with nothing else to say. "I guess I'm just upset right now," he said. "I didn't mean to get so carried away." Mary could hear the squelched anger in his voice as her husband said what he thought he must.

"I understand," Mayor Taylor said with a smile.

Rain began to fall heavier against the windows. The thunder became louder, and a few brief cracks of lightning flashed through the curtains in small bursts of electrified light.

SACRIFICIAL LAMB

The doors in the foyer opened as the Taylor brothers rushed inside, drenched from the rain. They set their rifles in the corner, and Liam held the safe, proudly entering the ballroom with Garret behind him carrying a large toolbox. They brought the safe to the center of the ballroom and set it down on the floor as the mayor watched with interest.

Garret shook the rain out of his hair like a wet dog, swiped his hand across the lid of the wet toolbox, and then paused dramatically, relishing the attention of the mayor and the other brothers. The security detail stood in their respective spots, looking as professional as trained militia and not interfering in any way.

Mary wondered just how much the mayor had paid them and others to look the other way over the length of his entire career. Like Deckers, all the rest must have sold their souls to help the mayor realize his wishes and ambitions. Beatrice emerged from upstairs to the sound of a toilet flushing and then looked down at them from the railing.

"What did they find?" she asked eagerly.

The mayor turned around and looked up at her. "A safe, my dear. Buried under Phil's barn."

Beatrice nodded with excitement in her eyes. "Ah, of course. He always had such fondness for that stupid barn. We should have known."

Mary watched them search through the toolbox with great anticipation, leading toward the big reveal. She hoped that its true contents were safe and that Theo had been able to secure them properly. Opening the safe had been a miracle in itself. The next miracle, she thought, would be surviving the coming ordeal. Her cell phone suddenly vibrated in her pocket, and she automatically reached down as if to cover the sound, but continued looking ahead.

Mayor Taylor hovered over the safe, offering suggestions and telling his brothers how slow and stupid they were and urging them to hurry up.

"Damn, Freddy. We're getting to it," Garret barked, kneeling down. "It's a four-inch-thick safe, not a freaking key box."

"Just do it," the mayor said. "Then we can move on."

Jeffery stood by and stretched, looking around while trying to shake the rain off his jean jacket. He looked to Mary with frustration on his damp face. "You got any towels around here?"

"Ah, suck it up, Jeff," Liam said as he pulled a crowbar and several long rods from the toolbox.

"Eat shit. I'm soaked here. Damn rain," he said.

"Nearest towels are in the kitchen," Mary said.

Jeffery thought to himself as he brushed back his wet gray hair. "You got any beer?"

"Go to hell," Curtis said abruptly.

Mary put her hand up for calm. "Yes. We should have a few cans in there."

Curtis whipped his head around to her, angered. "*Mary?*"

"It's just beer, Curtis," she said.

Jeffery seemed satisfied enough and walked past them toward the kitchen, down the hall. "I'll bring you one too. How about that?" he said with a laugh.

Curtis said nothing back and simply leaned forward with his head down. Mary wrapped her arms around him and rubbed his back. "We need to get you to a hospital as soon as possible."

"I know," he said. "I don't know how much more I can take of this."

"There's hope," she said softly. "Julie's near. I can feel her."

Curtis looked up and glanced at Mary, looking skeptical. She knew he had his doubts, just as even she was beginning to have hers, and with a storm starting to rage outside, she felt as though no one would be leaving the house for a long while.

"Get some lights on in here," the mayor said to the security detail as it got progressively darker in the ballroom. They searched for the switches and lit up every hall and room in the vicinity of their gathering.

Garret pulled out a welder and held it with the confidence of someone who had quite possibly cracked a few safes in his lifetime. Mary looked away as the welding tool flared against the safe door, sparks flying everywhere. With the lights on, she could see the injuries to Curtis's face more clearly. His fresh bruises made her gasp in pain for him.

"I'm so sorry," she said again, grazing the side of his face with her palm.

"Don't be," he said. "I told you that this isn't your fault."

Beatrice leaned over the railing, enjoying the show. "You're doing it all wrong," she said. "That's no way to open a safe.

Garret stopped the welder for a moment and waved her off, ignoring her. He then signaled for Liam to stick the crowbar into the side of the safe where the door was hung, and he brought the torch inches from the surface above the combination dial.

"What do you think's in there?" Curtis quietly asked Mary.

Mary thought to herself as Liam heaved at the side of the safe, pressing down on the crowbar. "Nothing."

A few moments later, the brothers managed to pry the door away with a distinctive-sounding pop, much to the relief of the mayor. "Wonderful," he said. "Now open it up."

He hovered over his brothers as Bob Deckers walked toward them. "What do we have here?" he asked. "You got it open?"

"Not a word from you," the mayor snapped. It would seem that the water was not yet under the bridge between the two.

With gloved hands, Garret adjusted the safe properly on the floor and grabbed a flashlight from the toolbox. He then pulled the safe door open. No one made a sound. Curtis watched as intently as the others while Mary pondered whether the distraction gave them their last opportunity to escape. One thing was certain: once the mayor and his entourage discovered what was really inside, they were going to press her even harder.

She stood up, reaching for her phone, as Garret shined his flashlight inside. He gasped as sand poured out and reached inside, grabbing a fistful, which he held up and allowed to drain through his fingers as the stunned faces around him moaned in growing panic.

Still watching from the staircase, Beatrice squinted and called out to the group, "What is it? What's wrong?"

Mayor Taylor instantly spun around to face Mary, angrier than she had seen him yet. "*This?* This is what you found? What is this, some kind of sick joke?"

Mary shrugged. "That's what we found. It was Phil's safe. Not mine."

The mayor took a step forward, enraged. "Then you didn't find the right one! *Where're the documents?* I know he had more! This is a travesty!" He knelt down, pushing his brothers out of the way, and then tore through the sand, tossing handfuls across the floor. "This... this is a decoy. That's what it is!" He then picked up the safe, lighter in weight now, and flung it as far as he could, sending it crashing onto the floor, with sand flying into the air and slowly settling everywhere. The mayor glared at Mary, Curtis, and his own men, as if blaming everyone for his disappointment. Out of fear, nobody spoke. Anything might happen now.

Curtis blocked Mary defensively as the mayor stopped inches away from them. "What's your problem?" he said. "She didn't put that sand in there."

"I don't know," the mayor said in a calm tone despite his heavy breathing. "Maybe she did, maybe she didn't. Either way, something isn't right here."

"Make an example of them," Beatrice called out from upstairs. "They're obviously not taking us seriously."

The mayor turned around to address Beatrice, seemingly distracted and confused. "Yes. I can do that easily." He spun to his brothers, Liam and Garret. They stood across from him, still surveying the broken safe on the other side of the room. "Grab your rifles. Things are going to get a little messy in here," he said.

Mary launched up, beside herself. "What are you doing? I had nothing to do with what was in that safe. All I did was find it!"

"I don't believe you," the mayor said.

"*We had a deal!*" Mary shouted.

"You're right," he said. "But I'm not about to walk away empty handed."

"Maybe Phil got rid of all this *blackmail* stuff," Mary said. "Did you ever consider that?"

"He didn't," the mayor said with assurance. "And don't try to convince me otherwise."

Liam approached, wiping his rifle with his wet sleeve. "Who do you want us to do first?"

The mayor looked at him with disbelief. "Who do you think, you idiot? The husband."

Liam nodded and aimed his rifle as Mary jumped in front of Curtis shouting, "No!"

"Get out of the way, Mary," the mayor said. "I mean it."

"I'll find it, okay?" she said, distraught. "Just lower the weapons, and I'll get you what you want."

The mayor put his hand up and brought Liam's rifle down. Garret watched the spectacle unfold, holding his own rifle against his shoulder.

Beatrice laughed from upstairs. "Oh, Frederick. You're such a softie."

"Start talking," the mayor said to Mary. "Where are the goods?"

Suddenly, a creaking noise sounded from the kitchen, attracting the mayor's attention. Shadows cast down the hallway moved closer as two men emerged, one holding a gun to the head of the other. Mary watched them get closer as the room fell silent and Theo came into view, walking behind Jeffery with a pistol pressed against the back of Jeffery's head.

"Everyone freeze!" Theo shouted, pushing Jeffery further into the ballroom "If anyone makes a move, I won't hesitate to shoot him right in the head."

Liam and Garret watched from afar, stunned, and aimed their rifles in Theo's direction. The mayor's security detail acted in kind and drew their pistols, aiming them in a kind of Mexican standoff. Mary's faith in Theo had never wavered, but she still couldn't believe his perfect timing. She and Curtis had been possibly moments away from getting shot.

The tension in the room increased as Theo maneuvered against the nearest wall, pulling Jeffery along and keeping a safe distance. "Drop your weapons!" he shouted. "You've got five seconds."

But no one moved. Mayor Taylor studied Theo for a moment as his eyes widened. "You..." he said. "You're that phony psychic. What in the hell are you doing here?"

Mary held back her smile. She couldn't believe Theo had actually gotten in, but her happiness was short-lived, with the admission that they were hopelessly outnumbered, just as the rain poured harder outside, beating against the window.

Theo pointed past the mayor, indicating Bob Deckers. "I recognize him. This is the asshole who tried to buy me off earlier, but it's not happening. You wanted me to deceive the Malones and keep them blind to what you're doing. But I know about all of you, especially you, Mayor Taylor," he said, standing behind Jeffery. "Now it's time for your motley crew to retreat before I leave you one brother short."

Liam, Garret, and the security detail all looked at Mayor Taylor for guidance.

"Five seconds!" Theo shouted, growing desperate.

Mayor Taylor passively pulled a pistol out from his coat and aimed it in Theo and Jeffery's direction. "I'm sorry, Jeff. You were one of the good ones."

He then fired two shots into Jeffery's chest without care, shocking everyone in the room. Jeffery slumped to the ground, causing Theo to trip and fall over, losing his pistol in the process. It skidded across the floor, stopping inches from Mayor Taylor's leather cowboy boots.

Mayor Taylor turned to Mary and Curtis with fire in his eyes. "It's time to come clean, Mary. You're going to help me this instant, or I will kill you, your husband, and that lump of shit in the corner."

He spun around to his dazed brothers and demanded that they subdue Theo immediately. Before Theo could even get up, the brothers were on him, pinning him to the floor. Liam and Garret lifted Theo up and carried him over to Mary and Curtis as he thrashed and twisted in their grip.

"You're not going to get away with this!" Theo shouted.

Mary noticed the vacant looks on both the Taylor brothers' faces. They were in an obvious state of shock. Jeffery's body lay only a few feet away in a puddle of blood. The mayor had made a definitive example. Mary hadn't imagined that it would be his own brother. She was relieved they hadn't killed Theo immediately but began to ponder why. Then the answer struck her: Theo and Curtis were leverage. The mayor was just getting started.

He signaled for Mary to get up from her chair as they brought Theo over and forced him to sit. "Bob," the mayor said, snapping his fingers. "Get that rope and tie them both up." Mary stood to the side helplessly, watching as the mayor looked at her with narrowing eyes.

"Any other surprise guests we should know about?" he asked.

"No," Mary said. "No one else."

"And just why didn't you mention your psychic friend before?" he asked, pointing at Theo. "Slip your mind?"

Mary nodded, feeling more hopeless by the second as Bob hurriedly wound a long line of nylon rope around Theo's wrists and ankles, binding him to the chair. With a cut of the rope, he then moved to Curtis, tying him up as before.

Upstairs, Beatrice seemed to enjoy the view, almost as though it were a type of dinner theater. "Frederick, it's getting late, and this storm outside is simply atrocious. Can we move on with it, please?"

"Here's the deal," the mayor said to Mary as she stood close by. "You're going to tell me where I can find Phil's files. And then, after that, you're going to help me find something that has eluded me for over forty years. You're going to help me discover the Bechdel fortune."

"Don't help him with a thing, Mary," Theo called out. "They have no intention of letting any of us live."

"Shut your mouth," the mayor said, snapping a finger in Theo's face. "She can make her own decisions."

Theo glared at the mayor, ignoring the water still dripping from his wet hair. "My mother, Elizabeth, and my uncle, Ben. What happened to them?"

Mayor Taylor stared back, confused. "The hell you talking about, kid?"

"Thirty years ago, my mother went missing. In 1985. She was last rumored to be investigating the Bechdel case. I want to know what happened to her."

The mayor leaned back, thinking to himself. His eyes suddenly lit up as though the memory had just come rushing back to him. "Oh yes. Now I remember! Young woman with three losers. They were trespassing on private property. We were only trying to send them a message. It was all an unfortunate accident really."

Theo's face went pale as the mayor recounted the terrible secret that had been lost for decades. "The woman. Her name was Elizabeth?" he asked. "Well, she was part of that little group of so-called investigators. Innocent inquiry, she had claimed. She tried to run. Attacked one of my men. Things got a little heated and..."

"And what?" Theo said, infuriated.

The mayor shrugged and wiped his hands together. "It was a mistake." He then took a closer look at Theo, marveling at his appearance. "Gee, so that was your mother, eh? Wow. Small world."

"You demonic fucking monster!" Theo shouted at the top of his lungs, shaking the chair forward.

He fell on the floor, helpless, unable to get up but filled with the rage of twenty men. "I'm going to kill you!" he cried. *"I'll kill all of you!"*

Beatrice laughed from the upstairs railing. "You're not going to let him talk to you like that, are you, Frederick?"

The mayor looked up and nodded to her. "You're right, Bea." He then turned to Garret and pointed to Theo, who was crying out in unbridled despair. "Go ahead and put him out of his misery."

"No!" Mary shouted. She rushed forward and grabbed an arm of the mayor's coat, pleading with him. "No, please. He's just upset. His mother died when he was an infant, and he never knew what happened to her."

The mayor yanked his arm away and shook his head. "I'm sorry to hear that, but you heard him. He intends to kill me." He then paused and backed away from Theo, pulling Mary along with him as she squirmed in his grip. "Take him out, Garret. We don't have all night."

"Don't do it," Curtis said, cutting in.

Garret stood between the two men tied to their chairs and the mayor, who maintained a safe distance.

"What are you waiting for?" the mayor said. "Do it!"

Garret stared back with vacant, unblinking eyes and lowered his rifle. "No..."

For a moment, the mayor was speechless, stunned in disbelief. "No? What do you mean, no?"

"I mean I'm sick of killing for you, understand?" he said, voice rising. Liam watched in wonder as Garret approached their powerful older brother with angry defiance. "You had us gun down that Bechdel family in this very room forty years ago. All for what? For some stupid curse and the family fortune? None of that exists! How long has it been? How long have we been searching? *No more!*"

"How dare you," the mayor shouted. "I've carried you three along for long enough. Without me, this family is nothing! Now do as you're told and shoot that man at your feet."

Garret took another step forward and handed the mayor the rifle. "You want it done? Do it yourself. Get your hands dirty for once. Only person I've ever seen you kill with your own hands is your own damn brother. We should never have listened to you. You're a spineless coward. That was as true forty years ago as it is today. Always getting people to do your dirty work." Garret spit at the ground, inches from the mayor's boots, and then turned away. "Let's go, Liam."

The mayor held the wet rifle in his hands, trembling with rage. Bob stood nearby, not daring to say a word. Not even Beatrice made a sound.

"You're right," the mayor called out, causing his two brothers to turn around. He then aimed the rifle at Garret. "I don't get my hands dirty nearly enough."

Though Mary was standing close to the mayor, everything happened so fast, Mary hadn't a moment to respond. The mayor pulled the trigger and blew off half of Garret's face. His body plummeted to the ground as Liam stumbled to the side, disoriented and losing his balance.

He fell against the china hutch and then raised his rifle, aiming at Mayor Taylor with a thunderous battle cry—but the mayor had beaten him to the draw. One shot from the rifle, and Liam's chest exploded and his body slumped to the floor in a bloody heap as glass shattered around his lifeless body.

The security detail looked confused and frightened, suddenly out of place, their pistols drawn but with an uncertain target.

"Don't just stand there," the mayor said, lowering the rifle. "Get these bodies out of here." He turned to Bob just as he was slowly recoiling into the hallway. "Where the hell do you think you're going? Give my men a hand."

The mayor's detail assembled in different positions in the room as though they had "disposed of" a few bodies before. Bob reluctantly walked to the wall below where Beatrice stood and helped one of the guards place Jeffery's corpse on a tablecloth ripped from the dining room table.

Curtis looked sickly pale, and even Theo went still. These were the beasts who had taken his young mother's life. Mary stood near the mayor, her hands slowly dropping to her side. She had just seen a man kill his three brothers over nothing. She had never seen anything so evil or known that such evil even existed. The mayor, however, was showing no signs of slowing down.

"Tell me now, Mary. Where can I find the documents? Where did Phil hide them?"

"I don't know…" she said in a soft, shaking voice.

The mayor shook his head in disappointment and then sighed. "That's just too bad. Now I'm going to have to go down the line until you change your mind." He stepped forward and held the barrel to Theo's head.

"Wait!" Mary said.

The mayor paused and looked up. "Yes?"

"The gazebo…" she said, barely audible.

"The what?" he asked.

Mary pointed toward the backyard. "The gazebo out back. That's where it's hidden."

The mayor leaned forward, intrigued. "Really? I would have never guessed. And what, pray tell, are we talking about here?"

Mary looked down, sounding ashamed. "Files. Photos. Written logs of the town elite, just like you said."

"And where's the map?" he said in a cold, demanding voice. "Could never get that family to talk. There's something in, or around, or under this house. A vast fortune, one beyond your wildest dreams."

"Yes..." Mary said. "There's a map and a key."

The mayor smiled and squeezed his fists in victory. "You're going to venture to this place, Mary. You're the only one that can, and you're going to tell me everything I want to know."

Tears streamed down her cheeks as she looked at Theo and Curtis, and Julie's image entered her mind. There was more to the Bechdel story than simple wealth. The mayor wanted power. He wanted a legacy. He wanted immortality. And even with the threat against her life and that of Curtis and Theo, she knew she couldn't go along with it, no matter what happened.

"I can't help you," she said.

The mayor stopped and leaned closer to her. "Excuse me? Come again?"

"I heard her just fine from up here," Beatrice said. "She's refusing to help you. I think you know what to do."

More lightning flashed outside as the lights flickered above them. Doors creaked from afar and Mary could see that the chandeliers were gradually coming alive, swinging back and forth.

Mary wrestled with her options and the consequences, then rose from her seat feeling more empowered than ever before. "I will never help you. I'm here to help Julie Bechdel. To find peace for her, and in the process, justice for her death."

The mayor glanced from Theo to Curtis with amusement while caressing the trigger of his gun. "Well. If that's how it's going to be, I have no choice but to provide you some incentive."

Suddenly, all the lights went out in unison as thunder and lightning boomed and flashed all around the house, illuminating the ballroom in intermittent spurts. The chandeliers rocked from their mountings and chains. Doors slammed shut, booming closed on both floors in startling synchronicity. The very ground they stood on trembled.

The mayor's six-man security team looked ready to bolt as they inched toward the foyer in the darkness. Bob Deckers backed against the wall, cowering behind the nearest sofa. Beatrice Thaxton gripped the guardrail, paralyzed with fear. The mayor lowered his rifle and scanned the room, frantic, as lamps and tables fell over and furniture shifted, scraping against the floor.

Theo lay on the ground, pulling at his ropes with growing panic. There was no doubt in Mary's mind that the spirits had returned in full force, with a chaotic entrance she knew only too well. And it was at that moment that she knew what she had to do.

She stepped forward, approaching the mayor with a steely and determined focus. As the lightning flashed around the mansion in deafening blasts, the mayor took several steps back from Mary, holding his rifle close and searching for his security team.

"Mayor Taylor," she began. "Your time has come. You are hereby charged with conspiracy for murder in the deaths of George and Anabelle Bechdel and their children Travis, John, Alex, and Julie, and Victor and Holly Drake and their daughter, Katelyn. You are also charged with the deaths of Harrison Grant, the Bechdel's doorman, Allison Comey, their executive chef, servers Ryan Lutz and Nicholas Freely, and cleaning staff Meghan Bowe and Rose Attwood."

"What is this? What are you doing?" he said, aiming his rifle at her. "You better stop this, or so help me God, I'll shoot you where you stand."

Mary maintained her steady pace, backing the mayor into a corner. His staff was thrown to the ground by an unseen force upon entering the foyer, pinned down against their will. One of the largest men attempted to break free and run down the nearby hall, only to be thrown high into the air and crash down onto a table, breaking his neck instantly.

"I can't control them," Mary said, raising her voice over the booming thunder and bursts of lightning descending upon the mansion. "I don't even know what they want, but I sure as hell have an idea."

"Frederick, what are you waiting for? Shoot her!" Beatrice yelled from upstairs as she ducked down behind the railing. "End this now!"

Suddenly, a window blasted open in the room next to her, followed by an overwhelming gust of wind that sent a screaming Beatrice over the railing head first and onto the hard floor below. Her skull split open and her body smacked the floor like a bag of bricks, silencing her screams instantly.

"Oh my God!" Bob said, gripping a sofa chair. "We've got to get the hell out of here." He ran to the nearest window and tried to open it, desperately pulling on it to no avail.

"Where the hell do you think you're going, Bob?" Mayor Taylor shouted.

Bob turned around, grabbed a stone Mozart bust, and threw it at the window with all his strength. The bust shattered the glass and sent a typhoon of wind and rain into the ballroom, further adding to the chaos. Mary ducked as the mayor steadied his aim directly at Bob. "You're a part of this too, damn it."

Bob stuck his arm through the shattered glass, slicing his lower bicep, and fell back screaming in agony as blood gushed from his arm. Theo's chair suddenly levitated ten feet above the ground and then came crashing down, splintering in a dozen pieces. He crawled away from the wreckage, finally free, and then tried to steady Curtis's chair while untying him.

With growing panic, the mayor fired several shots indiscriminately into the air. Mary fell to the ground and rolled to the side. Bob rose, clutching his arm, and then ran at Curtis, terrified, just as Theo pulled the ropes loose.

"Help me, please!" Bob shouted.

Curtis raised his foot and kicked Bob's face, sending him backward, up and through the air. Mayor Taylor fired another shot, blasting through the chain of a chandelier directly above Bob. It dropped down like a missile and crashed down on Bob, glass spears and shards shredding his flesh with brutal ferocity. Curtis then fell back in his chair, hitting the ground as Theo jumped over him, shielding him from the mayor's random rifle blasts, furniture stuffing raining down on them from above.

Not finished with the mayor, Mary put both hands on the floor and pushed herself up as he backed into a wall with the rifle shaking in his hands. Several more names entered her mind along with a vivid vision of the past that froze her in her tracks:

Bob Deckers reentered her mind. He was wearing a suit and tie and sitting in an elegant office with dark wooden walls filled with plaques and framed pictures of the Taylor family. Mayor Taylor paced around the office near a large mahogany desk with an American flag on a pole standing in the back.

"It's about that time, Bob. I need you to locate this couple and get them into the Bechdel property," Mayor Taylor was telling him.

Bob nodded. "I've been compiling a list, but it's getting to be a harder sell. Especially with the Internet out there."

"Never mind that," the mayor said. "These two. These are

the ones. We'll finally be able to get inside and get to the fortune. Who would have thought that *this* is what it takes?"

"You don't really believe that, do you?" Bob asked.

The mayor slammed his fist on the table, irate at the question. "You want to make a joke about this? I'm not in the mood. Did you know that Pastor Phil tested me once? And one time was all it took. We got his children out of town and left him a widower, but I just couldn't bring myself to quite finish the job. He's on thin ice, though."

"Why not just let him leave?" Bob asked.

The mayor leaned forward, stunned at the question. "You know as well as I do that no one who knows anything about what's going on here is ever allowed to leave." He grabbed the half-smoked nearby cigar, jammed it into an ashtray, and re-lit it, puffing away. "I've been waiting forty years for this moment, Bob. Don't deny me. Some have said that hidden somewhere on that property is the key to immortality. A spiritual void between life and death."

Bob shook his head. "That's all fine and well. As long as I get that loan you promised, I'll make things happen."

The mayor smiled and took another puff. "Consider it done. Just don't gamble it away again."

"That's slander, Mr. Mayor. I've been clean a long time. I'm currently in touch with a Realtor in Chicago. He knows the husband, Curtis. But he warned me that it wasn't going to be that easy getting them here. They have a life in Chicago, careers and the like."

"Well, there you go," Taylor said with his arms out. "We'll just have to do what's in our power to *convince* them otherwise."

Bob leaned back with a reserved smile. "I'd sure hate to see what you have in store for them."

"They'll come around," he said, stubbing the rest of his cigar out. "I guarantee it."

Mary snapped out of her trance to see the mayor rushing toward her. He then smacked the rifle's buttstock against her head, sending her to the floor as lightning flashed around them. The mayor stood over her, aiming his rifle ahead at Theo and Curtis, keeping them at bay.

"Don't fucking move! I only want what's mine."

He then brought the barrel down, sweat dripping from his face, and held it to her temple. "I never wanted it to come to this, Mary. All I want to know is what's buried beneath this house. I had high hopes for you, and you let me down. Well, if I'm going to die tonight, I'm taking you with me!"

Mary sat up, flinching in terror. She gasped and took a deep breath. The air began to swirl around her. She thrust her head back and began to scream: "Julie! Julie!" at the top of her lungs.

The house rumbled again, the gradual tremors of an earthquake building. "Julie, where are you?"

Suddenly, the rifle flew from Mayor Taylor's hands and smacked against the wall. He studied his empty hands as his gray hair flipped wildly in the wind. Mary rose with resolve, staring at the mayor, fury in every cell and muscle of her body. Frightened, he backed away, searching for a way to escape.

"I'm not done with you yet, Taylor," she said. "I wondered what the spirits meant when they said to 'bring you to justice.' Now I see that all they needed was someone to bring you to them and formally charge you for decades of crimes against innocent human beings. Alisha Evans, wife of Pastor Phil. Pastor Phil. Deputy Ramirez. And Theo's mother and uncle, Elizabeth and Ben Stone—their friends Scott Pinkerton and Adam Wesley."

"I didn't kill them!" the mayor shouted. "I didn't kill any of them."

Mary continued, unabated. "You didn't pull the trigger,

but you were responsible for their deaths nonetheless. Their spirits are here, and they've come for you, Mr. Mayor. There is no hidden treasure. No immortality, only justice."

A fireball burst of light suddenly exploded in their midst, blinding everyone in the room. Mary closed her eyes as her body trembled with static. Several bursts of light continued exploding at intervals, pulsing through the air. Furniture flew across the room, and a blinding light exploded and traveled across the floor, searing and burning everything in its path, racing from the wall, and one-by-one targeting Mayor Taylor, burning through him, his petrified security detail, and the bodies of his brothers, Beatrice Thaxton, and Bob Deckers, reducing them to ash.

After several blinding minutes of deafening static, Mary opened her eyes to silence. There was nothing left of the mayor or anyone else who had intruded on her home. Curtis and Theo remained unharmed but dazed by the brief but explosive phenomenon that had swept through the house with a vengeance.

The room went dark as the storm began to die down, providing a moment of relief and relative peace. Mary walked over to where Theo and Curtis lay on the floor and crouched down beside them.

"It's over," she said, touching Curtis's leg. "It's over."

"What the hell just happened?" Curtis asked.

Theo stood, feeling around the room. "I think we should get out of here."

Before he could take another step, a bright light beamed at the staircase, instantly beckoning Mary. She turned and walked toward it, in a trance, and Theo and Curtis called out to her. Suddenly, Theo placed a hand on Curtis's shoulder, holding him back.

"She's okay. Let her do this," he said.

The light formed an image of a young girl, floating above

the ground in her nightgown. Tears streamed from Mary's face as she took the first few steps, approaching the transparent being before her.

"Julie…" she said. "Are you okay?"

"I'm leaving," Julie said. "I don't know why, but I know I may never see you again. Thank you, Mary. I've been waiting for decades for this moment, ever since I first met you as a child."

"Did I do what you needed me to?" Mary asked.

"Yes," Julie said. "That and more. I would never let anything happen to your child. You're going to be okay. So will your daughter. This home is yours now. We are at peace, and so is this town. Thank you."

"But I didn't do anything," Mary said. "Nothing changes. You're still dead. How is that justice?"

"You did everything," Julie said, her image fading. "And perhaps we'll meet again on the other side. Until then, enjoy your life. Do good for yourself and others. Raise your daughter and be happy."

Mary sobbed as Julie's image faded from sight. "Julie?" Mary asked. "Where are you?"

There was no response, and the room went dark again. Theo and Curtis stood in place, surveying the damage all around them. No one was sure what had transpired, but the danger, it seemed, had been eliminated.

"Mary," Curtis called out, approaching her. She turned and ran into his arms, and they shared a loving embrace.

"I'm so sorry, Curtis," she said as he stroked her back. "We need to get you to the hospital."

"We need to leave," Curtis said, "leave this house and never come back."

"No. This is our house. We're not going anywhere." The thunder outside faded as the rain slowly died down. Theo turned and left the house without saying a word. They never spoke to him again.

“Why on earth would we stay here after what has happened?” Curtis asked, holding Mary close.

“Because I have a map and a key,” Mary said. “And we’re going to get the truth about this house and this entire town out there. It’s the least we can do for the victims.”

Sirens blared in the distance. The police were on their way. What would Chief Riley think about it all? Would he even begin to believe it? He had to. The evidence was there. No reputation would be left unscathed. Redwood needed to answer for its past.

Curtis and Mary held each other for what seemed like hours, happy with the thought of returning to their normal lives, lives with true hope for their future and the prospect of bringing another life into a world where darkness was vanquished, a world of justice and peace.